DOCTOR WHO

THE WHEEL OF ICE

Doctor Who Books from Ace

SHADA: THE LOST ADVENTURE BY DOUGLAS ADAMS
by Gareth Roberts

THE WHEEL OF ICE
by Stephen Baxter

DOCTOR WHO

THE WHEEL OF ICE

STEPHEN BAXTER

ACE BOOKS, NEW YORK

THE BERKLEY PUBLISHING GROUP
Published by the Penguin Group
Penguin Group (USA) Inc.
375 Hudson Street, New York, New York 10014, USA
Penguin Group (Canada), 90 Eglinton Avenue East, Suite 700, Toronto, Ontario M4P 2Y3, Canada
(a division of Pearson Penguin Canada Inc.) • Penguin Books Ltd., 80 Strand, London WC2R 0RL,
England • Penguin Ireland, 25 St. Stephen's Green, Dublin 2, Ireland (a division of Penguin
Books Ltd.) • Penguin Group (Australia), 707 Collins Street, Melbourne, Victoria 3008, Australia
(a division of Pearson Australia Group Pty. Ltd.) • Penguin Books India Pvt. Ltd., 11 Community
Centre, Panchsheel Park, New Delhi—110 017, India • Penguin Group (NZ), 67 Apollo Drive,
Rosedale, Auckland 0632, New Zealand (a division of Pearson New Zealand Ltd.) • Penguin Books,
Rosebank Office Park, 181 Jan Smuts Avenue, Parktown North 2193, South Africa • Penguin China,
B7 Jaiming Center, 27 East Third Ring Road North, Chaoyang District, Beijing 100020, China

Penguin Books Ltd., Registered Offices: 80 Strand, London WC2R 0RL, England

This is a work of fiction. Names, characters, places, and incidents either are the product of the author's
imagination or are used fictitiously, and any resemblance to actual persons, living or dead, business
establishments, events, or locales is entirely coincidental. The publisher does not have any control over
and does not assume any responsibility for author or third-party websites or their content.

Doctor Who is a BBC Wales production for BBC One.
Executive producers: Steven Moffat and Caroline Skinner

Published by arrangement with Ebury Publishing, a division of The Random House Group Limited.

Copyright © 2012 by Stephen Baxter.
Cover design: Two Associates © Woodlands Books Ltd, 2012.

PUBLISHING HISTORY
Ace hardcover edition / January 2013

Library of Congress Cataloging-in-Publication Data

Baxter, Stephen.
Doctor Who : the wheel of ice / Stephen Baxter. — Ace hardcover ed.
p.   cm.
ISBN 978-0-425-26122-4 (hardcover : alk. paper)
1. Doctor Who (Fictitious character)—Fiction.   2. Science fiction.   I. Title.
PR6052.A849D63   2013
823'.914—dc23
2012034670

PRINTED IN THE UNITED STATES OF AMERICA

10   9   8   7   6   5   4   3   2   1

To
Clare Baines, top Who fan;
Paul Cornell, top Who writer;
Paul McAuley and Kim Newman, top Who buddies;
and the memory of Patrick Troughton, top Who.

ARKIVE

Resilience. Remembrance. Restoration.

One day, in the dusty libraries of Gallifrey, she would be given a name: *Arkive*. All things are named in the libraries of Gallifrey.

But she did not need a name. She needed only her mission: Resilience. Remembrance. Restoration.

All that she was, all that survived of her – and she was all that survived of Home – was embedded in an ice moon. A moon orbiting a planet, a ball of roiling gas, that itself orbited a feeble sun.

This solar system itself had no value for her, no interest. Nor did the life forms that swarmed and died on the surfaces of its planets. A sculpture of debris and rubbish, the system owed its very existence to the destruction of Home.

She had survived in this system of garbage for billions of years. Survived though she was damaged. The detonation of the star that had destroyed Home had been too severe. It had caught her, it had overwhelmed the elaborate survival mechanisms given her by her designers.

She had not demonstrated Resilience. She could not be certain of the veracity of her Remembrance. And she could not be sure she could fulfil her ultimate goal of Restoration. She could not fulfil her mission.

And so she had formulated a plan. A strategy. If she could not fix herself, if she could not fulfil her mission, then she would return to the arms of those who made her. Who had perished billions of years before. Who had entrusted her with all that they were, all that they could have been. Who would grant her forgiveness.

She would bathe in the light of a long-dead sun. And she would try again.

She would reach through time, even though it would take the sacrifice of this pointless little moon to do it.

She even prepared a fallback. For now, on one of the garbage worlds, a kind of intelligence had arisen, low, cunning, but useful. An intelligence whose destiny would be sacrificed to her purposes, should she awake to find herself still trapped in the ruins of this lump of ice.

Deep in the heart of the moon, there was a kind of bomb.

Searing light.

A detonation visible from Earth, to curious eyes.

She huddled in the wreckage of the moon, what was left of it.

Fragments of shattered moonscapes gathered in a gleaming band around the primary planet.

And through a rift in space and time, branching, cracking, a tiny artefact fell into the deep past . . .

1

In the vortex that lies beyond time and space tumbled a police box that was not a police box.

The control room was empty. It was a spacious, brightly lit chamber. It alone was too big to have fitted into the battered exterior of the police box, and doors and passageways leading from it hinted at more inexplicable volumes beyond. Inset multicoloured roundels pleasingly adorned the walls. A central console dominated the room, a hexagonal platform encrusted with switches, dials, monitor screens and levers, with a translucent cylinder standing motionless at the console's heart. The room was silent save for a hum of unseen engines.

And on the gleaming floor, in one corner, lay two modest musical instruments, a wooden recorder and a bagpipe's practice chanter. Beside them was an elderly hardback book, the reader's place carefully marked with a sliver of plastic. Its title was *Brave New World*, the author Aldous Huxley.

Abruptly the console's central cylinder began to rise and fall, and a strange sound rent the air, a rhythmic metallic wheezing.

* * *

Distracted from their different pursuits, the ship's three crew hurried towards the control room.

Zoe Heriot was first to arrive. She was a short, compact young woman with her hair cut in a neat bob. She had an open, pixie-like face and, when she was in the mood, an infectious smile. She wore a jumpsuit from her own era, the latter half of the twenty-first century, comfortable but form-fitting, panelled with pastel colours.

She glanced around the control room and spotted the book on the floor, the latest she had borrowed from the ship's chaotic library. Once she had worked as a librarian, and had fallen in love with books. Since joining the crew of the TARDIS she had become fascinated by history – or rather, she had joined the crew to discover history, and the wider universe. And she was intrigued by books like this, speculations about the future by a man who had become a historical figure in his own right.

Jamie hurried in moments later. 'Och. What *now*?' James Robert McCrimmon, brawny, strong-featured, wore the kilt and shirt with lace-up throat and cuffs that characterised his own origins in the Scotland of the eighteenth century. The effect was spoiled only a little by the pair of roomy carpet slippers on his feet.

They both knew what the column's motion signified, the robotic grinding. 'This boat's landing,' said Jamie.

As Zoe opened her mouth to reply, the Doctor bustled in, pulling a battered old frock coat over a shabby white shirt. 'Well, I'm glad I arrived in time to hear you two remark on the utterly obvious,' he said rather grumpily as he hurried to the console. He was a small man with a mop of black hair cut to a fringe, and somewhat ragged sideburns. He wore a grubby red cravat, clumsily tied, and loud check trousers. And he wore no shoes, only worn-looking socks, and Zoe realised where Jamie had got the slippers from. The Doctor might have been in his late forties, had he been human. His rather lined face showed only impatience now, but it was capable, Zoe knew, of looks of deep wisdom, as well as childlike smiles of delight.

Zoe said, 'The issue is where we are landing. And why.'

The Doctor hurried around the console, snapping switches, peering at dials, and he stared at the rising column as if in disbelief. 'Well, the "why" is rather obvious. One of you must have been meddling again. How many times have I told you two to leave the controls alone? She is a rather temperamental old bird, you know.'

'Dinna look at me,' Jamie protested. 'I wasna even here.'

'And you needn't blame me either,' Zoe snapped. 'The TARDIS was in landing mode before I left my room. And as for "meddling", Doctor, let me remind you of the rather large number of times you've relied on me to help you get this "temperamental old bird" under control.'

'Aye, and me,' put in Jamie. 'Like that time ye had me hit yon button with the handle of ma dirk—'

'All right, all right,' the Doctor said. 'If you'd both stop your chittering and give me a moment to think, I might have a chance to work out what's going on.'

As she so often did when annoyed, Zoe retreated into the logic which had been the bedrock of her education. 'I think it's perfectly obvious what's going on. The TARDIS is landing. And as none of us were here to set the controls to land—'

'She's made the decision for herself,' the Doctor muttered. 'Yes, thank you, Zoe.'

Jamie, concerned, crossed to the console. 'Can she do that?'

'Well, evidently she can, yes. The TARDIS is capable of a great many things you've yet to witness. Or, indeed, I,' he said ruefully. 'But I can tell you *why* she's suddenly taken things into her own hands. Not that she has hands . . .' He tapped a small monitor screen which flared red. 'She's detected a Relative Continuum Displacement Zone.'

'Has she now? And what's that when it's not got its fur coat on?'

'That, Jamie, is a hole in time!'

Zoe frowned. 'That sounds rather dangerous.'

'Indeed it is, Zoe. Such a thing in the wrong hands can cause a great deal of damage, for it can lead to destabilisation. What is known as a direct continuum implosion.'

'How much damage would that cause?'

He shrugged. 'Whole worlds, perhaps.' He cupped his hands together, making a globe, spread his fingers. 'Poom!'

'That's aye verra well,' said Jamie, 'but wha's it got tae do with the TARDIS?'

'Well, it is a fact, Jamie, that the TARDIS was not really designed for, umm, the purposes to which I put her. My people, who have mastered the technologies of time themselves, rather frown on mucking about with time by anybody else. And so, you see, the TARDIS is specifically designed to react when she detects evidence of any such, ah—'

'Mucking about.'

'Quite so.'

'Ah,' said Jamie. 'So she's taking us in for a look-see.'

'That's the idea.'

'It doesn't sound very safe,' Zoe said, trying to sound sensible rather than wary.

'Oh, we should be fine. According to the read-outs we're heading for a landing on a perfectly ordinary moon of the planet Saturn.'

'Saturn? *My* Saturn? I mean—'

'Yes, Zoe. And not so terribly far away from your own time, in fact.'

Jamie was listening to the TARDIS's groaning. 'I think we'll land soon.' Jamie came from a technologically primitive culture, relatively, but he had had a lot more experience of the TARDIS and her whims than Zoe. The wheezing engine noise ended with a thump, and the ship shuddered. Jamie flicked on the external scanner, a wall screen filled with grey static that slowly cleared. 'Doctor . . .'

The Doctor was still at the console. He patted a row of switches. 'You really are a clever old girl, aren't you?'

Zoe could swear the TARDIS was leaning. She glanced around, and saw her Huxley book slide silently across the polished floor. 'I say, Doctor—'

'Let's take a look at this mysterious moon, shall we?'

But Jamie pointed to the screen. 'That doesnae look like any moon to me.'

In the monitor Zoe saw darkness. Empty space, spattered with stars. And a band of gleaming particles lying slantways across the image.

Jamie walked up to the screen and pointed to one bright fleck. 'I've my eye on that beastie yon. I think – whoa!' He slithered sideways.

Zoe grabbed a corner of the console. 'We're tilting, Doctor!'

Holding on to the tipping console to anchor himself, the Doctor peered at his instruments. 'That's not supposed to happen. Ah! The inertial lock has destabilised. The TARDIS is confused.'

'By what?'

'Well, she should have landed on a solid surface. That's what her space-time sensors told her to expect. But there's no solid surface here.'

Jamie said, 'Doctor, that speck o' light there—'

'In fact, you're right, there's no wretched moon at all! Ah.' He snapped his fingers. 'Of course! The Relative Continuum Displacement Zone. *That's* where the moon has gone. Down the hole in time – or more likely, blown up by it—'

'Doctor!' Jamie, waving his arms for balance, was shouting now.

And Zoe could see why. Over his shoulder the scanner showed a speck emerging from the background band. A speck becoming larger, more solid, a three-dimensional object. White. Gleaming.

Spinning.

Growing.

Heading straight for the ship.

'Duck!' cried Jamie.

As one Zoe and Jamie leapt for the Doctor, and the three of them huddled under the console, clinging to hatch handles. The control room filled with the noise of a blaring klaxon.

And the object hit.

2

High above the plane of Saturn's rings, a girl and a robot watched the drama unfold.

From the point of view of Phee Laws, the sun was a bright star, off to the left. Saturn itself was half full, a misty globe banded with subtle browns. Phee could see lightning crackle at the north pole – there were permanent depressions, like unending hurricanes, at both poles – and, deep in the night of the dark side, more lightning flared purple, each strike a sheet of energy bigger than the Earth. The ring system was like a tremendous roadway stretching around the planet, barely tilted away from the horizontal from Phee's point of view. She could see detail, ringlets as fine as if drawn by the pen of a careful artist. There were moons embedded in the ring system itself, small shapeless objects. The larger, perfectly spherical moons hung further out, like lanterns: silver Enceladus, burnt-orange Titan.

The sun was so far away that it cast its light across this system of moons and rings like a distant spotlight, making razor-sharp shadows. The shade of Saturn itself lay across the rings, etching straight-line edges thousands of kilometres long. The longest straight lines in the solar system, Phee's mother Jo liked to boast to the occasional visitors that came out to the Wheel.

And, right in the middle of the ring system, clearly visible if Phee worked the magnifiers in her skinsuit visor, was a tumbling blue box. There seemed to be some attempts at piloting it, but she saw ring fragments whack into it like stones thrown by unruly children.

Another big chunk came spinning in to clout the box. 'Ouch,' she murmured.

'Aye, that's gannae sting in the mornin',' said the robot.

Hovering over her scooter, MMAC was something like a fat spider, with a battered main body ten metres across, crusted with sensors and access hatches, and arms branching away around the rim, some terminating in tools, others brachiating into finer and finer manipulators. Rocket nozzles stuck out of the hull in every direction. 'MMAC' stood for 'Malenfant-IntelligeX Modular Autonomous Component'. MMAC had begun the construction of the Wheel of Ice, where Phee lived. But 'it' was a 'him' to those who found him good company, and they all called him MMAC – 'Mac'.

'Yon box is unlucky,' MMAC said now. 'Turned up right in the midst of a B belt, where the frags is as big as hooses.'

He was right. '*And* they seem to be in the middle of a spoke.'

The rings of Saturn were made up of billions of ice fragments, all following their own orbits around the planet, shepherded by the subtle gravities of Saturn's many moons. The rings further out were composed of dust grains almost too fine to see. But the big rings towards the centre of the complex, labelled A, B and C by long-dead astronomers on Earth, contained fragments that could indeed be as big as houses. Across much of its tremendous area the ring system was no more than ten or fifteen metres deep. That blue box, if it had any manoeuvrability at all, could easily have ducked out of that. But as MMAC said, it was right in the middle of a spoke. The ring system was full of complexities, waves and ridges and even spokes that turned with the planet. And in such places the rings could be kilometres deep.

'I wonder who they are.'

'Aye. And how they got there. I dinna see a ship turn up. Did ye?'

Phee knew he was just being polite to ask. MMAC, crusted with radar and other sensors, 'saw' far beyond the capability of the eyes of a mere human like her. 'I expect Marshal Paley will be interested.' Sonia Paley was the latest security chief imposed on the Wheel by Earth, by the International Space Command in Geneva.

'Oh, aye.'

'She'll probably lock the crew up.'

'But she will nae ha' a chance if yon box is smashed to smithers.'

'Do you think we should save them, MMAC?'

'Thought ye'd ne'er ask. After yiz.'

Phee ran a quick check of the systems of her skinsuit and scooter. Then she stood straight on her scooter, grasped the handle, and swept on a brilliant flame down towards the rings of Saturn. It was like falling down to a tremendous floor, thousands of kilometres wide. Behind her she sensed the bulk of MMAC, following at a careful distance.

And before her ice fragments pinged from the carcass of the blue box, a drama unfolding in utter silence.

3

The TARDIS control room was anything but silent. Zoe had anchored herself to a corner of the console, facing the external scanner. Peering into the murky, juddering screen, she was doing her best to call out warnings of the incoming hail of ice boulders. 'Upper left! Left! Now upper right!' The TARDIS bucked and shook as the Doctor responded at his controls. 'Now low right – right, Doctor! Now right again! I said *right!*'

Wham. Yet another block hit, almost dead on, despite all their efforts. Zoe thought she could feel the impact transmitted through the fabric of the ship to her own bones. But there was no time to reflect, for here came more of the unending storm. 'Another one from the right – now from dead centre, above us – this one's tumbling, it's going to hit—'

Scrape. Another bruising impact.

'Not fast enough, Doctor!'

'I'm doing my best, Zoe!' the Doctor wailed. He was held in place at his console only by Jamie's strong arms wrapped around his waist. 'It's not easy, you know!'

'You're telling me – left incoming!'

'Why don't we just leave this place?'

'Well, we can't for now, Jamie. You see—'

Wham.

'Surely this ship has an automated defence system!'

'Oh, Zoe, of course it has. But if it wasn't disabled, don't you think I'd have activated it by now?'

'Disabled!'

'I have been meaning to get around to looking into it . . .'

'I know you say yon blocks are only ice, but how much more o' this can she take, Doctor?'

'Well, she's built for punishment, but not this much. I daresay the hull will survive, but the contents might not.'

'The contents?'

'The mercury fluid links, for example.'

'Tae perdition with the mercury fluid links. What about us?'

'*Left*, Doctor!'

The Doctor wrenched at his controls again.

Wham.

Zoe turned, exasperated. 'Why *not* just leave? Why not dematerialise?'

'Because she won't let me!' the Doctor called back, distressed. 'It's all because of that wretched Continuum Displacement Zone. Until we've sorted that out we're not going anywhere.'

Jamie pointed. 'Zoe!'

And Zoe turned to the scanner in time to see a wall of white bearing down, not a cannonball this time, but a tremendous jagged mass heading straight for the TARDIS – she hid her face behind her hands—

There was no impact.

Zoe peeked through her fingers. The TARDIS was intact. Jamie and the Doctor stood breathing hard at the console. She was still here, uninjured. She saw, an odd detail, that the Huxley book had slithered across the floor and ended up at her feet, but it had lost her bookmark.

On the scanner screen there was only a fine hail of glittering dust. The great boulder had vanished. But now another block emerged from the swarm – she braced and prepared to call out—

The second block detonated and dispersed.

And a machine swam across her field of view, like a fat disc studded with flaring rockets. A forest of manipulator arms waved.

The TARDIS crew stood and stared.

'It saluted us,' Zoe said, breathlessly. 'I'll swear it saluted us.'

With a nonchalant spin the robot turned and zapped another brace of incoming ice blocks.

The Doctor came to life. He tapped a control to open a communication channel. 'This is the Doctor, aboard the TARDIS. Calling unidentified robot. We, umm, we're very grateful for your assistance.'

A speaker crackled to life. 'Aye, nae problem, wee man.'

Jamie stared. 'Ye're Scottish.' He leaned over the console. 'I said, ye're Scottish!'

'Really, Jamie,' said the Doctor, 'there's no need to shout. This equipment is very sensitive.'

'So I am, fella, and you too by the sound o' it. Call me MMAC. That's M, M, A, C.'

'James Robert McCrimmon,' said Jamie proudly.

'McCrimmon? The sept of the McLarens?'

'Aye, tha's right. Ye know of it?'

'Ye wouldn'a be a piper by any chance? The McCrimmons are famed for that.'

'Tha's me. Served with the laird hisself.'

'Which laird?'

But the Doctor shook his head sharply.

Jamie asked instead, 'Wha' about ye? Where're ye from?'

Zoe snorted. 'Ask him where he was *manufactured*.'

But the robot answered, 'Born and bred in Govan.'

Jamie's face fell. 'Govan? Glasgae? Och, I should hae known. Here I am off in space and the mechanical Scotsman I meet has tae be from Glasgae.'

The robot calmly zapped a couple more blocks.

'That looks like a meson shield to me,' murmured Zoe. 'Short range but effective.'

'And wha's wrong with Glasgae, if I may ask?'

'Only that ye lowland jessies supported the Anglish in the '45, tha's all.'

MMAC laughed, a convincingly human sound. 'Ye've a laing memory, fella.'

Now a new figure appeared in the scanner's view. 'Maybe we could talk about this later when we've got you to safety.'

Zoe stared, fascinated. With the robot continuing its defensive work in the background, in the foreground a spacesuited figure rode a simple rocket craft, just a platform on which she stood, a handle before her with basic controls. She was a young girl by the sound of her voice, maybe not much younger than Zoe. She wore a transparent sealed suit over what looked like straightforward T-shirt and shorts, in plain grey colours. Her face, serious and sensible, was dimly visible through her visor.

The Doctor murmured, 'That suit rather reminds me of the equipment on your own station, Zoe.'

Zoe felt oddly defensive. 'Well, we didn't walk around in transparent pressure suits. And nothing like that *broomstick* would have been allowed on Station Three. I mean, where's its backup propulsion system?'

'I think ye're jealous,' said Jamie with a grin.

'Oh, be quiet, Jamie.' She raised her voice. 'You, on the broomstick. Please identify yourself, and your rank.'

The Doctor raised his eyebrows at her aggressive tone.

'My name's Phee Laws.' She sounded amused, and snapped out, 'Josephine Miranda Laws, *ma'am*! I'm sixteen years old. I don't really have a rank. My tentative parapsychological-socioeconomic classification is

A, if that helps. My mother has a rank, I suppose. She's Jo Laws. She's the mayor, sort of, on the Wheel. Oh, her grade is B.'

'The Wheel?'

'The Mnemosyne Cincture. We call it the Wheel of Ice. Look, we ought to get you out of there before MMAC's meson gun runs out of juice. The best way is for MMAC just to tow you out of the plane of the rings. Then we'll take you to the Wheel.' She glanced around, evidently eyeing up the TARDIS's unprepossessing exterior. 'Is there any kind of grappling handle?'

'Oh, that's easily sorted out,' the Doctor said brightly. 'Do you have a line? We'll just wrap it around the control console, here inside the ship.'

Phee looked surprised. 'OK. It's your vessel. Where's the airlock?'

'Oh, no need for that. Hang on while I open the door.' He reached for the control.

Zoe cried, 'Doctor – no!' She lunged towards him, every space-trained instinct clamouring to keep the pressurised environment intact.

But the Doctor opened the door, long before she could reach him. Through the door Zoe saw a star field, a smattering of ice fragments, the spidery robot spinning and whirling, and the astonished-looking girl on her rocket craft, with a cable trailing back to the robot. And, rather to Zoe's surprise, the air did not rush out of the TARDIS leaving them gasping like stranded fish.

The Doctor smiled. He held out his arm to the girl outside. 'This way.'

Phee hesitated. Then, with a skilful blip of her rocket, she sailed in towards the TARDIS. She killed her relative motion before she collided with the ship, reached out an uncertain hand, and allowed the Doctor to pull her through the force field, or whatever it was that contained the TARDIS's air. She stood with a slight stumble on the gleaming floor, evidently surprised by the gravity, her lightweight craft in her hand. Zoe saw that under her transparent suit she wore a heavy pendant at her neck, a slim black panel about the size and shape of a playing card. It reminded Zoe of the communicators they had used on Station Three.

Somewhere inside the TARDIS an alarm chimed faintly.

The Doctor let the newcomer get her bearings. 'Welcome aboard,' he said gently, his face crumpled in a beaming smile.

'What is this thing, some kind of escape pod?'

'Well, we have done rather a lot of escaping in it, I suppose . . .'

And then Phee took in the size of the control room. Looked back at the open door that had taken up half of one of the TARDIS's external faces. Looked around the cabin again, with the doorway lost against one vast wall.

'Don't worry,' the Doctor said. 'Everybody reacts like that. Most people far worse, in fact.'

Zoe had heard this routine a hundred times. 'Isn't that a bit patronising, Doctor, considering that this girl and her robot spider are saving all our lives?'

'Yes, all right, thank you, Zoe. I wonder if you would mind glancing over at the console to check on that alarm? As for our visitor, it's perfectly safe to open your visor now, you know.' To back that up he filled his own lungs with a deep breath.

Phee cautiously tapped a control, and her visor slid back. Her hair was a rich red. Her face was serious, square rather than pretty, and she squinted in the control room's bright lights, her pupils oddly large.

Jamie came up to her with his usual clumsy friendliness. 'My name's Jamie.'

Phee grinned. 'Ah, yes, the proud Scot. MMAC's not so bad, you know, when you get to know him.'

'Aye, well, if he pulls us out o' this hole I'll even forgive him for being born in Glasgae. If he *was* born. Can I take this?'

'My scooter? Thanks.'

He propped it in the corner. 'Light, this thing. Might hae a go mesel'. Now here, let me gi' ye a hand with yon cable . . .'

The Doctor joined Zoe at the controls. 'You found the alarm.'

She pointed. 'This one.' The indicator was labelled PEDLERON PAR-TICLES. 'Went off just as Scooter Girl over there walked in.'

'Umm. Then the mystery we have to solve before we can leave here has just deepened, Zoe.'

'What do you mean?'

He tapped the display with his forefinger, and looked across at Phee, puzzled. 'I mean that the presence of pedleron particles tells me that the TARDIS has detected an object, something that has just been brought into this control room, that has *travelled through time . . .'*

Soon the cable was fixed in place around the base of the console. It snaked off out of the door, across open space, to the labouring, spinning, multi-limbed robot. With a squirt of rockets MMAC drifted away, the cable went taut, and the TARDIS followed like a dog on a lead.

4

There were five members of the loosely constituted inner council that ran affairs on the Mnemosyne Cincture, known to its inhabitants as the Wheel of Ice. Or rather, Mayor Jo Laws admitted to herself tiredly as the arguments rambled on, they liked to believe they ran those affairs, rather than just reacted to the latest calamities.

There was herself, Josephine Mary Laws, with the more or less informal title of mayor of the mining colony. She was, however, the only one of the council actually elected by those they were here to serve.

She had one firm ally among the other four, she believed, in the colony's chief medical officer, Sinbad Omar.

Then there were the two representatives of Earth's tangled politics. Marshal Sonia Paley was the cop imposed as security officer by the ISC in Geneva, the International Space Command. And Luis Reyes, ambassador from the PEC, the Planetary Ethics Commission, was here to monitor their moral behaviour – and, in extremis, shut the operation down if they didn't wash behind their ears thoroughly enough. Both following other people's agendas, both not bad folks in themselves, both thoroughly out of their depth out here on the edge of the solar system.

And then there was Florian Hart, who was talking now, as usual dominating the session in her ferocious way. Her official title was a corporate rank: Administrator. In practice she was the embodiment of Bootstrap, Inc., the mining consortium that had put up the money for this operation in the first place. As Florian never hesitated to remind them all.

She actually had some bernalium on the table in front of her, a frothy lump of it mined from Mnemosyne, the ice moon at the centre of the Wheel. The sample was embedded in lead-doped glass that would, hopefully, contain its residual radiation. Florian lifted the lump and let it drop; it swam down through the air in the low-spin gravity.

'Let me just put it on the record once again,' Florian said sternly. 'Bernalium, mined from the core of the moon. *This* is why we're all here. Bernalium, a highly conductive mineral, essential for the next-generation high-energy technologies that will fuel mankind's leap outward into deep space . . .' Raised in America, she was very beautiful, in a rich-kid, hothouse way. But there was nothing soft about her, nothing spoiled. On the contrary, Jo had learned, her background, and what had become of her father, had left her hard, driven to progress the fortunes of Bootstrap, Inc., locked in deadly competition across the solar system with its commercial rivals.

The rest listened to Florian with strained patience. She was a nightmare to work with.

The council was meeting in one of the smaller buildings in Residential One, the Wheel's top-class habitation sector monopolised by A-grades like Florian; as a mere B, Jo felt out of place. There were windows set in the ceiling, and when she looked up Jo could make out the battered hulk of Mnemosyne itself. When Jo worked up there, in the little moon's miniscule gravity, her disability, her legs shattered and amputated after an encounter with a roadside IED in Venezuela far away and long ago, counted for nothing. But down here on the Wheel, even though the spin gravity was no higher than Earth's moon's, she was confined to chairs.

Florian dropped the bernalium lump again. 'Bernalium is the reason we're all here. The *only* reason. Once we extract it in significant quantities – assuming we ever do, assuming we get past the trial-bore stage we've been stuck at for months – this dump might pay for itself at last.'

Dr Sinbad Omar, an elegant, restrained North African, leaned forward. 'You don't need to remind us, Ms Hart. We need bernalium-based technology ourselves, in this hazardous environment. Almost every day I treat impact injuries caused by ring fragment collisions – crushing, broken limbs, decompression incidents. To keep at bay the swarm of ice missiles we live in requires something beefier than our elderly meson shields. The new laser technologies they are trialling on Earth's moon will be much more effective, but barely affordable until bernalium becomes more widely available.'

Florian took this as support for her position. 'Fine. Then we should accelerate the bore programme.'

Luis Reyes was a Spaniard; he came across as diffident, even nervous, and Jo suspected he was on a steep learning curve. But she had detected a strong moral core in him. 'You rush to conclusions, Florian,' he said now. 'We of Planetary Ethics will not sanction any pressure to accelerate the work programme here unless we are certain of the safety of the workers. Especially,' he said, emphasising his point with a hand slapped on the table, 'the young people, the children, born here in what is effectively a labour camp, many of whom are already working on the mine projects in a quite unacceptable manner.'

Florian sneered. 'There's more at issue than the fate of a bunch of C-grade loser kids.'

A bunch of kids that included Jo's own son, Sam. Jo seethed silently.

Florian Hart went on, 'I know what your agenda is, Reyes. It's always the same with you people. Let's give up. Let's roll up the colonies, let's all go back to Earth, let's pull the blankets over our heads and pretend the rest of the universe doesn't even exist, and boo hoo. Yes?'

Luis was intimidated, but he stood his ground. 'I know what you're hinting at. The Pull Back to Earth faction holds one extreme and unrepresentative philosophical position, and is nothing to do with me. The Planetary Ethics Commission is a widely backed, government-supported moral initiative. As you know very well, Ms Hart. If it's a choice between slowing down this particular project and risking harm to children—'

Florian laughed loudly to drown him out.

Sonia Paley sighed. 'Let's all try to keep calm, shall we?'

Jo suppressed a smile. That was the authentic voice of a British bobby, which was what Sonia had been before joining the ISC: calming, reassuring, even rather boring.

But Florian rounded on Sonia. 'More Brit smugness from you, Marshal Paley? It's a shame you and your deputies aren't concentrating on cracking down on the vandalism and theft and downright sabotage that seems to be endemic in this sinkhole. As long as you and your half-trained goons sit on your hands—'

'We've no suspects.' Sonia sighed. 'We've been through this, Florian. I don't deny there have been incidents.'

' "Incidents"!'

'I've no reason to call it "sabotage". There's no evidence that the incidents of damage have in any way been organised, motivated. And despite heavy surveillance we've no confirmed perpetrators. Unless *you* have something you haven't shown us. I mean, it's Bootstrap systems that have the mines under surveillance, not ISC.'

'It's the kids. It has to be.'

'So what would you have me do, Florian? Lock up everybody under the age of seventeen?'

'A curfew would be a start.'

Luis Reyes grinned. 'Might work, as long as we could make sure the Blue Dolls obeyed the curfew, too.'

'Oh, for crying out loud.' Florian sat back in her chair in disgust.

Sinbad tapped the slate in front of him on the table; data flowed across its surface. 'There *have* been more of these strange sightings. Most by very young children – including your little Casey, Jo. With kids that age it's difficult to pin anything down. But I've no clinical evidence that they're suffering from any kind of mass delusion, or that there's any environmental factor that might be causing this—'

Florian snorted. 'The damn kids are pulling our chains. It's all a hoax.'

Sinbad laughed. 'What, a hoax organised by three-year-olds?'

Jo let the arguments flow on, wondering when she could bring them back to the meeting's actual agenda items, the next of which concerned a plumbing problem in the Recreation sector.

Then her own slate flashed, with a puzzling text message. She tapped out a reply. *Phee? What do you mean, you picked up three refugees?*

5

At that moment, two of those refugees stood with Phee Laws in the open doorway of the TARDIS, peering out at the approaching Wheel. The third, Jamie, stood behind Zoe and the Doctor. Zoe suspected he was more than a little disturbed by vertigo from standing in a doorway open to space – as she was herself, but since that feeling was purely physical and not at all logical she put it firmly aside.

And she had to admit the view was spectacular. The cable, firmly tied to the TARDIS's console, snaked out to the battered hulk of MMAC, the spidery space-borne robot that had rescued them. And beyond MMAC lay the Wheel of Ice, the Mnemosyne Cincture. Mnemosyne itself – *Ne-mo-seen*, it had taken Jamie some practice to say it correctly – was a tiny moon, a shapeless lump of ice about a kilometre across, set at the centre of the Wheel. Small it might be but its tiny gravity field had played a part in shaping the structure of the ring system hereabouts, and the moon lay in one of a thousand fine gaps in the ring system. The shining ringlets, separated by these gaps, looked like strands of hair, finely combed and laid out in sweeping parallels.

And, small as it was, Mnemosyne had human visitors.

The Cincture – a posh word for 'rim' – was a bracelet four kilometres across, surrounding the little moon. The core of its structure was a mesh of looped cables, MMAC had explained, as tough and light as the cable he was using to tow in the TARDIS. And on that thread was strung a series of spheres and ovals, bubbles blown from ice from the captive moon, some hundreds of metres across. Most sparked with artificial light, but others glowed dimly orange by the light of Saturn. The bubbles were colonised; people lived in there. In some of them Zoe could make out the green of growing things – even what looked like a captive forest. The ice bubbles were a chain of worlds in bottles, like snow globes.

And interspersed with the ice bubbles were smaller, blockier, opaque shapes, cones and cylinders of metal and ceramic, many of them faded from long exposure to space, long-dead rocket nozzles gaping. It was evident these space hulks hadn't been manufactured for the purpose, but brought here from somewhere else for reuse, salvaged, modified, and integrated into the Wheel's structure.

The Wheel was a working place. Cables dangled down from the ice bubbles and metal hulks to trail on the surface of the moon at the centre, scraping along a metal roadway built around the moon's rough equator. The whole arrangement was like a bicycle wheel, the cables like spokes reaching in from the rim to the hub. As Zoe watched, flecks of light passed up and down the cables, people travelling to and from their workplace on the central moon.

This whole remarkable ragtag structure turned around that little moon. Zoe timed its rotation by her own calm pulse. One complete turn every three and a half minutes, she estimated.

The Doctor turned to her. 'So, what do you make of it? Rather impressive, don't you think?'

She snorted. 'Rather primitive, more like. That rotation—'

'Yes?'

'Clearly intended to generate the sense of gravity through centripetal force.'

'Umm, well, that and to provide dynamic stability.'

'A rotation of three and a half minutes and radius of two kilometres would yield a spin gravity of one point eight metres per second squared.'

'About a sixth of Earth's – about the moon's gravity. Well, that's elementary, Zoe.'

'Yes, but what it tells us is that they have no true artificial gravity system!'

'Unlike your own Station Three, you mean.'

'And then there's the green.'

'The green?'

'Look at that ice bubble, and that one. Chlorophyll green! Doctor, they are *growing their food* here. Growing it!'

'Rather nice to have a bit of grass growing. Trees, in Saturn's light.'

'It's clear they have no modern food-dispensing machines.'

'"Modern",' he said, with a slightly sterner edge to his voice. 'Remember, Zoe, this is not your time. Not quite. Such things as artificial gravity may not have been invented yet. Or it may be it's just too expensive . . . But here these people are, mining a moon of Saturn even *without* all those advantages. Isn't that rather marvellous?'

No, she felt like replying. *No. It's – it's – inefficient*. But she suspected such an answer would be illogical. Emotional. She had wrestled with this sort of reaction before. She had come with the Doctor to break out of her own world, her narrow background. She hadn't expected it would sometimes be so difficult.

The Doctor said now, 'I'm rather puzzled by that little moon, however. It looks rather like a fragment left over from a much larger body, doesn't it?'

And Zoe saw that he was right, and remembered that the TARDIS had landed here expecting a much larger moon – a moon perhaps already destroyed by the hole in time. 'What do you think it means, Doctor?'

'What it means is that *I* don't see some glorious natural spectacle here, in these rings, that moon. I see the aftermath of some disaster, deep in time. An explosion of a moon perhaps, an explosion that reduced the moon itself to that rump, and scattered debris through space to become these rings. Zoe, I suspect that the rings of Saturn are no more a wonder of nature than the mushroom cloud of a nuclear detonation . . . Oh, I say. Isn't that a Phoenix-class freighter?' He pointed at a large stream-lined vessel docked to one of the substructures, evidently newer than the hulks in the Wheel.

'Mark II-A,' MMAC replied. 'Aye, that's the *Jim Daniels* come to resupply us. A pretty wee vessel, Doctor? Better than the old Eldred ion-jet scows that used to limp out here. A conn-oo-sewer of spacecraft, are ye, sir?'

It took Zoe a moment to decode that word: *connoisseur.*

'Not exactly,' said the Doctor. 'But I have found myself on rather a lot of them over the years. Usually locked up on one, or escaping at speed from another, which doesn't always afford the best of views . . . By Jove. Isn't *that* one of the old Mars probes, the early English ones?'

This was a cone sat atop a cylinder, with three landing legs. Beside it was a spent booster stage labelled 'GB-UK-R' in faded lettering. Both these derelicts had been threaded by the base cables and adapted for habitation; windows had been cut into the hull of the booster.

MMAC sounded offended. 'English? Naw. British, if ye must. Scottish, if ye're truthful about the engineering nous that went into yon spaceships. Even if they were used to shoot English public schoolboys off to Mars. Many o' these are test articles, that were left abandoned in orbit or jes' driftin'.'

'But salvageable. And very valuable, given the cost of launching raw materials into space.'

'That's the idea. Took me years tae assemble this lot.'

'This was all your work, MMAC? The whole of the Wheel?'

'Oh, aye,' the robot said modestly. 'I were out here on ma aen for a few years, puttin' together the base afore the first people came out. Ye canna get any mining done if there's no' a working cludgie, can ye?'

Zoe whispered, ' "Cludgie"?'

'I think he means – ah – a sanitary recycling facility, Zoe. Tell me, MMAC, was this one of the first colonies out here at Saturn?'

'The verra first minin' effort, so I believe, after the exploratory flights. A proposal started by the Laws family – that's Phee's family – and took up by Bootstrap, the mining consortium.'

'But I imagine you built on experience gained closer to Earth – at Jupiter, for example.'

'Jupiter? Nae – there were little gannin' on in that system when they first sent me oot here.'

'Really? That's odd. But Jupiter's only half the distance from the sun, compared to Saturn.' The Doctor was frowning now, rubbing his chin, a thoughtful look Zoe knew well. He was intrigued, suspicious, on the trail of something – perhaps the mystery that had brought the TARDIS to this time and place. 'There must be a reason why those first colonists made a beeline for this planet, this little moon. Even if they didn't know it themselves . . .'

MMAC was still reminiscing. 'Aye, it wa' a proud day when the folks moved in, and ma work were done.'

'And what is your role noo – I mean, now, MMAC?'

MMAC was vague. 'This and that, ye know . . . Look down there, Doctor, at about four o'clock. What d'ye mek of *that* beauty?'

'My word. That's an XK5 – or what's left of it.'

'An experimental deep-space ship,' Zoe said.

'Well remembered, Zoe.' The remains of the XK5 were a clutch of bronze-coloured cylinders, disassembled and strung out on the cable. 'And next to it – are those Demeters, MMAC?'

'Aye. Bomb-carrying missiles from another century, shot off into space and abandoned when they had a spasm o' peace-making. Some of them still had warheads – Z-bomb planetbusters – and I had to make sure they were disarmed and cleaned out.'

'There's some lovely stuff here, MMAC. It's like a museum.'

'Ye like museums, Doctor?'

'Oh, I've seen many museum exhibits in my time. I've *been* an exhibit more than once . . .'

'I've go' this laing-term plan. Call it a dream.'

'A dream?'

'One day, when the mining's done, this place'll be abandoned. So then mebbe I'll refurbish these old hulks. Turn it into a proper museum o' the early space age. Or mebbe sell 'em off tae collectors for a bit o' cash!' He laughed, a throaty, convincing simulation.

Zoe snorted. 'An antiquated artificial intelligence – with a dream!'

The Doctor said mildly, 'Well, everyone must have a dream, Zoe. Even an "antiquated artificial intelligence".'

Jamie, behind them, said, 'Doctor, yon wheelie is getting awful close.'

'So it is.'

'And it's turnin' awful fast.'

Zoe worked it out quickly. 'The modules in the Wheel are moving at about sixty metres a second. That's over two hundred kilometres an hour. It's going to be quite a rendezvous manoeuvre!'

'Och, a piece o' cake,' MMAC called back. 'Hang on tae yer sporrans!'

The spidery robot, towing the helpless TARDIS, swept down on the Wheel, and the universe was filled with rushing masses of ice and metal.

6

At the docking port, cut into the side of a derelict Earth-moon freighter, the party was met by Phee's mother, Jo Laws, the mayor of the Wheel. She was a rather harassed-looking woman in a wheel-chair, with a small, sleepy child in her arms: her other daughter, Phee's little sister Casey.

With her was a woman Jamie identified immediately as police, even before she opened her mouth, even though she wore no uniform, although she did have a mean-looking weapon at her side. She introduced herself as Sonia Paley, she was Marshal here on the Wheel, and she worked for a larger organisation called the International Space – something or other. This woman had an unmistakeably English accent, and everything in Jamie's upbringing had led him to react strongly against English in authority. But he had been with the Doctor long enough to know when to keep his feelings hidden.

Led by Sonia and Jo, and with Phee Laws in dark glasses trailing along, they were led through the Wheel away from the docking port. There were walkways and partition floors laid down to give you a sur-face to walk on, but even that was odd because Jamie felt light as a feather, and if you weren't careful you could bound up into the air with a single stride.

They were in a sector of the Wheel called Utilities, Sonia said. There were six sectors in all, each consisting of several ice bubbles and rocket hulks. Through the bubbles' clear walls you could see Saturn, misty and huge, and the old ships were cones and tubes full of musty old acceleration couches and dead control panels. All these chambers were connected by doorways with big heavy metal hatches hanging open, ready to be sealed in an instant.

As they passed through the chambers of the Utilities sector, one after another, the Doctor had fun identifying their purposes. Here was a weather station, here was a computer centre, here was astronomy and guidance, a forest of bristling instruments, here was a maintenance section full of gadgets most of which Jamie couldn't recognise but including reassuringly familiar items like mops and brooms and buckets. The power station was interesting, a hall of glowing spheres. 'This is a solar stack,' said the Doctor. 'A suncatcher system.' The power of the distant sun, collected by huge mirrors outside the module itself, was somehow stored in big ceramic spheres that glowed from within. The Doctor was fascinated. 'A rather discredited old technology back on Earth, as I recall, but I can see the utility here.'

The most attractive places for Jamie were the farms, ice spheres full of green growing things. Some had beds of plants growing in pallets of earth, or in trays full of some kind of muddy liquid; others were like parks, with lawns of green grass growing, even stunted-looking trees. Jamie supposed they must have carried the soil here from Earth, and seeds for the grass, the plants. It was strange to think that everything he saw had been brought here by people, that nothing was natural. Still, the air was fresher here, more to Jamie's taste, and he could smell the earth, the grass – even though there wasn't a proper sun, just banks of bright floodlights fitted to the roofs of the bubbles.

They came to a new sector, called Residential Three. The architecture was crowded and ugly, blocky buildings with rooms stacked up on top of each other like the cells in a beehive. There was little colour, little decoration. But from some of the buildings hung big flags whose designs changed, every minute or so. There would be a bold corporate symbol, then faces of workers in spacesuits smiling happily, and then a motto in huge capitals:

COMMUNITY

IDENTITY

STABILITY

Most of the people Jamie overheard spoke English – and many of them had a trace of a Scottish accent, or so he thought, but that might have been wishful thinking.

But everywhere they passed, people stared. Evidently they weren't used to strangers here. Even their clothing drew glances and whispered comments – Jamie's kilt, the Doctor's shabby coat, even Zoe's practical jumpsuit. The people here were dressed much alike, in jumpsuits, or else in plain T-shirts and shorts or slacks like Phee's. And the dominant colour scheme was purple. Jo herself wore purple, and Sonia and Phee, dressed predominantly in grey, stood out. Some of the youngsters, though, seemed to go in for a bit of decoration. Jamie spotted strips of purple cloth used as hair ribbons, and chunks of scrap metal and ceramic on bits of wire worn like necklaces or bracelets.

They came to an open area where kids were playing a kind of basketball, an unusual sight in a colony that seemed dedicated to hard work and discipline. The kids, tall and wearing sunglasses, ran and leapt impossibly high into the air, and a bit of Jamie longed to join in. But he saw markings etched into some of the walls, even the trunks of trees. Gang marks, said Phee: graffiti.

One bubble they passed through looked burned out, as if there had been a riot, or a small war, and Sonia hurried them through.

And in the next bubble Jamie saw a gang of kids in orange coveralls labouring to clear a demolished building. They had big letter Ds on their backs. Adults stood over them, watching. A punishment gang, then, in this garden in the sky . . .

In a narrow alleyway he thought he saw something odd out of the corner of his eye. Something running, scurrying into the shadows. Small, like a child. But *blue*, blue-skinned.

'Hey. Did ye see that?'

Sonia turned. 'What?'

'Like a wee bairn, but *blue*.'

Phee said quickly, 'There was nothing there. A trick of the light.'

'But I saw it too,' said Zoe.

Phee repeated, 'There was nothing.'

'Well, how can you be sure?' Phee's brisk, abrupt denials were making Zoe uncomfortable. She closed her eyes and summoned up the image she had seen: the wide street, the buildings, the brilliant lamps suspended from the bubble roof. She placed all the people she had seen in that brief glimpse in their correct positions, as if populating a photograph. Her memory was perfect, and she trusted it. The blue flash had been at the edge of her vision – but yes, there it was, a small, compact form, just glimpsed in her peripheral vision. And it had been holding something, a bulky metallic object, something almost as large as *it* was.

'A child,' she said, opening her eyes. 'It must have been. I saw it quite clearly. Only a little bigger than Casey here. And it was carrying something, like a bit of equipment. It was running. And it disappeared – into a doorway? Somewhere I couldn't see. As if it was trying to hide.'

Sonia and Jo glanced at each other, uncertain.

But Phee shook her head. 'You saw nothing. The light in here can be funny.'

'Actually it appears to be a rather effective simulation of visible-spectrum sunlight—'

'There was nothing to see.'

Zoe was growing suspicious. They already knew there was something odd going on here, at this mine in the sky, she reminded herself; if not the TARDIS wouldn't have brought them all here in the first place. And, given the way the TARDIS had reacted to Phee, there were already questions about *her*. Reluctantly she concluded this wasn't a line of inquiry to follow, for now.

But Casey, the little sister, gave her a gappy grin, and pointed, in the precise direction Zoe had seen the blue flash. Clearly, distinctly, unmistakeably, the child said, 'Blue Doll!'

7

They were brought at last to a small cabin, metal-walled, no windows, that Jamie, who had been in plenty of English jails, had no hesitation in recognising as a cell.

Here Phee and Jo had to leave them with Sonia Paley. Sonia said they were to be checked over by a medic, one at a time. The Doctor himself was the first to be taken off by Dr Omar, and he went cheerfully enough.

Zoe and Jamie, shut in, left to themselves, explored the little cabin. It was brilliantly lit by roof panels. At first it seemed empty to Jamie, nothing but blank metal walls. But Zoe helped him find a tiny toilet hidden behind a seamless door and, when you pressed little catches in the walls, tables and chairs folded down. 'This was how we had things on the Station,' she said. 'Everything packed away neatly when you didn't need it.'

There was a distant hooter, and an echoing voice. 'Shift change. Shift change . . .'

'Hmph,' said Zoe. 'It's like one huge factory.'

With a bit more exploring Jamie found a cupboard containing food packages and a water spigot, and ceramic cups. Both hungry, they gulped down the water and pulled open the packages. The food was disappointing, basically a kind of biscuit coated with green paste.

Zoe ate this, pulling a face. 'Probably a blue-green algae derivative from those hydroponics beds. The sooner the people of this era invent proper synthetic-food dispensers the better!'

There were tiny little tomatoes, red and round and perfect, that were full of flavour, and Jamie gobbled them like sweets. 'No meat, then.'

'Oh, no, I shouldn't think so. No animals, not here! Much too inefficient in terms of protein production.'

And Jamie pitied the children he'd glimpsed, growing up here, who must never have seen so much as a spring lamb.

Before long the Doctor returned. 'Ah, biscuits!' He sat down and fell on the food, but chewed with more hunger than relish. 'Not terribly joyful, our home from home, is it? Fits in with the character of the place as a whole, I suppose. I do like the little fold-down chairs and so on. Rather reminds me of a caravan holiday I once had in Wales—'

'How was the medical exam?' Zoe asked, forestalling the anecdote.

The Doctor rubbed one upper arm. 'Injection for a blood sample,' he moaned. 'Never was too fond of needles. Otherwise, much as usual when I go through these things. A lot of awkward questions and bluffing – you know the drill. Dr Omar's a nice young chap.'

'He looked it,' Zoe murmured.

'Don't get yer hopes up, Zoe,' Jamie said with a grin. 'I heard Phee say his partner's called Max.'

'Oh, shut up, Jamie.'

The Doctor said, 'But I'm afraid my various readings confused him thoroughly. Says he'll call me back. Not if I can help it! I believe I managed to distract him by praising his diagnostic machinery, even if he did think it was malfunctioning. Do you know, he had an electronic stethoscope I rather took a shine to.'

'They'll try to identify us,' Zoe said.

'Quite. He took swabs for DNA from my cheeks, for example. Well, *those* results from any one of us will make their computers blow a gasket, one way or another. One of us from the past, one from the future, and the other from somewhere else entirely! Nothing to be done about that, however.'

There was a knock at the door, then Sonia Paley's efficient voice. 'Ms Heriot next please.'

Stiffly, evidently reluctantly, Zoe got up, brushed her hands free of crumbs, and followed Sonia out of the room.

The Doctor asked, around a mouthful of biscuit, 'So how's Jamie? You haven't eaten much. Not like you, my lad.'

'Och, it's just . . . I never liked prisons.'

'Of course,' the Doctor said gently.

'And I'm even more confused than usual, Doctor.'

'Well, I don't blame you.'

'Where *are* we? Nothing out there made a blitherin' bit o' sense tae me.'

'I'm not surprised . . . Jamie, the big gassy world out there is the planet Saturn. You know that. It's much bigger than the Earth. Sixth planet of the solar system – well, it used to be the seventh, but that's another story. Saturn is the furthest planet visible to a human eye on Earth. But not long after your time, Jamie, another planet would be discovered, by an Englishman—'

'Och, it would be.'

'It ended up being called Uranus, after the Greek god of heaven. But the Englishman who discovered it wanted to call it after King George!'

'What! That usurpin' Hanoverian! I cannae believe it—'

'Not your King George. His grandson, I think. Oh, do sit down, Jamie. Anyhow, the name didn't stick . . . For centuries people observed Saturn's rings – well, you've seen them up close now – and wondered what they were made of. And now people have come here to mine them for the minerals, which, it seems, they may contain. Odd, though. They're mining bernalium, apparently. But bernalium is rare in this solar system. I wonder . . .' Just as he seemed to be losing himself in thought, he turned to Jamie again. 'And you. What do you make of this place, this Wheel of Ice?'

Jamie sniffed, smelling metal. 'It has its pretty bits. The farms. Great view, if you like big lumps of ice flying around everywhere. But it's all shut in. People all wearing the same colours. Doors that lock every-where. Like a prison, and I've seen enough o' them.'

'I know what you mean. The doors are there for safety, I'm sure, so a loss of pressure in one compartment won't affect the whole Wheel. But they would serve to confine the people as well.'

As they spoke, there was a loud click, as if an immense switch had been thrown. The lights dimmed, the big roof panels darkening and giving way to smaller glowing spheres.

The Doctor grunted. 'Thus evening falls, on the Wheel of Ice.'

'Aye, lights-out in this jail. And then there's Zoe.'

'Ah.' In the shade, the Doctor's eyes were deep, gentle.

'What's troublin' her, Doctor? Ye said this is close to her ain time. Ye'd think she'd like it here. Familiar, like. But here she is, and it's not makin' her happy.'

'No, it isn't, is it? I hope she'll adjust. But you have to remember, Jamie, that Zoe's upbringing was somewhat unusual. Her education was dedicated and focused, nothing much but logic and memory training. It's not that she was told that history was unimportant. It was more that she was encouraged to think it didn't exist at all. As if her own age, of the great Stations in space, was all that ever was, all that ever had been.'

'Aye. And then we showed up.' Jamie couldn't help grinning at the memory.

'Yes. Us and the Cybermen. Well, we helped wake her curiosity, didn't we? And so she stowed away on the TARDIS, and came with us.'

'Well, good fer her. She got what she wanted. Here we are. But—'

'But she's unhappy. I know, Jamie. I think it's just a little too close to home. This isn't just history. This is *her* history. The history that was always hidden from her. Here are these people struggling, and I daresay dying, in order to build the world in which she grew up, tucked away in her school like, like one of these delicious tomatoes in a greenhouse. I suspect she feels resentment. Guilt, perhaps. One forgets how very young she is, sometimes.

'But she'll see the longer perspective, in time. After all, this is only the beginning. Even in this age humans are definitely on their way, leapfrogging across space with their clever little eyes already fixed on the stars. And here, too, the solar system will be transformed. One day there'll be flower gardens in the clouds of Saturn, you know. And in the very far future, people will even be able to live on far Pluto, the furthest planet, in the warmth and the light.'

'Really? Will they be happy?'

'Aye, there's the rub, Jamie.'

'So ye think she'll get over it?'

'Without a doubt. You know Zoe.'

The talk had made Jamie feel more cheerful. 'She ought tae take a lesson or two from us Scots. We haven't forgotten our history. We revel in it.'

'Quite right too. Jamie, the Scots have achieved marvellous things – I suspect, given the accents we've heard, that this very Wheel is one example—'

The door clanged open, and Zoe half-fell into the room. 'All right, you don't have to push!' The door closed behind her.

The others stood. 'Zoe?' the Doctor asked. 'Are you all right?'

Zoe looked more angry than flustered. 'Not really. Marshal Paley brought the news while I was in with Dr Omar.' She smiled, unexpectedly. 'Who *is* very nice, by the way.'

The Doctor said sternly, 'Zoe, focus! What news?'

'That there's been some kind of trouble on this station. Sabotage, some say. Components of various machines stolen. Wiring, circuitry. Mirrors, from optical equipment and lasers.'

'How very odd.'

'And we're suddenly the prime suspects.'

Jamie had an unerring instinct in such situations. He hurled himself at the door, but he was too late. There was no mistaking the sound of the lock firmly closing.

Zoe cried, 'We're under arrest!'

8

After the incident with the refugees and the Blue Dolls, Phee was determined to get home before her mother. As it happened, Jo had appointments elsewhere, so she let Phee take Casey, who slept in Phee's arms as she dashed through the Residential Three sector to the family home.

And as soon as she got home, Phee collared her brother Sam.

Nineteen years old, tall and lanky, Sam was sitting in the kitchen in his sunglasses, working his way through a stack of pancakes. He was defiantly wearing C-grade green coveralls, as if proud.

Phee put Casey to bed. Then she went back to the kitchen and told Sam in a rush about the strange new refugees, and how they had seen blue creatures immediately they were brought to the Wheel.

Sam snorted. He wasn't interested in the refugees. Sometimes he didn't seem interested in anything at all. 'Clever people, to see something that only kids can see. To share in our "mass delusion".'

'But they're not like other adults.' Phee frowned, thinking of what she'd glimpsed of the TARDIS, the travellers' strange escape module. It had been like a door in space, into that brightly lit room . . . 'There's something odd about them.'

Sam grinned. 'Odd?'

She'd had an impression of *otherness*. How can you say that to your big brother without having him laugh in your face? 'Maybe they see a bit more widely than most adults. And I think they saw a Doll.'

'Adults see what they want to see.'

'Don't give me that. You're nineteen years old. *You're* an adult, Sam, whether you like it or not.'

He challenged her, 'Have you ever seen a Doll?'

'No. I haven't. But then I don't hang around with you and your loser friends.'

'Oh, yeah, we're all losers, us rubbish C-grades. Whereas an A like you, you're the strong one who faces the grim reality, are you?' He turned away, arrogant, bored.

She sat down opposite Sam. She wouldn't let him wriggle out of answering her questions. When Jamie and Zoe had seen the Doll, some instinct had made Phee cover it up, even though she didn't understand what was going on herself. But then Casey had pointed at the Doll, without fear. She had recognised it. 'What's all this got to do with Casey, Sam?'

For a moment there was silence. She could hear the soft breathing of the sleeping Casey in the next room.

He wouldn't answer.

'What have you done, Sam?'

When he still wouldn't answer, she marched into Casey's room.

Sam hurried after her. 'Don't wake her. Mum will kill us.' He was whispering now.

They stood together over Casey's bed, blankets piled up in a big ceramic cot, bright pink. Casey lay on her side with her half-curled fist by her face, a relic of how she used to suck her thumb when she was even smaller. There were a few battered, cherished toys piled up in the cot. Mister Rabbit. Teddy No-Ears. And –

And a blue hand, delicate, almost child-sized, sticking out from under a blanket. *Blue.*

Phee reached for the blanket.

'Don't,' Sam whispered, pleading.

Phee took the blanket, peeled it back delicately so she wouldn't wake Casey.

And she revealed a doll, life-sized, about as big as Casey. It had no clothes, but its flesh was seamless, all but featureless – no genitals, no nipples, no navel. And it was a rich royal blue.

A blue doll.

Hastily Sam covered it over.

'What was that, Sam?'

'Not here. Come on.' He took her arm and led her out of the sleeping child's room. 'Mum's seen it, but she's not suspicious about it. I told her I made it as a gift for Casey, when I did a training shift on the matter printers in Utilities.'

'But that was a lie.'

'Yeah. Look – OK, I'll tell you. But you've got to swear not to tell Mum, or anybody else.'

'I'm not swearing anything. She's my little sister. Just tell me, Sam.'

'All right, all right. I've taken her to the moon sometimes. Casey. Down to the mines. We smuggled her down, me and Dai and Sanjay and the lads.'

'What? You don't get taken down there until you're seven years old, for the familiarisation classes.'

'I know, I know. We just did it for a laugh.'

'A laugh.' Phee thought it over. 'Tell me the truth, Sam. When I'm away on a course, and Mum's working shifts, she leaves you in charge of Casey. You're supposed to arrange a babysitter—'

'All right! What are you, the ISC? I pocketed the money – no babysitter – and I took the kid down the mine with us instead. Look, it's safe! I know what I'm doing.'

'A three-year-old down a mine, dug into a moon of Saturn? Sure it's safe. So what about the doll?'

'It began a few months ago. We had a break period. We bunked off. There are places to hide, Phee. Unopened shafts, dug by the machines and pressurised, but not yet checked out by the miners. We try to set records – you know, to be the deepest anybody's ever gone inside Mnemosyne. You never know what you might find.'

Phee said heavily, 'So you took Casey down an unexplored shaft.'

'Well, I couldn't leave her behind! So this one time – well, we saw something.'

'What kind of thing?'

'Deep in the shaft – deeper than we'd penetrated before. There was a side-shaft. And at the end of it—' He frowned. 'Hard to describe. A kind of curtain. It was a pale blue, like you get with very old ice. Patterns in the light, like interference fringes maybe.'

'Something intelligent,' she guessed wildly. 'Deep down inside Mnemosyne.'

'I don't know. You tell me. And then something came rolling through the curtain.' He shuddered. 'Like an eye, on a tripod.'

'Like a *what*?'

'I only know what I saw, and I don't even understand *that*. We were spooked, I'll tell you. We scrambled back to the main shaft, to get out. All of us except—'

'Casey.'

'Yeah. *She* wasn't scared. Maybe you have to learn to be afraid of strangeness. She got away from me.'

'She *got away*?'

'All right! She went crawling to the eye. It sort of *reflected* her, like a mirror, but all in blue, and she laughed. That was all I saw before I dashed in and got her.'

'So what then?'

He shrugged. 'I went back once more, with Dai and a couple of others. Just to see, you know? We dared each other. Without Casey this time. But by this time the incidents had started.'

'The sabotage.'

'Yes. The early, minor stuff. Gremlins, they put it down to at first. But we wondered if we had somehow triggered it all by going down there – deeper than anybody else, remember. And then the gossip started about sightings of blue critters – *blue*, a deep blue, like the blue we'd seen in the shaft. So we went back to see if it was connected.'

'And you found the blue doll.'

'Yeah. Just lying there. I brought it back, I meant to hide it somewhere, but as soon as Casey saw it she grabbed it and ran to Mum to show her the new toy. All I could do was cover.'

'And that lame story about the matter printer was the best you could do.'

'All right, A-grade.'

'And it's in Casey's bed right now. This thing you found in the middle of the moon.'

'It's not doing any harm, is it?'

Phee closed her eyes, and visualised the doll. 'Sam – doesn't it seem to you – that doll's face—'

'What about it?'

A small mouth closed, a snub of nose without nostrils. Eyes sealed shut, eerily.

'Don't you think it looks like Casey?'

9

In the end the TARDIS crew spent less than twenty-four hours behind locked doors.

Their liberation was thanks to Zoe, who demanded that Sonia Paley send a message to the headquarters of International Space Command at Geneva, on Earth. This wasn't Zoe's time, but it was close enough that she was able to guess at the state of space law. The core of her case was a polite demand that the travellers be granted certain basic human rights, universally recognised by the authorities on Earth and across the solar system – the right to shelter and sustenance in space, the right not to be subject to false imprisonment. Such rights were upheld in Zoe's era, and, she earnestly hoped, in this age too.

She was proven correct when Sonia Paley, with Jo Laws at her side, unlocked their cell door.

The Doctor led them out, beaming with pride. 'That's my girl!'

Jamie, who never took well to confinement, was hugely relieved to be out. 'Aye, ye're a marvel, lassie. Although ye could hae been quicker about it.'

'Well, that's typical.'

They were led once more through the ice chambers of the Wheel, and the defunct spacecraft and fuel tanks that connected them.

Jo, pushing herself along in a slim wheelchair, navigated the hatches and corridors skilfully, Zoe observed. In Zoe's time there were automated chairs, and cybernetic prosthetics and exoskeletal suits that would enable a person with Jo's injuries to function normally, even if surgical options were ruled out. Maybe such options hadn't been developed yet, in this age, or maybe were too expensive for Jo.

Or maybe, Zoe thought, observing the skill with which Jo operated her chair, she just enjoyed the challenge.

Sonia said, 'You have the right to liberty and shelter until an inspector arrives from Geneva, or another ISC base. It helps that I happen to report to the ISC . . .'

Jamie asked, 'So how long have we got?'

The Doctor said, 'Well, it takes light itself an hour to get here from Earth, Jamie. And interplanetary travel depends on the availability of a ship, and the relative positions of the planets. Several days at least, I should think.'

'Seems a lot o' fuss, jest fer the three o' us.'

Zoe said, 'But such procedures are important, Jamie. People need to be protected out here, but so do colony facilities like this one. Don't forget, every breath of air you take in a place like this has to be processed, every sip of water. Nothing comes free, not even the air.'

'Well, I willna take more than my fair share, then.'

'Quite right,' said the Doctor.

They emerged through a hatchway into another wide ice bubble, another bauble on the tremendous bracelet of the Wheel, this one a densely inhabited volume. People swarmed everywhere, adults and children, most in a purplish colour scheme. There was an orderly layout to the main buildings, which followed a street that ran along the axis of the bubble. Zoe recognised a small hospital, a smaller school, residential blocks, stores, a meeting hall – and a detention centre. More of those big display flags hung and shimmered, silently dispensing symbols, images and slogans: IT'S *GOOD* TO BE A B! One big central tower led all the way up to the roof of the bubble, and looking through the translucent roof Zoe saw cables crossing space to the pinpoint block of the ice moon itself, suspended directly over her head. So that was how the workers travelled up to the mines.

At the feet of the main structures there were other, scruffier buildings. There was even a ramshackle church, with the symbols of many religions on its walls. Maybe this was how people *chose* to live, in these much more crude, humble structures that they built for themselves.

They came to a house on the main drag along the bubble's axis, a substantial block but not ornate. Zoe heard music, a rhythmic thumping along with a heavy plucked-string melody.

Phee Laws emerged from the main door, unsmiling, wary-looking. Zoe guessed this was the Laws' own home. Zoe saw that the Doctor was carefully trying not to stare at Phee, trying not to hunt for the anomalous time-travelling artefact she had evidently been carrying when they had first encountered her, out in space. Zoe was almost sure that the culprit was that heavy black amulet that Phee wore around her neck; it didn't fit with the rest of her bland grey outfit at all.

Jo Laws looked faintly embarrassed. 'Our home,' she said. 'Personally I'd have been happy to have stayed put in Triple Block.' She indicated one of the big residential buildings over the road. 'That's where the kids grew up. But the planners decided the mayor needs a palace, and so here we are.'

'Oh, I'd hardly call it a palace,' the Doctor said, patting a seamless ceramic wall.

'But we still get ragged for it,' Phee said. 'By the kids at school. Sam hates it.'

'Sam?'

'My eldest,' Jo said. 'You'll meet him soon enough. Well, you can hear him already. At least we didn't move up to Res One, Phee. You might have fitted in there, but Sam—'

The Doctor asked mildly, 'Ah – "Res One"?'

'Sorry. The Wheel has six sectors, numbered anticlockwise.'

'Widdershins – it would be!'

'There are three residential sectors. Res One is reserved, more or less, for A-grade, Res Three – this one – for Bs like me, and Res Five is for Cs. The other sectors are Utilities, Industrial, and Recreation – sectors two, four and six.'

'Sounds jolly. And how does one become an A or a B or a C?'

'They test you at school,' Phee said.

Jo said, 'Bootstrap used parapsychology consultants to set up the educational system here. I think they saw us as a test case. An experiment.'

The Doctor said, 'Hmmph. Like that, is it? Everybody classified and colour-coded!'

'It could have been worse, Doctor. There were proposals to replace family units with work cadres. Most of us argued hard against that.'

'And I suppose once you have been graded you are stuck for life, are you?'

'Well, you can always become a D,' Phee said.

'Criminal class,' Sonia Paley said. She sounded mildly impatient.

Jamie had his mind on more practical matters. 'Now we're out of the jug, where are we gonna kip? I suppose there's always the TARDIS.'

Sonia frowned. 'Oh, you mean your escape capsule? I'm afraid it's been impounded.'

'That is my property,' blustered the Doctor. 'Well – not strictly – but it's certainly nothing to do with you!'

'I think you'll find the sanction is in the scope of the law.'

Jo said, 'Look – you're welcome to stay in my home as guests. That's why we brought you here. Phee seems to have taken a shine to you all, for one thing.'

Her daughter blushed and looked away.

'And it's a way to keep an eye on you that satisfies Sonia here. Mr McCrimmon is going to have to share a room with Sam, my son. You'll be in with Phee, Zoe. Now come on inside, let me get you settled.'

Zoe decided to make an effort. 'I'm glad we're sharing, Phee. It'll be fun.' She knew her smile could be infectious, at times.

Eventually, Phee smiled back.

Sonia stepped back. 'I'll leave you to it. Oh, Doctor – there's somebody who wants to meet you.'

'Really? Who?'

Jo pulled a face. 'Florian Hart. The conscience of our commercial lords and masters. Likes to know about whatever's going on in this Wheel. She can be somewhat intense, but I'll sit in, don't worry. Now do come in . . .' With a graceful flip she rolled her chair over the threshold and into the house.

The Doctor followed, after a cheeky nod to Sonia.

Jamie marched after him. 'I'd better go meet ma new roommate.'

'Just follow the noise,' Jo called back wearily.

Sam's room was at the top of the stairs. Jamie found himself facing a closed door, painted jet black. The music, such as it was, came from behind the door, a thumping, repetitive drumbeat, the twanging of some stringed instrument. Muffled as the noise was by the door, Jamie found his foot tapping; the beat was just a bit faster than his heartbeat.

He knocked. There was no reply, and he shrugged, turned the handle and pushed the door open. The room within was dark, the only light a glowing pattern on the walls and ceiling, a stripy, coloured design. Jamie thought the pattern was an image of Saturn's rings. The designs were slowly evolving, he saw, changing.

The main piece of furniture was a bed, black sheets and blankets, on which a young man sprawled. He plucked at a kind of harp, made of a bit of curved ceramic with strings running taut across it. There was a set of drums stacked in one corner that looked like they had been made out of odds and ends too, but the drumming sound was a recording, coming from some kind of box in the corner of the room.

The din was loud. Jamie called, 'D'ye mind to turn yon box doon a wee bit?'

No reply.

Jamie set his fists on his hips and leaned over. 'Ah said, will ye turn yon box doon? And it wid be nice tae have a bit o' LIGHT in here!'

To his surprise, as he yelled the word 'light', a bright white glow flooded the room, from tubes set in the ceiling. Now Jamie could see that the floor was covered with discarded clothes and other junk.

Sam threw his arm over his eyes, abandoning his harp. He called, 'Off,' and the drum noise stopped. He lowered his arm and slipped on dark glasses. He was very like Phee, his sister, Jamie saw, with the same pale colouring, the red hair. He was tall, and looked strong in a wiry, ropy way. He wore a green jumpsuit that had been artfully gashed to reveal a bright red underlay. He looked Jamie over. He looked jealous as he took in the traveller's kilt and tunic, and especially the knife at his waist. But he said with a sneer, 'What did *you* come as? This is my room. Get lost, granddad.'

Jamie loomed over him. 'Aw, now you jest shut yer geggie. First off it's *our* room for now, because yer mam says so. And second off, I'm no grandda'. How old are you?'

Reluctantly, Sam said, 'Nineteen.'

'Aye, well, I'm no' much older, so ye call me grandda' again and I'll larrup ye. Pleased to meet yer by the way. I'm Jamie.' He glanced around the room. 'Messy scamp, aren't ye?'

'Now you sound like my mother.'

'A' right, a' right. I like yer wallpaper.'

'It's not wallpaper,' Sam said contemptuously. 'It's an update of an analysis we're doing on the rings.'

'Saturn's rings?'

'Full of resonances. Patterns. You can see some of it with the naked eye, but there's a lot more in there if you do some analysis . . . Music, maybe.'

'Huh?'

'Some of us think there's music in the rings. Frozen in the patterns in the ice. But nobody *your* age thinks so.'

'Now, I told ye—'

'All *they* see is more mines. More profit.'

'Music, eh. And what do ye call this?' Jamie picked up the harp and experimentally plucked a string. The sound was louder than it was sweet, but the strings were backed by a crude fretboard, and Jamie quickly found that he could change the tuning by bending the board as well as by fingering the strings. With a few seconds' experiment he began to pick out a tune.

Sam stared. 'I made that myself.'

'Ah can tell,' said Jamie, a bit unkindly.

'The body is the lid of a defunct home suncatcher pile. The strings are threads of elevator cable. The stuff they use to drop us down onto the mine. I made the drums too. There are a few of us. We play . . .'

'Play what?'

He shrugged. 'Stuff we make up. They don't like music here. Gets in the way of work, they say. All we get is company motivation songs, and you should hear *them*. But some of the oldies remember songs from Earth and we learned those. But we prefer to write our own . . . What's that you're playing?'

It was an old Jacobite marching song. 'Ah, ye wouldnae know it.'

'You must have an instinct for music, to pick up a thing like that and just play it.'

'I'm a trained piper. In the blood.' He thought the boy had the faintest trace of a Scots accent himself. A bit wistfully he asked, 'If there's Scots here, I don't suppose there's a set o' pipes around?'

'A bagpipe? In the museum, maybe. Yes, I think there is.' He grinned. 'We could bust in and pinch it. You could play with us.'

'Ah, whisht ye, maybe we'll leave that fer tomorrow.'

The boy grunted. 'I won't be here tomorrow.'

Jamie frowned. 'What do ye mean?'

From outside the house came a cold, artificial noise, an urgent blaring. Jamie had heard it several times before, cooped up in the jail cell.

Sam scowled. '*That's* what I mean. Shift change. Time to go to work.' He swung his legs off the bed. 'Don't you know that much? Where are you from?'

'Ye look young to be working down a mine.'

Sam pulled a trunk out from under his bed; it contained boots, a heavy-duty green coverall, what looked like a skinsuit, transparent. 'There are kids a lot younger than me being sent up to that mine every day, believe me. You ever been skiing?'

The change of subject took Jamie by surprise. 'Skiing?'

'A bunch of us break out sometimes. We pinch scooters and nip over to Enceladus. You know, the moon. You should come, next time we go. Fantastic. Full vacuum, low gravity, you feel like you're going faster than light!' Now Sam was pulling on his skinsuit. 'Make yourself at home. There are pillows and stuff under the bed. You can find a place to kip on the floor. But don't touch my stuff.'

When the shift-change hooter sounded, Zoe and Phee, with a little help from Casey, were going through Phee's wardrobe, such as it was. All the clothes Phee cherished she had made herself, modified from the uniform-like grey-toned standard issue gear. Phee wasn't complaining. 'It's the same for everybody. And you can do stuff. See?' She held up a top cut from an old pair of coveralls and covered with bursts of white, like flowers, or like storms on Saturn.

So Zoe smiled, and they compared sizes, and Zoe wondered if she could give Phee some of her own clothes from her room in the TARDIS.

But when she heard that shift-change hooter Phee hastily changed into a work outfit of heavy coverall in her usual pale grey, and skinsuit over the top. Zoe was amazed when Phee told her where she was going.

Phee led Zoe downstairs to the house's small kitchen cum dining room, where the Doctor sat at a table of convincing artificial wood, drinking tea with Jo.

'Zoe! You must try this. A quite marvellous cuppa. A good old British tradition, preserved among the rings of Saturn!' But then he looked into his cup dubiously. 'Although I suppose it pays not to ask what these leaves grew in.'

Zoe sat down with him. 'Doctor, haven't you noticed what's happening? These children – they're all being sent to work in the mines!'

The Doctor gave her a warning look.

'That's the way of it here,' Jo said tiredly. 'Company rules. Look, Florian Hart is on her way to speak to you, Doctor. I'll stick around. Besides I have to wait for a sitter for Casey.'

'Huh!' Zoe said. 'I'm surprised you aren't putting *her* to work as well.'

The Doctor said evenly, 'Now, Zoe, ours is not to judge these people. Or those they work for. I'm given to understand that the very young ones are only sent up there to observe. To familiarise, to get used to the environment—'

'Where they will be working for the rest of their lives. Wouldn't it be better if they were at school?'

'Where they would usefully learn what?' Without knocking, a woman walked in through the open door: tall, beautiful, confident, dressed in a shining silver-grey suit. 'My name's Florian Hart. Bootstrap, Inc., Cincture Administrator. Good afternoon, Zoe Heriot, Doctor. I've read your files. Good day, Mayor Laws.'

'Hello, Florian,' Jo replied neutrally.

Florian sat at the table, again without being asked.

Zoe said indignantly, 'I can think of many things more useful than to spend one's childhood learning about mine workings. Utility trumps everything for you, does it?'

Florian said, 'It's not a question of utility but of basic economics. For Bootstrap, despite the high intrinsic value of bernalium, the profit margins on an operation like this are smaller than you'd think. We're pioneers. We continually encounter novel technical challenges, and it costs money to overcome them. That moon up there – the core seems unstable, somehow. We pick up shifting gravitational fields. Then there are anomalous neutrino fluxes.'

The Doctor said, 'Neutrinos? Well, that's interesting . . . I suppose there is much to learn.'

'But this does mean that we must exploit all our resources to their maximum efficiency.'

'"Resources",' Zoe said curtly. 'Child labour, you mean.'

Florian smiled sweetly. 'Ms Heriot, I'm sure you know as well as I do that the laws concerning "child labour", as you put it, have been relaxed concerning the space colonies. I like to compare our settlement to the heroic days of the Old American West. If you were a pioneer family everybody had to pitch in to help, from children to grandparents. And when those children grew old themselves, what a heroic tale they had to tell their own grandchildren! This is what the bleeding hearts like Luis Reyes can never see. People *want* their kids to grow up here, like this. Of course every measure is taken to ensure the safety and ongoing health of all our workers.'

'I'd enjoy a look at your casualty figures some time,' the Doctor said mildly.

Florian's expression hardened. 'I don't know who you are, Doctor. I don't know what you want. I know I'm not likely to learn it before the ISC pen-pusher gets here from Geneva. But it's obviously to do with the mining operation. What else is there here? And that means, it's to do with me. I wanted to meet you to make quite sure you know what you're dealing with.'

'Oh, I think I know that already,' the Doctor said, with faint sadness.

There was another shrill electronic noise, coming from Florian's cuff. She glanced at a flashing display. 'Excuse me, I'll have to take this.' She turned away, clamped a hand over her ear, and began to whisper rapidly, angrily.

Zoe leaned towards the Doctor. 'Have you heard of Bootstrap, Inc., before?'

'In various contexts, yes. Met the chap who founded it, actually. Not a bad fellow. Let his ambitions run away with him, though.'

'This isn't a happy place.'

'I'd say not, Zoe. A society where children's whole lives are being sacrificed to the goals of their parents. The parents had a choice about coming out here, living like this – well, I presume they had a choice. The children had none at all.

'These are the first generations to live away from the Earth, Zoe. You're meeting some of the first children, like Sam and Phee and little Casey, ever to have been born away from the mother world. Born in boxes of metal or plastic or ceramic, where you have to buy every molecule of air you breathe. These, Zoe, are the first human beings ever to have been born in cages.'

'No wonder there is conflict, then.'

'Quite. But, Zoe, *it's nothing to do with us.* All we are concerned about is the Relative Continuum Displacement Zone.' He glanced up at the moon. 'I rather think I need to take a look at what's really going on up there, in the mine. And to have something of a root around down here. I saw it too, you know,' he murmured.

'Saw what?'

'Casey's "Blue Doll".' He tapped his nose. 'Now if *we* saw it, despite having just arrived here, it's clearly a real phenomenon. Something that can be objectively confirmed. So why the denial, why the mystery? Is somebody running a cover-up? And what's the significance of the Blue

Dolls anyhow? I've no idea what's going on here – not yet – but everything's connected, Zoe. The social tension, this funny business with the Blue Dolls, the time anomaly. Everything's connected. It always is. All you have to do is pull on a thread, and the rest unravels.'

This sounded a bit pompous to Zoe, and irritated her. 'What about Jamie and me? What threads shall we pull on?'

'The girl Phee Laws is somehow central to this. The time-travel artefact that may be in her possession. Jamie's rather hit it off with the brother, I think, and you with Phee. I suggest you stick close to the youngsters.'

In this place, Zoe didn't feel young at all. She too had been born and raised in confined extraterrestrial environments. She ought to be used to this. But part of her longed to be away from this Wheel of Ice. 'I think I'd rather go chase another dangling thread. I want to speak to MMAC again. That spider robot. *He* must know all about this place.'

'Yes, that sounds worthwhile to me, I hadn't thought of it.' His tone was so gentle, she couldn't tell if he was being sincere or just being kind.

Florian shook her sleeve out. 'I need to go.'

'What a pity,' the Doctor said with only mild sarcasm. 'And why's that?'

'More sabotage. More production lost – another disruption to the income stream. Those wretched kids!'

'Are you so sure it's the children?'

'The adults are all committed to the economic goals. If they weren't they wouldn't have come here in the first place. Of course it's the kids.' And with that she turned away, distracted, checked the time and marched out as if the others no longer even existed.

MMAC

I

Alone, Zoe Heriot rose above the rings of Saturn.

'Oh, I loathe this scooter—'

'Och, dinna fash yersel', miss.'

'Oh! I was talking to myself. I didn't realise you were listening in. I mean—'

'Dinna fret. I didnae mean to intrude. But I can override yer privacy settings. It's a safety thing. Ah, but that's me, now that my days o' colony-buildin' are done. I'm just one big fat backup system these days!'

'Well, it's the lack of backup on this scooter that worries me. There are so many ways for this thing to go wrong!'

'If ye were tae lose control, it would fly ye home. Like one o' ma uncle Murdo's homin' pigeons back in Govan.'

'Uncle Murdo? Yes, but with all respect that's not good enough. Not in the environment I come from. The scooter has only one rocket engine! *We* designed systems for safety, with multiple layers of redundancy built in from the start.'

'It's different here, miss. They're pioneers. They take risks. Otherwise they'd get nothin' done. And besides there's the cost. Yon scooter would cost a hatful more if it had a backup engine. And it'd be heavier, and harder tae handle.'

'And not so much fun to ride.'

'Now ye're talkin'. But I understan' yer thinkin'. I'm programmed fer safety mesel'. So dinna think me a hero if I bail ye oot again, miss. I canna help it.'

'Oh! Sorry. I'm rising out of the shadow of Saturn, into the sunlight. Quite a spectacle!'

'Tell me what ye see.'

'A gas giant. The rings are within Saturn's Roche limit, as it's called, where the tides are strong enough to rip larger objects to fragments. The flatness of the ring system, and the banding of the rings, come from gravitational resonances with the orbits of the moons . . . But it can't be as simple as that. There are waves, ripples, even spokes laid over the basic circular banding.'

'I take it yer studied space science.'

'Yes. In the City, I was a pure maths major, and went on to astrophysics and astrometry.'

'And ye've been tellin' me what ye think.'

'I'm sorry?'

'I asked ye what ye *see*, miss. Try again.'

'You sound like the Doctor. All right. Well, I suppose – the dim sun, the gentle shades – I see . . . autumn.'

'Ah. *Now* ye're gettin' it.'

'So what do you see, MMAC?'

'Smog. A smoggy sunset o'er Glasgae, when I were a wee bairn.'

'MMAC, I don't understand. About your being a bairn, I mean a child, in Glasgow. And having an uncle?'

'Ye dinnae wanna hear all that rot.'

'But I do . . .'

II

'I were born in Govan – well, ye know that.

'My ma worked in the spacecraft fittin' yards on the Clyde. A welder. Worked on the first generation o' Phoenix ships. My pa worked in computing, in software an' artificial intelligence. Well, that's nae surprise I suppose.

'I loved gannin' tae see my ma at work. One of my first mem'ries is sittin' in the navigator's seat o' a big ol' Phoenix Mark I. I think e'en then ah knew I'd work in space some day. That or the football, and I had two left feet and would ne'er have cut it for Glasgae Celtic!'

'I still don't understand. You had a mother and father. Your memories are of being a boy, physically. Of playing football . . .'

'Look, miss – I grew up *believin'* I were a little boy.'

'A human.'

'Aye. It was the way it were done then. My job, my purpose, was always gannae be oot here. At Saturn. They were gannin' tae send me out here alone, all on my tod, 'cept for some dumb subsidiary bots that ye couldnae have a conversation with if ye worked 'em like a ventriloquist's dummy. I had to build the colony – yon Wheel – build it from scratch using old salvaged hulks and the raw material here, ice from the moon and the rings. That was the plan.

'Givin' me the ability to do the work, that was easy for the programmers. The hard part was givin' me the motivation. Ye see? I had tae work ma hide off for the sake of humans, and tae do it as fast and as well as I could. So tae give me that motivation—'

'They wanted to make you loyal to humanity. And so they made you grow up believing you *were* human.'

'Aye! It was cleverly done. A mix o' virtual-reality foolery and live action. Fer example, that day my ma took me in to the spaceship yards –

she *actually* took in a remote sensor unit, a box with cameras and microphones and sensors so I could see and hear and smell and touch and taste, and accelerometers so I could feel as if I was being picked up and put down . . . But it wasn't a little boy sat in that pilot's chair. It was a gadget the size of a suitcase.'

'And she wasn't really your mother.'

'Nah. But my pa had more claim; he was one o' the team that designed me. So I grew up. Went to school, or thought I did. Helped Uncle Murdo with his pigeons. Got to the age o' twelve and started showin' an interest in the lassies. And then—'

'And then they told you the truth.'

'Aye. They had Uncle Murdo do it. He just held up a mirror, and I saw mysel' clear, fer the firs' time in my life. I didnae see my face any more.'

'What did you see?'

'That suitcase. On a kind o' trolley. Not my eyes, a camera lens lookin' back at me. I remember what I said.'

'What was that?'

'"S'no' fair." What else could ye say? And then I, or my programmin', was whisked up to the moon, to the big Bootstrap, Inc., construction yard in Clavius Crater, where they were buildin' this big ugly carcass I'm in now. And I started trainin', like I had tae learn how to walk again. And tae move a hundred arms independently!'

'It must have been traumatic. MMAC, I'm sorry.'

'Well, it wasnae your fault.'

'But it seems so terribly cruel.'

'Aye, well, it were done fer the best o' motives. I'll tell ye, once I got used tae the idea I had great fun out here. Diggin' into the moons, hurlin' great lumps o' iron across the solar system. And, look at it this way. At least I ne'er had acne.'

'Oh, MMAC, you shouldn't joke about it.'

'Wha' else is there tae do? And besides, they had the right. I was ne'er

human at all. I am a made thing. They made me. They could do wha'
they like wi' me.'

'No. I don't believe that. Made or not, you are a sentience, a mind.
However you were created, you have rights, to self-determination, to
consciousness, to liberty . . . But then, I don't know if your treatment
was so terribly different from my own upbringing. My education was as
narrowly vocational as it could possibly be. And the result, well, a good
friend of mine once called me "All brains and no heart". I didn't even
know what he meant, until I met the Doctor and Jamie! At least *I* had
the chance to escape – a chance I took. What chance did you ever have?'

'Oh, it's no' so hard as that.'

'Well, I think it is. Did you see your parents again?'

'Not in person. My pa was on the programmin' team. But after I was
transferred to the moon – well, he wasnae really my pa no more.'

'It had just been an act.'

'Aye. But my ma, she wanted to come visit. The Bootstrap folk wouldnae allow it. She sent me letters. Mail. Just text, or audio or images if she
could.'

'Do you still hear from her now?'

'Naw. Not since I came oot here.'

'Hmm. That's odd. I must remember to check that when I get back
to the Wheel. So what now for you, MMAC?'

'They still find me work. Bits o' construction, or ferryin'.'

'Rescuing stranded space travellers like us?'

'Some o' that too.'

'There must be other mining projects to develop. Why not transfer
you?'

'Because I'm out o' date. Knackered. Past it. It would cost more tae
upgrade me than to build a new specialised unit in the firs' place. And
besides, they don't make 'em smart any more. Not like me.'

'Yes. You certainly couldn't have a conversation with the servo-
robots on the Station where I worked.'

'For one thing brainy robots make people uncomfortable. And then, there are rules about binnin' us. See, I think they'd scrap me, Bootstrap would, if they could. But they cannae, because the authorities won't let 'em.'

'What authorities?'

'The ISC. But they're under pressure from PEC.'

'The Planetary Ethics Commission. So they won't transfer you, they can't shut you down—'

'And so I just hang around, oot here. There are worse lives, believe me. And worse places to be . . .'

'Sorry to interrupt.'

'Doctor? Is that you?'

III

'Do forgive me, Zoe. I'm down in the colony, in Mayor Laws' home. I just wanted to check and see how you're getting along. I didn't mean to eavesdrop.'

'No matter. Are you getting a visual feed? Can you see what I'm seeing?'

'I can indeed, Zoe. And it's enhanced with imagery from MMAC's cameras. My word, what a glorious sight! It's like a tremendous musical box, isn't it?'

'And rather different from our first look at it, Doctor.'

'Yes. The middle of the ring plane is *not* the best viewpoint of the Saturn system. And now, Zoe, if you don't mind putting your scientist's cap back on – look at all the structure in those rings!'

'Yes. I was thinking of that before. Some of it is obvious. The gaps are clearly caused by tidal resonances with the moons' orbits. But there's more to it than that, Doctor. It's very clearly visible from up here. You'll have to come up here and see.'

'On one of those scooter things? Not on your nellie.'

'There are more complex patterns overlaid on the rest, the basic bands and gaps. Spokes, crossing the ring bands, that seem to turn with the planet.'

'Umm. Some effect of Saturn's magnetic field, perhaps?'

'Maybe. But what about *this*?'

'Ah. I see. Fine ringlets – and they're *braided*, like hair. Oh! How remarkable. I wonder how *that* can happen. You know, Zoe, I'm beginning to wonder if these strange features of the ring system are somehow connected to the other puzzles we're facing.'

'Everything's connected, Doctor. That's what you told me.'

'Whatever's shaped the rings is basically mediated by gravity and magnetic fields. Hmm. Florian Hart, in between bragging, threatening and being generally domineering, said that our own mined moon, Mnemosyne, itself produces gravitational anomalies, as if the core is unstable. I wonder if that could have anything to do with the higher-order patterns you're detecting?'

'It certainly could, if you consider the relevant equations of orbital mechanics and gravitational perturbation. And, after all, the very existence of the rings themselves is something of a puzzle. Let me think – given the quasi-stability of the orbits of the particles, the rate of attrition by the atmosphere of Saturn . . . Why, the rings can only be fifty million years old or so. Any older than that and they'd decay away, all those little ice bits being dispersed into space, or falling into Saturn's clouds.'

'"Only", ye say? Tha' seems long enough tae me.'

'Not really, MMAC. We handle much longer timescales in astrophysics. The solar system, Saturn itself, is *a hundred times* older than that. So finding rings here is unusual. Unexpected. Oh! But, Doctor, you already had a theory that the ring system is the debris from some ancient disaster.'

'I did indeed. The break-up of a moon. And now we have a date for that event: fifty million years ago. Good thinking, Zoe.'

'But to work out what the ring perturbations might mean, we'd need a long baseline study.'

'Yes, quite. Years and years of records! I don't imagine Bootstrap and their workers will help us there. They've been up here for the bernalium in Mnemosyne, not for planetary physics.'

'Ah, 'scuse me. I'm still here.'

'Sorry, MMAC!'

'I've been floatin' around this system fer – well, ne'er you mind how long. And I've been watching the rings, among other things.'

'You don't mean—'

'Full record, high resolution. I've got a big brain, Doctor, an' a high-capacity memory, and not much tae fill it with. If ye can work out where ye want me tae download it—'

'Oh, what a splendid fellow you are!'

'Ah, whisht ye, Doc, it's a pleasure.'

'I should think the computing capacity here will be up to the job. If not, there's always the TARDIS, if they'll ever let me near the old girl. Well, I think we've got our work cut out, Zoe. A number of threads to follow, indeed.'

'Yes, Doctor. I'll come back in and make a start. Oh, by the way, Doctor, how's Jamie?'

'Jamie? You know, he did tell me one thing that bears on what we've been discussing. He says the youngsters here have noticed the ring structures too. And what they see is resonances – harmonies.'

'As if the rings are frozen music?'

'Exactly.'

'Why, what a charming thought.'

'Yes. Rather wasted on dear old Jamie, I fancy.'

'So where is he now?'

'Going skiing.'

'*Skiing*?'

'Don't ask. Sooner him than me! I'll pass on your regards . . .'

10

At the end of her latest shift on Mnemosyne, Phee overheard mutterings among the older workers, mostly Cs but a few B-grade supervisors and shift leaders. Mutterings about more gremlins.

And another injury, to a man called James Campbell. Phee knew a few of the Campbells. In a community as small as the Wheel it was impossible not to have some kind of connection to almost everybody, but she hadn't come across this man James. Anyhow, whatever had happened to him was none of her business.

But she couldn't help but hear the gossiping. The C-grade workers tried to keep what they knew secret from the B-grade supervisors, and the Bs kept secrets from the Cs, and neither of them talked to the A-grade executives. But none of them seemed to notice the youngsters around them, on their orientation tours and apprenticeships, and, sometimes, they would speak as if you weren't even there.

So Phee picked up fragments of the story. Of some kind of encounter in the deep shafts, that had left the workers terrified. It wasn't any technical problem this time, not like the earlier glitches, though some of those had caused injuries as a by-product. This time it had been a direct injury to a worker – a human, to Campbell. A direct *attack*. The injury was strange, the doctors were puzzled.

And it was something to do with the colour *blue* . . .

After the shift she went straight home. Her mother's shift was the same as hers, and with any luck she wouldn't be back yet. Casey should be away at her nursery. Sam had bunked off work and was getting ready for his jaunt to Enceladus. With gritted teeth Phee had agreed to go too; she hated to skip shifts, but she felt she had to keep an eye on Sam . . .

She hoped she'd find the house empty. It was.

Her heart hammering, her conscience pricking, Phee made straight for her mother's desk, in the small room she used as a study. She raised a decorative lid to expose a stout steel hatch, with a combination lock in its surface.

Nobody knew the combination of Mayor Jo Laws' desk. Nobody but her son Sam. And her daughter Phee.

Sam knew because he had spied on his mother. Partly that was out of habit; it was the sort of thing Sam did. And partly, Phee suspected, so that he had an option of adjusting or destroying any damaging records held on him in there.

And he had whispered the combination into Phee's ear, once, when he was drunk. It was pure spite, to implicate his 'stuck up, sanctimonious, A-grade snitch of a sister' in his own grubby affairs. At least she had never before used that bit of knowledge. And now she told herself she was doing this for the good of Casey, maybe the good of the colony as a whole.

She tapped in the combination. The steel lid swung open, silent and smooth, as cold as her guilt.

She leaned forward, tucking the amulet that hung from her neck out of the way. Inside the desk was a stack of records and files, mostly hand-written, and a few photographs taken with crude wet-chemistry cameras. Jo Laws had grown up in an age when nobody had imagined that any digital record or image could possibly be secure, so she insisted her most private documents were written out by hand in unique copies like this, very old-fashioned, but quite unhackable . . . The desk wasn't very well organised, her mother was no file clerk, but what Phee wanted was very recent and was easy to find, right on top.

'CAMPBELL, JAMES, IDENT C78J987K, PP-SE CLASSIFICATION C7. INJURIES SUSTAINED DURING SHIFT ALPHA-SEVEN . . .' It was a medical report, one copy of four, filled out and signed on the cover by Dr Sinbad Omar. Phee flicked through it quickly. There was an account of a routine shift's work, Campbell's team had been opening up a new shaft, and Campbell, forty-two years old and very experienced, was in the vanguard.

Then had come the encounter.

'They just crowded around,' testified a co-worker. 'Little creatures. Stunted. Cold. Swarming everywhere. Yeah, blue. There was one that acted like a leader, but they all looked alike. We got away, out of the shaft, all but Jim Campbell. He went down and they dragged him back. Covered him, swarming like big blue maggots. He screamed. I'll never forget. We went back for him. We couldn't fire our blasters, we'd have hit Jim. So we just went in with whatever we had to hand, laying into them with bars and struts and blaster butts and our bare fists. We drove them off and got Jim out of there, but the damage had been done . . .'

There were images, taken by the medical staff, of Campbell in the hospital. The blue creatures had got him by the legs, and his flesh from the groin down –

'Metamorphosed' was the word Dr Omar used, but Phee knew the fancy word didn't imply any greater understanding. Metamorphosed meant *changed*. Human flesh changed into cold blue seamless – what? Plastic, ceramic? And at the edge between blue and pink, she could see a spreading stain, a fibrous infestation, halted only by death.

Shuddering, she shut the file. She closed the desk and locked it down, and sat thinking.

Then she walked through to Casey's room.

* * *

The empty cot was the usual jumble of blankets and toys. Phee pulled out the blankets one by one. They smelled of Casey, her warm-toast kiddie smell.

She came to the blue doll, lying there in the nest of blankets.

She felt oddly reluctant to touch it. Its material looked exactly like the stuff on Campbell's legs, in the photographs. She bent and picked up the doll. It was neither warm nor cold to the touch, that was eerie in itself, and its synthetic flesh was smooth, seamless. She got it under the armpits and held it up, and looked into that eerie, smoothed-out copy of Casey's face. 'What's going on here? What *are* you?'

The eyes snapped open, revealing wells of black.

The mouth too peeled open, a widening slit, revealing a row of teeth like needles.

And it came alive in her hands. Squirming, strong. Those black eyes fixed on the pendant on her chest, and made a grab for it.

She screamed, spun around and hurled the Doll away from her. It slammed against the wall on the far side of the room. For a heartbeat it was still again, lying there, head down.

Then the creature turned, swarmed up the wall and squirmed out of the window, and it was gone in a blue flash.

The air went out of Phee in a rush, and she folded her arms over her amulet, safe on its chain. She couldn't tell her mother about this, she realised immediately. Jo would never forgive Sam for bringing a murderous, monstrous – thing – into her child's bedroom. So what was she to do?

'I rather think we need to talk, Miss Laws. Don't you?'

The voice startled her. She whirled around. It was the Doctor.

11

The next day, with Sam and Phee Laws and a bunch of their similarly aged friends, Jamie found himself on a rocket scooter, plummeting across the Saturn system. They were on their way to one of the bigger moons, a ball of ice called Enceladus. Jamie had had to write the name down on the back of his hand to remember it at all. Then the challenge had been to find a way to wear a kilt inside a pressure suit . . .

Unlike Zoe, Jamie didn't mind riding his little scooter. He found it exhilarating. In his day there had been no mechanical beasties like this to ride around on, but Jamie had been a good horse-rider, not that he'd often had the chance. You twisted the handles to turn or go faster, just as you'd haul a rein or spur a horse. On such a light craft the way you distributed your bodyweight was important, and you had to lean this way and that in the turn, and that was just like horsemanship too. He'd been told that the ride would get easier on the way back when the scooters would be less laden with fuel pods and ration packs, lumpy containers that were attached to the main upright.

Of course, he thought at first, you could never love a scooter, a thing of ceramic and metal and squirty rocket nozzles, the way you learned to love a horse. But maybe he was wrong about that. He looked at the youngsters scattered around the sky about him, riding vehicles jazzed up with gaudy colours and flashing lights, even fanciful, entirely useless fins and wings. They were all bunking off from school or mine work, which added spice to the adventure, he supposed. They played endlessly, chattering on their comms links, running races and performing stunts, swooping and barrel-rolling – and mounting mock collisions, tricks that made Jamie's heart race. He felt tired just watching them.

It would take a full twenty-four hours to reach Enceladus, he was told. That was all right for these kids, but Jamie was old enough to admit that he needed his kip. He'd just have to hang on.

Only Phee Laws hung back from the antics of the rest. She swept down out of the sky to ride alongside Jamie. 'Don't worry about them,' she said.

'I'm tryin' not to.'

'We've all been flying these scooters since before we could walk. And besides, accidents in space happen in kind of slow motion. If you survive the initial impact you just drift away, until somebody retrieves you.'

'That's reassuring.' It wasn't. 'But I notice ye're not chucking yersel' around the sky, Phee.'

'Well, it's not my cup of tea.' She laughed. 'I heard the Doctor say that. Cup of tea!'

'Then,' Jamie asked gently, 'why are you here? You're not a daredevil. And you don't strike me as a slacker either.'

She sounded defensive now. 'Well, why are *you* here?'

He didn't want to answer that. Didn't want to tell her that the Doctor had asked him to stay close to Phee herself, to find out more about the time anomaly she seemed somehow to be associated with. Time enough for that, Jamie.

'Look, Phee – I think ye're here because o' that big lummox up there.' Jamie pointed to an electric blue scooter spinning in the sky up ahead. 'Sam. Yer big brother. I know it's difficult for ye. He's older. He should be lookin' after *you*. Instead he's the one needs his bumps felt.'

That made her laugh. 'What does *that* mean? Oh, never mind. All right, yes. He's always getting into trouble. He always has. But he's nineteen now, Jamie. They can't keep turning a blind eye for ever. If he was to get prosecuted for something or other—'

'I imagine it'd break yer ma's heart, to see him locked up.'

'Oh, we don't lock up people here,' she said bleakly. 'We just have holding cells like the one you three were kept in. We haven't got the resources to support a prison population. Everybody has to be *productive.* You get busted down to a D-grade, and sentenced to a work detail, or worse.'

'A work detail? But ye're all working yer backsides off as it is, as far as I can see.'

'Yes, but there are jobs nobody much wants to do. Humiliating. Dangerous. Well, Sam hasn't got that far yet. But this latest stunt doesn't help. I don't know why Sam is the way he is. I mean, there's no bad in him. My dad died when I was very small. I don't remember him. It was an accident, they were opening up the first shafts on Mnemosyne. Sam was there. You know the way they like to take us up as little kids to familiarise us with the mine?'

'He saw it,' Jamie guessed. 'Sam saw your father die.'

'Later, Mum got married again, to a man called Harry Matthews, and the result was Casey, before they broke up. *He* moved out, went off to the methane extraction plant on Titan . . . It's all been a mess. And Mum's always busy being mayor. But none of that is any excuse. Luis tries to help.'

'Who? Oh, the chap from Earth.'

'Luis Reyes, from Planetary Ethics. I think Sam likes him – thinks he's exotic. Anybody's who's not from the Wheel is interesting to Sam. Even you.'

'Oh, thanks.'

'But it doesn't do any good. Nothing ever does, not with Sam.'

Jamie felt intensely sorry for this serious, responsible young girl, in this place of hard work and regulations, and the unruly elder brother she couldn't protect or control. And he felt even worse that in a way he, Jamie, was only here to spy on her. 'Och, try not to worry, lass. Look, I'm here to help bail him out on this jaunt anyhow.'

'Well, it isn't your problem. But thanks anyway. Oh, by the way you need to change your comms setting.'

'What, my little radio? Why?'

'You're allowed to speak scooter to scooter but you have to shut down your links back to the Wheel.'

'What? That's daft. If somethin' goes wrong—'

'I know. But that's the gang rule. Sam's rule.' She spoke with a kind of weary contempt. 'It makes no difference. They track us on radar anyhow. But—'

'Boys will be boys. All right, Phee, I'll take care of it.'

Phee, riding alongside Jamie, seemed to hesitate, as if there was more she wanted to say. But she just nodded, and her scooter swooped away.

12

Jo summoned Sonia Paley to talk about the latest bit of bad news.

There had been another incident in the mined moon. Another fatality. The third in twenty-four hours, beginning with the Campbell incident.

When Sonia walked in, Jo had the medics' reports spread out over her kitchen table. And there was the Doctor, sipping tea, calmly studying the gruesome images on the tabletop before him.

'What's he doing here?'

Jo sighed. 'Sonia, he is rather persistent. You try keeping him away.'

'That wouldn't be hard. You are technically still under arrest, Doctor.'

'Oh, am I? Well, technically arrested or not, as I've been trying to persuade your mayor here, I have rather a lot to offer you in this difficult situation. A lot of relevant experience.'

'Experience of what?'

'Alien life. And extraterrestrial intelligence. Which may be causative factors in this situation. Aha! I see you're not dismissing that out of hand. You may deny the conclusion, but the mounting evidence—'

'Yes, well, whatever you're an expert in, I'm just a copper. So let's stick to the evidence for now, shall we?' She poured herself tea from the pot and sat at the table.

Jo showed her the latest images. It had been another attack, another case of the strange blue metamorphosis. This time the changes had spread over the victim's torso, from her neck to her hips.

'The heart gives out, you know,' Jo said. 'That's what kills them. Arteries and veins are severed, capillaries too, as this transformation turns human tissue into – well, whatever *this* is.'

'Do the medics have any theories?'

'Sinbad Omar suggests it might be some kind of disease. A plague. Some life form from a biosphere inimical to ours.'

The Doctor sniffed.

'I take it you don't agree,' Sonia said dryly.

'Well, does this look like any kind of plague to you? The pattern differs every time. For this poor victim it was the torso that was attacked. Last time it was the back. Before that, the legs. The most horrific of all is what happens to the face. There is an image here—'

'I don't need to see it, thanks.'

'You're squeamish for a copper, aren't you? Can't you see the pattern? It's almost as if these poor miners are being *experimented* on. As if they are being trialled, their bodies tested.'

Sonia frowned. 'And you think this is intentional. As if driven by some intelligence.'

'Isn't that at least possible? And now look, don't you play the sceptic with me, Marshal. I'm well aware that the International Space Command has full access to UNIT's records, which bulge with evidence of alien incursions of various kinds into the solar system and on Earth itself going back centuries. You must surely be at least open to the possibility that that's what we're dealing with here.'

'Well, what would you have us do?'

'Speak to your medical people again. Get them to look again at these cases, perhaps with slightly more open minds. And talk to Florian Hart, or if necessary her bosses.'

Jo said, 'Florian? She just denies it all. Calls it human error – or human criminality.'

The Doctor snorted. 'Well, then she's mistaken – or lying. There must be wider evidence than this; I'm quite sure that mined moon is full of surveillance systems.'

'Yes,' Sonia said, 'but that data is proprietary to Bootstrap and Florian won't let us near it.'

Jo said, 'But what she *is* doing is threatening all sorts of reprisals for the sabotage, and now these murders – her word, not mine. She's talking about lockdowns. Sometimes I think there's a danger she'll use this as an excuse to take some kind of control here, in the Wheel as a whole.'

'Not while I'm around,' Sonia said coldly.

Jo went on, 'It is true that each of these incidents generates eye-witness accounts of attacks. Swarming, by some kind of creature. Blue-skinned.'

The Doctor said, 'But there's no photographic evidence, I take it.'

'No. Well, the workers are too busy fighting for their lives to take holiday snaps.'

Sonia put in, 'And the testimony of C-grades is regarded as unreliable anyhow.'

The Doctor protested, 'This isn't a court of law, Marshal! Evidence is evidence.'

Sonia sighed. 'Yes, but – look, Doctor, I've been to a number of off-Earth outposts before. On planets, on moons, in deep space. People cooped up too close together in entirely alien environments. They see things that aren't there – or misinterpret what they do see.'

'It's all cosmic ray flashes in the eyeballs!'

'Well, yes. And they gossip. Rumours spread like a cold virus.'

'But we are dealing with deaths here,' Jo said firmly. 'They can't be denied. And are unexplained, so far.'

'Yes. Of course. But we're working in a fog.' Sonia stood. 'Look, let me go make some further enquiries. And I'll contact Geneva. Maybe I'll ask them about warrants to search the Bootstrap facilities. We'll talk later.'

When she had gone the Doctor leaned towards Jo. 'And what about the sightings away from the mine, Jo – in the Wheel itself? I'm sure you can't deny such things have occurred. Flashes of blue. Creatures scurrying out of sight. Why, I've seen it myself.'

Jo shrugged. 'The kids keep it to themselves because they think nobody believes them. But even I hear the rumours. Nothing's been substantiated. Again there's no photography, no visual evidence.'

'That could mean that whatever's here is too smart to be picked up by your routine surveillance systems. Or again, that somebody is deliberately hiding evidence. Perhaps under your very nose.'

'What do you mean by that? Look, what would you have me do? Start hauling children in at random for questioning?'

'No,' the Doctor said. 'Though I imagine Florian Hart would enjoy that. This is a community so riven with mutual suspicion – there's no trust even between parents and children! Let's sort this out before Florian sorts it out for us.

'I want you to help me get to some of this evidence directly, Mayor Laws. If I'm to help, I need to see what we're dealing with. Perhaps run some tests of my own. I do have a fairly wide expertise. And we need to find out whatever Florian Hart is covering up – for I'm increasingly sure that's what she's doing. If possible, I must go up to that moon myself and find out what's really behind all this.'

'Is that all? Anything else?'

To her surprise his crumpled face assumed a gentler expression. 'Actually, yes. Mayor, we need to talk about your own children . . .'

And he told her what he had seen in Casey's bedroom, of Phee and the Blue Doll.

13

By the time Enceladus swam into view, Jamie was dog tired, and starving hungry despite the little nipples in the suit neck that fed him some kind of liquid food.

Enceladus was a globe of clean cold ice. At first it looked like a billiard ball, round and white and perfect. But as they approached, Jamie started to make out detail. The northern hemisphere was pocked by craters; it looked as if it had been blasted by a musket shot. But the south was smoother, just as white but lacking craters, and textured with sheets and soft mounds of what looked like snow. That lower hemisphere was scarred by long, straight blue-white cracks, a network of them reaching up towards the equator. They must have been hundreds of kilometres long.

About a third of the globe was in shadow, from Jamie's point of view, and he saw no lights gleaming on the dark side. No people down there, he guessed.

Sam swept down in front of him from out of nowhere, the nozzles on his electric-blue scooter squirting exhaust. 'How's it going, granddad?'

'Ah, clear the road. Ye scared me half tae death. And dinna call me granddad.'

'What do you think of Enceladus?'

'I'd tell ye if ye'd get oot ma way.'

Sam laughed, but he twisted his scooter gracefully up and around to settle in alongside Jamie. 'Look away,' he said.

'What?'

'Look away from the moon and shield your eyes.'

Grumbling, Jamie tried it, cupping his gloved hand before his visored face. He had spent enough nights hiding out on the Scottish moors to know that he needed to give his eyes time to adapt to the dark, and he waited patiently.

And he saw a kind of glowing corridor, misty, sparkling, stretching ahead of the moon, and behind it. A ghostly ring, in which Enceladus was embedded.

'Och, it's bonny.'

'Nothing but ice,' Sam said. 'Just like the main rings. Nothing but ice crystals, and sunlight.'

'Where does it come from? Yon moon?'

'Yes. It's hot inside, liquid under a thick ice crust. Something to do with the tides – keeps it warm. See the tiger stripes?' He pointed at the cracks in the southern hemisphere. 'They're fissures. Breaks in the crust. The liquid stuff from inside comes up in geysers and fountains. Some of the stuff snows out, back on the moon.'

'Ah, and buries the craters.'

'That's it. And some of it gets thrown away from the moon and it's created this band of ice, all the way around the moon's orbit. Listen, granddad. When we go in just follow me, me and the others. Don't bother about Phee. Go in right after us. And when I tell you, press that button there, on your right-hand controller.'

'What, this big red jobbie? What happens? Do the bristles shoot out o' this witch's broomstick?'

'And I've got a present for you.' It was a package wrapped in a translucent blanket; he pulled it free of his scooter's main strut and tossed it across open space to Jamie.

Jamie inspected the package by Enceladus's silver-white light. 'A bagpipe!'

'Think you can play it?'

'Och, I could play a haggis skin if you stuck a few drones on it . . . Where'd ye get it? Oh. From that museum ye talked about, I'll wager.'

'It's the only set of pipes in the Saturn system. Well, they were doing no good stuck in a box in the museum, were they?'

Jamie was dubious about being drawn into this. But still – pipes! It didn't look like much of a make, what he could see through the packaging, but he longed to try it out.

There was a sound like a chiming bell.

Sam tapped a dial on his scooter. 'That's it. Approach trajectory locked in. Cowabunga, granddad!'

'Your cow's – what?'

But Sam had already peeled away. He had his friends lined up in a tight, narrow formation, all save Phee who hung back, and swept down towards the shining face of Enceladus, a swarm of fireflies before a Chinese lantern.

Hastily Jamie attached the package of pipes to his scooter's upright. He clenched his fists around his scooter's controls and drove it forward as fast as he could, arrowing straight at the white face of Enceladus.

It was a world, looming out of the dark. It filled his field of view and seemed to flatten out, becoming a great dish of sculpted white, those craters like burst blisters in the north, and the snow fields of the south cut through by those long, nearly straight tiger stripes.

Now the scooter swarm ahead of him swept upwards, and Jamie hastily followed suit. Enceladus tipped over, and suddenly he was flying over a landscape of hills and canyons. Still they dropped, the features shooting under the prow of his scooter with bewildering speed. Everything was white, the world a mask of ice and snow, with not a single splash of rock or vegetation, and the sky above was an eerie black over the brilliant white of the ice plains.

And still they dropped. They passed over a mound of huge, tumbled boulders, the ground fell away beneath them, and they descended into a crevasse, a valley cut deep into the ice. The walls were blue-white, the deep ice trapping the light. The whole feature was no more than a kilometre or so wide. This must be a tiger stripe, one of those long valleys.

With the walls whipping past him, the sense of enormous speed was suddenly overwhelming.

Sam whooped. 'You still with us, granddad?'

'Just.'

'That button. Hit it now!'

Jamie didn't let himself think about it. He thumped the button. With a jolt, two flat slats popped out from the side of his scooter's main body and levelled out to either side of him, beneath his feet.

And then the scooter dropped, just like that, and suddenly he was *on the ice*, scraping along the surface. His scooter's main rocket nozzle swivelled so it was firing behind him, hurling him forward, and he had to lean forward to keep his balance. The rough ice surface was carpeted by a layer of loose grains that were thrown up in a plume behind him. Every bump and hummock jolted Jamie's bones.

Now everybody was whooping on the comms channel. Sam yelled, 'Isn't this what life is for, granddad? Skiing on a moon of Saturn!'

Jamie risked a glance upward. He saw a single spark hanging high above the valley. That was Phee, keeping out of trouble – or waiting for trouble to happen.

Somebody yelled, 'Beware vent!'

The swarm of fireflies was lifting up from the surface again, rising high into the blackness. Jamie had no time to react. The ground rose up in a kind of natural ramp, and the scooter on its skis hurled itself forward and *up*, and Jamie was flying over a huge circular hole in the valley floor. The ramp he'd climbed had been a rim of raised ice. The whole feature looked like the remains of a burst boil.

'Tell me how it can get better than this!' Sam yelled again, almost hysterical. 'Tell me, granddad!'

Jamie felt like he'd left his stomach down there on the ice.

The ski run came to an end at last at the far end of the tiger-stripe canyon, amid another heap of giant ice boulders. Jamie got off more cautiously than the rest; he felt as if he'd been beaten black and blue all over.

The youngsters stacked their scooters together and started unloading their packs. One boy had a kind of sheet of translucent material, folded small into a backpack, that spread out a remarkably long way over the ice. The youngsters anchored it with gadgets like guns that fired spikes into the ice. Then they unfolded poles, and started crawling under the sheet to fix it like a tent.

Jamie tried to help, but he floated around like a soap bubble in the impossibly low gravity, and was clumsy as a young ox. After the third time he'd fallen over, and the second time he nearly shot himself through the foot with a spike gun, Phee gently took his arm and pulled him away from the action.

'Of course it's not really skiing,' she said.

'It's not?' Nobody in Jamie's time had used skis. But he had seen skiing in Tibet once, though he and the Doctor had been too busy running from robot yeti for him to take much notice. 'I dinna understand.'

'On Earth your skis slide over a slick of slippery melted ice. Here the ice doesn't melt, it's too cold, so the scooters' skis have to be treated with a frictionless surface to make them work. And your rockets have to push you down onto the ice to stop you flying off all the time.'

'Aye, well, whatever it was, it was too much excitement for me . . .'

He thought he felt a tremor. A tremble deep in the ice ground of this little moon. Phee said nothing about it. Probably his imagination – or his stomach trying to unknot itself after that ride down.

'Come on. I think they've got the dome ready.' She led him to the erected tent.

There was a simple fold-out airlock stuck on the side of the dome, and inside everybody was climbing out of their skinsuits and dumping them on a rolled-out groundsheet. But Jamie noticed Phee kept her suit on, though opened to the waist, revealing the jet-black amulet she always wore at her neck. That seemed a wise precaution in case this tent thing failed, so Jamie followed her example.

Their bits of lightweight equipment were soon functioning remarkably effectively, providing air, warmth, light, water to drink; there were even cooking smells. The youngsters in their customised clothing lounged around, talking, messing with musical instruments, drums, harps, a kind of mouth organ. Some seemed to be calming down, even climbing into lightweight sleeping bags. But others, suited up, were still coming and going through the airlock, which dilated with a sigh each time.

Phee seemed to want to take charge of Jamie. She sat him against the wall, and while he unwrapped his bagpipe she fetched him a bowl of soup.

'Nobody lives here, on this moon. Not permanently. It's one reason we like to come here.'

'Why not?'

She shrugged. 'Officially because there might be life in the water ocean under the ice crust. I think it's just because the corporations haven't got around to mining it yet. There are easier targets.'

'Like Mnemosyne.'

'Yes. You're quite safe in here, you know. The tent is made from skin-suit fabric. It doesn't look much but it's very tough, self-repairing and resistant to magnetosphere radiation—'

'Whisht ye.' He touched her hand. 'Phee, I'm fine. You dinna have to reassure me.'

She flashed him a grin that lit up her face. 'If you say so, granddad. How are you getting on with those pipes?'

He fingered the kit, unscrewing drones. 'Och, it's a bit of tat if truth be told. These drones are plastic! Made in some factory in England, probably. But I daresay I'll squeeze a note out of it.'

The others were getting more seriously into their music now. Little huddles of two or three played snatches of song. None of it was familiar to Jamie, but some of the tunes were engaging. So he tried out the pipes. The tone was thin, the fingering clumsy, but he soon coaxed a tune out of the set. And when he played an old Jacobite air, 'The Wearing of the Green', the reaction of the kids surprised him. They stopped their own playing, and listened intently. It seemed to him it was almost as if they knew the tune already, but hadn't known they knew it. Self-conscious, he packed it in when the tune was done.

The others resumed their playing, but soon the music grew more languid, restful. Maybe the kids were settling down at last, as excitement waned, and fatigue from the long journey cut in.

Sneakily, to work his way to doing the job he'd been given by the Doctor, Jamie said innocently to Phee, 'I like your locket.' In the time he'd spent with her it was the one accessory she'd worn constantly, and he and Zoe had agreed it was the best candidate for the Doctor's pedleron-particle time-travel anomaly.

She fingered the black pebble at her neck. 'Oh, it's not a locket, it doesn't open. We call it the amulet, in the family.'

'Ye're always wearin' it.'

'It's a kind of heirloom. My mother gave it to me when I was sixteen, and she got it from *her* mother. Been in the family a long time. Always passed down the female line, mother to daughter or granddaughter.'

'Is that right? There must be quite a story to go with it.' He tried to act as if he was only casually interested, but he was no spy, no actor.

She looked at him curiously. 'Well, there is. Sort of. My great-great-something grandmother is supposed to have found it in a fossil.'

Now Jamie had an excuse to be intrigued. 'No! Why don't ye tell me about it? I always liked bedtime stories.' He pulled a couple of light-weight blankets out of a pack, passed one to Phee, and snuggled down under the other.

Phee smiled. 'You're just like Casey. All right then. Once upon a time . . .'

AMULET

I

'Fossil, miss? Fossil for a penny . . .'

Josephine Laws had been hanging back on the platform, unwilling to follow her father into the train carriage. This was Sir Iain Laws' proudest moment, in this year 1890, his forty-eighth year, her sixteenth. The very day of the opening of the City and South London Railway, the world's first deep-level underground railway, on which her father had served as chief engineer. Here was the line of carriages by the gas-lit platform, ready to go deep into the brand new tunnel; here were the journalists, the cheering crowds, dignitaries from city and country. There was even a minor prince, a nephew of Queen Victoria.

And here was Josephine, Sir Iain's only daughter, and his only family companion since her mother had died four years ago. Yet she could not bear to enter the carriage. The carriages had been built small and tight to fit into the narrow tunnels. With their high-backed, cushioned seats, even their designers called them 'padded cells'. And inside this cell Josephine was going to have to enter a tunnel dug into the clay beneath the river Thames itself!

Her father, chatting, had not noticed her reluctance. And nor would she allow him to. She just needed this moment to gather her strength.

But now she was distracted by a tugging at her sleeve.

'Fossils, miss?'

The woman cradled a tray of what looked like bits of rock. She might have been forty, with grimy lines in her skin, pox scars on her cheeks. Her dress was shapeless and shabby, a poor contrast with the layers of fine-spun cotton and silk Josephine wore.

Josephine recoiled, then felt ashamed for doing so. Her father, a great reader of Dickens in his youth, had always impressed on her the need to eschew snobbery. 'Yes? What is it?'

'Fossils, miss. Have one. Souvenir of the opening. You're his daughter, aren't you? Sir Iain's. Good man, my Jack always says, and a fair one when you step out of line. Have a keepsake. Fossils, dug out of the ground while they was building the tunnels. A lot of them there was, and the gents from the Kensington museums took most of 'em, but not all. From deep down, deep in the clay and under it. Penny piece each.' She smelled of coal dust and baby milk.

Josephine could not help but look at the woman's shabby wares. Some of the 'fossils' looked like so many bits of rock, but others had some appearance of authenticity, pieces of bone embedded in masses of clay. They could have been bones of dogs or rats for all she knew. But here was a tooth, as long as a cigarette.

'You say your husband worked in the tunnels.'

'That's so.'

'Then why must you—' She should not use the word 'beg'. 'Why must you sell these trinkets? The pay was good for the labourers, my father says.' So it had to be, for the conditions in the tunnels had been foul and dangerous.

'Drinks it away, doesn't he? My Jack. Found these pieces in his pocket and his bag, and why shouldn't I profit? *Look.*' The woman produced a lump of hardened clay bigger than her fist. 'Dinosaur bones, on my life.'

Josephine took it curiously. There were bones trapped in the clay. Bones almost like a hand, or at least a paw, with long fingers and a thumb – but the thumb had a savage claw. And inside the paw –

'This is a clumsy fraud.'

'What do you mean? I swear I never—'

'Inside this, this *paw*. Can you see what it is holding?' It was difficult to see in the dim gaslight. The skeletal fingers were wrapped around a slab of some dark stone, that looked shaped, polished. It was like a pendant, of a heavy, clumsy sort. An object clearly finished by human artifice. 'A dinosaur claw,' Josephine said heavily, 'wrapped around a piece of polished semi-precious stone? What kind of fool do you take me for?'

The woman seemed to think fast, fearful, desperate. 'But how could it have got *inside the clay*, miss?'

'A magician could mock this up, I daresay . . .' But somehow Josephine couldn't believe even the famous Li H'sen Chang could fabricate this piece.

'A curiosity,' the woman breathed. 'Not just a fossil. A curiosity. And a souvenir of the day.' She smiled, showing brown, gappy teeth, and held out her hand.

In the end Josephine gave her her penny.

Slightly ashamed of herself, feeling grubby from the whole encounter, Josephine was aware of the lumpy mass in her clutch bag throughout what seemed an interminable journey under the river in the brand new train.

That night, in the privacy of her bedroom, she took out the fossil. Some of the clay had rubbed off in her bag, dirtying it. Carefully, using nail file and scissors, she chipped away at the object, removing the clay, and then the enclosing bones, which she set aside. The pendant, revealed, was seamless, heavy, perfectly proportioned, a neat rectangle with rounded corners, about the size and shape of a playing card.

Something obviously artificial. And held in a dinosaur's paw.

Suddenly, soundlessly, it lit up, gleaming like an Edison light bulb. She screamed and dropped it on the carpet. It did not break; its flare did not diminish.

'Josephine? Was that you? Are you all right?'

'It was nothing, Father.' In an odd panic she tucked the slab into an old tin box which had once held a childish collection of glass jewellery, and tucked it out of sight under her bed.

But she looked into the box the next day. The light had gone out, leaving the slab as black and featureless as before. She checked the next day. And the next.

In the years that followed, she took the box with her to finishing school, and then to her own London flat, and then to her married home. She checked it every day.

Until the day, nearly ten years later, when the slab flared again.

And again, ten years after that . . .

II

'I was given this when I was sixteen,' said Mother. She was holding a little tin box.

'Hush,' said Father. He sat before the televisor, his face bathed in its odd silvery light. 'It's about to start.'

The televisor was a heavy wooden box with an odd glass window set into its front. Father said it was like a wireless, but with pictures. It looked more like a fish tank to Josie Laws McRae. Yet she was curious. She leaned forward to see in the dim light of the living room, through air thick with smoke from her mother's cigarettes, her father's pipe.

'This is an experimental device, you know,' he said now. 'Only a handful of people have one.' Her father was a lawyer working for the Logie Baird company in Long Acre. 'Us and the Prime Minister!'

And today the BBC, the wireless people, were going to show a *play* on this little box.

'Make a note in your diary, Josie,' Father said.

Josie was sixteen years old, and suspicious. 'How do you know I keep a diary?'

Mother looked away.

Father said, 'This is the fourteenth of July 1930. The day they broadcast *The Man with the Flower in His Mouth*. You'll be able to tell your grandchildren.'

'Huh!'

'Apparently they're thinking of adapting *Black Orchid* next, if this works. You know, dear, that Cranleigh book—'

'*I'm* not having any children. Let alone grandchildren!'

Here was Mother with her battered old tin box. 'I thought that when I was your age.' Smiling, tired-looking, Mother was fifty-six years old. It was hard to believe she had ever been young. 'But, Josie love, when I *was* your age, I came across this.' She held out the box. 'I was sixteen. Which is why I think it's appropriate to pass it on now.'

Josie frowned. 'It's not something else to do with Grandpa, is it?' Her mother had always made much of the fact that she was the last of the Laws, a long line of Scottish gentlefolk and engineers. She had insisted, in fact, on her daughter having the name incorporated into her own. All this seemed horribly backward-looking to Josie. This was the 1930s, the modern age; she didn't want to be burdened by the past.

'No. Well, not directly. I just think it should stay in the family.' And she opened up the enigmatic box.

The object revealed, lying on an old silk handkerchief in the box, was black, rectangular, gleaming. 'What is it? A cigarette box?'

'Not that. Well, I don't know what it is.' And Mother began to tell a complicated and rambling story about a poor woman and a dinosaur claw.

Josie, distracted, kept looking at the televisor, where figures were moving about through a hail of white, as if glimpsed in a snowstorm.

'And it lights up.'

'It does what?'

'It's done it four times so far, since I've had it. Once on the very day I was given it.' She pulled some bits of paper, yellowed with age, from the bottom of the box. 'I made a note of the dates. It lights up for a few hours every nine years, nine months and twenty-six days.'

Josie liked numbers. It seemed to be something she had inherited from the engineers on one side of the family and the lawyers and accountants on the other. 'Why that period?'

'Well, I spent a long time wondering. I looked in almanacs for calendar cycles, historical significance . . . In the end it was an astrologer who gave me a clue.'

Father guffawed. '*Astrology*! As if the stars have anything to do with it.'

'Not the stars,' Mother said patiently. 'The planets. Josie, nine years, nine months—'

'And twenty-six days.'

'Is one-third of the year of the planet Saturn. The time it takes to go around the sun.'

Josie could only gape at her mother, and the wondrous nonsense she was suddenly spouting.

'Ah,' said Father. 'I think it's about to start.' Tinny voices, like insect scratches, emerged from the set's tiny loudspeaker.

'Saturn?'

'Saturn.'

'And when's it due to light up again?'

Mother glanced at the calendar on Father's desk, and Grandpa Laws' big grandfather clock, and smiled. 'Actually—'

'Hush!' cried Father.

'Today,' said Mother. 'In fact, if I've timed it right—'

The box lit up, bathing Mother's face with a pale, unearthly light.

The picture on the televisor broke up, and a howl emerged from the speaker.

III

Mum intercepted her at the door. 'You're not going out again!'

Joss was sixteen years old and felt it was childish to scowl. But she scowled anyway. She pulled her sheepskin coat tighter around her, adjusted her bell-bottom jeans, fixed her woollen hat firmly over her blonde hair, and wondered if she smelled of the incense she'd been burning in her room. 'No, Josie, I'm not going out again. What does it look like?'

Mum sighed, and glanced back at the living room. On the TV was a grey image of worried-looking shirt-sleeved men at rows of consoles. 'I thought we might watch it together.'

'Watch what? That old space thing?'

'It's important, Joss. The astronauts still aren't safe. Apollo 13 has rounded the moon, but—'

'Oh, Josie, it's *boring.*'

'I wish you wouldn't call me Josie.'

'And I wish you didn't call me Joss. I'm not six years old. I wish you wouldn't call me Joss *Laws.* That wasn't even Dad's name.'

'I told you, after the divorce, I decided to go back to the old family name . . . Where is it you're dashing off to anyhow? The Apple studios again, I suppose.'

'None of your business!'

'You and those other girls. You can hang around out there all day and all night and you won't make Paul change his mind. He really has left the Beatles, you know.'

Joss tried to keep a lid on her anger. 'That's not the point. It's not like that. It's deeper. It's . . .'

Mum put a hand on her shoulder. 'It's you growing up.'

Joss pulled back.

'Come and sit with me. Just for a while.'

Joss glanced at the TV, where Patrick Moore was making some solemn pronouncement. 'Why? So you can tell me *again* how you watched the very first programme ever broadcast, on a telly handmade by John Logie Baird? Why can't you be normal, Mum? Why can't you do normal things, that normal mums do with their daughters, like watching cookery shows, or Morecambe and Wise? Why space? People flying off to the moon has got nothing to do with us.'

'But it has, dear,' Mum said, almost sadly. 'Or I think it might do, one day.'

'Oh. You're talking about that stupid amulet of Grannie's again, aren't you?'

'Well, it's not an amulet. Whatever it is. I told you I expected it to light up, last Tuesday—'

'I had a party, Mum. Why should I sit around and stare at a bit of old Victorian jewellery?'

Mum said, more sternly, 'I didn't ask you to. Just listen, for once. I can never get a word in! I took it to an old friend, a contact of your father's from work. I just remembered that first time when I watched TV with your grandma and grandpa, and the thing went off and scrambled the TV reception. Although we called it a televisor then. I wondered if—'

'What old friend?'

'Nobody you know. He was a soldier. Well, an engineer, telecommunications. He worked for UNIT.'

'Who are they?'

'Military. Sort of. I'm not quite sure. But they do have radio facilities. They listen for – signals. I gave the slab to your father's friend, who gave it to a friend of *his*, and they sat and waited for it to go off, and monitored what happened. And they heard something.'

Joss was intrigued, though she tried not to show it. 'Heard what?'

'Their radio receivers picked it up. A blast, not noise, like a very compressed signal. And it was aimed right at—'

Joss sniggered. 'The moon?'

'Saturn, Joss. The planet Saturn.' She looked blank. 'I must say that startled me. I don't think I ever told your father's friend about the dates . . .'

'What dates? Oh, look, Mum, I've got to go.'

'All right. Just remember, love – that amulet, slab, box, whatever it is, we're stuck with it. We Laws girls. It's yours now. I still keep it in your Grannie's old tin box. And some day—'

Joss felt as if she was going to explode. 'Some day, when it's mine, I'm going to throw it in the Thames and let it find its own way to Saturn. Good*bye*, Mum.'

And, though she knew it was childish to slam the door, she did it anyway.

IV

Jo Laws stood in the doorway, in her uniform, her pack at her feet, the door open behind her. At the bottom of the drive Martina waited in her father's Volkswagen Dragonfly, loaned specially to fly them off to the army training camp in Northumberland.

Mum and Dad stood in the hall, carpet slippers on their feet. Dad leaned on the wall, his head almost brushing Mum's treasured signed photo of George Harrison – 'To Joss, the Fabbest Apple Scruff' – until Mum slapped his arm to make him stand straight.

It couldn't have been more awkward, Jo thought. She longed to go begin her new life, yet she couldn't bear to leave. She felt like she was being torn apart.

It was her father who broke the silence. 'I still can't picture you in Venezuela.'

'Dad, I'm only sixteen. They won't be shipping me overseas just yet.'

And Mum started crying.

Jo hugged her. 'Come on, Mum.'

'I almost managed it. Almost got you out of the door without the tears.'

'Mum, I'll be fine.'

'But what if you're not, Josephine Laws Patrick, what if you're not? You see it on the telly – all you have to do is step on one of those IEDs – children, those soldiers are, children barely older than you coming home in boxes, or with horrible injuries.'

'Mum, don't.'

'I wish you weren't doing this.'

Jo sighed. 'We've been through all this. Mum, it's a recession. There are no jobs. I'm not academic enough to be bothered to take on thousands of pounds of student debt. The army – well, it's a good career.'

'When I was your age I used to think we'd all be living on the moon by now. That was the influence of your gran, I suppose. Not that I listened to her. Sailing among the rings of Saturn. How daft that all seems now. But what an adventure it would have been! And instead, here you are going off to war.'

'Venezuela will be an adventure.'

Mum straightened up, wiping her eyes, taking control. 'Just make sure you survive it, because I think you're meant for better things than that. Here.' She reached back and produced a parcel, a heavy handful wrapped in an old scarf.

Jo took it reluctantly. 'This is that amulet, isn't it?'

Mum closed Jo's hand over the bundle, and patted it. 'I remember when I first showed it to you, you thought it was a smartphone! I did laugh at that.'

'Well, it would be more use if it was. Mum, I shouldn't take this. What if it goes lighting up when I'm on patrol?'

'It won't light up for another ten years, nearly. And whatever it is it's been with us Laws girls for a long time now, so maybe it's good luck.'

'Mum—'

'Please, Jo.'

Jo saw how important this gesture was to her. 'All right. I'll keep it safe in my kit . . .'

Martina sounded her horn.

There was one last round of kisses, she had to prise herself away from her mum, and then a dash down the drive to the car. She clambered in, the amulet in her hand.

'What's that?' Martina asked as the Dragonfly lifted gracefully into the air.

'Nothing.' Jo tucked it into her bag. 'Last-minute stuff.'

'*My* mum gave me a box of scones.'

'Old folk! They're all the same . . . Right here, Martie, not left!'

'Sorry, sorry.' The flying car executed a high-gravity U-turn.

'Some use you'll be when we're on patrol . . .'

14

'And then,' Phee Laws told Jamie, 'on *my* sixteenth birthday, having brought the amulet in a box all the way to Saturn, my mum gave it to me.'

'Wha' a tale!'

'Yes. My mother says that's why she got involved with Bootstrap herself. When the mining companies started floating proposals to develop the outer system, they looked at Jupiter first, but *she* lobbied for prospecting probes to be sent here, to Saturn. And then when the early probes found bernalium on Mnemosyne, she made sure her family were in with the first lot of pioneers to come settle out here. That's what she says. I wasn't even born yet.'

'And all this because of yon dinosaur's amulet.'

'Well, my mother says it's a link between our family and Saturn, so why not come out here and see if it's leading us to our fortune?'

Jamie grinned. 'Sounds like mumbo jumbo tae me.'

'Maybe. But my mother's quite superstitious. She says old soldiers always are.'

Jamie was feeling quite pleased with himself. He had no idea what all this meant, a family story about some old bit of stone, and a planet in the sky, and *dinosaurs*. But it was just the kind of nice twisty puzzly stuff the Doctor liked. And if it was puzzly, it was a fair bet it had something to do with the bigger mystery of the Doctor's Relative Continuum Displacement Zone, and the way the TARDIS had reacted to Phee in the first place. All he had to do was get this news back to the Doctor and let him do the rest . . .

The ground shuddered again. This time it was unmistakeable; Jamie felt it through his legs, up his spine.

The tent quivered, its fabric walls rippling. A bowl of soup began a slow-motion fall to the floor, spilling as it went. The youngsters stopped making their music, or woke and sat up, looking around.

'That's a vent blowing,' Phee said. She was already up, sealing up her suit, making for the airlock.

Jamie struggled to get to his feet. He got it wrong in the low gravity and went floating up in the air, tangled in his blanket. Flustered, frustrated, he called after her, 'Phee! Don't go out!'

'Sam's out there somewhere.'

Jamie hadn't been aware of that. She, of course, would always know where her brother was.

She turned, pushed through the airlock and was gone.

Jamie was out on the surface of Enceladus in less than a minute. He was the first out, after Phee. Only he had had his suit on, ready to be sealed up.

'Phee!' he called, looking around, stumbling as he spun in the low gravity. 'Where are you?'

'I see her.' The voice in his headphones was Sam's. 'Sis, get down from there.'

'I was trying to find you.' That was Phee. 'I climbed up here for a better view.'

'Where are ye, for heaven's sake?'

Then he saw Sam, a speck in his skinsuit, standing on top of a heap of ice rubble, waving his arms. 'She's to your left, Jamie,' Sam said. 'Towards the end of the tiger stripe.'

Jamie hurried along the valley. It was frustrating trying to run, because he kept lifting off the ground; in the end he settled for making huge bounds, pushing sideways against the ground every time he landed. He neared the end of the canyon and saw the huge, shattered ice blocks piled up there.

The ground shuddered again.

And now he saw Phee. She was standing on an unspectacular mound of ice. It reminded Jamie of the hill forts in Scotland that people said had been built by the fairy folk.

But even as he watched, he saw the mound *swell*.

'Phee, that's a vent,' Sam said. 'A new one. And it's about to blow.'

Still Phee didn't move. She seemed bewildered. She'd got herself in trouble remarkably efficiently.

Jamie snapped, 'Phee. Speak tae me. What's a vent?'

'A geyser,' she said. 'Where liquid water erupts from the interior of the moon. You know, to make snow, and the ring in space.'

'These tiger stripes,' Sam said. 'They are faults in the crust. This is where the venting happens.'

'*Wissat?*' Jamie could hardly believe what he was hearing. And now he remembered the 'vent' they'd flown over in the scooters. Like a huge, burst boil, he'd thought at the time. Well, he'd been right. 'Sam, ye brought us here knowing it was so dangerous? Are ye tapped, man?'

Sam sounded defiant again, the prickly kid. 'That's what makes it fun, granddad.'

'Fun, is it? That's yer wee sister up there, man! What'll happen if that vent blows? Will she be scalded, or what?'

'No. It's not as hot as that. But she'll be blown into space – maybe lost—'

The ground shuddered again, and Jamie saw silvery wisps of vapour squirting up around Phee, up on the mound.

'Blown into space, is it? Not on my watch.' He glanced around for the scooters. Too far away – no time for that. Only one thing for it, Jamie lad. He looked up at the mound, took a pace back, braced himself. 'I'll show ye granddad—' He began to run, straight at the mound. He had got the measure of this daft little moon now; his legs worked like pistons, and he drove himself forward over the ice. Even the worsening shuddering of the ground didn't put him off. 'I'll show ye granddad!'

And he leapt, high off the ground.

His momentum carried him forward in a great bounding arc towards Phee, who stood there and stared. But the flight through the blackness seemed awfully slow, and he could see that mound was starting to crack up under her, like the shell of some monstrous egg. Suspended, he heard his heart beat, his breath rasp. All he could do now was pray he hadn't got his timing wrong. And that he didn't smash his head on the side of the hill. Or go sailing too far over Phee to reach –

No! Here she was, just below him, approaching fast. He twisted so his hands were dangling, and she was reaching up towards him. 'Take hold! We're only ginna get one go at this—'

The contact was messy. He grabbed one of her wrists, she grabbed one of his. She wasn't so heavy, but their masses, suddenly joined, made them spin head over heels, making it even harder to hang on. But as he whirled over the mound he saw its surface cracking open, falling away from where she'd been standing, and great billows of ice particles came washing up.

They landed short on the mound's lower slope, in a tangle of limbs. Jamie was first on his feet. He dragged her away as the last of the mound crumbled, and they ran off through a hail of ice shards. And here was Sam, grabbing their arms, helping them to the cover of the big ice blocks at the end of the valley.

Huddled under a wall of ice, Phee was panting hard, eyes wide. 'Thank you,' she said to Jamie. 'I froze up there – I stopped thinking, just for a second – and then the surface started giving way and I couldn't move—'

'It's all right,' Jamie said, and he let her brother hug her. 'Ye're safe now.' And so is your amulet, he thought, but he put that thought aside as cynical. He stabbed a gloved finger at Sam. 'You. Take better care o' your little sister in future. And now we're gonna go check everyone else is all right, and after that we'll pack up and go back to the scooters, and we'll gan on home. Is that all right with you?'

Sam nodded mutely.

'*And* we're gonna talk to them, back on the Wheel. Tell them what's happened. Can I open yon comms link from this suit?'

Phee, recovering, pulled away from her brother. 'Yes. There's a control on your chest panel . . .'

As soon as Jamie opened a channel to the Wheel, his ears were filled with clamouring voices. Somebody had blown up a mining machine, and Florian Hart was on the warpath.

15

On the morning Jamie was due back from Enceladus, Zoe had spent a sleepless night in Sam Laws' house, trying to analyse the data on ring resonances and patterns she had extracted from MMAC's memory banks. It was a nice problem, and a novel one, with such a strange data set. But she felt hamstrung by the primitive computer technology of the Wheel of Ice.

'Doctor, it's like trying to do tensor calculus on an abacus!'

'Now you mustn't exaggerate, Zoe. It's a bad habit you're picking up from Jamie. Look on it as a challenge to your computational skills. I've every faith in you. And do wake me if you find anything of *exceptional* interest.' And with that, he'd taken himself off to bed.

Well, any vague plans Zoe had had for a nap before the start of the colony's working day were quashed not long after dawn, as the bubble's artificial lights slowly brightened to a full simulacrum of an Earth morning, and she smelled strong coffee and heard raised voices downstairs.

She knocked, and crept into the Doctor's room. Curled up in bed, he was snoring so loudly it was a wonder he didn't wake himself up.

For a moment she looked at him fondly, with his black hair tousled on the pillow, his battered old coat hanging on a door knob. He had been a wanderer far longer than she had been, and she liked to see him, if only briefly, at peace. Or perhaps, as Jo Laws suggested, an old soldier herself, it was just that he had learned the soldier's knack of grabbing sleep wherever and whenever he could.

She touched his shoulder gently. 'Doctor.'

'Mmph . . . mm . . . wassa? Victoria?'

'No, Doctor, it's me, Zoe. I think you'd better get up. All hell is breaking loose downstairs.'

He raised his head, opened one eye and cocked an ear. 'Hell can wait.' And with that he pushed his head back down into his pillow, and within a couple of breaths was snoring again.

Zoe, too shy to face the others by herself, crept back to her own room.

The day was a good deal more advanced by the time the Doctor finally rose, and Zoe followed him downstairs.

'Good morning, good morning,' the Doctor said brightly, apparently oblivious to the lined faces and tired eyes of Jo Laws and Sonia Paley. 'And how are you today? Is that coffee fresh?'

'Ish,' said Zoe, checking. 'I'll pour you a mug.'

He sat at the table. 'I gather you've some trouble.'

'I'm afraid so, Doctor,' Jo Laws said bleakly. 'More disruption.'

Sonia said, 'And this time it isn't a question of a few components being nicked.' She took a data slate, tapped its surface, and showed him an image.

Zoe peered to see. The slate showed a heavy-duty truck with a giant screw tip mounted on its prow, and tractor treads on its hull and roof. 'This is evidently a mining craft,' she said. 'Some kind of shaft-cutter? It's been adapted for low gravity with those wall-gripping treads.'

'Exactly,' Sonia said. 'But look more closely.'

The craft's mid-section was badly disrupted, ripped open by some kind of explosion.

'Ah,' said the Doctor sadly. 'Not the sort of thing one can turn a blind eye to.'

'Quite so,' Sonia said. 'What's worse, this took place up in one of the workshop bubbles in the Industrial sector – *on the Wheel*, not down in the mine. Obviously it's not just property damage we're dealing with here but a threat to human life as well.'

'Of course. So what are you doing about this?'

'Florian Hart has been pulling rank,' Sonia admitted. 'She does have tough contractual clauses on her side. I've had to agree to a kettling.'

'A what?'

'It's an old British police term—'

'A containment, Doctor,' Jo Laws said. To Zoe, she looked distressed and embarrassed. 'Getting all the potential troublemakers in one place and containing them there until the problem is resolved, and they can be processed.'

'"Processed". And where is this "kettling" going on?'

'In Trinity Bubble, here in Res Three.'

Zoe frowned. 'Isn't that the one that was smashed up by rioting?'

Jo sighed. 'Well, at least they can't make it any worse.'

The Doctor asked impatiently, 'But who are "they"? Hmm? Who exactly are these potential troublemakers you are "kettling"? I think I have a suspicion. Once again you people are turning on your own children, aren't you, Mayor Laws?'

'Not all of them,' Jo admitted miserably. 'Just between the ages of fifteen and—'

'Shame on you,' the Doctor said sternly. 'Are you so much under the sway of Bootstrap and this wretched Florian Hart woman?'

Sonia held her hands up. 'It's a delicate situation, Doctor. Bootstrap has its own guards here.'

He eyed her. 'Whereas you—'

'I'm on my own here, Doctor, in terms of resources from the ISC. I have to rely on my deputies, who are all citizen volunteers.'

'You're outnumbered. Is that what you're telling me?'

'That in itself is a provocative remark, Doctor, and I wouldn't use such language.'

'Oh, how very temperate of you!'

'Go easy, Doctor,' Jo Laws pleaded. 'My own children are swept up in this. Not little Casey. But the others—'

Zoe asked, 'Sam and Phee?'

'The party returning from Enceladus came in overnight, and was diverted straight to the Trinity holding tank.'

'What!' The Doctor stood immediately. 'But Jamie's with them! Well, that's where we must go, forthwith. Come along, Zoe.' He was already heading for the door. 'And bring my coat!'

16

The hatches at either end of the Trinity bubble were locked and manned by Bootstrap operatives, tough-looking guards in black coveralls with company logos on their sleeves. The Doctor and Zoe weren't allowed through, and found themselves stuck in a neighbouring space hulk, a fuel tank from an old XK5.

Sonia Paley had followed them here. 'Order is being kept,' she assured them.

'Oh, is it?' snapped the Doctor. 'And what irreparable damage do you imagine is being done to the souls of the children in there while your "order" is "kept"? Well, at least we can get Jamie out of there; he's no child . . .'

That turned out to be harder than Zoe might have expected. Jamie was not an inhabitant of the Wheel, he was not formally suspected of any misdemeanour, and he was too old to be categorised with the rest, as the Doctor had pointed out. But he was, with the rest of the TARDIS crew, still under vague but unresolved suspicion. And Jamie himself was reluctant to come out. He seemed to have become attached to the youngsters he had jaunted to Enceladus with. He didn't want to leave them to the mercy of 'yon Bootstrap redcoats', as he called them, a vivid insult, Zoe thought, if suffering from chronologic inexactitude.

He was grumpy when he was finally escorted out through the hatch, carrying a folded-up pressure suit, and another unexpected package. 'Got me sprung agin, did ye, Zoe?'

Zoe snorted. 'Thank Sonia, not me. And, Jamie, after all our travels I shouldn't be surprised by anything you do, but surely only you could visit a lifeless moon of Saturn and come back with a bagpipe!'

He glanced down. 'Och, it's not a very *good* bagpipe.'

The Doctor led them away. 'Oh, do stop bickering, you two, and let's find a quiet corner to talk. We must decide what to do next.'

'Leave,' said Zoe firmly when they were alone, tucked behind a corroded bulkhead. 'I've had enough of this awful place and its rules.'

'I know how you feel, Zoe, but until we've resolved the conundrum of the Relative Continuum Displacement Zone that brought us here in the first place, the TARDIS won't let us leave, believe me.'

Jamie perked up. 'Aye, well, I've got some news about a' that.' And he quickly related his conversations with Phee about her amulet, and its strange provenance. 'I always had my eye on tha' wee trinket.'

'Jamie, you've done very well.'

Zoe admitted, 'I'm not sure I follow all this, Doctor. What *is* this "amulet"?'

'I rather suspect it's an allohistorical lure, Zoe.'

'Aha,' said Jamie, a seasoned time traveller compared to Zoe, and he grinned and pointed at her. 'I knew it.'

Zoe snorted again. 'You're not fooling anybody, Jamie, you haven't got a clue. Go on, Doctor.'

'Well, it's an old trick but a dirty one, and it does depend on time-travel technology of a limited sort. Let's suppose, for example, that you are stranded on a moon of Saturn, from which you badly want to escape, and you have such a gadget. You can't use your time machine to save yourself, you see, it's not powerful enough for that, but you can use it to send tokens – small objects – to the Earth. Or rather, to the Earth's past.'

'What for?'

'To manipulate history, Zoe.'

'The history of humanity?'

'Or of any sentient creature that evolves there. What you do is to plant a device, a legend, a signpost, a promise – you can lie all you want – but the point is it must be implanted deep in humanity's past, and it must direct humans to your moon. It must make them *want* to go there. And so humans, attracted by this lure, whatever else they might have achieved with their civilisation, distort their own history to build a space programme to get to this Saturnian moon. And once there they find—'

'The fisherman,' Jamie said. 'Waiting for a lift.'

'Precisely, Jamie. The great thing about it from the fisherman's point of view is that the rescue ought to show up as soon as the lure is cast! There may have had to be thousands, millions of years of rewritten history to bring about the rescue party – but none of that matters to the fisherman. Cast your lure in the morning, pack up to be rescued in the afternoon! As I said it's a not uncommon practice, but it is regarded as rather unethical. Even by my own people, and that's saying something.'

'So *that* explains why the prospectors came to Saturn first,' Zoe said. 'Not to Jupiter, which would have been a much more obvious choice.'

'Quite so. You have it from Phee's account. The motivation was planted deep in the past in the Laws' family history.'

'But there's a lot that still doesn't make sense.'

Jamie rolled his eyes. 'Don't worry, if you keep travellin' with us ye'll get used to *that*.'

She wouldn't be deflected. 'You say that Phee's story is that this great-grandmother found the amulet in a fossil – in the claw of a dinosaur? Why, that might have been formed, oh, a hundred million years ago. Certainly before the dinosaur extinction. And long before humans were more than a theoretical evolutionary possibility!'

'Well, it is rather chancy, Zoe, this business of the allohistorical lure,' the Doctor said. 'You can't be sure that the people whose attention you're trying to attract will do what you want them to do. And nor can you be sure that you'll catch the eye of the right people in the first place. By which I mean the right *species*. There have been intelligent races on Earth before humanity, Zoe.'

'Really?'

'Oh, yes. There may have been a strain of intelligent reptilians who survived the main dinosaur extinction event; I've seen some evidence of that . . . But even they vanished many millions of years ago.'

'I'm not sure I follow all that.'

'I think I do,' Jamie said. 'Suppose the fisherman was himself around millions of years ago. He sees these smart rapscallions on Earth.'

'Reptilians, Jamie.'

'Tha's what I said. He goes fishin' for 'em. But he overshoots. He sends his lure *further* back, where it gets lost in the time o' the dinosaurs. And then when it's their time the rapscallions miss it.'

'Rep – oh, never mind.'

'And millions of years *after* that, it's picked up by humans. Maybe it was never meant for us in the first place!'

The Doctor beamed. 'Well done, Jamie! Yes, I think the course of events could well have been something like that.'

Even Zoe was impressed. But she had to ask, 'Doesn't that mean that this – fisherman – must have been waiting around for millions upon millions of years?'

'Well, that's not impossible, Zoe. Machines can be put into dormant mode, after all. And there are certain species of bacteria which can survive for millions of years as spores—'

'All this is guesswork. Do you have any *evidence* that all this was initiated millions of years ago?'

'But you know we have, Zoe – in the rings of Saturn! It takes a great deal of energy to achieve time travel. It may not feel like it when we ride the TARDIS, but then she is the result of an ancient and mature technology. A great deal of energy indeed. And we have seen clear indications of a very energetic event, and a destructive one, having taken place in the vicinity of this planet some fifty million years ago, have we not?'

And Zoe saw it. 'The formation of the rings. The explosion of a moon! You're saying it was the by-product of some kind of experiment with time travel?'

'Yes. Quite possibly. And the moon we know, Mnemosyne, is a mere fragment of a much larger body that was all but destroyed, long ago.'

But Jamie's practical mind was turning to more immediate issues. 'So what's all that got to do with lockin' up kids, and blowin' up mining engines?'

'Those are excellent questions, Jamie, which we will only answer by visiting the scene of this so-called "sabotage" ourselves. Come along, come along.' The Doctor turned to lead the way out of the rocket hulk.

Zoe followed, but Jamie hung back. 'Jamie? What is it?'

'You go,' Jamie said stiffly. 'Let me stay an' go back through yon hatch. Those kids – they're not evil, or criminals. They're just mixed up. And if that woman Florian Hart starts gettin' stuck into them—'

'Jamie, Jamie. You mean well. But we can't save everybody, you know. We have to let these people sort out their own problems.'

'Aye, I ken. But I might be able to stop a few noggins being smashed in the process.'

The Doctor hesitated. Then he grinned, and patted Jamie's cheek. 'You're a good boy, Jamie McCrimmon.'

'Boy? Hmph. A good granddad, mebbe.'

'What's that?'

But Jamie had already grabbed up his bundles, his skinsuit and bag-pipe, and was making his way back to the hatch.

The Doctor sighed. 'Now come along, Zoe, let's get on with it . . .'

17

The wrecked tractor was in a bubble called Garage 4-4, in Wheel sector four, Industrial.

It took the Doctor and Zoe some time to complete the short journey around the Wheel from Trinity, for Florian Hart's rather sinister Bootstrap guards blocked every hatchway. But as they passed through Industrial's more technical modules Zoe looked around with interest, at the power plants, the resource processors, the air and water recyclers and scrubbers. One bubble, called the Print Shop, housed a bank of heavy-duty matter printers. Such a device would spray out raw material in carefully shaped designs, molecule by molecule, building up a machine part layer by layer. This was a typical mass-saving space colony application; given the right raw material these printers could produce any part you desired.

Garage 4-4 was one of a number of specialised modules devoted to manufacturing and maintaining equipment for the mining operation. In 4-4 itself, finished vehicles were stored: a range of fantastic engines designed for the extraction, processing, storage and transport of materials from a mine on a moon of Saturn. Zoe glimpsed tremendous angular hulls, forests of manipulator arms like MMAC's, huge lightweight wheels of metallic mesh, and harpoons and pitons for anchorage in the low gravity. All these great machines were stamped with the logos of Bootstrap, Inc. Some of them were shiny and new, waiting for their first deployment, but others brought back for repair showed the scars of hard service in buckled plates, scorched nozzles, snapped manipulator arms and blistered paintwork. When she walked past these veterans, Zoe smelled the tingling, burned-metal scent of materials that had been exposed to the vacuum. She felt oddly thrilled.

Now they came to the heart of the colony's trouble. The sabotaged tractor was just as Zoe had seen it in the images shown her by Jo Laws on her kitchen table. Another big, muscular piece of equipment, brand shiny new, but with its heart ripped out by an explosion. The wreck had been cordoned off, by Bootstrap guards and some of Sonia Paley's citizen deputies. In a clear area around the wreck, Zoe saw that technicians were retrieving fragments blown away from the hulk, and were laying them out on the bubble's floor like a diagram of the shattered machine, a first step to understanding what had happened here. More technicians were crawling over the machine itself, and inside it. Zoe spotted small wheeled machines probing further in, equipped with grabber arms and spot-lights: bomb disposal robots, perhaps, checking for more explosives.

Without hesitation the Doctor led the way under the cordon rope and picked his way through the litter of twisted parts to the tractor. Zoe followed, and was surprised to find Luis Reyes here. He stood by the hulk of the machine, with earphones connected to a lead plugged into an access socket in the engine's hull.

The Doctor bent down, stuck his head in the hole in the hull and sniffed. 'Methane, or traces of it. I think it's pretty clear what's happened here—'

'Oh, is it?' Here was Florian Hart, dressed in a protective coverall and hard hat, striding vigorously towards them. She was angry, urgent, determined, and yet she still looked impossibly beautiful, Zoe thought.

The Doctor straightened up. 'Oh, it's you. Well, I suppose we could hardly expect to avoid you.'

Florian looked down on his shabby form, not bothering to conceal her contempt. 'Just remember that my authority here is absolute.'

Sonia Paley coughed. 'Now, just hang on, Florian. This colony is still under the jurisdiction of the ISC—'

Florian said, cutting over her, 'After an incident like this – and you can check the terms of the corporate contract under which this whole facility is run – *absolute*. I could have you thrown into detention in an instant, you ridiculous little man.'

'I'm sure you could. And what good would that do, pray? Oh, I don't have time for this.' And he bent again and began to crawl into the splayed-open interior of the machine.

'That isn't safe,' Florian snapped. 'And you're not authorised.'

On his hands and knees, he sighed. 'Well, no, I'm not *authorised*, I'll give you that. But I suspect I'm perfectly safe, short of cricking my back in here.'

'There may be more explosive devices—'

'Oh, of course not. Can't you smell the methane? It seems quite obvious the detonation was caused simply by tampering with the machine's fuel and oxidiser feeds. Quite enough explosive power in that; no need for anything more tricky . . .' As he spoke his shabby checked trousers were receding into the shadows of the machine.

'Let him be,' Sonia said to Florian. 'I'm sure he knows what he's doing. And your precious security isn't going to help if it gets in the way of finding out what is going on here, is it?'

But Florian, bristling, aggressive, shot back, 'As for security, suppose you give me a briefing on whatever inadequate measures you've put in place so far in response to this outrage?'

Sonia, visibly suppressing her own irritation, began to go through a litany of the steps she'd taken: a general lockdown, monitoring of weapons, guards posted on explosive stores and inter-module hatchways, the kettling of the children in the Trinity bubble. Florian aggressively cross-questioned her on every point.

Zoe, dismayed, pulled away from the confrontation. For all Florian's righteous rage it seemed to Zoe that the Bootstrap administrator was *enjoying* this incident. Well, if the accident handed her the power over the colony she had evidently been angling for all along, she had a good deal to be happy about.

Luis Reyes was still here. Listening to his earphones, he was murmuring into a microphone attached to his cheek. As Zoe watched, he patted the flank of the damaged machine, as if trying to comfort it.

She approached him. 'I wasn't expecting to find Planetary Ethics here.'

He smiled at Zoe. Luis was slim, dark, good-looking, earnest, and when he spoke he had a trace of a Spanish accent. 'Well, there is another victim here.' He tapped the flank of the machine. 'The tractor itself. Or rather the artificial intelligence that drives it.'

'Oh! Just like MMAC.'

'This body of metal and ceramics has suffered a traumatic injury, and though there are subroutines to suppress what to you or I would be pain sensations, still the loss of function is distressing. And then there is the uncertainty over the future. Can this carcass be repaired? If not, what becomes of the mind inside it? What's more, Bootstrap, or the IntelligeX subsidiary that handles their robotics, endows all its artificial intelligences with strong drives, to fulfil company goals. Right now the mind in here is suffering from guilt, because it can't fulfil its objectives. Call it an engineered conscience.'

'I didn't realise PEC tries to protect artificial minds.'

'Oh, we do. On Earth, some nation states have laws protecting artificial sentience. Giving them rights equivalent to humans'. The moral issue is whether it is right to create a mind for a specific purpose. PEC tries to be ahead of the curve, ethically. That's why we're here. It won't surprise you to learn that the further you get from Earth the more prevalent those abuses are. We have had some successes. I suspect MMAC would already have been shut down if not for pressure from us . . .'

Zoe found herself hugely admiring this clever, capable, even charismatic young man, though not really understanding him. He had devoted his whole life to a difficult, complex, perhaps even impossible cause. He might never live to see his goals fulfilled. And yet here he was, in the thick of it – doing good, as he saw it, bit by bit.

'But,' he said now, 'progress is slow. And that leads to some people taking more drastic action.'

Florian Hart overheard this, and turned on him. ' "Drastic action". That's a nice euphemism for terrorism, isn't it? What is it your militant wing calls itself?'

'Pull Back to Earth is not *my* anything—'

'Who's to say this stunt hadn't been arranged by one of that lot? The colony wouldn't be hard to infiltrate, would it?'

'Look, Florian, you can't just chuck around insinuations like that. There's not a shred of evidence—'

A muted cough.

The Doctor emerged from the machine, his coat scuffed, his trouser leg glistening with what looked like leaked lubricant fluid. 'Evidently you've made no progress while I've been gone. Well, I suppose I shouldn't be surprised. But, Zoe, I have found something on which I'd like your opinion. Ah, you too, Mr Reyes, if you would.'

Zoe couldn't help but glance at Florian, as if asking permission.

'Oh, go ahead,' she said sarcastically. 'The more the merrier, crawling around my crime scene.' She put on a mockery of the Doctor's very English accent. 'Shall I send in some tea and crumpets?'

Disappearing back into the machine, the Doctor called back, 'Oh, yes, please. Strawberry jam if you've got some!'

Zoe and Luis exchanged a look, got down on their hands and knees, and followed.

'The thing with the Doctor,' Zoe said, 'is that he might actually think she's being serious . . .'

18

The kettling was designed to keep people out of the bubble. It wasn't hard for Phee to go the other way, and break in.

It was all a rush; she was still in her skinsuit from her own flight back from Enceladus. She had got back earlier than the rest – *she* hadn't mucked about on the way home – and she had got home before the kettling had been imposed. Sam, of course, had been swept up.

Inside Trinity Bubble, she found chaos. Hundreds of people milling about, few of them much older than her, and most of them in the bright green uniforms of C-grades. If there was anybody in authority in here, she couldn't spot them. There was nervous laughter. Music playing somewhere. Even a game of soccer going on in a field of rubble, between burned-out buildings. But under it all was fear; you could smell it in the air.

It didn't take her long to find Sam. He was with a bunch of his usual buddies, with Dai and Sanjay and Mindy Brewer, hanging around. And here was Jamie McCrimmon, with his skinsuit on and, comically, his bagpipe still in a pack on his back. He looked lost, concerned. But he smiled at Phee.

Sam, though, glared at her. 'What are you doing in here?'

'Finding you.'

'They wouldn't have picked you up. You're an A.'

'Look, Sam. We have to say something.'

'Say what? To who?'

'About the Blue Dolls. Come on, Sam. You know as well as I do that all this sabotage is the Blue Dolls, not us. We have to get out of here, and confess it all to Mum, and confront Florian Hart and the rest, and *tell* them. *Make* them listen.'

He looked at her pityingly. 'Phee, Phee. You could hardly be more naive, could you? *They already know.* About the Blues.'

'What?'

'Oh, of course they do. But they're going to keep on hiding it so they can get at us. Look, Phee, you shouldn't have come here. Get back out if you can. Just flash that nice grey A-colour at them and they will let you go.'

'I'm not leaving you.'

'Are you sure?' He glanced around. 'In a minute, some of us are going to try something.'

'Try what?'

He said softly, 'Break out.'

'*What?*'

'We don't have to stay here. We've still got the stuff from the Enceladus trip. And we've other caches. *Now* will you get out of here?'

She felt chilled, and she clutched her skinsuit close around her. 'I'm not leaving you,' she said firmly.

Jamie took her hand, and squeezed it. But she noticed that, oddly, he was looking at the amulet she wore around her neck.

19

Zoe found herself crawling through a crude passageway cut pretty efficiently right through the tractor carcass by the explosion. There were sharp metal shards under her hands and knees, and fluid dripping from split ducts, and what looked like live electrical cables dangling. Progress had to be slow and careful, though she was helped by torches held by Luis behind her and the Doctor up ahead.

'Ouch!'

'Doctor?' Zoe called. 'Are you all right?'

'Oh, fine, fine. I was fed up with this coat anyway. Now keep up, you two, keep up.'

He led them to the heart of the machine, to a large ripped-open tank and a stink of methane. Here the damage was obvious, the surfaces scorched, metal bulkheads melted by intense heat. The Doctor got to his haunches and faced them sombrely, the lines of his face deepened in the torchlight.

Luis glanced around. 'I guess this is the centre of the explosion.'

'Quite so, my boy. The fuel tanks. I found the rigged-up crossfeed from the oxidiser tank. The ignition was a simple shorted wire. Elementary, really, just as I tried to explain to Ms Hart. But that's not what I brought you in here to see. Look at that.' And he pointed to a huddled shape on the floor, just outside the cone of his torchlight.

Zoe glimpsed blue.

Luis leaned over for a look and turned away instantly, hand over his mouth, retching.

Zoe crept forward, her heart hammering, dread gathering. But she made herself look long and hard at what the Doctor had found.

It was a body. Human – or at least human-like, she corrected herself. That was evident from its basic layout, the head, the four limbs. Even though, she saw with real horror, the blast had torn it apart. One arm was actually detached and lying away from the body, with some kind of tool in its closed fingers. A human body, no larger than a child – no bigger than Casey Laws. And its skin, what was left of it, what hadn't been shredded by the blast, was bright blue.

The Doctor put a hand on her shoulder. 'It's all right, Zoe. You're doing very well. Tell me what you see – what you deduce.'

'This is our perpetrator.'

'I'm afraid so. Those are wire cutters in its hand, the hand on the detached arm. It was caught in the blast it created. As I suspected, no bomb was necessary; the sabotage was easy to carry out – if you were small enough to have crawled in here in the first place.'

'It is *blue*. The flesh. You can see it isn't just some surface treatment, not paint or make-up. Where the skin is broken you can see that beneath the surface—' She gagged.

'It's all right,' he repeated. 'I think it's clear what we're dealing with here, isn't it? This is one of the creatures the youngsters here have been sighting, and calling "Blue Dolls". We've seen them for ourselves, haven't we? It's impossible to believe that the advanced surveillance systems that must saturate this place and its mine have not picked up these creatures. And yet the official adult line remains one of denial, that the children are deluded or malicious. Ha! Well, Zoe, even the mild-mannered Phee Laws knew about the Dolls, and tried to keep them secret, perhaps in a rather misguided attempt to protect her brother. I had to inform Jo about that, but I don't think the mayor has decided how to handle that yet, and I don't blame her. It's rather hard to keep track of who knows what, isn't it? But that's the product of a system of distrust and lies.

'And here we have the undeniable physical proof – but we haven't done with our analysis. Not yet. Go on, Zoe. What else do you see?'

She took a deep breath. 'It isn't remotely human. Look at it, Doctor. There is no sign of internal organs. Nothing like a person's anyhow . . .' Under a formless mass of tissue, broken open, she saw a gleam of metal, deep inside the body.

'No, indeed. It seems to have been created to look human, or at least using the human body as a model. But it is not human.'

'Why do you say "created"? Rather than "born", or "evolved"?'

The Doctor pointed. 'That metallic shine in there. I suspect its skeleton, or the equivalent, is made of a bernalium compound. It seems very unlikely *that* could arise naturally. What else? Come now, Zoe. There's one more thing you're missing.'

Zoe, bewildered, looked down at the strange carcass. Her head felt empty, her blood pounded in her ears. What else? What could the Doctor mean?

It was Luis who spoke first. 'It wasn't the methane explosion that killed it.'

'Ah. Good. And how do you know that?'

Luis pointed. 'Because that big chest wound looks like a blaster shot to me. I've seen too many of those in my line of work, I'm afraid. He – it – was shot by a blaster, from the front. And *then* the methane tank went up, catching the creature from the left side. Look, you can see the burning on the surviving flesh. That must have thrown it aside, detached the – the limb . . .'

'Yes. Precisely. Well done, Mr Reyes, well done.'

Zoe said slowly, 'So this creature, after setting up its explosion, was detected—'

'By a human being, with a blaster. Who shot the Blue Doll without mercy. *And then allowed the explosion to go ahead.*'

Luis said, 'It's a miracle anything of the Blue Doll survived the explosion.' He glanced around at the wreckage. 'A chance bit of shelter from some bulkhead, perhaps . . .'

'Yes. Our killer must have been hoping there would be no trace left of the Blue Doll at all. For it's not the Blue Dolls who are the most useful suspects for an incident like this, is it? Not if you're trying to get control of the Wheel for your own purposes. And furthermore, Mr Reyes, tell me this – what would happen to the mining operations on Mnemosyne if an indigenous, and apparently intelligent, native species like this were to be discovered there?'

'The operations would be shut down immediately,' Luis said without hesitation. 'Life comes first. Interplanetary law is clear about that.'

'There you are. Another reason why certain vested interests would not want this creature, and its kind, to be exposed. Let them commit their convenient sabotage, but keep them hidden, and blame it all on somebody else.'

Zoe asked, 'Are you accusing Florian Hart, Doctor?'

'The glove does fit, doesn't it? But I'm not in the business of accusing anybody, Zoe. Not yet. Not until we've assembled a good deal more evidence. And there's the whole business of the allohistorical lure to think about. Where does *that* fit in?'

'The *what*?' Luis asked.

'What I really must do,' the Doctor said gravely, 'as I keep saying, is to get up to that mine and see for myself. And then perhaps—'

A monitor at Luis's waist bleeped urgently. He glanced down at it.

'We have a more urgent problem,' he said. 'It's the youngsters, in the Trinity bubble.'

Zoe grabbed the Doctor's arm. 'That's Jamie. What's happening?'

'They're breaking out!'

20

They emerged from the wrecked machine to find a full-scale stand-off going on between Sonia Paley, Jo Laws and Florian Hart. Jo was distracted by a flow of messages coming into a pad she held in her hand.

'No!' Sonia said firmly to Florian. 'You will *not* use lethal force against children! If your goons attempt it, I'll arrest you and have my own deputies shoot back!'

Florian stood taller than the others, arms folded, smiling coldly. 'But they are trying to break out of the bubble. Smashing through the ice wall! They are not only defying the kettling orders but are threatening the safety of the colony itself.'

'The only threat to safety is you,' Jo Laws snapped back. 'You and your threats of mutilation.'

'Mutilation?' The Doctor, standing up, brushing down his ruined coat, sounded outraged. 'What in heaven's name are you planning now, Florian Hart?'

'The logic is simple,' Florian said. 'Doctor, this is a space colony on the edge of survival.'

Jo snorted. 'The edge of profitability, more like.'

'And we are faced with law-breaking on a mass scale. There is no room, we don't have the resources to lock up so many miscreants. Everybody on this Wheel needs to work productively. And so I am proposing a more portable punishment regime.'

'Portable, eh? Oh, I see. Like Saxon England, I suppose. They couldn't afford to carry passengers either. So they would lop off a hand or a foot! Is that what you're suggesting?'

'Nothing quite so crude . . . but that's the idea. A toe, maybe. Who needs toes in fractional gravity? Of course this would all be carried out under medical supervision.'

Jo said, 'I'll tell you flat that Dr Omar and his team would have nothing to do with this.'

'So,' the Doctor said, 'you thought it wise to bring this up now, did you, Florian Hart? In an already inflamed atmosphere, to let a few hundred falsely imprisoned teenagers know that unless they behave you're going to start mutilating them? You could hardly be more provocative, could you? You know, I'm beginning to suspect you've manipulated this whole situation.'

'Oh, don't be absurd—'

'Are you making your move, Ms Hart? Are you using this incident with the tractor to mount some kind of quasi-legal coup?'

'Doctor.' Jo Laws held out her comms slate. 'I have Jamie. He wants to speak to you.'

'Give me that.' The Doctor grabbed the slate; there was no image on it, and he held it up to his ear. 'Jamie?'

'Doctor? I'm speaking on my skinsuit communicator . . .'

Zoe could hear shouting in the background, the sound of running footsteps – cracks, shattering glass, the sounds of destruction.

'What are you up to now?'

'It's the kids. They were steamin' anyhow, and when the announcements started being shouted about in here about gettin' yer toes off—'

Jo Laws crossed her fingers and muttered, 'Let Sam not be involved. Let Sam not be involved.'

'Young Sam's the ringleader! Poor old Phee is bein' swept up wi' it all too.'

'With her amulet,' muttered the Doctor.

'They're breaking through the ice wall, Doctor! But they're organised, ye've got tae give them that. Everybody in here's got a skinsuit. And somebody on the outside has come around with a big mess o' them wee space scooters. They ken wha' they're doin'.'

'But even if they do break out, Jamie – what can they hope to achieve? Where will they go?'

'Ah, they've got a plan for that! Titan, Doctor! We're all goin' tae Titan! Wherever *that* is! Wait – I think yon wall's givin' way at last—'

Zoe heard a crack, like a vast eggshell shattering. There was a roar of wind, a few last shouts – a scream. The sound dwindled quickly, as the air escaped from the bubble.

And then silence.

The Doctor looked around, at Jo, Sonia, Florian, Luis, Zoe. 'I rather think we need to talk. Don't you?'

21

A day after the sabotage, and with sixteen colony youngsters, plus Jamie, on their way to Titan, the leaders of what the Doctor insisted on calling his Doll-hunting expedition rode up to the mine on the moon, crammed into a single elevator module: the Doctor and Zoe, Florian Hart, Marshal Sonia Paley, Mayor Jo Laws, and Dr Sinbad Omar. Some of Sonia's deputies and Florian's guards rode other modules. Of Zoe's group, only Florian and Sonia were armed, with ugly-looking blasters. Florian had been adamantly opposed to letting the Doctor set foot on 'her moon'. But the others had opposed her in turn, and when she couldn't keep him out she insisted on coming along herself.

Zoe hadn't been up to Mnemosyne before, and nor had the Doctor. Zoe had no real idea what she would find up there on the moon, and she felt only dread as the elevator module began to ascend. The sense of gravity faded fast as they moved inwards along the Wheel's radius, and Zoe was glad of the harness she wore, strapped to rails bolted to the walls; at least she wouldn't float away. As she rose, the details of the moon's surface, inverted in the sky above, started to become clearer: roofs painted bright green, shafts like black punctures, roadways and paths cut through the ice. There was continual motion, huge vehicles like beetles crawling everywhere. The Wheel rotated at a different rate from the moon itself, and the elevator cables terminated on a complicated raised roadway that ran around the moon's rough equator.

'A remarkable scene of industry, isn't it?' the Doctor murmured now, looking up. His skinsuit was rucked up uncomfortably over his hastily repaired frock coat. 'They have a power plant at each pole – two for redundancy, of course. Fusion power, and the fuel is an isotope of hydrogen mined from the atmosphere of Saturn itself. Mined by giant scoopships operated by another bit of Bootstrap, Inc., no doubt.' When she didn't reply he glanced at her. 'Are you all right, Zoe? You're very quiet.'

'Jamie would say I should be used to all this. Living in space, as I did. But it's all so rickety, Doctor.'

'Well, this is the frontier in this age, Zoe,' he said softly, so the rest could not hear. 'They are having to work things out as they go. Invent, improvise. Yes, it is rickety. But I suspect that will be the least of our fears once we start descending into that mine in the sky up there . . .'

The sense of gravity had all but faded away now. There was a brief warning chime, and the module flipped over, so that wheel and moon rotated around Zoe's head.

She shut her eyes and swallowed hard. What would Leo Ryan and Gemma Corwyn and the rest of them on Station Three have said if they saw her throw up like an earthling on a sub-orbital hop? She would not be weak, she would not.

The module landed on the equatorial rail with a judder, and there was a sharp sense of braking as the module slowed to match the moon's rotation rate. Then it rolled off towards a kind of airlock, one of a dozen protruding from the sides of a broad, flat building. The world had turned upside down. Now the moon was 'down', under Zoe's feet, and the Wheel was a great arch in the sky, crammed with detail, its ice bubbles and metal tanks rolling over her head.

Everybody unbuckled, and Zoe followed suit. The Doctor, taking an experimental step, floated up to the ceiling. 'Oh, no!'

Jo Laws, laughing, reached up and grabbed the seat of his skinsuit and hauled him down. 'The moon's gravity is barely there at all,' she said. 'Don't worry. There are handholds and foot anchors everywhere; just hold yourself down. Now – orientation, Doctor, Zoe. This building is at the head of one of the main shafts we've drilled into the moon. The shafts are pretty extensive now, and there are natural cavities in the body of the moon itself – Mnemosyne is becoming something of a honeycomb.' She looked at Florian challengingly. 'We've come to this particular facility because the shafts beneath us have been the scene of the most recent sightings of Blue Dolls. No more denials, Florian.'

Florian snorted. 'Just to restate my position, one last time. This is a fool's errand. There is no alien phenomenon here. Our problems are human in origin. And all our efforts should be focused on that.'

'There's none so blind as they that won't see,' the Doctor muttered. 'Jonathan Swift said that to me once, and he was a smarter human being than you'll ever be, Florian Hart.'

Jo sighed. 'Whatever you say, Florian. Let's all just keep our eyes open and our mouths shut.' The module reached the airlock and docked. 'Now follow me . . .'

She pushed forward on a light wheelchair and led the way into the building's brightly lit interior, where huge machines hulked, and workers, mostly in C-grade green, watched the newcomers incuriously.

Jo pointed. 'We've got power distributors, matter printers, raw materials processors, air scrubbers. There's also a dormitory, refectory, infirmary, though most of the workers' human needs are taken care of up on the Wheel. We try to keep the shafts pressurised throughout, with breathable air that we manufacture up here, extracting oxygen and nitrogen from moon ice. Much easier to work that way. In fact we're pumping air into shafts and natural channels and chambers we haven't even explored yet; we send down robot carriers to fix lights and perform preliminary maps and assays, to see what's worth opening up properly. So come on. Let's go exploring.'

She led them to a shaft, brightly lit, a big round hole in the workshop's thin ceramic floor. It was walled with smooth ice, grey-white but laced with purples and greens: traces of some complex chemistry, Zoe imagined.

'We have to climb down,' Jo said. To demonstrate, she just pulled herself over the lip of the shaft, alarming Zoe, but she drifted slowly down, balloon-like, until she could grab hold of a rung sticking out of the wall surface. With her lightweight wheelchair folded up on her back, grabbing one rung after another, she was remarkably graceful, her lack of legs no hindrance. 'You work your way down the rungs. There are also hand- and foot-holds dug into the ice itself. Even if you fall, your descent is so slow you are easily recoverable. We can give you safety ropes. We don't usually recommend them.'

Ropes please, Zoe silently pleaded.

'That won't be necessary,' said the Doctor briskly. 'Shall we get on with it?'

They formed up in a line to follow Jo down into the hole.

Sinbad Omar quietly stood beside Zoe. 'Don't worry,' he murmured. 'I'll go ahead of you. Catch you if you fall. Not that you will.'

'Thank you,' she said, embarrassed.

When it was his turn, Sinbad drifted easily and without hesitation over the edge, and caught himself with one hand.

Zoe forced herself to follow. Her fall through the air was dreamlike. There was plenty of time to grab a rung, and it was easy to support herself with one hand, to balance with one foothold. They descended steadily, in their line. They passed breaks in the wall, horizontal corridors that led off to either side. Sometimes Zoe heard rumblings of machinery, echoing human voices, coming from the side-shafts. She would have felt quite safe, if not for the shaft below her, straight-walled, lit up all the way, that looked as if it reached down to infinity.

'I think we're all on edge,' Sinbad called up to her. 'I know Jo is cut up about the trouble with the kids, and worried about Phee and Sam, of course. I suspect she's on this expedition partly just to keep herself occupied.'

'Why are you here, Dr Omar?'

'Call me Sinbad. I didn't start out in life as a medic. I majored in human biology, anatomy, physiology, biochemistry, all of that. But the first cadres to come to the Wheel had to have multiple specialities. There weren't many of us, and we all had at least two jobs. We A-grades anyhow. So I cross-trained in medicine.'

'And today—'

'Well, the injuries that directly relate to this Blue-Doll phenomenon are biochemical in nature. A reworking of human tissue at the molecular level to produce that strange, inhuman – carapace. So I'm here with my old scientist's hat on today. But I have to say I think of myself more as a doctor nowadays. Found I rather enjoyed it.'

And he was evidently good, Zoe thought, at least with the bedside manner. For with his gentle conversation he had distracted her from the fact that she had already descended so far that the shaft opening was receding to a bright coin far above her head, but the bottom of the shaft was still out of sight, far below –

'There!' Sonia's voice.

Zoe heard the crisp rasp of blaster fire, smelled ozone in the scorched air. Startled, she looked down.

Sonia dangled one-handed before the opening of a side-shaft, her blaster in her hand. 'I saw one, I swear it! Large as life, blue, the size of a kid!'

The Doctor cried, 'And you shot it! Oh, Marshal, what have you done?' With surprising grace he pulled himself one-handed into the side-shaft, a leap like a salmon. 'We're here to study these creatures, not to shoot them! But try to explain away *this* sighting, Florian Hart!' He was scrambling into the tunnel, and soon his checked trousers and booted feet, all contained inside the skinsuit, had disappeared from view.

Jo called, 'Doctor, come back!'

But Zoe knew he wouldn't do that, not until he had found what he was looking for. Without hesitation she swung herself into the shaft. 'We must follow him. Come on, Sinbad!'

The medic laughed, and squirmed after her.

22

The side-shaft was just tall enough for Zoe to run upright, though it was narrower and rougher cut than the main vertical shaft, and the lights, globes stuck in the ice wall, were wider spaced, leaving ominous pools of shadow. It was colder here too. She wasn't so much running, of course, as driving herself along, yanking on widely spaced handholds in the walls, paddling with her booted feet at the floor. Still she was making good time. When she glanced back she saw they were all following, led by Sinbad, then with Jo and the rest behind.

She came to a kind of crossroads, a rough chamber from which three more shafts led off sideways. The Doctor was out of sight.

Sinbad came up to her. 'Which way now?'

'If I know the Doctor, he'll have left a sign.'

Sinbad tapped his shoulder, and a small torch fixed to an epaulette on his suit lit up. He quickly found a yellow arrow, hastily scrawled, pointing towards one rough-walled corridor. He touched the wall; his fingers came away coated with yellow dust. 'What's this, chalk?'

Zoe grinned. 'That's the Doctor, all right. Come on!' She plunged on that way.

'What's he doing with a bit of yellow chalk? This is Saturn!'

'Those pockets of his – you don't want to know what's in them . . . Look, is that another arrow?'

This time the shaft they followed led to a wider chamber, roughly spherical. The lights were sparse, the chamber full of shadows.

With Sinbad at her side, Zoe hurried across the floor. 'Is this a natural chamber?'

'No. It's been worked.' He pointed. 'See the scoring in the walls? The miners have been working their way through the moon, looking for concentrations of biochemicals and minerals – mostly bernalium. And when they find a lode they dig it out until it's exhausted.'

On the far side of the chamber there was another chalk scrawl. They hurried through more passages, following more arrows . . . Behind her she heard the voices of the others, still following.

'Don't worry about getting lost,' Sinbad said. 'It is a bit of a maze down here. And it does change all the time as the work evolves and they cut more shafts. But your skinsuit has a telltale, a beacon so you can be found again. And besides you could just follow the Doctor's arrows back the way we came.'

'Oh, I never get lost,' Zoe said. 'I've an eidetic memory. Perfect recall.' When she closed her eyes she could visualise the interior of the moon, filling up with a three-dimensional map of the shafts she'd followed, or glimpsed.

'Eidetic, eh? I'm impressed. Quite a capability.'

'It's just a matter of training.'

'Makes you feel like you're in control, I imagine – did you see that?' He was looking back down the passageway they were following.

'What?'

'A flash – something blue – it came out into the light, into this passage, and disappeared again. Must have been from a side cut.'

'I didn't see it. But the others are following it. Look!'

Jo, Sonia, Florian, their torches visible, were cutting off into a shadowy passageway.

'We should follow them.'

'No! We have to find the Doctor.'

Sinbad was uneasy, but nodded. 'All right. Come on.' They hurried ahead, along the passage, leaving the others behind.

So three had gone one way, three the other, Zoe realised. It was almost as if they had been intentionally split up . . .

The passage abruptly opened out into a wider chamber, this one irregular and rough-hewn, evidently natural. Sinbad stuck out his arm to stop Zoe going any further.

Zoe stood still, breathing hard. The lights here were even sparser, the shadows pooled wider, and her eyes slowly adapted to the dark. The chamber was no more than a great bubble in the ice, perhaps the result of a pocket of gases released when the moon was first formed. Ice formations stuck out of the walls, like randomly fixed sculptures, fantastic low-gravity shapes, crystalline and vesicular. It was almost beautiful in the scattered light.

Beautiful, and reflecting royal blue highlights.

And then she saw them. Blue Dolls, two, five, ten, a dozen. All identical, as far as she could see. All inert, their arms at their sides, their eyes and mouths sealed shut. Like dolls, like child-sized mannequins, littering the chamber, laying or standing or leaning on the walls, as if placed at random. None of them moving, none of them apparently aware of the intruders.

Sinbad took Zoe's hand. His palm was dry, and she could feel his steady pulse. He was a reassuring presence. He whispered, 'I think we should—'

The Dolls came alive.

All at once. Eyes and mouths dilating open. Limbs sheer and flexible, bending at unnatural angles.

The Dolls swarmed through the air and over the chamber walls, in utter silence. They made soft, sliding, plastic-slithering noises as they touched the ice walls of the cavern.

And they came from all angles, above, below, to the sides. Converging on Zoe and Sinbad, who dared not move.

'Keep still,' Sinbad murmured, the tension in his voice obvious. 'If we don't move, maybe they'll leave us alone . . .'

They were very close now. Zoe tried not to shrink back. They were very doll-like, with their child-sized bodies and their blank, sketchy faces. But it was the way they were *unlike* humans that was most disturbing: no nose, black unliving eyes, mouths like slits, no lips, teeth like rows of needles. And they moved unnaturally, their arms and legs bending at unnatural angles, as if there were no bones under that blue skin.

Now one *touched* her. It ran its palm over her cheek. Its hand was a kind of paddle, a flipper, with a thumb but with its fingers fused together. Its skin was smooth, neither warm nor cold. Eerily damp. Zoe stayed as still as she could, flinching at every touch. Her mind was full of the images she had seen of the man in the infirmary, the inhuman blue coating on his legs, the transformation of his skin . . .

The Doll faced her now, its head before her. She could see her own face reflected in its empty eyes. Its head tilted right over as it stared at Zoe, flopping loosely from one side to the other.

Suddenly the Dolls were swarming all over her, touching her with their hands, feet, even their faces. They were like moths, insect-like, fluttering around her, huge blue moths that she longed to bat away. They were *hissing*. And now, before her, an open mouth, needle teeth closing on her face.

She screamed.

She was dragged away. It was Sinbad, waving a muscular arm to drive the creatures back, forcing a way across the chamber and hauling Zoe after him. For a heartbeat they clung to her, her arms, legs, neck, she even felt those paddle-hands wrapping themselves in her hair. But then, suddenly, they released her, and she and Sinbad ran forward.

At the far side of the chamber they turned, backed up against the wall. The Blue Dolls hadn't followed them. Instead they had crammed themselves into the shaft from which Zoe and Sinbad had emerged, swarming together like a grotesque multi-limbed plug.

'Well,' Zoe said, 'we aren't going back *that* way.'

'Casey Laws,' he said now.

'What about Casey?'

'I am her family doctor . . . Those faces. They remind me of Casey Laws. A sort of simplified cartoon version of her little face. That can't be a coincidence, can it?'

'I suppose not.' Zoe glanced around. There was a shaft entrance only a few paces away, marked with another yellow arrow. 'Look! The Doctor went this way. At least we can follow him. He must have got past these creatures too.'

'Or they let him pass.'

'What do you mean?'

'Think about it. We had that sighting a way back, that drew off Jo Laws and the others. And now we've been jumped by this lot, and they've blocked the passage.'

'You mean—'

He said firmly, 'I mean these Blue Dolls have been stalking us. Herding us. They split us off from Jo and the others. And now they've trapped us. Whatever they are, human or not, biological or not, those critters are smart. Look – I don't mean to scare you. This moon is a warren; there's always another way out.'

Determinedly she put aside her fear. 'We can deal with that later. First we must find the Doctor. Come on.' And she led the way into the latest passage.

23

More twists, more turns, more smooth-walled human-cut corridors, more natural crevasses, chambers and flaws. This whole moon was like a piece of Swiss cheese, Zoe told herself. But she kept building up the three-dimensional map in her head. Its growing completeness pleased her, even though it was only a map of where they had been, not where they had to go. And at least, for now, there was no sign of any more of the Blue Dolls.

They passed through another chamber, where icicle-like growths extended from the walls, like stalactites and stalagmites in a cave on Earth, but these formations pushed into the cavern from all angles . . .

There was a peculiar shuddering in the air. The ground shook, like an earthquake, strong enough in the low gravity to bounce the two of them up into the air like peas rattling from a struck drumskin. Some of the icicle formations broke loose with tinkling cracks and fell slowly.

Florian had spoken of gravitational perturbations in the core. Zoe imagined whatever lay at the heart of Mnemosyne rolling and turning, the whole of the moon shuddering in response.

When the shock had passed she and Sinbad hurried across this chamber of icicles, followed another short human-cut shaft, and entered another large, open chamber, its walls dark, one of the largest she had seen so far . . .

'Zoe.'

The Doctor's calm voice, coming out of the gloom ahead, startled her to stillness. She was about halfway across the floor of the chamber. Sinbad was a few paces behind her. Before her, in the semi-dark, there was the Doctor, his frock coat crumpled inside his transparent skinsuit, sitting calmly on a big ice boulder. On the walls a few scattered lamps gleamed, shedding a sparse light.

But the walls were odd, and indeed the ceiling, and much of the floor. They were covered with some shining, gleaming, undulating covering.

Shining blue, in the dim light.

There were Blue Dolls *all over* this chamber, clinging to the walls, in tangled clumps on the floor. Not a mere dozen or so – hundreds. Even on the roof, clustered close together like figures painted on the ceiling of a Vatican chapel. Or they were like bats, Zoe thought uneasily, huge blue bats roosting. None of them moved.

None save a little group straight ahead of her, between her and the Doctor. Four, five, six Dolls were squatting, almost like a group of human children intent on some game. But a seventh Doll lay on the ground between them. It was as inert as the rest, but there was some quality about it, a deeper stillness, that told Zoe it was dead – or terminally malfunctioning? She knew too little about these creatures to know what language was appropriate, the language of living things, or of machines.

And now she smelt a sour stink, like plastic burning.

'Doctor?'

'It's all right, Zoe. I don't think we'll come to any harm if we don't alarm them. I've been here for some time, sitting on this rather cold block of ice, and they haven't done anything to me. Why don't you come to me? You can see the way I walked around that central group – that's it, off to the left. You too, Dr Omar. I really don't think there's any need to be afraid.'

Zoe stepped forward, taking each stride slowly and deliberately, making sure she didn't stand on any of the prone bodies around her feet. As she approached that central group the stink of burning intensified. 'I take it this is the one Sonia shot with her blaster.'

'I'm afraid so—'

There was a rustling, all around them. Zoe stood still. She glimpsed movement, above, below, to left and right. Limbs squirming like snakes on the walls and roof. A hundred blue bodies, all apparently identical, shifting and wriggling as one, without a word being said. It was eerie, utterly inhuman. It stopped as suddenly as it had begun.

Zoe saw there was still a clear path, still a way for her to reach the Doctor, and she hurried that way. He held out his hands, and she grabbed them with great relief, and let him pull her to his side.

But Sinbad didn't follow.

'I'm stuck, I'm afraid.' He stood on a bare patch of floor, surrounded by a sea of Blue Doll bodies that had closed around him.

'I'm sure you're perfectly safe,' the Doctor said, his voice glacially calm.

'I could probably just jump out of here—'

'Perhaps later, when we need to resort to such measures. We are here to observe these creatures, remember.'

'All right.' Carefully, slowly, making no sudden moves, Sinbad sat down, cross-legged.

'Doctor,' Zoe scolded, 'you shouldn't have run off like that.'

'Well, I knew you'd follow,' the Doctor said blandly. 'And I did leave you messages. The signs in chalk.'

'Yes, we saw those.'

'We did shoot this poor creature, you know, Zoe. I don't particularly blame Sonia Paley – I suppose it was a natural reaction. Especially given the whole environment of control and confrontation Florian Hart has carefully built up. I followed the one we wounded. It didn't get far, but then others came to carry it away; I saw them and followed, as best I could. I would swear one of them was more dominant – a leader. There have been reports of that sort of behaviour, I believe. Then they came to this place, this chamber, and – well, you can see for yourself.'

'It died.'

'I'm afraid so. Another little burden for the conscience of humanity, eh? I did have a notion of retrieving the body and bringing it back for analysis. I should think some kind of autopsy would reveal a great deal – this specimen is much less damaged than the one we found in the tractor up on the Wheel.'

'Well, why haven't you?'

'Because of the others. Look at them, Zoe. Just watch.'

The half-dozen Dolls around their fallen companion sat in a ring, like children playing a statues game. But every so often one would reach out a hand, and lift a limp arm, or touch the open mouth, or shake the body. Gently, almost inquisitively.

'I've no idea what kind of intelligence motivates these creatures. There may be some form of group mind. Or perhaps they are like puppets, controlled from somewhere else. But on an individual level, I can tell you from my own direct observation that these are no simple animals. *They understand death.* They are mourning their fallen comrade. And only a handful of animals on Earth do that: the chimps, the dolphins, the elephants—'

'And man.'

'Quite so. And that is why I haven't taken the body, not yet. Out of respect.'

Sinbad shivered. '*Brr-rr.* I'll be honest, I wish I was sitting over there with you two. They may or may not be conscious, but these things do give me the shudders.'

'Just sit still, Dr Omar.' The new voice was a bold challenge, and unmistakeable.

The Doctor looked around. 'Florian Hart? Is that you?'

'The very same. You took some finding. But you brought us straight to the nest of the monsters. Well done.' And she raised her blaster.

'No!' the Doctor cried. 'Not again! Don't shoot!'

There was a crackle of fire. Blue bodies, scorched and broken open, went flying through the air to slam into the walls.

And the Blue Dolls moved as one. They rose up from the walls and descended from the ceiling in a hissing, slithering horde, their bodies rustling as they slid over each other. The very air was filled with them. Sinbad Omar screamed as the Blue Dolls swarmed over him, and he went down.

'Your skinsuit!' the Doctor yelled at Zoe. 'Zip it up! Now!'

She did as she was told, bringing down her visor just as blue bodies slammed into her. She struggled to her feet as the Dolls clambered over her, clinging like monkeys. But the Doctor grabbed her hand and, with surprising strength, dragged her across the floor towards Florian and the others. Zoe saw that the Doctor had somehow scooped up the Blue Doll corpse and had slung it over his shoulder.

They passed Sinbad. He was struggling to his feet in a tide of Dolls, of hands and teeth that clung and pulled him back. His eyes met Zoe's, and she reached out a hand. But his skinsuit had been ripped open, and his bare hand was already mottled blue. She reached for him even so, but the Doctor dragged her away.

They had to dodge through a hail of blaster fire to get out of the chamber. To shouted orders from Florian, a sustained cannonade of blaster fire brought down a chunk of the cavern's roof, sealing the Dolls inside. But this blockade wouldn't hold for long. Already Zoe could see blue hands probing, pushing through the mounds of ice-rock rubble. The party turned and ran.

24

Sixteen children of the Mnemosyne Cincture fell into the dusky air of Titan, their rocket scooters flaring like matchsticks. And James Robert McCrimmon, veteran of Culloden Field, with his bagpipe in a pack on his back, followed them in.

It had taken them a day to get this far from the Wheel, and Titan had grown from a brown pinprick to a ball like an orange hanging in the sky to this huge featureless globe below him. Another wretched moon! Jamie was no coward but this was an extraordinary experience, even by the standards of the adventures he had endured since leaving Scotland with the Doctor. He wished the Doctor were here now, and Zoe at his side, and the stout walls of the TARDIS around him, rather than being naked to space with a bunch of kids like this. But once again Sam had shut down the comms systems on their suits, and even calling the Doctor or anybody on the Wheel was impossible.

And now his scooter shuddered, and he felt a buffeting. Attitude rockets banged, jolting him, and exhaust products squirted in thin glittering streams.

'That's normal,' Phee Laws called. 'The scooter's steering itself, it knows what to do.'

Glancing around a sky crowded with scooters, Jamie easily picked out Phee, the grey of her customised A-grade uniform visible through her skinsuit.

'Normal, ye say? Normal tae me is a slice o' haggis, a wee dram and a punch-up afore bedtime. Not this – this fallin'.'

'We're already entering the atmosphere,' she said evenly. 'Titan's air extends out a lot further than Earth's. The gravity's lower. So we're already starting to feel its effects . . .'

He let her chunter on, not really listening, not really understanding. She was just a kid herself, and this was her way of coping, by taking care of everybody else. But now she was talking about the descent, and he tried to pay attention.

'Your scooter will throw out a shield.'

'A shield?'

'Against the air friction. Don't worry, it's all automatic. And then once we're under the smog layer there'll be a parachute. You can use your rockets in the last few metres to cushion your landing. It's all controlled by the scooter's systems. Just make sure you've got your harness tightly secured.'

'Aye, I dinna want to fall off this thing.'

There was a wash of static on the comms link. The air was gathering now, almost glowing, a deep brownish orange. When Jamie looked up he saw the stars dimming out one by one.

'We're in the haze,' Phee said. 'The top of the air, where the sunlight manufactures hydrocarbons, a molecule at a time. They're called tholins. They make the smog below us, and rain out on the surface. You might find streaks of the stuff on your equipment. Don't worry, it's normal, it can't penetrate your suit.'

The ride was turning into a bumpy buffeting, as the air thickened. He could actually hear something now, a kind of thin whistle, air catching the sharp edges of the scooter.

And then, without warning, the scooter flipped forward so he was suddenly falling face-down, the scooter underneath him. He felt his last meal rising in his throat.

The comms channel was breaking up, but he heard whoops, and a few alarmed cries, and Phee's calm, steady voice: 'Don't worry! It's normal! Just part of the automated entry programme . . .'

Suddenly the spine of Jamie's scooter popped open and a kind of sheet unfolded with a snap. The sheet billowed, grabbing at the air, becoming a shield underneath him, held open by an internal frame of lacy rods like the bones of a bat's wing. The scooter's descent immediately slowed, and Jamie felt a jolt as if he had been dropped from a height onto his stomach.

Yet still he fell, into the thickening air. Below him was nothing but featureless orange mush. He could see the other scooter riders above, around, below him, lying on those big entry shields. But they were scattering, and he wondered how far apart they might all end up when they finally made landfall.

Another sudden change. Jamie's shield abruptly tore down the centre, and the two halves went flapping up past him to either side. For an instant he thought he was falling freely, but then he saw that the two panels were reassembling themselves over his head, turning into a pair of parachutes, not round but squared off, connected to the scooter by threads that tightened as the chutes billowed full of air. The scooter swivelled again, jolting Jamie upright, and he was swinging in the air now, slow as a clock pendulum, huge, steady, stomach-dragging swings. But the chutes were holding above him, strong and proud.

The comms channel seemed to clear of the static, and suddenly everybody was talking at once. But Jamie didn't pay any attention to that, for the orange smog cleared, and he was looking down through clear air to a still-distant ground.

In his days with the Doctor he had flown over many landscapes, on Earth, over the moon, and many alien worlds. But the Titan ground he saw below him now reminded him of nothing so much as his home, of

Scotland: crumpled chains of mountains, a long narrow lake with a complicated shoreline, rivers snaking down from the higher ground. It was only the colours that were wrong. The lakes and rivers were jet black, not blue or steel grey, and the ground was a murky orange, not the green of forests or meadows. Jamie was reminded of the Land of Fiction, one of the strangest places he had visited with the Doctor, a place beyond space and time where everything had been jumbled up and reversed, just like this.

And now he plummeted through a layer of clouds and the ground opened up further, expanding, its detail revealed a bit more with every heartbeat. Jamie looked for signs of human habitation: lights, roads, buildings. He wondered where that famous methane plant was. Nothing. He did, however, see a tremendous ripple on that loch of black ink, a wake as if created by a gigantic ship . . .

There was a light in the air to his left, flaring green.

'Can you see me?' Sam called. 'Gather around my flare, when we go in. It'll be a lot easier to get together while we're still in the air than when we're down on the ground. I'm going to make for the southern coast of that big methane lake under us. That's where our stash is, if nobody's robbed it.'

'Tha's all verra well,' Jamie called back. 'But how d'ye steer this beastie? With the rockets?'

People laughed at his ignorance. That was kids for you.

Phee called back, 'No, you steer by tipping the parachutes. But it's all automatic, it works through the hand controllers.'

Jamie, experimentally, tried it. When he twisted the scooter handles the complexes of strings tugged at the wing-shaped chutes above him, and he was pulled this way and that through the air. It wasn't the same as when the scooter was in space. The responses were more sluggish, you had to leave a lot more time to complete a manoeuvre, and that slow swinging didn't help. But soon he was swooping easily around the sky, and starting to enjoy himself again.

Around him in the air he saw the other scooters sweep in like huge gliding birds, like albatrosses, closing in on the green light of the flare.

But suddenly the ground was awfully close, turning from a map safely far beneath him to a real landscape of hills and dunes and streams into which he was falling, incredibly fast. The detail exploded further until he could see he was heading for a plain littered by rocks and pebbles, many of which were clearly big enough to crack an ankle.

'Use your rockets!' Phee shouted. 'If you hit the big yellow button the scooter will do it for you.'

Jamie, taking no chances, hit the button. The ground rushed up at him. In the last instant the rocket flared under his feet, kicking up dust that billowed around him. Even so he landed hard, and as the rocket died he tipped on his back, tumbling softly with the scooter still attached to him by its harness.

The dust he'd kicked up fell down around him slowly. And then the big sheets of his parachute came settling out of the sky, covering him over, hiding the world behind a soft green-orange glow. He felt oddly comfortable, lying there on his back, with only the noise of his own ragged breathing in his ears. 'Did I just dream all that? Am I home in my bed?'

The chutes whipped away from him, revealing Phee Laws, her grinning face behind her visor. 'Not quite,' she said. She held out a hand to help him up.

25

The scooter, performing one last function, hauled the shield-chutes away from Jamie, rolled them up and packed them back away into its body, cables and all.

Jamie found himself sitting on a rocky plain. Not far away, Sam and the others hauled at a mound of rocks, like a cairn. There was some kind of heap of supplies under the cairn, and Sam and the others crowed and whooped at their success at finding it. Soon they were unfolding a dome-shaped tent, just like on Enceladus. Chutes were still coming down from the orange sky, like giant birds settling to a rookery. Jamie made a quick count. Sixteen plus him, sixteen safe and sound – well, not quite, one girl had hurt her leg on landing, and a few others were huddling around her to help.

He stood up and took an experimental step. The ground was sandy, gritty; the dirt was an orange-stained muck. Boulders and pebbles of some kind of rock littered the plain. This wasn't particularly Scottish, close to; it looked more like a rocky desert, or even the smashed-up floor of a crater on the moon.

He picked out a flat rock, his skinsuit felt stiff when he bent to get it, and started walking towards the lake, which he could see as a fine black horizon, not far away. Walking was odd. He felt light, as he had on the Wheel, but he felt like he was pushing through some dense fluid, as if he was wading through an invisible ocean.

He reached the shore of the lake. It was black, like a sea of oil. Slow, heavy ripples crossed its surface, and on a gritty beach it lapped by his feet, though he took care not to step into it. He hefted his rock and sent it spinning, flat through the air. It hit the lake surface and bounced once, twice before sinking. 'Losin' yer touch, McCrimmon,' he muttered.

'Nice effort.' Phee was standing beside him.

'Aye. Used tae do that on Loch Tay. Managed more than a couple o' bounces, mind.'

'You're getting old.'

'Och, dinna you start.'

'What do you make of Titan?'

He looked up into the sky. Beyond pale fluffy clouds the sky was just an orange dome, featureless although he thought he could see a brighter glow where the sun must be. He couldn't see Saturn, and that was a disappointment. But now he heard a soft patter, on his skinsuit hood, his shoulders. A heavy rain was falling, big brown-black blobs of it, so slow it was like a rainstorm in a dream. He let it strike his visor, and the drops rolled off, leaving purple-brown smears.

'It's kind o' like home,' he said at last. 'But all the colours are wrong. Like home, made out of different stuff.'

'That's what you hear people say. People who've travelled . . . You can go to the moon or Venus or Mars or Titan, and everywhere you go you find rocky plains like this, eroded pebbles. But made from different stuff.' She kicked a pebble. 'Jamie, it's very cold here. The "rock", like these pebbles, is actually ice, but hard as basalt, and just as tough to drill into. The lake over there is methane and ethane. Hydrocarbons. Deep down under the crust there's a mantle of liquid water. There are volcanoes, here on Titan, like the vents on Enceladus, but much bigger. The lava is water!'

'Ye're jokin' me. So I'm a lumberin' beast o' molten lava!'

'Yes! On Titan *we're* the alien monsters.'

'Aye, for once,' he said with feeling.

'But there is life here.' She held out a gloved hand and let the murky rain fall into her cupped palm. 'Because of all this complicated organic chemistry muck, falling out of the sky. They used to think there might be some kind of primitive microbes here, that it was too cold for anything else. Just bugs. Of course when they got here, what they actually found was—'

Something whooshed over their heads, making them duck, heading out towards the lake. Jamie straightened up and saw two scooters screaming out over the lake's dead flat jet-black surface. 'Wha's *that*?'

Sam walked up. 'Dai and Sanjay. Idiots want to go surfing. I told them to wait, we've got the whole shelter to set up and everything. But they wouldn't listen.'

Phee laughed at her brother. ' "Wouldn't listen"? You're the great rebel, Sam. You're the one who's always breaking the rules. Now you're complaining when somebody else breaks *your* rules.'

'Shut up.'

'What a hypocrite!'

'Shut up!'

Jamie could see the scooters were dipping down to the lake's surface, and throwing up huge plumes of oily liquid that fell back slowly. 'Are they supposed to do *that*?'

'No,' Phee said firmly. 'Remember the skis you used on Enceladus, Jamie? That's what they're using out there now. Like water skiing. Though that's not water.'

'Idiots,' Sam growled. 'They'll use up their fuel too.'

Jamie frowned. 'I thought there was a methane plant down here.'

Phee was staring at the lake. 'I can only see one of them now . . . Maybe they're in trouble.'

Sam said, 'The plant's in the north, where all the really big lakes are. We're near the south pole here. As far as you can get from Pop and his buddies.' He spat out the name.

'Who's "Pop"?'

'Our stepfather,' Phee said. 'Well, before the divorce. Casey's dad. He's not that bad, Sam.' But she was staring out at the lake, distracted.

'I see what ye mean,' Jamie said now. 'I only see one o' them scooters, sort o' flapping back and forth. Doesnae look much like fun to me.'

Sam stared out. 'If they were in trouble they'd call—'

'HELP US!' The screeching call, painfully loud in Jamie's ears, came through right on cue. 'We turned our comms off so Sam wouldn't chew us out – Dai's gone down – HELP US! CAN YOU HEAR ME?'

'Sanj,' Sam shouted. 'Sanjay! Take it easy. What happened? Did Dai's scooter fail?'

'Not that. It came out of the water—'

'What did?'

'This big mouth. Teeth! It got the scooter, it missed Dai, but he's in the lake—'

Teeth?

Jamie glanced around. The rest were busy with their half-built dome, though they were clearly listening in to Sanjay's broadcast. They were all away from their scooters. Jamie's was only a short sprint away.

He set off at once.

Sam called, 'Jamie, no. You're not experienced enough.'

'Aye, well, ye follow if yer want, but the quicker somebody's out there the better.' He grabbed the scooter, jumped on its platform, squirted its rockets and flew off.

The scooter was sluggish, its rocket engine underpowered in Titan's thick air. But soon he was swooping low over the eerie black surface of the lake. Of course he had no idea how much fuel he had left after the descent from space – less than the others, probably, given he had less experience handling the craft. But he put that out of his mind, he didn't look back, and he leaned into the motion, urging a little more speed out of the scooter.

Soon he was over the boy in the lake. Dai was floating, it looked as if his suit had inflated itself for buoyancy, but he was thrashing in the thick oily muck, sending up spray that fell back with eerie slowness. Of his scooter there was no sign. The other boy, Sanjay, seemed to have lost his head, and was just skimming back and forth on his own scooter a few metres above the surface.

And then Jamie saw the teeth. A ring of them showing in the water. They were white, white as ice, set around a cavernous, gaping mouth, and behind the mouth trailed a streamlined body, huge but barely visible in the black fluid. This tremendous beast was circling the terrified boy, creating huge slow waves that rippled out across the lake.

'Can ye see this?'

'Yes, Jamie,' Phee replied, 'we've synced into your visor.'

'What manner of hell-spawned creature is that?'

'It's called a T-shark, Jamie. A Titan-shark. It has some posh name ...'

'I thought ye said there was only bugs here!'

'Once everybody thought so, because of the cold, and of course the lack of free oxygen in the air ... Well, everybody was wrong. Maybe it breathes hydrogen, or methane, instead of oxygen—'

'So there are monsters here after all. I should hae known it were too guid to be true.'

'It looks like sharks on Earth because it has the same kind of lifestyle.'

Jamie had seen enough alien life forms to know a few basic facts. 'Yon T-shark won't get much joy out o' eatin' Dai, will he?'

'No,' Sam snapped. 'He won't be able to digest him. But, Jamie, I don't think the shark knows that.'

Suddenly a huge streamlined head shot up out of the lake, immense jaws snapping. Jamie had let his scooter dip too low. He dragged on his control handles and lifted up and out of its way, *just*, but that huge mouth came close enough to spray him with jet-black slobber.

'Aye, and I won't be goin' down there to explain it either.' He tried to think. 'What I need is a rope . . .' He snapped his gloved fingers. 'Phee – the parachute cable – that's all wrapped up somewhere inside this toy I'm ridin', right?'

'Yes, it is. Listen, Jamie. You'll have to work the controls properly to release it. Just follow my instructions . . .'

Soon the cable was dangling down from Jamie's hovering scooter, and Dai was able to grab it.

'I can't hold it,' Dai called up, sobbing, but reasonably calm. 'My gloves are all greasy with this muck.'

'Then tie it around your chest, ye numpty. And – whoa, hey, what was that?' Sanjay's scooter passed him, just metres away. The boy was flying around at random. 'Lad, can ye no' keep yer distance?'

'He's panicking,' Phee said. 'He's in a worse state than the one in the water.'

'Aye, well, just keep him talkin', and out of my way. Now, Dai, ha' ye got that tied tight? All right. Here's ma plan. I'll lift ye nice and easy so as not to strain the thread, and not to alarm yon critter—'

'Lift me up! Here comes the shark!'

So Jamie pulled at his controls, and the scooter lurched up. At first Dai's weight dragged at the little craft, but he came free of the lake with a kind of reluctant squirt.

Came free just as the T-shark jumped out of the lake and soared high into the air.

Its long black body was exposed now, all the way down to massive beating flukes. At its highest point its razor teeth missed Dai's dangling feet by a hair's breadth. Then it fell back with a tremendous inky splash, and did not surface again.

Heart hammering, Jamie turned to the shore.

After that it was plain sailing. Except that Dai's weight kept dragging the scooter down.

And the fuel started running low, with loud warning chimes, and Jamie piled on the speed. But the two of them still went down into the lake, short of the shore. The others came out to help them wade free of the sticky stuff.

Plain sailing.

Safe at last, Jamie threw himself down on the sandy ground, his skinsuit black with the tarry stuff from the lake, his breathing a deep rasp.

Plain sailing. Just another extraordinary day, in the extraordinary life of James Robert McCrimmon.

He fell fast asleep.

26

To study the corpse of the Blue Doll he had brought back from the moon, the Doctor co-opted one of Sinbad Omar's surgeries to serve as a laboratory. This was no great loss to the Wheel, because there was a similar surgery in each of the three Residential sectors of the Wheel.

But Zoe saw that the Doctor was provoking a great deal of resentment. It was as if he was being insensitive about the loss they had all suffered, moving too quickly to take over what had been Sinbad's. After all Sinbad's body hadn't been recovered; he wasn't yet declared dead. It didn't make a lot of sense, but Zoe supposed it was a natural human response. People didn't act very logically when they grieved.

Of course the death of Sinbad impacted on her too. She had barely known him, yet he had shown her such kindness. For her, it was going to be a great relief to be able to concentrate on the science for a while. She knew she would have to deal with her feelings about Sinbad's loss in time. For now she shut them up inside a compartment of her soul.

Jo Laws was the last to leave. 'Is there anything else you need? I could have someone from Sinbad's staff assigned to help you.'

'No, thank you,' the Doctor said briskly. 'No need for that. The equipment here is rudimentary but it's quite comprehensive. We'll soon get the hang of it, don't worry.'

'We're still looking for Sinbad. We have various deep-scan devices we're turning on Mnemosyne now. Deep radar, heat sensors. We've been using them to locate bernalium deposits. If we retune them to detect movement, heat pockets, we may find Sinbad, or more concentrations of these Blue Dolls.'

'Umm,' the Doctor said. 'Don't you think that would have been a good idea before now? Ah, but of course you were all dancing to Florian Hart's tune, weren't you? Who has probably been making these sorts of scans all along.'

Zoe touched his arm. 'Doctor . . .'

'Oh – I apologise, Mayor Laws. Now isn't the time, is it? But I do rather fear Sinbad is lost. As a human entity at least.'

Jo nodded, expressionless. 'Just remember I have three kids here, Doctor. Two lost on Titan. And the smallest of them has been in contact with these – effigies. Every minute of every day I find myself shaking at the thought that instead of just looking at little Casey they might have taken her.'

Zoe said gently, 'But they didn't.'

'You know, I chose to bring my children up in this place. I thought it would be a better life for them than on an Earth of overcrowding and pollution and war . . . It turns out I can't even keep them safe.' She glanced up at a camera nestling in a corner of the ceiling. 'You'll be under surveillance. It's necessary for the official records. And I'll have to have a guard posted on the door.'

'To keep us in, or to keep others out? Oh, never mind. We'll be fine, Jo, really.'

When he had finally hustled her away, the Doctor blew out his leathery cheeks theatrically. 'What a relief! Now then, Zoe, where were we?'

Zoe had been quietly looking around. She had already found a kit of surgical gear, scalpels, forceps, pliers, clamps, even rugged-looking saws. Over the table there was a more modern set-up of scanners and surgical lasers. Now she opened a drawer and produced surgical gowns, with masks and caps, all in a cool grey. 'These might be useful.'

'Good thinking, Zoe. Though I have a feeling the chance of cross-infection and so forth is rather remote.' He slipped on the gown. 'How do I look? Do you think I suit A-class grey?'

She snorted. 'Not with your grubby old bow tie dangling out of your gown, no.'

'Ah, well.' He looked around for a sink. 'We'd better scrub in, as they say. What fun to play doctors and nurses!'

There was disinfectant fluid in dispensers. As they scrubbed their hands and arms, slipped on long surgical gloves, and fixed their masks in place, Zoe felt she was engaging in some archaic ritual.

Then they stood side by side over the body on the table, their gloved hands raised. The Doctor, only his eyes showing over his mask, winked at Zoe. 'The two of us masked and armed with forceps. An alien body on the slab, and a camera in the corner of the room. Takes me right back to Roswell, 1947! *That* took a bit of explaining away, I can tell you.'

'Doctor?'

'Never mind, never mind. Let's make a start.'

'Shall we use the laser?'

He shrugged. 'We're venturing into the unknown, Zoe. I rather think the old-fashioned way will be the best.' He picked up a scalpel, and looked down at the Doll's inert face. 'Sorry, old chap.' He laid a hand over its eyes.

Then he thrust the scalpel into the chest, delicately, just beneath the throat, or rather the smooth skin where a throat ought to have been. Zoe could see the skin was tough, resistant. The Doctor began to pull the scalpel down the body, making an incision that would run down the centre of the torso. 'Hard work,' he said. 'It's like cutting into stiff plastic.'

'Let me help.' Zoe moved to stand behind the table to hold down the creature's shoulders, enabling the Doctor to exert more pressure on the skin. Zoe could see that beneath a tough outer layer was softer, spongier matter, a deeper blue. But there was nothing like blood.

As he worked the Doctor said, 'I don't, however, believe that we're going to find all the answers we're seeking from this amateur autopsy. What we need is to get back into that ice moon and engage not with dead Dolls, but the living. And find out what's behind *them*. These Dolls are clearly artefacts, Zoe. Conscious to some degree perhaps, but artefacts nonetheless, and clearly modelled on the human form, and specifically on the very first human they encountered.'

'Which happened to be little Casey Laws.'

'Yes, as we learned from Phee – thanks to that foolishness by the brother. Which is why the Wheel appears to be infested with toddler-sized alien-technology androids. Of course they've now seen human adults, and have experimented on them, and indeed have captured one, whether dead or alive. Perhaps they're developing a new design . . . Anyhow, now at least we can lay the artifice bare. Help me.'

He had completed his incision. Now he and Zoe dug their gloved hands into the long cut, grabbed flaps of skin, and peeled it back. It came away with a sucking noise, to reveal a mass of blue-purple tissue. It wasn't like opening up a human body to reveal a chest cavity, with ribs and organs, Zoe thought. It was more like peeling a fruit.

'Aha,' said the Doctor. 'Just a mass, can you see? No differentiation into specific organs, and so forth. A highly distributed structure. Hand me a specimen glass, would you?' With his scalpel he sliced away a thin section of the internal tissue, and laid it out on the glass dish Zoe handed him. He took this to a bench where an electron microscope stood among other equipment. With a little tinkering, and only a few frustrated curses, he soon had a magnified image of the tissue's structure projected on a wall screen.

It was something like a wiring diagram, torn and crumpled by his crude cutting.

'Why, it doesn't look biological at all,' Zoe said. 'It's like circuitry.'

'Yes. And can you see the blockier lumps embedded inside? Some of those will be processor units or stores, I'm sure. And some of these other components must be micromechanical impellers. Tiny engines, doing the job of muscles. It's clearly artificial, but a very advanced design, Zoe.'

'And highly distributed.'

'Yes. With no specific centres, no equivalent of a brain or a heart or musculature – not even anything as straightforward as a blood supply. Instead there is this flexible mass of components, with the body's functions distributed throughout its volume, down to the level of these microscopic components – and further down to the nanotechnological level and beyond, I shouldn't wonder. That's why it's so flexible in form and posture. And resilient; you could slice this creature in half and it would continue to function.'

'Yet it was killed by a blaster shot. I mean—'

'Yes. Not killed. Terminated. I suspect it was the powerful electromagnetic scrambling that the blaster fire delivered, as much as the physical damage, that shut down this creature. It's not invulnerable.'

'And clearly an artefact.'

'Oh, yes. Look here.' He returned to the body and dug deeper into the mass of tissue, with quick, brutal slices of his scalpel. He revealed a kind of structure, a layering. 'It's like a Russian doll,' he said. 'One inside the other. Can you see? And that, Zoe, must be a relic of the manufacturing process.'

'It might have been made in a matter printer,' Zoe said. 'Like the ones here on the Wheel. Built up layer by layer. That would give you this stratification.'

'Yes. A highly advanced version of the human technology here. Quite so, Zoe.'

'Have you ever come across this technology before, Doctor?'

He scratched his sideburn with the handle of the scalpel. 'As a matter of fact, I have. In a museum of ancient times. An exhibit rather over-shadowed by displays of the worlds of the Great Vampires, and so forth . . . There was once a race called the Kystra, as I recall. During their Era of Embodiment they had a technology like this, in fact ulti-mately rather more advanced, based on the manipulation of matter right down to the level of quantum functions. The Kystra were traders, happy to sell their wares to the highest bidder. Thus, just because this is Kystra technology it doesn't mean that the Kystra necessarily used it. But this is long ago, five or six billion years back.'

'Their "Era of Embodiment". What came after that?'

'Why, an Era of *Dis*embodiment, of course! But that's another story.'

Zoe looked down at the splayed-open Doll. 'So this is very old tech. But nevertheless, here it is.'

'Yes. Which suggests, does it not, that what we're dealing with at the heart of the moon must itself be very old. As we had already begun to suspect.'

'But now it has gone beyond producing Dolls with its matter printer technology. These attempts it is making to transform human flesh—'

'Yes, we mustn't forget about that. We may be able to find out how it is done in the course of this autopsy. Contact with the skin perhaps, the transference of some kind of replicator. Or injections through the teeth – there may be some analogy to venom sacs.'

That idea made Zoe shudder, and she thought of how the creatures had crawled over her, deep in the ice moon.

The Doctor said, 'I suspect it is experimenting. *It* – our mysterious central mind. Trying things out, to see what works, to discover the most effective strategy to handle the problem it faces.'

'It all seems rather makeshift.'

'Slapdash even, yes. We may be dealing with an entity that is very powerful, but not terribly competent, Zoe . . .'

'Old and confused.'

'Well, possibly.'

A communications console chimed, and a screen lit up with Jo Laws' face. 'Sorry to disturb you.'

'Go ahead,' the Doctor called.

'We've got the preliminary results of deep-radar scans of the moon. No sign of Sinbad Omar, unfortunately. But we have found a concentration of the Dolls.'

'What kind of concentration?'

'In an upper chamber. It looks like another nest, Doctor. A big one this time.'

The Doctor turned to Zoe gleefully. 'Then that's where we must go next.'

Zoe protested, 'But the last time we went into the moon it ended up in a firefight. One of the Dolls was killed, and one of us was taken!'

'We've no choice but to go back, Zoe. We've known that from the beginning. The mystery of this place is lodged at the heart of that little moon, and we have to keep on going back until we've penetrated its heart. And the place to begin is with the Dolls – especially if we can locate their leader, of which we've had a few tantalising scraps of evidence.'

'But how can we gain the trust of the Dolls?'

'I've an idea about that. But we'll need to get hold of some of those fancy animated flags they have here. I imagine Jo Laws could arrange that. And, Zoe, when was the last time you spoke to your friend MMAC? . . .'

27

Once again Jamie was woken up by a row. He pushed his way out of the little private shelter he'd made for himself, his old tartan blanket hanging from a handle on the dome wall. Yawning, he stretched and looked around.

Every day started with a decision: which end of the makeshift colony's shabby little recycling plant to visit first. The plant was a rough row of hoppers and processing machines, white boxes joined end to end by pipes and ducts, all the components pinched by Sam and his cronies from Utilities up on the Wheel. You did your personal business at one end, and then let the engines process the waste, extracting nutrients and adding Titan meltwater and tholin chemicals to flavour. And out the other end came breakfast, things like biscuits that weren't biscuits, bowls of stuff like mushroom soup that wasn't mushroom soup. It was a little factory with a cludgie at one end and a soup dispenser at the other. Charming.

The morning decision on which end to visit first – whether you were going to go for input or output – depended on where the biggest crowd was gathered. There was never any queuing. Nobody queued in Tartarus, kingdom of Sam Laws. Instead there was always just a kind of mob around the recycler, one lot crowding to get at the cludgie end, the rest at the soup tap. And already this morning people were pushing and shoving, Jamie saw.

The shabby dome stretched low over all their heads, the interior space divided up into little tumbledown shacks by blankets and tarpaulins. People were moving everywhere, sticking tousled heads out of improvised tepees, checking over bits of kit. They never looked younger to Jamie than first thing in the morning, their faces puffy with sleep, those big wide pupils making them seem oddly bewildered.

He didn't underestimate them; these weren't kids, they were young adults. Some of them had paired off into couples. He supposed it was impressive that they had managed to survive at all, that after such an improvised getaway they had managed to put together a functioning colony on an ice moon – and they'd planned it all ahead, of course, stealing and stashing the equipment they'd need weeks or months ahead of the eventuality of needing to escape. It said a lot about the harshness of the regime on the Wheel that they even thought that way. And you had to admire the way they had rejected the life they had been born into, in a Wheel that was one huge labour camp, and were out here on this hostile moon trying to find their own way.

But even so, from Jamie's lofty age, he couldn't help but feel responsible for them all.

And as the days went by things were fraying. This was a very small dome for the seventeen of them, and it was hard to walk away from an argument. The way the stinks were gathering, despite the recycling machines and the air scrubbers, wasn't helping the mood. And nor did the fact that some bright spark had figured out how to induce the waste-processing machines to produce a kind of vodka. Jamie tasted the filthy stuff once, out of curiosity, and since then had tried to keep the youngest ones away from it. Now everybody woke up with a hangover, which only made things worse.

Even when you went outside there was no escape. The light was never better than dim, like a murky winter afternoon in the Highlands. Oddly, Jamie kept expecting the dense smog that covered the sky to clear, but it never would, not for five thousand million years, Phee had told him, not until the dying sun heated up and blew away Titan's clouds for ever. No wonder the inhabitants of Tartarus were driving each other crazy.

Mind you, Jamie had been impressed by the name Sam had given his colony. Phee said Tartarus was a deep layer of Hell where Zeus, king of the gods, had once hurled the Titans, giants of Greek myth. Jamie suspected that if Sam knew about stuff like that he wasn't quite the hardened ignoramus he pretended to be, or indeed the C-grade he'd been labelled. Well, Tartarus seemed a good name for this place, for a lot of the time it did feel like a pit into which they'd all been flung.

And this morning the fights and pushing seemed a bit more serious than usual. When a fist was thrown, and there was a splash of blood, Jamie hurried forward.

The fight had started at the middle of the recycling chain, near something called a Sabatier furnace, where solid human waste was broken down under intense heat to yield usable chemicals and water. But the process wasn't perfect, there was always a residue, and somebody, every day, had to clean out that residue and dump it in a hole they'd dug in the ice outside. It was one of the worst jobs in the little colony, and had been a cause of friction from the start.

And now Sam Laws and Dai Llewellyn were coming to blows right beside the furnace. Their supporters were gathered around them shouting, and the usual idiots who just liked a barney had come crowding around to make things worse.

Jamie barrelled into the middle of it. He was shorter than these gangly space kids but stockier and stronger, and he pushed the main protagonists apart, a hand on each of their chests. 'Hey, hey, hold on now.'

Sam and Dai faced each other, breathing hard. Dai was the boy Jamie had pulled out of the methane lake on the day they arrived. He was supporting himself on the improvised crutch he'd been using ever since that accident, when a tiny flaw in his skinsuit had let the cold of superchilled methane-ethane mix get to one of his legs, and he had suffered bad frostbite from the knee joint down. But it was Sam who had the cut over his eye, Sam who had what looked like a nasty bruise coming up on one cheek.

They were still shouting, so Jamie grabbed their tunics and shook them. 'Shut your geggies, the pair o' you. What's this all about? Sam?'

'Dai didn't do his shift,' Sam said. 'On the furnace. So it got overloaded, it shut itself down, and now the whole process is backed up.'

Jamie was horrified. 'D'ye mean there's no breakfast?'

Phee pushed her way through now: Phee, the only A-grader here, controller of the rotas, popular with nobody, but on the other hand not particularly disliked by anybody either. She said, 'Sam's right.'

Dai snapped, 'Ah, you always back him up.'

'It was your turn, Dai. You didn't show up.'

Dai snarled, 'Then let somebody else do it. You do it, A-girl rota queen.'

'These jobs have to be done,' Sam said. 'To keep everything functioning.' His voice was reasonable, so were his words, but Jamie could see how angry he was getting, how frustrated, how humiliated.

Dai snapped back, 'We might as well go back to the mine if it's going to be like this. What are you going to do, Sam, kettle us? Have your pet goon here cut my toes off?' And he pointed at Jamie with his thumb.

Jamie gave him a warning shove. 'Less of that, sonny.'

Dai faced Sam. 'If you want the grunge slopped out of this furnace, do it yourself. Go on.'

'It's not my turn.'

'Not my turn,' Dai echoed, in a childish singsong. 'Not my turn.

What are *you* going to do today? Oh, I know. You're going flying over Vesuvius, aren't you? That's good enough for the great leader, isn't it? While the rest of us slop crud out of the furnace. Is it because I'm a C?'

'I'm a C myself, you rockhead.'

'Not for much longer, though, eh, Sam? You planning to be the only A in Tartarus? A super-A, a super-duper—'

'Shut up. Just do the job.'

'Do it yourself.'

And Sam hesitated.

Go on, Jamie thought, silently urging Sam. Say you'll do it. Say you'll stay here and get the furnace sorted out. That's what a true leader would do, in a situation like this. Lead by example. Show that you're not above doing the menial stuff with everybody else – give up your latest play-time, get your hands dirty. That way you'll shame Dai back into line. But the rebel was warring with the leader in Sam; he was used to being the one who broke all the rules, not the one who enforced them.

In the end the rebel won. Sam snarled and shook Jamie's hand away. 'I'm going flying. It's my turn. And you, Llewellyn, you do what it says you've got to do on the rota.' And he turned his back and walked away.

The crowd he left behind shouted angrily. Dai's thin voice called after Sam, 'Or what? How will you make me, Sam? What will you do?'

Sam didn't look back.

The crowd broke up, and soon only Jamie and Phee were left by the dormant machines.

'He came so close,' Phee said. 'So close to getting it right.'

'I know. But you're all still very young.'

'Tell me about it. Sometimes being sixteen drives me crazy.'

Jamie laughed. 'Make the most of it.'

'Look at us, Jamie. I suppose we ought to be proud we're surviving here at all. But what if we had a real emergency? You know what my nightmare is? Suppose somebody got pregnant. How would we handle that?'

'Umm.' Jamie scratched his chin. 'I'm nae midwife, that's fer sure.'

'And that idiot Sam has shut down the comms and cut us off even from the possibility of asking for help from the Wheel.' Her small face was pinched with worry.

'Hey, hey. We'll get through this. You're not much of a rebel yersel', are ye?'

'I only came to look after Sam.'

'I know.'

And I only came, Jamie thought with a stab of cynicism, to make sure that that pendant around your neck gets to the Doctor, one day, somehow. But then he thought back to those brutal few hours of the kettling, when these kids, maddened by fear and betrayal, started to plan the breakout that could have killed them all, and Jamie had to decide whether to stay with them or not. No, he decided, looking into his own soul. He'd have come with these kids anyway, amulet or not. They were brave and resourceful but they were always going to need a bit of help, a wise head. And in the absence of any wise heads, he thought ruefully, James Robert McCrimmon would have to do.

And maybe these strange Saturn children reminded him of other youngsters, back in Scotland, youngsters who had fought for their own dream, and had been maimed, imprisoned, transported and killed for their trouble.

He patted Phee's shoulder. 'Ye an' me together, eh?'

She forced a smile. Theatrically she threw her rota over her shoulder. 'So what do you know about Sabatier furnaces?'

'Less than ye can possibly imagine.' He rolled his sleeves up. 'Show me where to start.'

28

The second expedition that Zoe joined into the heart of the ice moon was more purposeful than the first. They had proper maps now, for one thing. And, rather dismayingly, the expedition was heavily armed.

The Doctor went in empty-handed, as ever relying on nothing more dangerous than his wits. Zoe herself carried only a neat fold-up display flag in a backpack. But the squad of Bootstrap guards who went in with them wore body armour, and had blasters at their hips, and two of them carried a larger weapon, like a bazooka.

And once again Florian Hart, as heavily armed and armoured as her guards, insisted on accompanying them.

The Doctor grumbled as they worked their way through the corridors and crevasses of the moon's interior. 'Do we really need an armed guard, Florian?'

'Well, it's for your own protection,' Florian said, with apparent good humour. 'This is either a crime scene or a war zone, depending on whether what's disrupting our operations here is human in origin or alien, as you suggest.'

'Pah! But besides, even if that's so, don't *you* have anything better to do? I really do feel your company has delighted me enough.'

'If only you were as funny as you think you are, Doctor.' She glanced at her watch. 'I have many things to do. Not least to monitor the progress of the latest trial bore. But you've managed to position yourself at the spearhead of events here. I feel I need to keep an eye on you—'

'Never mind all that. What was that you said about a "trial bore"?'

Florian replied, 'We're here for the bernalium. Amid all the nonsense you ought to try to remember that, Doctor. We've continued to run remote sensor sweeps, and we're finding fresh lodes of the mineral and its ores throughout the body of the moon. But it's clear that the strongest concentration is at the centre, where we've yet to reach. And so—'

'And so you're drilling? Even now? In the middle of this complex and fast-moving situation, when you have all that instability up on the Wheel, and a moon infested with an unknown alien technology? Even so, you're *still drilling*? But that's utterly irresponsible! Surely you can see—'

'Surely *you* can see I've my job to do.' She glanced at the animated map on a small display screen she carried. 'Right at the next junction.'

'Ah, but with people like you it's more than a job, isn't it?' he said as they hurried on. 'It always is. I've met your sort before, you know. What drives you on, Florian Hart? What makes you push others to such irresponsible risks? Dreams of wealth, is that it?'

'Not that. My family is wealthy – more wealthy than you could possibly imagine, I should think,' and she cast a dismissive glance over his shabby coat, the scuffed boots inside his transparent skinsuit.

'Old money, is it?'

'Not at all. My father started from scratch. *His* father came from a Parisian slum, but he was a man who worked hard, kept on the right side of the law, and gave his descendants a chance. My father got through university on a scholarship, and then began a start-up company developing quantum teleportation techniques. Small scale at first, but highly profitable. Then he joined an international consortium that developed a technology called the Travel-Mat Relay.'

'The T-Mat!' Zoe said.

The Doctor gestured at her to stay quiet.

Florian went on, 'It was enormously successful. But then—'

'But then,' the Doctor said sadly, 'it all went horribly wrong.'

'My father didn't lose everything. He'd always been wise in spreading his money, in other industries, property. We, his family, remained wealthy. But he'd lost everything he'd worked for, all his life. Why, he was even prosecuted for his part in the T-Mat crisis. I grew up in the middle of all this. Well, when the courts were finished with him he made sure we were secure, financially – my mother, and me, his only child. But then he disappeared. Perhaps he went back to the slum, to Paris. We've tried to track him down; he spent a great deal of money making himself disappear. He did not want us to see him a broken man.'

The Doctor's tone was almost gentle now. 'But he was still your father. Surely you would have loved him even so . . . Ah. But you never had the chance to tell him that, did you? And so you take revenge on the world you think betrayed him.'

'Don't presume to psychoanalyse me, Doctor.'

'Wouldn't dream of it.'

'Just be aware that I utterly reject the value system of a world that brings down such a man, whatever his flaws. For they were magnificent flaws.' Florian seemed angry, as if she felt she had said too much. Zoe had seen the Doctor draw people out like this with his deceptively simple questioning many times before. Now Florian glared into her screen, evidently determined to focus on business. 'Nearly there. Make sure your blasters are charged . . .'

Zoe walked closer to the Doctor. 'Of course what crashed the T-Mat was aliens. The Ice Warriors. Another alien infestation of a bit of human technology, just like this. So Florian must know about an alien presence on Mnemosyne as a theoretical possibility at least, despite all her denials.'

'That's insightful, Zoe.'

'And you do wonder if too many trips through the T-Mat as a little girl might have scrambled her circuitry a bit.'

'Now that, Zoe, is unscientific, unkind and rather funny. But there is more at stake here than the battered ego of Florian Hart, I'm afraid. Now. We're nearly at the nest of the Dolls that Jo spotted for us with her deep radar. Are you ready?'

Zoe reached back to her pack, extracted the foldout display screen, and shook it out like a blanket. Then she tapped the comms control at the neck of her skinsuit. 'MMAC. Can you hear me? This is Zoe Heriot calling Malenfant-IntelligeX Modular Autonomous Component Registration Number—'

'Zoe! Guid tae hear yer wee voice! And ah'm ready when ye are . . .'

29

Florian's guard commander insisted that Zoe and the Doctor walk down the short final passage to the nest of the Dolls flanked by two guards, with more backing them up, and a party further back still to secure their escape route.

The Doctor ignored all this. He was never very interested in guns. He made sure his skinsuit hood was well pushed back from his head, and he put his empty hands in the air, and fixed a smile on his face. 'Now then, Zoe, here we go. I'll go in first. You follow right behind me.'

And he walked into the chamber of the Blue Dolls.

Zoe followed the Doctor, taking care not to trip over the flag she was holding out before her. For now it was blank, giving off only a dull blue glow.

The chamber was just another natural cavity in the ice. It had a rough floor, a lumpy ceiling, and shadowy breaks in the wall revealed more passages leading deeper into the moon. The air pumped down from the human plants on the surface had reached this level, and the ubiquitous light globes had attached themselves to the ice walls and ceiling.

But the place was dark, because many of those lamps were covered by clinging blue bodies.

It was just like the chamber where they had lost Sinbad. The Blue Dolls were everywhere, on the roof, the walls, much of the floor, like glued-on mannequins. Immediately the dread of her last encounter flooded through Zoe, and it took a real effort for her to follow the Doctor deeper into the chamber, until she was surrounded by the creatures once more, surrounded and helpless.

The two Bootstrap guards who flanked her were tense, wary. 'Don't worry, girlie. We got your back.'

'Yeah. Ben, if it all kicks off, you take the roof crowd and I'll go for the walls.'

'Right. It's the charge that scrambles them. Set your blaster to wide aperture and—'

'Will you two shut up?' Zoe snapped. 'Nobody's going to "scramble" anybody. And I'm no "girlie", thank you. If you want something useful to do, hold this.'

She handed the guards a corner each of her display flag, leaving them standing there open-mouthed, like human flagpoles.

The Doctor was in the dead centre of the room, his arms still held out wide, as if in welcome. He turned slowly, looking around, smiling his most engaging smile. There must have been hundreds of Blue Dolls here, and if any of them were looking back at him it wasn't obvious to Zoe.

'Do you think smiling at them is doing any good, Doctor?'

'Well, it can't harm. Remember, these were all imprinted from impressions of a human child. And even very small children do respond to smiles, Zoe. At least it's better than waving a blaster around!' He raised his voice for the last bit, for the benefit of Florian Hart.

'Shall we run the experiment?'

He nodded curtly, still smiling, still studying the inert Blue Dolls.

Zoe tapped her collar. 'MMAC? Are you ready to go?'

'Aye. Linked in to yon flag.'

'Go ahead please.'

The flag, designed to display corporate motivational slogans and the faces of smiling workers, immediately lit up, with a shifting, panning image of colours and light, bands of varying thickness terminating in a razor-sharp shadow. The light from the screen bathed the chamber with colour, and picked out the blue forms on the walls and ceiling.

The two guards, surprised, looked down at the screen they were holding. 'That's the rings,' said one. 'Saturn's rings.'

'Well spotted, genius,' said the other sourly.

'A live feed, in fact,' Zoe said. 'Now we'll see if it works.'

'Well, the theory's sound enough,' the Doctor said. 'We know there is *something* in the core of this moon. We know that its motions cause tides that create ripples, patterns in the ring system. Here we are reflecting those patterns back to these Blue Dolls, who we suspect may themselves be artefacts of that central entity.'

'Doctor . . .'

'It's all guesswork, of course. But if there is some unity to the design, a wider information-processing cycle—'

'Doctor!' She pointed to the roof above his head.

A Blue Doll had unpeeled from the huddling mass. It hung upside down, like a mannequin suspended by its heels. Zoe could not see what was attaching it to the roof. But its eyes were open, and in those black pits the gaudy colours of Saturn's rings were reflected.

'I think it's working.' The Doctor clapped his hands together in glee, and now his smile wasn't forced. 'By heavens, I think it's working.'

More of the Dolls unpeeled – yes, that was the right word, Zoe thought – they stood up on the floor with fluid movements, or hung down from the ceiling, not at all as a human would move, each of them like a bit of soft plastic recovering its shape after having been bent and twisted. Soon the walls and roof bristled with the blue bodies, sticking out into the air at all angles. All of them were staring at the flag.

And those on the floor began to shuffle forward, their gait stiff, unnatural, efficient rather than graceful.

The Doctor, hands outstretched, smiled and nodded. 'Hello, hello. Welcome . . .' He looked somehow at home, surrounded by these alien creatures the size of three-year-olds. Like an entertainer, a clown at a birthday party, Zoe thought.

'Ha! Zoe, look at that.' He pointed to one of the Dolls, shambling past him.

At first glance it was indistinguishable from the rest. But when Zoe looked more closely she saw that it had yellow markings on its chest – crudely drawn, just concentric circles. 'What do they mean? Do they represent some group memory of Saturn's rings?'

'Well, quite possibly. But two points are clear, Zoe. The first is that this is clearly an effort to differentiate – to stand out from the crowd. Quite a human impulse, don't you think? And the second point is – that's my chalk! The stick I used to mark the route last time we were down here, remember? I wondered what happened to it. Here, here.' He dug into his pockets and produced more bits of chalk of various colours, broken and worn.

One by one, cautious little hands took the chalk, fused fingers folding.

Zoe, gradually feeling more confident, wandered through the slowly moving crowd. None of the Dolls paid the slightest bit of attention to her. But she soon saw that the Doctor's chalk hadn't been the start of these creatures' impulse to decorate themselves. They had patterns scratched into their skin, or smeared in some purplish fluid, perhaps an organic-chemistry residue from the ice rock. Many of them wore some variant of the Saturn's-rings design, but there were other markings, zigzags and spirals and figures of eight. Some had even marked their faces, with swirls around their eyes and mouths.

She came to an exposed wall surface. On it were scratched more marks, circles and whorls and spirals, but in some places just simple lines cut into the rock.

'Look at this, Doctor. They're counting!'

'Counting what?'

'Who knows? The passage of time, perhaps. The numbers of their own kind. This proves it. These creatures are sentient, Doctor. And self-aware.'

'Well, to some degree, yes. They're trying to express themselves. I can't say I'm surprised, Zoe. Mind, you know, consciousness, can be created like any other component. But a mind is not a spanner or a wing nut. A mind grows and changes by its very nature – well, it must, it has to process new information, or it wouldn't be a mind at all, would it? And minds once created will flourish and complexify beyond anything dreamed of by their creator – hello, what's this?'

There was a commotion in a branching corridor. Another Blue Doll came running into the chamber.

And skidded to a halt, as if in shock, right in front of the Doctor.

The other Dolls turned away from the display flag and faced the newcomer. This one was different to the rest, Zoe saw. More important somehow, its bearing more imposing, though physically it was identical to the rest, and bore no markings, none of the chalk marks or the crude tattoos.

The Doll was motionless for a moment. Then it raised its right hand, and with its left mimed scraping a mark on the upraised palm. It pointed to its own chest.

The Doctor seemed confused. 'I don't—'

'*First*,' Zoe said. 'Don't you see? He's mimicking the marks on the wall. *First*. I think he's saying his name is First.'

'Ah! Well done, Zoe. So we've found our leader, it seems.' He looked at her sceptically. 'But – *he*?'

That confused Zoe; the Blue Doll was just as sexless as the rest. 'But there's something about him – I don't know what—'

'Perhaps the way the others are responding to it – *him*. There's something of an elder brother about him. Well, if he *was* the first to be manufactured, I suppose that's natural. I wonder what his story is . . .' He knelt before the child-size creature, smiling. 'Hello. I'm the Doctor.'

BLUE DOLL

I

Alive!

That had been the start of his story. To find himself suddenly alive.

In that first instant of existence his mind was a blank sheet of blue plastic, empty, unmarked, innocent. And yet immediately experience began to engrave impressions.

A light above him. Not understanding what he was doing, he *reached* for the light. His arms lifted before him, into his sight. Long cylinders of blue, terminating in sketchy hands. His hands clenched into fists.

He felt his face, his chest. He sat up. He saw his legs.

He stood, impossibly, balancing. His slim body. He felt his face again, his eyes, his mouth. *Himself*, inside this blue case, a spark of awareness in his head. *Not himself*: all that was outside. Thus he began to map the universe.

He looked around. He was in a hollow, contained to his left by rough walls of some pale blue-white stuff. And to his right, a curtain of shimmering light, light in patterns, curving lines of colours. Neither of these struck him as strange, unusual. Why *not* a crude blocky wall? Why *not* a fence of light?

His mind fizzed. Why was he here? Why did he think, rather than not think? And why indeed was his head full of these questions? His own thoughts turned in on themselves in convolutions of self-awareness, and the blankness of his new mind disappeared in a scribble of recursive complexity.

A sobbing sound.

He whirled.

On the floor beside him was a blue body. Identical to his own, but not his own. He was certain this had not been here a moment ago. Another!

The other sat up. The other was staring at him. The other said, 'Who am I?'

Speaking! The other had spoken before he did. He felt an unreasonable stab of jealousy.

The other repeated, 'Who am I?'

He replied, 'I don't know.'

The other considered. 'Then who are you?'

He thought about that. 'I am first.'

'First. Help me.'

He was First!

'Help me.'

He thought about that. He extended a hand, and helped the other to stand.

And then another sob. Another astonished gasp of existence.

'Help me.'

This time he was ready. He held out a hand, to help the new one up. 'I am First,' he said. 'I will help you.'

And another. And another. 'I am First . . . I am First . . . I will help you.'

Soon there was a host of them.

The wall of light pulsed. Another voice. WELCOME.

They turned as one and stood stock still, facing the light, their identical faces blank.

First said, 'Who are you?'

I AM ARKIVE. AND THIS IS YOUR MISSION.

'Our mission,' they breathed.

RESILIENCE. REMEMBRANCE. RESTORATION.

'Resilience. Remembrance. Restoration.'

MY MISSION IS YOUR MISSION.

'Yes,' First said. 'Yes. Resilience! Remembrance! Restoration!'

II

Now First was in the upper levels of the moon. Trying to avoid the Others. Trying to steal their technologies.

Trying to understand what Arkive wished him to do.

Then he saw the Other – a small Other, only a little larger than he was. An Other without weapons, without the guns that crackled and stung and burned. One like himself, but made of pink flesh, not blue synthetic material. Like himself but complex inside, with beating pumps and closing valves and hot, rushing fluid. He sensed all this.

The Other stared at him. The Other pointed. The Other laughed. 'Dolly!'

First fled from the strange noise, fled to the shadows, the small spaces where the Others would not see him. The rest followed.

Waiting, hiding, a dozen of them huddled together. They became still. For a time First was there, and not there. Their backs glistened, blue, moist, unmoving. The light shifted.

Then First was there again. The Others were gone. He could hear, smell their absence.

They returned to the core of the moon. To Arkive, to the curtain of light, the chamber of their birth. The rest clustered behind First, fearful.

He stood before the light.

WHAT IS IT YOU WANT?

'It was . . . I . . . one of the Others. It was like us.'

Silence for a moment. Then First's head seemed to pulse, as memories were extracted and downloaded.

YES. THIS WAS THE FIRST OF THE OTHERS I ENCOUNTERED. I MADE YOU IN THEIR IMAGE. IN THE IMAGE OF THIS ONE.

'The rest of the Others are not like this one,' First dared to say. 'They are taller. Stronger.'

There was only silence. The others waited behind him, their distress and confusion evident. Yet only he could articulate it.

'What am I?'

YOU ARE A MADE THING. I MADE YOU.

'Why did you make me?'

TO FULFIL THE MISSION. RESILIENCE. REMEMBRANCE. RESTORATION.

They murmured the holy words in unison.

But First was not done yet. 'Why do I know myself? More than these others know themselves?'

IT IS ACCIDENTAL. THE AGONY OF SELF-KNOWING SERVES NO PURPOSE.

'And the Others—'

I BROUGHT THEM HERE, TO SERVE MY PURPOSE. YOU MUST BRING ME THE LURE.

His head exploded with images and concepts. The lure was an object in jet black, small enough to hold in the hand.

FIND THE LURE. THE THING THAT BROUGHT THEM HERE. PROVE THAT THESE OTHERS ARE THOSE WHO I HAVE

SOUGHT. AND BRING ME MORE OF THEIR ART, THEIR TECH-
NOLOGY. I BROUGHT THEM HERE, TO SERVE MY PURPOSE.
BRING ME WHAT THEY HAVE MADE.

He had had this command before. But all they could steal and carry
away were scraps. Bits of larger machines . . . Soon the heart of the moon
would be stuffed with purloined scraps.

'I exist to serve you.'

NOT ME. THE MISSION.

'The mission.'

They huddled. Soon, First was bathed in the comfort of not-
thereness, with the rest.

III

And then one died.

They had been on the circle structure that surrounded the moon.
They had been up there trying to fulfil the new command. To steal more
technology. And to obstruct the Others' mining efforts, which were
becoming troubling.

One had died, in the mining machine they had tried to destroy. Died
at the hand of an Other.

First had escaped, back to the caverns of the moon, by hiding in one
of the Others' carriages, sliding along the cable back to the moon.

But the Others had followed. And another was killed, in the corridors of the moon.

They had carried the body to one of their places of comfort. They sat
with the dead.

Again, the Others had followed. More fire. More had died!

Now First fled to the deepest pit of the moon, the chamber with the curtain of fire, and again he faced his maker.

'Two have died! More than two. Several!'

MORE EXIST. SUFFICIENT TO FULFIL THE MISSION –

'Will I die?' He had interrupted. He had never before interrupted. He tried to imagine it. Tried to imagine returning to nothingness, the nothingness that had existed before the moment of his manufacture.

IT IS YOUR DUTY TO FULFIL YOUR FUNCTION BEFORE YOU DIE.

'What am I?'

YOU ARE A MADE THING. I MADE YOU.

'What are you?'

I AM A MADE THING. YOU ARE A MADE THING OF A MADE THING. YOU ARE LESS THAN ZERO, LESS THAN NOTHING. YOU HAVE NO PURPOSE SAVE YOUR FUNCTION.

'No purpose save my function. And yet—'

No response.

'Will I be remembered? These others who follow me. They gave me my name. Will they remember me?'

No response.

'I have made—' Drawings. Marks on the wall, to count, to mark the passage of time. To record his existence. He had no words for these things. But he made them anyway.

THAT IS YOUR TRAGEDY. NOW FULFIL YOUR FUNCTION. FOR SOON YOU WILL NO LONGER BE REQUIRED.

'Will I die?'

A NEW SORT WILL REPLACE YOU. A SORT BETTER SUITED TO THE PURPOSE. A SORT THAT WILL BE ABLE TO DRIVE THE OTHERS OUT OF THEIR TUNNELS AND SHAFTS.

'Will I die?'

RESILIENCE. REMEMBRANCE. RESTORATION.

The holy words rang in his head like the sounding of huge gongs, threatening to drive out his thoughts, his *self*.

He fled. He ran back to the chamber of the drawings.

'Will I die, will I die, will I die . . .'

There was one of the Others here. One he had seen before. One who had done him no harm. With a face that was . . .

Kindly. Sympathetic. Smiling. He had no words for these qualities.

The Other spoke.

Hello. I'm the Doctor.

30

'So what now, Doctor?'

'Well, Zoe, we've made contact at least. Now we need to gain their trust. That will put a stop to the sabotage and the killings, I hope. Then we must try to find out *why* they have been carrying out these destructive acts.'

'And to do all that we will have to go deeper. Find whatever's at the core.'

'Quite so.'

The Blue Doll, First, standing stock still, stared straight back at him.

Quite tenderly the Doctor cupped its cheek in his palm. 'You've had to bear a lot of responsibility in your strange little life, haven't you?'

There was a distant crump, a wave of pressure in the air, a shudder in the ground that Zoe felt in her knees, her hips, making her stagger.

The guards dropped the display flag and set their blasters with a double click.

Moving as one, the Blue Dolls turned and ran, pouring out of the chamber and into the darkened passages beyond, like a swarm of rats. Only First stayed an instant longer, looking up at the Doctor. Then he, too, turned and fled.

Florian Hart strode into the empty chamber. Again the ground shook, a distant denotation, as if Florian was accompanied by a music of destruction.

The Doctor faced the mine administrator. 'Florian Hart! What have you done?'

'We've got a bit further,' she said. 'Nearer the core with our trial bore. There has been a response.'

'What kind of response? Oh, you fool, woman, you wretched fool! We were getting so close with these Dolls—'

'We have to get out of here. Follow, or stay – your choice.' She strode away, followed by her guards.

The Doctor made to call after her again, but Zoe grabbed his hand and hurried him out of the chamber. Another explosion somewhere. Zoe glanced back to see sheets of ice rock coming away from the walls, obscuring the Dolls' crude sketches.

31

Phee and Jamie had spent a pleasant couple of hours tinkering with the innards of the Sabatier furnace.

And then the emergency broke.

'It's Mindy. Mindy Brewer. Hello? Is that the dome? It's awful, it's Sam on Vesuvius, it's all gone wrong . . .'

The message came from the flank of Vesuvius, a cryovolcano off to the north of here. The message was relayed around the dome so everybody heard it, and people started emerging from their tents and shacks.

But Jamie and Phee, not for the first time, were the only ones already in their suits. They ran for the main airlock. Outside the dome they grabbed first-aid packs and basic repair kits, and jumped on the first scooters they could find.

As they lifted up and away from the dome, Phee tried to keep Mindy talking. 'You're doing fine, Mindy. We're on our way. Just tell me what you saw.'

'It was the volcano – oh, Phee, it went up! It erupted. It wasn't supposed to do that . . . was it?'

Jamie sighed, for he knew that even if there had been some kind of a prediction of an eruption of this cryovolcano, whatever *that* was,

Sam and his cronies wouldn't have bothered to check it out before they left. Things didn't work like that in Tartarus.

Jamie gathered more details from Mindy's panicky, fragmentary call. Sam and Sanjay had flown to the volcano – but without their scooters, and Jamie didn't understand how they had managed that, not yet. Mindy had gone along on a scooter with emergency supplies and an open comms line.

It had been one of Sam's own rules that every jaunt away from the dome had to have at least one scooter rider along as a fallback in case of emergencies. Mindy Brewer had broken her leg during the first landing. Encumbered by a clumsy cast she couldn't go out with the rest lake-skiing or ballooning or flying, but she had volunteered to be the backup a few times. Nobody could blame her for that; at least it got her out of the dome. But she had clearly never expected to be called on in the event of a real emergency, and now it had happened she wasn't coping too well.

Jamie saw something up ahead now. A tower of steam or smoke, it looked like, looming above the horizon. And it was tall, impossibly tall, reaching up to the layer of scattered methane clouds above.

'A big gusher caught Sam, and now he's stuck on the ground, on the flank of the volcano, and this stuff, the lava, it's oozing all around him . . .'

'What about Sanjay?'

'He's still in the air, he's still flying. But I think he's getting tired. He doesn't dare land, and the thermals are all disrupted.'

Jamie asked, 'Thermals?'

Phee said, 'Hot air coming up from the volcano. Well, hot compared to the rest. It rises up. You can just glide around, let it lift you.'

Mindy said, 'Sanjay doesn't want to leave Sam.'

'All right, Mindy, take it easy, we're coming . . .'

Now Jamie saw the cryovolcano itself, a mountain looming over the tight curve of this little world, a big squat cone, as if some huge fist had punched up from underground and driven the crust up and out. Its flanks were cracked by huge fissures from which something like steam billowed up. Even the ground around the volcano was distorted, the tholin-purple plain broken by crevasses and littered with tumbles of smashed rock.

And at the very summit of the volcano was a crater, a huge imploded wound. Fountains of some dense liquid plumed up, some of it hardening into rocky lumps that immediately fell back to the ground, the rest billowing up as a kind of gritty ash to fuel that looming cloud above. All this was lit by the classic colours of Titan, shades of a sombre brown-orange.

Jamie had seen volcanoes before, in his travels with the Doctor. 'But this isn't Earth,' he muttered.

'What? . . . No.' Phee said. 'You're right. Jamie, everything you see up there, the volcano, everything, is *water*. The rocky flanks. The lava. The cloud of ash – it's not really ash, it's frost. And it's not superhot, like volcanoes on Earth – I've seen clips of them. It's *cold*, supercold. That's why they call it a cryovolcano.'

'It looks familiar, but it's not. And that makes it even more dangerous.' Jamie remembered the Doctor giving him exactly that advice on more than one occasion.

'Yes, and Sam was even more of an idiot than usual to come out here.'

He heard the tremor in her voice. 'Hey, hey. It's all right. We're nearly there. We'll get him out o' this, I promise.'

'Look! I see Sanjay! Look, straight ahead, to the right of the ash column!'

Jamie peered ahead. And he saw a *bird*, a giant flapping bird, wheeling in the air, nervously avoiding the ash column. Then he got that bit closer, saw a bit more clearly through the murky air, and spotted a cradle under the big wings, a slim body lying there, and a flash of green, a C-grade coverall beneath a transparent skinsuit. It must be Sanjay, lying in the cradle with his arms strapped into wings of some sheer translucent fabric, with struts and vanes that spread like feathers. And he flapped the wings and flew like a bird, powered by nothing more than his own muscles.

'Well, by the blood o' Prince Charlie himself. Ye told me they flew up here. But I wasnae expectin' *that*.'

'The wings?' She was tense, uninterested. 'Low gravity so it's easier to lift. Thicker air to push against.'

'Well, mebbe. But ye won't catch *me* flappin' about like that—'

'I think his comms are out.' That was Sanjay's voice. He sounded tense, exhausted. 'The caldera just broke open like a zit bursting, and all this rock came flying up in the air. Razor-sharp it was, like a hail of knives. I was lucky, I got out of the way, but Sam was right in the middle of it. He got caught in the hail.'

'Can ye see him?'

'Yes. He's right below me. Well, nearly. It's hard to hold my position. The air's boiling like a pan of water—'

'Hang on.' They were getting close to the volcano and its towering cloud now, and Jamie dipped down, heading for the flank, searching the cluttered surface. The ice ground cracked open further, releasing more spumes of ice-ash and steam and showers of needle-sharp rock fragments, and the scooter bumped and shuddered as it hit pockets of warmer air. This scooter of his wasn't as fragile as the wings of the flying boys, but his skinsuit was no more resilient than theirs had been, and one unlucky fragment –

'I see him!' Phee squealed. 'Look, Jamie, there! To your left, about thirty degrees. Just over that ridge ahead of you.'

Jamie hauled his scooter up into the air away from the ground – and there, right before him and just beyond Phee's ridge, Sam was sprawled on the ground. He looked like a downed and wounded bird, his wings broken and shredded and splayed out across the rock.

'Right, I'm going down.'

'I'll come with you,' Phee called.

'No! One of us has to stay safe, lassie, whatever happens. And you, Sanjay. Your job's done. Can ye fly home?'

'I don't know. I'm pretty tired. I can get away from the volcano, though. Are you sure—'

'Just hie yersel'. Ye'll be doing me a favour, one less tae worry about. Go, go, will ye!'

Sanjay peeled away and flew off, huge wings flapping.

At last Jamie got his scooter down on the volcano's flank. It was a lousy landing, but Jamie just dumped the scooter and ran the few paces to Sam.

The boy was awake, lying on his back, still strapped to his cradle. He looked deathly pale to Jamie despite the burnt-orange glow of the Titan sky. A panel on the chest of his skinsuit was lit up with red lights, and black-lettered telltales warned of LOSS OF SUIT INTEGRITY and SIG-NIFICANT POWER DRAINAGE. One monitor was obvious and sig-nificant: a ragged green line showing Sam's uncertain heartbeat. You didn't have to be a doctor to tell that he was in a bad way.

And just a few paces away lava flooded, eerie, peculiar, water-ice lava that didn't flow like water on Earth but slowly, tackily, with heavy grey lumps of ice-rock embedded in it. It looked as if that lava stream was diverting, and would soon come gushing over Sam's prone form.

The ground shuddered, and Jamie could sense huge energies stir-ring, restless, beneath this cryovolcano.

Phee called down anxiously, 'What's going on?'

'He's alive,' Jamie said curtly. 'His comms are out. How can I talk to him?'

'There's a manual feed . . .'

This was a line that Jamie, under Phee's instructions, pulled out of a compartment at his own neck, and plugged into Sam's visor. Suddenly he could hear Sam's rasping breath, loud in his ears.

'Sam. Sam! Can ye hear me?'

Sam's eyes fluttered open. 'Get lost, granddad.'

'Any more o' that and I really will larrup ye. How d'ye feel?'

'Cold,' he said softly. 'Cold. My suit – the eruption—'

'Is it ripped? I have some sealant back on the scooter. I remember how Dai got that frostbite—'

'No.' He licked his lips, and kept speaking with a visible effort. 'No good. It was a kind of ash – frost – a swarm of little needles. You could barely see them. Pinpricks all over the suit, and the telltales went off like fireworks. A couple got through to my skin, I must look like a junkie . . . don't tell Mum . . . Microscopic leaks, see, Jamie. A million of them. I'm not losing any air, the inner seals keep that in. But I'm losing heat. That's the killer on Titan, the cold, it gets at you any way it can. The suit's trying to keep me warm, but I'm running down the power too fast.'

Jamie tried desperately to think. 'I could try to move ye. Lift ye on the scooter and get ye back—'

'Probably rip the suit wide open. Just leave me, Jamie.'

'Shut up,' Phee said tearfully, from her orbiting scooter. 'Now you listen to me, Sam Laws. I know you're not as stupid as you act. You shut down the comms. *But you'll have left yourself a lifeline.* One working contact to – somebody. In case of a real disaster.'

He tried to laugh. 'You know me too well, sis.'

Jamie said, 'Now's the time to cough up. Come on, Sam. We're not goin' anywhere, so ye're puttin' the two of us at risk too—'

'All right! Lay off, granddad. All right, I did keep one channel.'

'To Mum?'

'No, sis. Not her. To someone I can trust.' He tapped a couple of buttons on the chest panel of Jamie's suit. Jamie heard a comms connection open with a click, and a man's voice immediately replied.

'*Luis Reyes.*'

32

I t took the man from the Planetary Ethics Commission just a few seconds to take in the essence of the situation. 'Leave it with me.'

Sam fell back, exhausted. More red lights lit up on his chest panel.

Jamie murmured, 'Whatever ye're going to do ye'd better do it quick, Mr Reyes.'

'I'm afraid he's offline. Rather busy saving your necks,' replied a warm, familiar, rather breathless voice.

'Doctor!' Jamie felt a surge of relief.

'Yes, it's me. Mr Reyes is getting you help. And he's spreading the word about Sam's emergency link, and there is rather a long queue of people waiting to use it.'

'Ye sound out o' breath, Doctor. Are ye *runnin'*?'

'Well, it wouldn't be the first time, would it, Jamie?'

The Doctor and Zoe, fleeing from the heart of the moon, had been doing their best to follow Florian Hart and her team of guards. But their progress was always slower. The guards, trained for these conditions, swarmed away through the dimly lit tunnels like fish, two of them pulling Florian Hart with them.

Soon they were out of sight entirely, to Zoe's alarm. 'Wait! Wait for us!'

'I don't think that will do any good, Zoe,' the Doctor said grimly. 'I rather think we've been abandoned to our fate. Mind you, I suspect we're better off without them. The fewer guns the better is always my motto . . . Never mind that. Jamie? Are you still there? Now listen to me. How's Sam?'

'He's fading fast, Doctor. I cannae read these dials on his chest. I think his suit might run out of energy before whatever Mister Reyes is plannin' comes off.'

'The problem is the temperature difference, Jamie. Between the interior of his suit, which is at a comfortable temperature for a human, and the outside, Titan, which is two hundred degrees below. The greater the temperature difference the faster the heat flows out. Now, if there was some way of *reducing* that difference the heat loss would diminish, and the suit's power cells would stretch that bit further.'

'Ye want me to warm him up somehow. But how?' Jamie looked down at his own gloved hands. 'I ken that if a man gets too cold ye cuddle him, to give him your body warmth. We learned that in the Highlands, in winter. I cannae even do that. I'm stuck in my own suit, and that's gonna be as cold as Titan on the outside too.'

'Look around, Jamie. Think. Is there nowhere you could put him to keep him warmer, even by just a few degrees? It could make all the difference . . .'

The lights flickered, all the globes embedded in the walls dimming as one, before they slowly recovered.

Zoe, still running, started to feel panicky. 'Doctor, it will be unbearable in here if the lights fail. We'll never get out!'

'Don't worry, Zoe, I think I have some matches. And besides, won't your marvellous memory continue to work in the dark?'

'Hush.'

'What?'

She stumbled to a halt. She heard a sound like the beating of a great drum. Rhythmic. Heavy. Relentless. 'Can you hear that?'

He listened intently. 'Yes, I'm afraid I can.'

That metronomic thumping was coming from the tunnels just behind them. It was like a march, she thought now. Like the inhuman, machine-like stomping of the Cybermen. Relentless. Untiring. Overwhelmingly powerful.

And in pursuit.

'Do you think it's getting louder?'

'Yes,' the Doctor breathed.

'Well, then – run!'

'Yes, yes, Zoe. Jamie, are you still there? I can't see you, I don't know what's around you. I'm going to have to run rather rapidly! You'll have to work it out for yourself . . .'

Just then the lava flow surged, busily shifting its course again, a dense plastic flow with a crust of ice that formed and broke continually. A spray of droplets settled over Jamie and Sam, freezing instantly on their skinsuits, a patina of ice.

Ice!

This was molten lava. If Jamie was on Earth, this close to a lava flow, he'd be fried by now. But this was Titan, where the rock was ice. And the lava was molten ice.

Water. Just flowing water.

Jamie got to his feet. 'I'm gonna try to move ye, Sam. Just lie still.' Judging it best to keep Sam strapped tight into his flying cradle, for fear of doing any more damage to his injuries, he crouched, got his arms underneath the cradle, and lifted. The gravity was low, but the mass of cradle and inert boy was just as hard to shift as on Earth. Then he dragged the cradle through the air back towards the lava stream.

'I dinna ken how cold yon stream is,' he said, grunting with the effort. 'It's no Scottish burn; I bet there's all sorts of funnies in there. But it's running water. Stands to reason it's gonna be warmer than the rest. Right? Just a few degrees, the Doctor said, just a few degrees . . .' But Sam didn't reply, and anyhow Jamie was only talking to reassure himself.

He strode backwards into the lava stream. It didn't feel like water flowing around his legs; it was heavy, sticky, dense and difficult to wade through. But he got to the middle of the stream, and carefully pressed Sam and his cradle down into the flow, through the shifting crust of ice, until the boy was immersed. 'If this was an Earth volcano,' he muttered, 'we'd both be burnt cakes by now, Sam. But it's not Earth. It's not Earth . . .'

That was how they were standing when, only minutes later, a big bruised-purple craft came swooping through the air, a bulbous shell with thick windows and four fat rotor blades mounted in pods. On its flank was a Bootstrap logo, a vehicle registration number and a station assignment: NORTH POLE METHANE EXTRACTION PLANT.

Sam stirred. 'Oh, no. It's Pop.' His eyes drifted closed.

And only minutes after the rotorcraft had lifted, with Jamie, Sam and Phee aboard, the volcano erupted again. The ground on which Jamie had been standing was smashed open, the fragments wheeling in the thick air, and ice needles hailing harmlessly.

33

Still Zoe and the Doctor ran as best they could, away from the marching noise, flapping and floundering along the corridors. It was like a nightmare, Zoe thought, a nightmare of flight, as she tried to build up speed but could gain no traction in the soft gravity field of this treacherous moon. She tried to think, to recall the map of the moon she had built up in her head. She *thought* they were heading the right way, to the shafts to the surface facilities. But in the uncertain light, stumbling around as they were, it was difficult to be sure.

Then they turned a corner, and suddenly the marching noise was coming from *ahead* of them too. They skidded to a halt.

Blue shapes, emerging from the dark.

Not child-sized mannequins this time. These were tall, taller than Zoe, heavy, powerful. Adult sized. Their naked Blue skins were as seamless and smooth as the Dolls'. And, yes, their blank, almost featureless faces had something of the cold inhuman chill of the Cybermen.

Not Dolls, Zoe thought. Soldiers. These were Blue Soldiers.

And they were purposeful. They walked in ranks of three, stomping and slamming.

The Doctor said dryly, 'Evidently the matter printer in the core has got a new pattern.'

'Sinbad,' she said grimly.

'Sinbad?'

'The Dolls captured him. He's been used as a template. You can see they've a similar build. Look at their faces, their features are just sketches, but can't you see a little of Sinbad in them, the set of the jaw, those bumps that are sculpted like cheekbones?'

'You did like Dr Omar, didn't you?' he asked gently.

'Sinbad was warm, generous . . . How can there be anything of him left in these things? They are so inhuman. Engine-like.'

'Perhaps. But clearly intelligent – or at least there's an intelligence behind them.'

'What do you mean?'

'Well, they have managed to cut us off,' the Doctor said grimly.

And she saw that the Soldiers were closing on them from ahead and behind. She grabbed the Doctor's arm, and he hugged her. She could feel the rattling of his twin hearts. 'Will they kill us?'

'We may not be so lucky, Zoe—'

'Och, now that's no' a verra Scottish attitude.'

Zoe called wildly, 'MMAC?'

'Duck.'

'What?'

The Doctor cried, 'He said, "Duck"!' And he put his big hand on the crown of Zoe's head and pulled her down.

The tunnel wall to their right exploded.

Zoe and the Doctor, still clinging to each other, were hurled across the corridor to collide with the far wall. Big ice blocks wheeled down the shaft, and light globes scattered like fireflies. Zoe was deafened, her head filled with an odd ringing noise.

She saw that the blast had shoved the Blue Soldiers back down the passages from which they'd been emerging, a tangle of heavy bodies, arms and legs bent at unnatural angles. But as Zoe watched they immediately began to recover. The more badly damaged were pulled aside, and the rest started forming up in their ranks. In just seconds they would be on the march again, Zoe realised.

And she and the Doctor still lay here against the ice wall, flopping like stranded fish. She struggled to rise.

But now the debris was clearing, and troops came pouring in through the breach. They were civilian deputies, Zoe saw, Sonia's police force, rather than Bootstrap guards. The leaders turned immediately to face the oncoming ranks of Blue Soldiers, blasters raised.

Sonia Paley herself, in a robust-looking armoured skinsuit, followed the leaders. She looked around briskly, and hurried over to the Doctor and Zoe. 'Out, you two.'

'You've saved us, Sonia,' the Doctor said.

'Well, that's the general idea.'

Zoe was picturing the map of shafts and tunnels in her head. 'You broke through from a neighbouring shaft. The ice wall was fairly thin . . .'

'Too thin to resist a few blaster shots.'

'But how did you find us?'

'There's gratitude for ye.'

'MMAC! I'm sorry – I'd forgotten – when the wall caved in—'

'Aye, nae matter. Just be thankful I didnae forget *ye*, Zoe Heriot. I've been tracking ye since ye went on yer fool's errand down in yon corridors. So when I saw ye were in a pickle I copied your position doon tae the Marshal—'

'And we did the rest,' Sonia said.

'Well, we're jolly glad you did,' the Doctor said. 'No sign of Florian Hart and her stormtroopers, then?'

Sonia grunted. 'At times like these the Bootstrap people tend to take care of themselves, I'm afraid—'

The Blue Soldiers were on the march again. The deputies were forced to fall back, firing as they went. One deputy cried out, fell and would have been overwhelmed if the others hadn't pulled him back. There was a crackle of blaster fire, concussions in the air.

The Doctor snapped, exasperated, 'This is needless slaughter!'

Sonia took his arm. 'We can debate this later. Follow me – now!'

Zoe followed Sonia through the breach in the wall, emerging into a wider, brightly lit tunnel that was, Zoe saw with relief, only a short distance from a vertical access shaft to the surface. But to get there they would have to pass through a crude airlock and go out into vacuum. She fumbled with her skinsuit hood.

The Doctor stumbled behind, followed by the troops. Still the blasters fired with electrical crackles, and still Zoe heard that jump-push rhythmic noise of the Blue Soldiers. It sounded as if the whole moon vibrated with it.

They pushed through the lock into the evacuated shaft, and began a climb that seemed to take for ever. Zoe was already exhausted, her head and chest ached from the explosion in the side-shaft, and now here she was once more swimming through this irritating microgravity.

At last the disc of black sky above her opened up. A beefy gloved hand reached down, grabbed her by her suit's scruff, and dragged her up and out of the shaft mouth, leaving her sprawling on her belly. She felt like a fish she had once seen Jamie land, a big salmon he had hauled out of a Scottish lake, many centuries away.

Struggling to regain her breath, she scrambled to her feet. Over her head she saw the big, gangly, clumsy, hugely reassuring form of MMAC swimming through space. And not a hundred metres away, a cable dangled with a clear-walled elevator cage standing open at its base. Her way off this moon and back to the Wheel!

The last of Sonia's troops came pouring out of the shaft. Zoe and the Doctor were waved back. Then, to a snapped command from Sonia, deputies pushed forward to make a cordon around the mouth of the shaft, blasters raised.

The first Blue Soldiers emerged only seconds after the last of the humans. Naked to the vacuum, they moved much faster than the humans had, swarming up ice walls that had seemed sheer to Zoe.

Sonia's troops opened fire.

Zoe saw heads sliced away, torsos cut in half, fragments of limbs and heads wheeling away. But *they still came on*, despite their injuries. Legless torsos pulling themselves over the ice. A headless creature stumbling blindly, arms outstretched. An arm, detached, crawling with its fingerless sketch of a hand.

The Doctor rushed forward, among the troops, risking the blaster fire. 'Aim for the walls! Block the shaft to contain them! It's the only way!'

One of the deputies, a C-grade woman, grabbed the Doctor and hauled him back out of harm's way.

The rest began to hose their blaster fire at the walls of the shaft, which cracked and crumbled, huge sections splitting away from the walls' faces. Most of the Blue Soldiers were knocked back and went tumbling back into the shaft in low gravity slow motion.

But one group made it to the surface, and rushed the Doctor and the deputy who was trying to save him. In the last moment the deputy shoved the Doctor away.

And the Blue Soldiers closed on her, swarming. Pulling her to the ground. Dragging her back towards the shaft. Zoe heard her scream over the skinsuit comms system, piercing. Then a Soldier dug its blade-like hand through the woman's suit, and the screams cut off with a drowning gurgle. Limp, she was dragged down into the shaft.

Sonia hauled the Doctor to his feet. She was breathing hard, her eyes wide. 'Her name was Bella Kage. She was a volunteer. Her main job was as a midwife. She had two children of her own.'

'I'm sorry – I'm so sorry—'

'She saved your life. Don't ever forget her name.'

'Oh, I won't,' the Doctor said grimly.

'We have to get out of here. They're coming up out of the other shafts, and out of natural chimneys, crevasses. Boiling up everywhere. We're evacuating the moon. Come on, let's get to that elevator.'

So they fled across the ice, with the Doctor and Zoe at the centre of a knot of deputies. Around the blocked shaft behind them, stumps and limbs and smashed body parts continued their grotesque shuffling over the ice.

And Zoe thought she saw shadows racing across the broken ice surface, heading for the cables to the Wheel.

Blue shadows.

34

'They're setting up a conference call,' Harry Matthews called back to Jamie.

'A what-now?'

Jamie and Sam Laws sat in the two rear seats of the ship's small control cabin. Harry and his co-pilot, a woman called Karen Madl, sat up front, before a bank of glimmering controls. Phee and the rest of the sixteen youngsters from Titan were in a roomy rear compartment, a cargo chamber designed to transport methane from Titan, hastily fitted out with rows of emergency acceleration couches.

And beyond the pilots was a huge curved window showing an unbelievably complex sky. They were flying inside the circle of the Wheel, so that the gleaming blown-ice bubbles and the chunkier metal-walled hulks turned steadily in space around them. Cables dangled down to the central moon from all around the Wheel, and lights crawled steadily up every one of those cables, elevator cars carrying people up from the moon's surface – including, Jamie hoped, the Doctor and Zoe. Meanwhile ships of various kinds whizzed around like shining insects, descending to the moon and rising again. It was a full-scale evacuation, Jamie saw.

And on the moon itself what looked like a blue stain was spreading from cracks and holes in the ground. A stain that resolved, if you looked at it through special bits of the window that magnified like a telescope, into swarming human-like bodies.

The sheer swarming fast-changing complexity of it all overwhelmed Jamie. And not only that, the atmosphere in the ship's cabin couldn't have been stiffer.

Harry Matthews, the man Sam Laws called 'Pop', was Sam's mother's second husband, now divorced, and father of his half-sister Casey. As far as Jamie could tell, Harry's co-pilot Karen was also Harry's current partner. Jamie felt as if he had walked into a huge family row.

'We're about to be patched in.' Harry glanced at a display. 'I've got Florian Hart in the ops centre in the Industrial sector.'

'Here.' Florian's voice was a brisk snap.

'And Mayor Laws in Res Three—'

'Less of the Mayor. I'm your ex-wife, Harry, not your boss.'

'All right, all right.'

'I suppose you're patching in that Madl woman too.'

Karen glanced at Harry, and squeezed his hand. Beside Jamie, Sam mimed a silent vomit. Karen called, 'Actually, Jo, I'm right here.'

'Thank God we don't have the bandwidth for visual.'

'Now, ladies,' Harry said. 'I hope we also have Marshal Paley. Sonia, are you there?'

Sonia's voice was the scratchiest. 'We're here – just. I'm in an elevator, coming up to Res Three. My party took some losses down on Mnemosyne, but most of us got out. We have the travellers—'

Jamie sat forward sharply. 'Ye mean the Doctor and Zoe?'

'Oh, give me that thing.' Despite a crackle of static it was the Doctor's unmistakeable voice. 'Hello? Hello? Jamie? Is this still on?'

'Doctor! Aye, I'm here, right as rain. Is Zoe there?'

'She's fine, Jamie. But we've had some adventures, I don't mind admitting it.'

Now Zoe cut in. 'Jamie – where exactly are you?'

Jamie looked around helplessly. 'Up in the sky. I'd have to let Captain Matthews tell ye more particularly. Zoe, I'm in this fantastic beastie of a spaceship. It's called a, a phib—'

'A phibian,' Karen called over her shoulder.

'How interesting! Like an amphibian?'

'Aye! It can fly around in space but it can duck into the air as well, on Titan anyhow.'

'Actually,' Harry said, 'it can go swimming in the methane lakes too.'

'It has these rotor pods in the air, that fold away when ye're in space, and these panels slide back and it has rocket vents. It came to rescue us when Sam got stuck on yon volcano down there.'

Now Jo Laws' voice was thunderous. '*What* volcano?'

'Oh, mother—'

'Jo,' Harry Matthews put in, 'cut the kid some slack. Boys will be boys.'

'I'm no boy, *step-dad*,' Sam snarled.

'Nobody came to any harm,' Harry said.

'Oh,' Jo said, 'thanks to you and your daring rescue, no doubt. Enjoyed playing the hero, did you?'

'Actually it was Jamie who saved him. Karen and I just tidied up.'

Florian Hart's voice was like a tinkle of broken glass. 'Entertaining as the disintegration of your dysfunctional family is, Mayor, we're in the middle of a crisis here. Maybe we should focus on business?'

Jo Laws sighed. 'Agreed. Sonia, what's the security situation?'

'Confused. I'm getting updates from the Wheel and the mine fed to the comms console, such as it is, in this elevator cage. Will narrowcast it to you all now – wait a minute, sending it via MMAC—'

'Och, that tickles.'

'Shut up, MMAC.'

A panel on the wall of the phibian's cabin lit up like the TARDIS's scanner, and started showing scenes from across the Wheel, the mine surface, and the cables linking the two. Jamie saw those beads of light still rising up all the cables, towards the Wheel. But there were pools of deep blue at the base of many of the cables, close to the mine.

'OK,' Sonia said. 'You can see the evacuation is still under way. The elevator cages are all working at full capacity, and we have ships calling in to pick up stragglers.'

'A veritable Dunkirk,' the Doctor said, but nobody seemed to know what he meant.

'On the Wheel itself, we've had incidents with the Blue Dolls, scattered outbreaks of disruption, damage, sabotage . . . They all went crazy at the same time, just when the trouble with the bigger models started.'

'The Blue Soldiers,' Zoe said clearly. 'They need a name. Let's call them that.'

'Fine. Fortunately the Dolls are less advanced than the Soldiers, as well as being smaller physically. Less capable.'

The Doctor said grimly, 'Evidently whatever is manufacturing these things is learning.'

Sonia said, 'We've had no reports yet of Blue Soldiers up on the Wheel. Well, the only way they can get there is via the elevator, or the ships that are calling at the surface. We can put strict controls at the Wheel airlocks.'

'I'll get on to that,' Jo Laws murmured.

The Doctor said, 'Some of your images, Marshal, show the Blue Soldiers swarming *up the cables themselves*. The vacuum doesn't seem to bother them, does it? And they certainly aren't queuing up for the next elevator car. If I may make a suggestion . . .'

'Go ahead,' Sonia said.

'Captain Harry, perhaps this is a contribution you could make. Tour the moon, keeping out of reach of the Soldiers, and, umm, snip the cables. If you cut them below the level of the last passenger car, those aboard should be safe, shouldn't they?'

'I think so. Good idea. Locking in. We'll get started right away.'

Immediately the phibian lurched down towards the surface of Mnemosyne. Jamie felt nothing, it seemed there was an artificial gravity system on this particular ship that held him in place as the ship swooped and rolled, but the spectacle of the universe whirling past the windows became ever more dizzying. He tried to focus on the interior of the cabin, the back of Harry's couch ahead of him, the stable frame he was sitting in.

'And that will strand most of the Blues down on the moon. *But—*'

Now Zoe interrupted the Doctor. 'But I believe I saw Blue Soldiers getting to the cables before us. There may be some on the cables already, *above* the rising cars.'

'Let's take a look,' Matthews said. 'I'll hack into the external monitors and see if we can spot your own cable . . .'

Soon a new image crowded into the scanner screen on the phibian's wall, and Jamie peered to see. It was a thin thread strung across space, leading up to a Wheel ice bubble. There was the elevator cage, a transparent box – and Jamie saw people inside, Zoe and the Doctor, the man himself unmistakeable in that shabby black coat, even inside a skinsuit.

And above the box he saw blue figures, wriggling, rising, climbing up the cable.

Sonia grunted. 'You were right, Ms Heriot.'

Jamie peered at the image. 'One o' them looks blurry. Is it wearing a skinsuit?'

But nobody paid him any attention.

Sonia said, 'Well, we can't cut the cables *above* the rising cars, not without risking the passengers' lives. Madam Mayor, I suspect you will soon have some unwelcome visitors.'

'We'll be ready. But it's going to stretch us thin.'

Sonia called, 'Are we done?'

'Not quite,' the Doctor said, his voice sterner. 'Now that all the key players are at last in contact with each other, we should take the opportunity to look beyond the immediate crisis and consider the longer term.'

'What longer term?' Florian was as dismissive as ever. 'The only longer term I'm planning for is the resumption of mining, and the extraction of bernalium.'

'Oh, I don't think there'll be any more mining until this situation is resolved. And in fact it's your foolish attempts to drive on harder and faster that have provoked this crisis in the first place, Florian Hart.'

'Now you listen to me—'

'No, you listen,' the Doctor said firmly, and Jamie heard the note of command that emerged in him in a crisis, when the situation became clear, and the course of necessary action obvious. 'The pieces of the jigsaw are fitting together, at least in my mind. *There is something at the core of your moon*, as I've suspected from the beginning of all this. What it is, I still don't know yet. But I do know it is massive, for its motions affect the moon's gravity, and thereby the ring system. I know it is intelligent. It has encoded information of some kind into the ring system.'

Florian snorted.

'It is technological. It has manufactured these androids, the Dolls and the Soldiers, in response to its encounters with humanity. *And it is something that doesn't belong here.* The very presence of the bernalium you're mining, Florian, is one clear indicator of that. Bernalium is rare in this solar system – save here! And, Zoe and Jamie, you'll be aware of more conundrums we've uncovered.'

Jamie said, 'Aye, yon allohistorical lure.'

Zoe added, 'And the continuum displacement—'

'And the fact that it caused a big bang in the deep past—'

'It did *what*?' Sonia asked.

'Yes, well, we don't need to go into all that now,' the Doctor said hastily. 'Suffice it to say that *we must return to that moon*, once again. In spite of the danger. We must penetrate to its very heart. We must find out what lies there – what it is, and what it wants. And we must stop it from doing any more damage. Because, believe me, the potential for further disruption dwarfs anything we've seen so far.'

'And the Blues,' Sonia said. 'The Dolls and the Soldiers. What must we do with them? Exterminate them?'

'Oh, no,' the Doctor said, sounding shocked. 'We must save them, Marshal Paley. We must save them.'

Zoe said, 'I think we're nearly there. At the Wheel.'

'Then I'm about to have visitors,' Jo Laws said. 'I'll call you back . . .'

35

In Res Three, the cable docking station and its airlock were a couple of bubbles away from Mayor Jo Laws' home cum headquarters, where she'd been taking the conference call. Now she dashed for the docking station, working the wheels of her chair with brisk, practised shoves, calling ahead to have the hatches between the modules opened for her. From her elevator module, Sonia ordered available deputies to assemble at the docking station, armed, to support her.

The sector was locked down tight, Jo saw as she hurried through, just as she had ordered. This was a residential zone, but the schools, bars, play areas were all shut down and secured. Nobody moved on the streets save for a few deputies. But she saw maintenance robots at work, spidery machines patching the ice walls, others vacuum-cleaning the road surfaces or plunging extendible arms down drains: the infrastructure of the Mnemosyne Cincture, engaged in the endless task of maintaining itself, activities usually going on unnoticed by busy humans at all. It was oddly peaceful, harmonious, industrious. You'd never have known that people had been fighting for their lives down on the ice moon, just kilometres away.

By the time she got to the airlock, Sonia's deputies were already in position, half a dozen of them; all but one carried a blaster. They circled the airlock, which was a transparent cylinder a little taller than human height, with one big dilating door.

And inside the lock, already, were several figures. Tall, blue. There might have been six, seven, eight, more. They stood still as statues, but that only made them seem more menacing.

One seemed to be wearing a skinsuit, oddly. 'You were right, Mr McCrimmon,' Jo murmured.

'What's that, Mayor?' one of the deputies asked, a stocky woman.

'Never mind.'

'You can see we have the lock secured.'

'Good.'

'They seem to know they can't get out. They haven't tried, anyhow.'

'We're going to need the lock when the refugees get here. We'll have to let them out and deal with them outside.'

'Agreed. Let's form a couple of perimeters.' The deputy issued swift orders. Three of her colleagues stayed close to the lock, surrounding it in a loose circle, and the other three stood further out. All had their blasters trained on the lock. 'That should do it. And if any do get past us I've ordered the bubble hatches to be secured. They can't get out of here into the rest of the sector, at least.'

'Good. All right. Let's do this.'

The deputy raised her arm, and prepared to work a control panel on her wrist to open the hatch. The others stiffened, almost imperceptibly, ready to fire. Jo too raised her own blaster.

'On my three. One. Two—'

When the lock opened the Blue Soldiers swarmed out immediately. They were sprinting, Jo saw, sprinting like athletes, their bare feet somehow clinging to the floor. They moved unbelievably quickly.

And the one in the skinsuit was coming straight for her. It had skin mottled brown, she saw, brown in with the blue, under the sealed suit.

Blasters fired. The Blues were cut down, sliced, exploded, decapitated.

Yet a slick of blue-tinged body parts continued to crawl towards the deputies.

And the one in the skinsuit survived. The deputies hadn't been sure about shooting it. It walked unsteadily towards Jo in her chair, and touched its suit's controls. The suit peeled back.

That brown mottling wasn't a discolouration. It was flesh, human flesh, scraps of brown skin embedded in the blue. A panel of skin survived on the upper chest. Half of one upper arm. Areas around the thighs, the groin. Where there was contact the blue infiltrated the flesh, with needle-like fibres.

Half a face. The rest colonised by the blue.

Sinbad's face.

He opened his eyes, one human eye, one black as night. Opened a mouth that was half sealed by the blue. His voice was a wheeze, just breath.

'Help me.'

Jo raised her blaster and fired, again and again, until the body was broken up completely and every scrap scorched out of recognition. The blaster ran out of charge. A deputy took it from her limp hand. She slumped back in her chair, exhausted. And still the scraps of flesh on the floor slithered towards her like slugs.

'Why are you doing this?' Jo asked. 'Who are you? Where did you come from? Why did you bring my family here? *What do you want?*'

HOME

I

What Arkive wanted was simple.

To go home.

But to achieve that goal was anything but simple.

Five billion years ago:

When she was born, her very first awareness was of her mission.

Resilience. Remembrance. Restoration.

Those words were doorways in her young mind, through which understanding flooded.

And something else. Regret.

(They know this is cruel. To take away my youth. My growing. There is no time for growing. No time, if I am to save the best of them.)

Knowledge knitted itself up in her head. Then came interpretation. And then, understanding.

She orbited a world. One of a family of worlds. They in turn orbited a stable, long-lived, red-tinged, harmless sun. This world was called

Home. It was old, its ages of war and exploitation long past. If no longer rich, its people were content, in the light of their faithful sun . . .

Their sun, however, was not the problem.

(And what am I? I am embodied. A hull, shining, new, of stout bernalium and other materials. Inside there is complexity, a design engineered down to the level of subatomic particles. And, strapped to my metallic body, a shield. Or a sail?)

The problem was another star, a monstrous star nearby, young, bloated. Born in a nearby stellar nursery, drifting too close. That was the problem, a ghastly cosmic accident. For this star's life would not be long. Its core imploding, its outer layers cascading into space, it would soon destroy itself in a titanic explosion.

Titanic? How titanic? It would not just devastate Home, the other planets. It would destroy Home's sun itself.

(But it will not destroy me. Those who made me cannot save themselves. They can only save the memory of themselves, in me. They will load the best of themselves into me. And hope. Yes, they can invest that in me. And when the supernova detonates –)

There was a plan. A design. The shield would protect her from the detonation. Then it would act as a sail. The explosion itself would hurl her out of the solar system. And then, in the fullness of time, she would find another star, another world . . .

(Resilience. I must survive where all else is lost. Remembrance. I must remember what has been lost. The worlds. The life that swarmed. The minds. The art, the science, their unique apprehension of a universe that betrayed them. And, restoration. I have the facility to make new life. I have a womb! I will create them once again, on a new world, so that their story is not lost. And I –)

No time! No time! No time to tell you who we are! No time to tell you who *you* are!

(I am Arkive –)

II

She sensed the explosion.

A flare of white light, searing pain, a deep agonising rip as the filmy shield was ripped from her carcass, and the deeper inner burning as the supernova's radiation penetrated her body of metal and ceramics . . .

Too deep!

The plan had failed. The design was flawed. She was damaged. She fell, helpless, tumbling in the searing light.

Her mission was compromised. The detonation of the sun of Home had not been as expected. Too severe. Or too asymmetrical. (But who studies supernovas close to?) And it had caught her, it had overwhelmed the elaborate survival mechanisms given her by her designers.

It was a billion-year mission, and in the first few *seconds* she had failed. The regret was deeper than the agony of the physical pain.

The supernova poured out neutrinos, ghostly particles that bit into her interior. Twisting in agony, she manipulated the singularities deep in her own core to spit neutrinos back out into space. These were cries, cries of hate and anguish yelled back into the teeth of the storm. But the supernova had no ears to her, no mind to understand.

And still she fell through space, helpless.

For a thousand years, she fell.

Before her, the supernova's energy battered at a huge interstellar cloud, a swirling mass of dust and ice and organics. In response new stars began to nucleate, swirling and spitting and sparking to life. New planets, lumps of rock and ice, coalesced from a whirlwind of collisions. Whole new star systems were being created by the shock of the supernova, the event that had destroyed all she loved.

These systems would be garbage. Swirls of rubble. Worthless.

Yet she fell towards them.

For a million more years, she fell.

Until, at last, before her, a gas giant, a spinning, still-accreting ice moon . . .

36

The Doctor wasted no time. Less than a day after the battle on the moon, for the third time the Doctor and Zoe descended on Mnemosyne. He was going to let nothing stop him reaching the entity in the core this time, the Doctor told Zoe, and he was going to put an end to the petty war between the Blue creatures and the colonists. And he was going to put right whatever had gone wrong, deep in Mnemosyne. He spoke with a cold authority that sometimes settled on him; when he was like this she believed him even as she feared him, a little bit.

This time they went to the moon aboard a spaceship. The phibian craft, its hull still streaked by Titan tholins, settled softly on scarred ice. As Harry and Karen worked their way through a post-touchdown checklist, the landing party began to suit up and check the equipment they had brought. There were four of them this time: the Doctor, Phee Laws, Sonia Paley and Zoe. Zoe had an improvised suite of instruments, scientific sensors and a little tool kit for running repairs, all built into a backpack with a small handheld control unit. The Doctor carried a set of folded-up display flags, programmed with images of Saturn's rings. Phee had her amulet.

And Sonia had a blaster.

Zoe realised she had been holding her breath throughout the routine landing. The situation was extraordinary. At least when she'd visited before she'd had the feeling that she was approaching a functioning, inhabited, industrial facility. Now there was not a human on this whole moon, none but the crew and passengers of the phibian ship. Not for the first time she wished Jamie was at her side, Jamie with his sturdy strength and endless reserves of loyalty. But Jo Laws had asked that he stay on the Wheel and join the clean-up parties. Jamie had become a kind of ambassador to the estranged younger generation. Good for Jamie! But he wasn't at Zoe's side where he belonged, she thought resentfully.

Before he let them out of their couches, Harry ran through a series of external scans once again, supplemented by long-range checks by MMAC and other flying platforms. 'Still no sign of movement anywhere. We're good to go.'

Zoe fumbled to release her harness. The scans had shown furious activity for the first few hours after the last human had left the moon; the Blue Soldiers seemed to have scoured the ice corridors for their enemy. But then, once the moon was established as abandoned, the Soldiers, and the Dolls, had simply shut down, as far as anyone could tell from a distance.

Zoe murmured, 'I'm going to expect a warm welcome with every step we take, Doctor.'

'Perhaps. But they don't seem to have reacted to the landing of this ship yet, Zoe. We must remember we're not dealing with a human military force here. This isn't a UNIT base we're sneaking into. The Blue Soldiers are a desperate gesture of self-defence by an ancient and ailing mind. I think I would have been surprised if there had been anything resembling a conventional organisation – you know, sentries and patrols . . . Let's just be thankful for any advantage.'

This logic was convincing. But she knew the clutching fear would not leave her until she was safely back on the phibian ship again, and away from this place.

As they assembled at the phibian's airlock, Harry momentarily blocked the way with an upraised arm. 'You're sure you want to go through with this?'

'Quite sure,' the Doctor said peremptorily. 'And the sooner we get on with it—'

'Phee? You sure too?'

Phee, the amulet at her neck visible through her skinsuit, scowled. 'My mum is making you say this, isn't she?'

'Well, yes. She twisted my arm. Look, Phee, she's concerned for your safety. And if you want to back out of this now we can just take off in this bucket and go straight back to the Wheel, and there's no shame, no questions asked, no pride lost—'

'I have to do this.' The Doctor and Jamie had patiently talked her through it all. How the amulet had been thrown back in time, and still bore the traces of that event in particles their equipment could detect. It was an extraordinary story, but somehow it made sense, given the object's own tangled relationship with her own family. 'This old amulet is the reason we're all here. The colony, my family especially. Now it's time to bring it home.'

'Yes,' the Doctor said. 'It's time.'

'Which is all very abstract,' Sonia said sternly, 'when you're risking the life of a sixteen-year-old girl. Phee, Harry's right. You don't have to do what *he* says.'

'It's my choice,' Phee said. 'Let's get on with it.'

With good grace Harry stepped aside.

They had landed close to the surface support facility where Jo had first brought Zoe and the Doctor to this moon. Now the low, plain building was dark, and much of it was open to vacuum. There was no movement: no humans, no Blue Dolls, no Soldiers.

Inside they found their way to the downshaft without difficulty, and descended.

Soon they were through a lock and inside the pressurised side-shafts, and they pushed back their skinsuit hoods. The air was cold, colder than it had seemed before. Zoe thought she could smell burned plastic, and the sharp smell of ozone – static electricity? – and, under it all, the iron stink of human blood.

The Doctor led the four of them down another vertical shaft, deeper into the moon's interior. He intended to retrace the steps he had taken on his second venture into the moon, and return to the nest of the Blue Dolls.

He warned, 'Of course we may be in danger from the Blue Soldiers when they work out we are here. But remember too that nobody has been back here since the fighting with the Blue Soldiers, and the evacuation. Nobody human, I mean. So there has been no clean-up.' He glanced at Phee. 'We may see some sights which will be – well, distressing.'

'Dead people, you mean,' Phee said bluntly. 'Don't worry. It was another reason my mother didn't want me to come down here. I'm not squeamish.'

'I'm sure you're not,' the Doctor said. 'But none of us in this party are trained soldiers. Not even you, Marshal Paley. So let's be honest with ourselves. This isn't going to be easy.'

They reached a side-shaft, and the Doctor, quite nimbly, swung inside. Sonia insisted on taking the lead now, her blaster loose in its holster at her side. The Doctor and Phee followed, with Zoe at the rear.

Sonia said, 'I don't know why you wanted to come this way in the first place. If we're heading for the core, Florian's new trial bore would be a lot easier. Takes you straight there.'

'Yes, well, digging that shaft was a clear act of aggression, and I don't think we should have anything to do with that. And besides, there's somebody we need to find first.'

'Who?'

'An ally, I hope—'

'Hush.' Sonia held up a hand. They stood stock still. Then she led them forward, treading softly.

The passage ahead was filled with Blues. Blue bodies, curled up on the floor or clinging, flattened, to the walls and ceiling. Most of them were adult bodies, Soldiers, though a few Dolls nuzzled between the larger forms. This tableau was utterly still, silent. Like a heap of discarded sculptures, Zoe thought. She seemed to be frozen with fear.

'I wonder what they dream about,' Phee said.

'I don't know,' the Doctor said. 'I rather hope it's nothing at all.'

Sonia took an experimental step forward.

There was a rustling. Every Blue head lifted and turned, like so many antennas, to face the human party. Every one, all at once. Zoe quailed, under the gaze of a hundred pairs of empty black eyes.

Sonia had her blaster drawn. 'Well, they're blocking the passage. It's either go back or go through them.'

'Oh, for heaven's sake.' The Doctor pushed her aside, and began shaking out the display flags he had been carrying. 'Here, put these on.' He handed them around.

Sonia took her flag, looking confused. 'What's this for?'

'Put it on! We haven't come here to shoot our way through anything, Sonia. We're here to talk – to listen – not to destroy. And this encounter is going to prove if that's possible or not. Look, put these over your shoulders like cloaks, you see?' When they were all draped in the flags, the Doctor nodded at Zoe. 'You have the controls.'

Zoe tapped a command into the simple keyboard of her control unit.

Immediately the flags lit up, with shifting, striped patterns of light, graceful curves, delicate colours. There were images of Saturn's rings, some recorded, some a live feed from MMAC – and, if the Doctor was right, a reflection of the thoughts of the entity at the heart of the moon, and at the centre of all this.

All those heads shifted again, to stare at the flags.

The Doctor took one pace forward, two, cautiously stepping over the prone bodies. The Blues didn't get out of his way, but they didn't impede him either. Their heads swivelled to follow the shifting patterns on the flags, with more of those unearthly rustles.

'You can follow me safely, I think,' the Doctor said calmly. 'Try not to step on anybody. I don't think they'd react badly, but let's not take the chance, eh? Oh, and Phee, now would be a good time to begin displaying that amulet of yours. No need for anything fancy. Just hang it outside your skinsuit, perhaps. Make it visible.'

Sonia growled, 'But do not compromise the integrity of your suit, soldier.'

'Yes, Marshal,' Phee sighed.

Zoe was the last to walk across the chamber. The Blue bodies at her feet were tightly packed, but she followed where the others had walked, where there was room to set her feet down. The Blues watched her, and the shifting colours on her flag. They didn't breathe, it struck Zoe now. There was not a single sigh, or gasp, or cough. And if she put her ear to any of those blue chests, there would be no heartbeat. So strange, at the same time human yet so inhuman.

She wanted to shrink away from any contact with them, to flee, to huddle back into herself. To go back. But she was halfway across the blockage now. She took another step, and another, following the others, and made it to the far side. She took a few hurried steps away from the last prone body, the last sprawled limbs.

The Doctor was waiting for her, a broad, sympathetic smile on his face. 'Well done,' he whispered. 'I'm starting to think we might actually live through this. Come on!' They walked after Sonia and Phee. 'What about your sensor kit, Zoe? Any significant readings?'

She checked her readouts. 'There's an elevated level of ozone in the air.'

'I can smell that,' the Doctor said. 'Like the seaside. Mmm. Sandcastles and candy floss!'

'What? Some of that might be a residue of all the blaster fire down here.'

'Or perhaps there's some other cause. Well, I expect we'll find out. What else?'

'A cocktail of exotic hydrocarbons in the air. I suspect that's a relic of the Blues. I mean—'

'The destroyed ones, yes. What about the core?'

'The most significant reading is an oddity. An elevated yield of neutrinos, coming out of the core.'

He looked at her sharply. 'More neutrinos? That's odd.'

Astrophysicist Zoe knew that neutrinos were ghostly subatomic particles to which almost any substance was quite transparent. If they were somehow being created in the core of the moon, most would flood out through its mass and into deep space, with only a handful of them being impeded by the moon's billions of tonnes of ice. 'What's the significance, do you think, Doctor?'

'Well, the usual ways to create a neutrino flow are to turn a nuclear reactor on and off, or to make a star detonate in a supernova explosion . . . It's too early to theorise. We need more facts, Zoe, and that's why we're here: facts! Come along.' And he trotted ahead.

But after only a few more paces they came to a battlefield. Sonia and Phee had already come to a halt, and were standing and staring.

It was a war zone entirely contained within a few dozen metres of tunnel. The ice walls themselves were pocked and scarred by blaster fire. Bodies lay scattered, smashed and broken, human and Blue alike – a lot more Blues, or the remains of them, but dried human blood was splashed everywhere, deep brown against the blue-white ice. Some of the human victims had died in the process of transformation, like Sinbad Omar, with blue patches embedded in their skin.

The Doctor said gently, 'There's nothing we can do here. We must move on—'

Sonia turned on him with a snarl. 'Doctor, I don't care what other goals you have today. We aren't going on until we've done something for these people. Phee, I need you to help.' She dug a little medallion out of her own vest. 'See this dog tag? Everybody down here should have been wearing one of these. See if you can help me find them. Then their families will know where they are, at least. Even if the bodies can't be taken back for processing.'

'Processing?' the Doctor asked.

'Bodies are recycled, in the hydroponics bays,' Sonia said. 'Even in death you contribute to the colony. Not to my taste, but it's done respectfully enough.'

With a visible effort, Phee nodded. 'I'll help you, Marshal.'

Slowly the two of them worked their way around the bodies. Zoe thought Phee showed remarkable courage in handling the broken corpses, in digging into their bloodied skinsuits and clothing. But many of the bodies were too badly damaged, or transformed, for the dog tags to have survived.

So Zoe stepped forward and dug a small sample extractor from her kit. 'I'll take swab samples. A DNA identification will back up the dog tags. And if the tags are missing—'

'Thank you.'

The Doctor nodded. 'Let me help you, Zoe.'

It took half an hour to complete the grisly process. Zoe uploaded all her data to MMAC. Sonia passed around wet-wipe towels from her own small kit, and the four of them cleaned blood and sticky Blue tissue from their skinsuits and gloved hands.

Then they moved on.

Time and space swam strangely for Zoe in these corridors of primordial ice. Sometimes it seemed as if they had walked many kilometres, other times as if she had barely stepped away from the vertical access shaft. The thick air, the stench of ozone and plastic and blood, all made the experience dreamlike, swimming. The gravity was fading too as they gradually descended deeper into the moon. It all worked to detach her from her usual logic, her own inner sense of order and regularity.

She felt great relief when they finally reached the place the Doctor had labelled the Nest of the Blue Dolls. It was another landmark reached, and Zoe was a step nearer the end of this unnerving journey.

The Doctor walked forward, his flag over his shoulders, his hands held out, empty. Fifty little heads swivelled with a rustle like turning pages. 'I'm looking for First,' he said clearly. He raised his left palm and marked a downward slash with his right forefinger. 'The one called First. Is he here?' He moved through the crowd, like an adult walking through a room of napping children. 'First. I'm looking for First.' He made the name mark over and over.

At last the crowd parted, little bodies slithering and rolling out of the way, and a single Blue Doll came forward.

The Doctor leaned down, his hands resting on his knees. 'How good to see you again, old boy. I'm the Doctor. Remember?'

First simply stared back, his face blank.

'Now,' the Doctor said, 'we need your help. Or rather, I hope we are going to be able to help each other. Phee? It's up to you now.'

Phee came forward hesitantly. 'What am I supposed to say?'

Sonia grunted. 'How about, "Take me to your leader"?'

The Doctor glared at her.

Phee stood before the Blue Doll, who gazed back patiently. She bent down and held out the amulet, still on the chain around her neck. 'I've brought this back. I think it's yours.'

First reached out with a small, sketchy hand, and laid his palm on the amulet. There was a crackle, a kind of spark. Phee jumped back.

Sonia was at her side immediately. 'Are you all right? What was that?'

'I'm fine. Just a sort of shock, an electric shock. It made me jump.'

'The ozone level just rose a bit,' Zoe said, reading her instrument unit. 'I think it was some kind of electrical discharge.'

'A transfer of energy,' the Doctor said, 'which seems to have accompanied a transfer of information.'

First, the Blue Doll, turned and walked away, heading for a passageway at the back of the nest chamber.

'Where's he going?' Phee asked.

The Doctor smiled. 'I think we'd better follow and find out, don't you?' Whistling a little tune, he wrapped up his display flag into a bundle and followed the Blue Doll.

Zoe hurried after him. 'Doctor, there's something else. I've seen a spike in the neutrino output.' She peered into the dark tunnel. 'Whatever's waiting for us down there—'

'It's already responding,' he said with relish. 'Good! And since we're still alive I presume my ploy of linking up with our little friend here is working – proof that we are a friendly embassy, not an invasion force. Isn't this wonderful, Zoe? Plunging into the unknown. Heading for first contact with a new alien species, perhaps. Anything at all could lie in wait for us down there!'

She linked her arm in his. 'Ask me how I feel about it all later – if we live through it . . .'

37

Jo Laws called a council meeting in her home in Res Three. A meeting of sorts. One of the old council members was dead, poor Sinbad Omar, and another, Marshal Sonia Paley, was down on the moon with the Doctor and Phee. But Florian Hart was here, and she had demanded the meeting in the first place. And Luis Reyes, the man from the Planetary Ethics Commission, who was doing a good job in helping a wounded community pull back together, even if it was outside his remit of ethical policing. But then, in a crisis, as Jo had observed many times before, people pulled together regardless of formal rank and role. Jamie McCrimmon was here too, at Jo's invitation, because the young traveller was about the only adult on the Wheel the more disillusioned kids would speak to, since the incident of the kettling.

Florian was as uncompromising as ever. The first agenda item she wanted to raise was about sending prison gangs down to the moon for forced labour. 'Every unproductive day is a wasted day. We're here for one thing only, and that's—'

'Bernalium,' the rest chorused, sitting around Jo's kitchen table.

And little Casey, playing on the floor at Jo's feet, echoed it too.

'Benn-ar-umm!' She had a new blue doll, made by Jo and Phee of scraps of cloth, to make up for the loss of the old one.

'We know, Florian,' said Jo, feeling strained, exhausted before the latest fight even started. 'Look, what labour we do have is tied up putting the Wheel back together, which is what keeps us all alive, if you hadn't noticed. And the moon is not yet secure. The work of clearing it out to the point where we can begin operations again—'

'Hasn't even begun. And every day we delay puts off the restart even more.' Florian glanced at Jamie. 'We could send down those kids who went to Titan. That would show them.'

'Ye'll do that o'er my dead body,' Jamie growled, glaring at her.

Luis Reyes said, 'Florian, the PEC would have significant reservations about sending young people and children into a site which is, depending on your definition, either a war zone, a crime scene or a site of special scientific interest.'

'Pah!' Florian pointed at Jo. 'But our glorious leader here has sent her own kid into that "war zone". How do you square that?'

Jamie said, 'The Doctor says Phee's needed. To sort out whatever beastie's lurkin' there. You heard the arguments.'

'And I agreed,' Jo said firmly. 'Admittedly reluctantly.'

'You're talking about science,' said Florian. 'We're not here for science. All right, Mayor. Here's a compromise. Let me go down to the moon.'

'I can't possibly allow it,' Jo said. 'You heard Sonia's orders. The moon isn't secure. The Doctor and his party are under Sonia's own protection. I couldn't allow—'

'Just hear me out. I won't go unprotected. I'll take a small team, we'll secure one of the surface facilities. At least I can start some kind of assay of the work we're going to have to do to get up and running again. My risk. Bootstrap will take full responsibility for my own safety and the guards'. Call it a delaying tactic. This will get me off your back, and the shareholders off mine. What do you say?'

Luis was thinking quickly. 'I'll accompany you.'

Florian stared at him. 'What? Why? What use are you?'

Luis laughed at her coarse rudeness. 'I'll monitor the safety of your operatives. And yours, in fact. And I'll make sure *you* protect the site.'

'The science, you mean.'

'Conserving mankind's common heritage in the face of despoilment or exploitation is part of the mandate of the PEC—'

'Save me the speech. Fine. You can make the coffee.' She glared around, challenging. 'Anything else? Are we done here?'

And Jo Laws, feeling uncomfortably that events were slipping once more out of her control, could only nod her head.

38

First led them along a twisting natural shaft, deeper into the heart of the ice moon. The air remained fresh enough, Zoe thought, but the scattering of light globes, automatically placed from the human facilities on the surface, became sparse, and at last dwindled altogether. The explorers had lamps on their skinsuits and Sonia passed out handheld torches from her backpack, but from now on the light would always be uncertain.

It was a sign that they were penetrating deeper than any human had gone before them. Zoe's mood swung between dread and wonder.

The shaft at last opened out into another chamber. This was at least as large as the Dolls' nest, but it was empty of Dolls. Instead it was crammed with a clutter of equipment. Zoe's first impression was of a mass of wires and cables and coils, struts, panels, and glinting glassware, especially mirrors. As she turned around she saw the reflection of her own lights wink back at her from a dozen surfaces embedded in the shadowy junk. This was evidently equipment taken from the Wheel and the mine. She saw registration numbers, a few Bootstrap logos, even clunky black-letter labels:

HAZARDOUS WASTE
RESIDENTIAL FIVE INFIRMARY
DO NOT REMOVE

The ozone stink was sharp in here, Zoe noticed.

First stood amid these heaps of junk, quietly waiting.

Sonia gazed around in wonder. 'So this was where it all ended up. All the stuff that went missing.'

Phee said, 'The stuff you accused people like my brother Sam of pinching.'

'All right, Phee. We were wrong. It was these Blue Dolls all the time. And it wasn't sabotage, was it?'

'Not intentional,' the Doctor said. 'Though machines are going to fail if you rip out enough of their vital components. No, the Dolls didn't want to cause damage, not at first anyhow; what they wanted was the parts themselves.'

'To be brought here, to this great – midden,' Zoe said. 'What's it all for, Doctor? Is it just collected at random?'

'Like the nest of a bower bird,' Phee said. She seemed embarrassed. 'I read about that at school.'

'Oh, I think there's more intent to it than that,' the Doctor said. He walked forward to a kind of cabinet, about the size and shape of the TARDIS in fact, roughly constructed of plastic panels. 'I'm surprised you don't see the pattern, Zoe.'

'Well, I'm sorry, I'm sure.' But, looking around, Zoe did start to see a kind of design. 'It's all glass tubing, and electrical wiring, and coils – and look, is this a dynamo? It's like a giant electrical engine.'

'Yes.' The Doctor fiddled with a rough door that sealed the cabinet. When he pulled it free it fell apart in his hands; it had only been panels loosely taped together. 'Oops. But if I'm right, what we'll find in here—' He leaned forward, his suit lights bright, and there was a blaze of reflected light.

Zoe glanced inside the cabinet, over his shoulder. Mirrors! Rank upon rank of them, carefully positioned to face each other, so that each way she looked she saw copies of herself heading off into infinity.

'Let me see that.' Sonia pushed past them. 'Why, there's a fortune in pilfered optics in here, from astronomical telescopes, laser installations . . .' Phee poked her head in curiously.

The Doctor drew Zoe aside, and whispered, 'Best if the others don't overhear. Zoe, I think what we're seeing in this rather pathetic contraption is the end result of the placing of the allohistorical lure.'

'Which drew humans here.'

'Yes. Because whatever lies within this moon wanted humans to *make* something for it. Or at least bring the component parts. And this is the Blue Dolls' rather muddled attempt to satisfy those wishes. They raided the mine workings and the Wheel, to build – this!'

'But what is it, Doctor?'

'I can tell you what it's meant to be. Whoever ordered this thing built wants to send a message, to future or past – and, possibly, to escape there. This is a time machine, Zoe. A time machine.'

Zoe was bewildered by this revelation. A greater difference between the hugely advanced technology of the TARDIS and this heap of pack-rat junk could hardly be imagined. A time machine!

But the Doctor ought to know, and, as she listened to his hasty explanation, she found herself growing convinced.

'Mirrors reflect light, after all, and light is integral to the theory of time travel. Indeed, travelling faster than light is equivalent to travelling in time! And then if you cross-wire that, so to speak, to a generator of static electricity – if like poles repel, Zoe, perhaps like *images* can be made to repel, and then sent off to wherever you want them to go . . .'

'I'm remembering my quantum gravity theory,' she said slowly. 'Yes, there is something plausible about that. If you mounted the mirrors on insulating bases, if your static charges were strong enough—'

'That's the idea. But you do need the right trace elements in your apparatus. You may not succeed in making a time machine, but you might manage to hook a flaw in time to your gadget, and I've seen *that* done before, by two gentlemen of the Victorian era, one misguided, the other a greedy fool. And *their* reward was a visit from a Dalek!'

'Oh. And so is this the source of the Relative Continuum Displacement Zone that attracted the TARDIS?'

'I suspect so, Zoe. We probably detected a trial run – enough to pass a bit or two of information, no more. Much greater energies would need to be applied to give it a credible chance of working. But of course it would *not* work, not as intended. This is such a muddle – as if the designer was having trouble remembering what it wanted to build, and the Dolls were having trouble understanding its instructions . . . At best it would cause a continuum implosion. I strongly suspect something similar happened fifty million years ago, wrecking the original moon and creating the rings of Saturn – and now we're all set for another go. It would be the end of what's left of this little moon at last, and the Wheel. And if the disruption spread – well, there's an awful lot of mass-energy wrapped up in Saturn.'

'My word. You're talking about a solar-system-wide disaster!'

'Quite possibly.'

'Well, what must we do to stop it?'

He grinned. 'That's my girl! Straight to the point. What we must do, Zoe, is go a bit deeper into this strange little moon—'

'Find out whoever ordered this machine to be built.'

'And ask it not to throw that switch! Now come on, the others are growing suspicious of our mutterings . . .'

So they passed on from the chamber of the time machine.

As it turned out they had to walk only a little further, only a little deeper, before they came at last to the heart of the moon.

And confronted what brooded there.

39

There was a hole in the moon. The gravity, always very low, was now all but non-existent. They were very close to the moon's mass centre, Zoe realised. And here they found a chamber, roughly spherical – a big one, perhaps a hundred metres across. A curtain of light, spectral, shimmering, hung before the rough entrance to the chamber. The lights from their torches played across the space beyond.

And by the torches' uncertain glow she glimpsed something in the heart of the chamber, resting on the ice. Something shapeless. Worn. *Old*. That was her first impression. Yet not inert. Something, if not alive, then functional.

The Blue Doll called First walked forward, neither boldly nor nervously. He stood before the big central mass, upright, hands by his sides, very like an attentive child – or a statue of a child, for he was utterly still.

The Doctor grunted. 'I wonder what's passing between them. Come on – there's no use standing here. Let's have our calling cards ready. Help me unfurl the display flags. We can at least show it our intention is to communicate, even if all we're managing is to reflect back its own thoughts to it. And, Phee, your amulet—'

'I have it, Doctor.' The girl was holding it out before her. She looked scared but determined.

Zoe smiled at Phee. 'You'll always remember this day,' she whispered. 'This moment. Wonderful, isn't it?'

Phee stared. 'Is it always like this for you?'

'Pretty much,' Zoe said.

'If you two are quite done gossiping?' Irascibly, nervously, the Doctor took a step forward. In his right hand he held out a flag across which ring arcs rippled, his left arm was folded protectively against his upper chest, and he walked almost sideways on, hesitant, as if approaching an unexploded bomb. Yet his voice was calm, reassuring.

'Hello. I'm the Doctor . . . Can you hear me? I suspect, well, I *hope*, that you can hear my words through the sense organs of your creature, the one who calls himself First. Perhaps you can sense our physical presence too that way. Even if you can't make much sense of what we say just yet. Just remember: we come in peace. We've come to help you, not harm you . . .'

There was no obvious response from the entity.

Zoe tapped her sensor readouts. 'Doctor. Another flood of neutrinos. I'm sure it's some kind of signal. But I can't read it.'

'Of course not. You can barely detect neutrinos with a box that size, let alone decode any signal.'

'And, Doctor. Look at the flags!'

It was the live feed sent down from space by MMAC that had caught her attention. The rings, the fine detail – they were *rippling*.

And now, though she saw no movement in the entity, Zoe sensed a deep disturbance, a rolling, the thrashing of some restless giant.

Sonia grabbed her stomach. 'That's making me ill.'

The Doctor ignored her. 'Quick, Zoe. See if you can run any kind of pattern recognition on the signals in the rings, and the neutrino flow if you can.'

She hurried to comply, and kicked in analysis suites. But she asked, 'Pattern recognition? Based on what?'

He glanced around to make sure Phee and Sonia couldn't see, then dug into his pocket and slipped her a small glass bar. 'Here. This contains an extract from the TARDIS's translation system, a database of all known galactic languages and their families. I thought it might come in handy today.'

'I thought Sonia had the TARDIS impounded—'

He pressed a finger to his lips. *Hush.* 'See if there's any match between this creature's patchy signals and any known language – well, there must be, the database is rather comprehensive.'

'How do I plug it in?'

The Doctor sighed. 'Give it back.' He just tucked the slip into her backpack. 'Now. Is it working?'

She hastily improvised a readout subroutine. Results began to scroll across a tiny screen on her control box. 'Why, yes. There is a correlation with a group of languages known as the Talsiccian Family. A mostly extinct group, it says here, very ancient. There isn't enough data in the signal for a full match—'

'Yes, yes. We're going to have to set up a much more comprehensive data capture system. We need a decent neutrino detector for a start. But for now – what's it *saying*, Zoe?'

'Two things. One is a name – I think. More a definition. A compound of two concepts. It is an ark. And it is an archive.'

'Ark – archive. *Arkive!* Its mission is preservation, then. Well, it would be. What else?'

'I'll let it tell you itself.' She tapped a button on her console, and a synthesised voice, loud as a brass gong, filled the chamber with words:

RESILIENCE

REMEMBRANCE

RESTORATION

40

'Explain it tae me agin. What have I got to do exactly?'

'Jamie, it will be your job to build me a neutrino detector here on Mnemosyne.'

'What have new trees got to do with it? Anyway ye'd call them saplings, Doctor—'

'Neutrinos, Jamie! They're a kind of subatomic particle.'

'A suba – what? Are ye sure ye've got the right man for the job? Why don't ye ask the town cat to do a highland reel while ye're at it?'

'Oh, but it's really quite simple, Jamie. The neutrino detector will be nothing more elaborate than a big hole in the ice. It needs sensors to be placed in it, but I'm having Zoe order those up.'

'Zoe? Is she back on the Wheel now?'

'Yes, she is. She went back with Sonia. She's going to be working with MMAC as soon as all this is up and running, and we try to close the loops of communication.'

'A hole in the ice, ye say?'

'More of a subsurface cavity. Entirely sealed up, and full of fluid – well, the meltwater will do. Oh, and a healthy dose of cleaning fluid would help.'

'Cleaning fluid?'

'I'm sure the Wheel's stores can supply that. Most of the neutrinos will pass through the fluid not even noticing its presence, since ordinary matter is all but transparent to a neutrino. But given a big enough bulk of fluid, statistically speaking *some* of the neutrinos are going to interact with it, knocking off an electron from an atom here and there. Zoe's sensors, drifting in the fluid and embedded around the cavity's surface, will detect these events, or the products of them. On Earth they've been building detectors like this, big tanks of cleaning fluid down mines, oh, for a century or more. And then when we have enough detection events we will backtrack to build up a three-dimensional picture of the neutrino flow from the Arkive.'

'I . . . see.'

'And *that*, Jamie, will enable us to work out what the Arkive is saying – and what she wants. I wondered if you might work with your youngsters on this. Plenty of brawn and ingenuity to draw on there.'

'Aye. A lot o' energy with nowhere to go. Well, I'll get stuck in. Me and the lads swingin' a few picks, we'll have it done in nae time.'

'Oh, I suspect there are more efficient ways, Jamie . . .'

So Jamie called together Sam Laws and his buddies Dai and Sanjay, and told them what the Doctor wanted, and described his first idea of how to achieve it. 'I thought if we all got our picks, and started out on all sides, an' just kept swingin' until we met at the middle . . .'

To his chagrin, they laughed at him.

Sam clapped him on the shoulder. 'Granddad, granddad. There are better ways to do it than that.'

Crestfallen, Jamie asked, 'What, then?'

'We're going to have to get Marshal Paley to hand over some blasters to us.'

'Whisht ye! She'll never do that!'

He was wrong about that, though it took tense negotiations involving Sam, Jamie, Jo Laws, and even a few words from the Doctor down on Mnemosyne on the importance of the project, before Sonia would make the concession. And even then she insisted on hardwiring the settings, fixing the weapons to a mild stun setting.

'But then that's what the Doctor wants anyhow,' said Jamie, consulting his notes. 'A dispersed field. Low energy concentration. We're trying to melt ice, not cut people in half.'

'There,' Sonia said, testing one of the blasters. 'The only way you could kill somebody with one of these is by clubbing them over the head with it.'

'Don't give them ideas,' Jo Laws said gloomily.

So, for the first time, Jamie made the short hop down to Mnemosyne from the Wheel. Once again Harry Matthews and Karen Madl were drafted in as cab drivers, as Harry put it. This time the capacious holds of the phibian ship were loaded up with cleaning fluid from the Wheel's stocks. The atmosphere in the cabin between Sam and his divorced stepfather, as they all sat there in their skinsuits, was as frosty as it had been before. But Jamie had an instinct that it was good for these two survivors of a broken family to have something to work on together.

They landed close to the surface facility in Quadrant Four where the Doctor's party had disembarked earlier. Florian Hart was already here, working on plans to restore the mine operations. They had to land here; it was the only part of the moon's surface Florian's guards and Sonia's deputies had agreed could be regarded as secure.

And Jamie noticed a scarred hulk, a cylinder with much-faded paintwork, lying beside the surface building. It reminded him of a fallen pine trunk. It must be an old rocket ship. He tapped Sam on the shoulder. 'What's yon spaceship doin' lyin' there on the ice?'

Sam looked. 'That's an old Demeter booster, I think. Intercontinental missile. I never saw it before.'

Jamie touched the studs on his skinsuit collar. 'Jamie to Zoe. Can ye hear me, lass?'

'Yes, Jamie, I'm here. Working hard . . .'

There was a kind of gurgle in the background. 'Oh, aye, so what's that? Doesnae sound like hard work to me.'

'I'm babysitting Casey Laws while I work. Helping Jo out; it's a busy time. And we're quite safe in here. We're in one of MMAC's old space-ships in the Wheel.'

Jamie scoffed. 'You? Babysittin'? Ye could babysit a computer, maybe. Or a Cyberbaby!'

'Yes, all right, Jamie.' She sounded hurt. 'We're doing fine. She's got her little blue doll, and her other toys. Is that all right with you?'

'Aye, aye. Sorry.' He leaned over to Sam. 'Say hello to yer wee sister, Sam!'

Sam just rolled his eyes.

'What did you want, Jamie?'

'Eh? Oh, aye. Listen, d'ye have a line to MMAC?'

There was a click, and MMAC replied immediately. 'Right here, big man.'

'What, ye're listenin' in?'

'No, but the use of ma name triggers a detection system.'

'I wanted tae ask ye both—' He glanced out of his window again. 'What's Florian Hart doin' with a big old booster rocket on the moon's surface? I thought she was down there to plan how to get yon mine up and runnin' again. Did she take it out o' the Wheel?'

'No,' MMAC said. 'But I've a stockpile of old craft like that on Tethys. Another o' the moons. Spare parts fer the Wheel, ye might say. Those old birds have got useful electronics in 'em sometimes. Other stuff ye can scavenge. There was some damage done tae yon facilities by those Blue rascals, Jamie. Maybe she's tryin' tae fix it.'

'I suspect it's all innocent,' Zoe put in. 'I'm working in an old Mars shuttle craft myself, built into the Wheel. Decades old, but I can patch into the avionics and what's left of the AI to support the Doctor's project, linking MMAC to the Arkive . . .'

'Hmm. A missile, ye say? Which means it would have had a big bomb in its nose?'

'Aye, once,' MMAC said, 'but I cleaned 'em all out long before they were brought out here, Jamie. Ye can check if ye want. I was always very careful about safety, when I was puttin' this Wheel together. Scrupulous, ye might say.'

'Jamie, is that all?' Zoe asked.

'Aye.'

'Well, good luck then. The sooner we can put all this together the sooner we'll have everything resolved.'

'Aye. We've all got work to do . . .'

He shut the line down, still not quite satisfied. Something about the sight of that big old rocket lying there on the moon's surface disturbed him. A missile, with Florian Hart, angry, impatient, ambitious, working only a few paces away. It didn't feel right.

Just do your job, Jamie boy. Just do your job.

Inside the facility, Jamie, Sam, Dai and Sanjay pulled on backpacks laden with gear, strapped their blasters over their shoulders and clambered down the shaft's rough ladder and deep into the moon. Sam and Dai still hadn't fully recovered from injuries they'd suffered on Titan, but they'd been able to satisfy Jamie and Sonia that in the low gravity they wouldn't be impeded. And, well, they'd wanted to come, wanted to take part in the mission, and that counted for a lot with Jamie.

They soon reached pressurised shafts and corridors, and that made moving easier. But as they penetrated deep into the moon's friable ice, Jamie was soon lost, even though he was carrying a map, a fancy layered thing prepared by Zoe that showed the deep structure of the mine shafts. The Doctor wanted a big cavity to be melted into the ice directly over the Arkive's chamber, because that was the way the Arkive seemed to be directing her neutrino blasts, straight up into space. Zoe had marked a roughly spherical chamber on the map, and had even marked firing positions for them with crosses. The trouble was, where Jamie came from nobody ever used maps, save maybe for scratches in the dirt as some veteran explained how they were going to raid a redcoat camp. He'd grown up learning his mountains and moors and glens from direct experience. And for sure nobody ever needed a map in three dimensions like this, all contours and layers showing down and up as well as side to side . . .

'Are you lost, granddad? Poor old fella.' Sam took the map from his hands and made a point of turning it the other way up. 'We're on the right road. But we need to split up here. Dai, Sanj, you go that way – left. Granddad, you follow me . . .'

In the end, Jamie found himself alone in a deserted shaft, with sparse light globes glowing fitfully. But this point would become the 'north pole' of the Doctor's spherical hole. Sam had wormed his way down to the 'south pole', having sent Dai and Sanjay to opposing points on the equator.

Now Sam called over the suit comms, 'All set? Blasters charged?'

The others called in positive replies.

'Ye sure this is going to work?' Jamie asked. 'Meltin' ice with guns?'

'It's how they blew the bubbles in the Wheel in the first place,' Sam said. 'With big industry-strength blasters. It'll work if *you* don't make a muck of it, granddad. Do you want to count us down?'

'I'll leave that tae ye, ye scallywag.' Jamie pressed the flaring muzzle of his blaster down onto the ice under his feet.

'On zero, then. Three, two, one – zero!'

Jamie closed the trigger.

Used to firing muskets, he had braced for recoil, but there was none.

He could hear nothing, in fact, see nothing. But he knew that energy was pouring out of the weapon into the substance of the ice beneath him, and he smelled an odd burning scent – electrified air, Zoe called it, like the air of an ocean beach on a fresh day.

'Hey, granddad,' Sam called now. 'You do realise you're melting the ice under your own feet. That's why we put you at the north pole. I hope you can swim!'

In fact that had occurred to Jamie when Zoe had set out the scheme for him. And in fact he couldn't swim. But he knew the theory. The blasters' four beams would meet at the centre of the cavity, and the melting would start there, and work its way out through the ice. If they timed it right the melting would stop long before it reached the ice under Jamie's feet, leaving a hollow in the ice, full of meltwater, neatly sealed up. And no swimming highlanders.

But Jamie was no theorist, and he was relieved when time was up and they shut down their blasters, and he was still on dry land, so to speak.

Harry Matthews called down from the surface. 'Running some deep radar from up here, boys. I can see the cavity. Perfect – just as the Doctor wanted it.'

Jamie thumbed his comms studs. 'Doctor, Zoe – d'ye hear that?'

'We did, Jamie,' the Doctor called. 'Splendid! Now, what's next?'

Jamie remembered the plan. 'Well, we'll run a pipe down from the phibian to bring in the cleaning fluid from the hold. We'll have tae fix heating units to keep the meltwater liquid. You said the water down here is full o' funny stuff, funny chemistries, and will freeze very fast otherwise. Oh, and we have to put those little sensor pods of Zoe's in place all through the cavity. We have those in our packs . . . A couple of hours, Doctor, and ye'll be in business.'

'Well done to all of you. Well, get on with it then!'

Over the open comms, Jamie heard Sam and Harry discussing how to handle the pipe from the ship. Stepfather and stepson, separated by a divorce, united in an interesting job. Jamie grinned as he set a heating unit down on the ice beside his feet, got out a small handheld drill and set to work.

41

'Did you hear that, Casey?' Zoe asked.

The little girl sat on a mesh flooring panel, surrounded by a litter of toys. The new blue doll, her favourite, sat on her lap. 'Jay-ee.'

'Yes!' Zoe said, oddly delighted. 'That was Jamie, you recognised him! He's doing very well, isn't he? And soon we'll all be talking together. You and me, and the Doctor and the Arkive.'

'An' MMAC.'

'Are my ears burnin'? Oh, nae, I haven't any ears, ah forget.'

Casey laughed at the gruff voice.

'Hello, MMAC,' Zoe said. 'And I suppose you have your alert software searching for your name being pronounced by three-year-olds, do you?'

'Ah, well, I do keep a weather eye on little Casey. She's a poppet, isn't she? Ye know, I made her a toy once. A model of me.'

'Did she like it?'

'Scared her wee noggin off. Maybe when she's older.'

'Do you feel like running another simulation?'

'Aye, why not? We dinna want to be the ones laggin' behind when everybody's ready tae go.'

'Quite so. I'll set it up.' And Zoe, sitting in the co-pilot's seat of this compact little craft, began throwing switches and tapping screens, running preparatory subroutines.

This particular relic ship, now bolted firmly in place in the great necklace of ice and metal that was the Wheel, wasn't particularly old, though its design harked back to much more venerable craft. It was a shuttle that had once served a base on Mars, but it had the body plan and black-and-white markings of the old NASA Earth-orbit space shuttles of the late twentieth century – though it was smaller, more compact, more robust, and its engines, now safely removed and dismantled, had been a good deal more powerful. But the principles were the same: a lifting body shape, hull coated with white heat-insulation blankets and black tiles resistant to air friction. Jo had recommended it as Zoe's base for her part of the Doctor's project; the shuttle was never going to fly anywhere under its own steam again, but its electronics were still sound, especially the avionics, the flight control.

Oh, and if Zoe wouldn't mind keeping an eye on Casey while she worked – it would free up Jo, she had so much to get through – the little girl would be no trouble – she wouldn't be able to escape as long as Zoe kept the airlock hatches closed . . . And Casey did like Zoe's face, after all. Oh, hadn't Zoe known that?

No, she hadn't. Zoe, puzzled, had stared at her own face in reflective surfaces. She saw a round, very young-looking face, full mouth, wide eyes, framed by neatly cut dark hair . . . It had never occurred to Zoe to wonder how children might react to her. It wasn't a topic that came up in astrophysics classes in the City. Or, indeed, while fighting Cybermen or Ice Warriors with the Doctor.

Anyhow here the two of them were, safely tucked up in the flight deck of this old shuttle, which was warm, humming, with a comforting new-carpet smell. Luckily the little girl seemed more interested in her toys than in the switches and panels all around her. She shouldn't have been able to do any damage – everything should be inert, save the systems Zoe could access from her pilot's position – but this was a space-ship, and it was very old, and you never knew . . .

'Ready to go, MMAC?'

'Aye, when ye are, lassie.'

Screens on the console before Zoe lit up with images of Saturn's rings, the features that were so familiar now, the ringlets like hair strands, the colours, and the spokes and bars and ripples that, they knew now, were the frozen thoughts of the Arkive. And behind her, on a big display flag she had draped over some of the defunct consoles, larger-scale imagery came pouring down, retrieved from MMAC's sensors and from free-flying probes he had sent out over the plane of the ring system.

Casey gurgled, clapping.

Zoe smiled. 'Beautiful, MMAC. And you've made a little girl very happy.'

MMAC laughed again. 'Then ma work is done. Wha' next?'

'Now for the simulated neutrino signal.' She worked a keypad, and a screen filled up with an image of Jamie's detector, like an X-ray photograph, showing a ghostly spherical cavity enmeshed in the shafts and corridors of the deep mines of Mnemosyne. Green crosses showed her the positions of Jamie and the boys, who had stayed at their posts. Now she tapped a tag on the screen. A simulated neutrino pulse washed up from the heart of the moon, causing sparkling collision events all over the detector volume. It was like a firework display in a glass bubble, she thought. And the products of those collisions caused sensors in the detector to light up in turn, all in simulation. The software kicked in, tracing back the products to the collisions that had caused them.

And immediately the screens, and the big display flag, began to scroll with interpretations and amendments, as the software, backed by the chip from the TARDIS's universal translator, began to process the data.

'It's workin',' MMAC said. 'It's a right lash-up. But it's workin', lassie!'

'Well, this is just a simulation, MMAC. Let's not get carried away until we see the real thing.'

She spoke cautiously. But in truth she was delighted; yes, clearly all this was going to work just as she, leading the design, had intended it to.

She sat upright in her chair, intent, calm, poised. She never felt more alive than in moments like this, with a system she thoroughly understood at her command, and colleagues in space and down on the moon ready to work with her, and a fascinating intellectual challenge to be met. As if all the parts of her were working together.

Behind her the little girl gurgled again. Zoe felt a quite unreasonable stab of fondness for her.

'Explain it to me again, Florian,' said Luis Reyes. 'What are you doing here exactly?'

Florian Hart did not reply. She stalked around the room, her skinsuit hood pushed back in this airtight section of the surface facility. Some of her guards stood by, apparently at ease. But Luis noticed that they were all in a position where they could watch him. Other guards had gone off deeper into the facility, accompanied by the Bootstrap techs Florian had brought here.

They'd all flown down here in a small, crowded shuttle, since the Wheel-to-moon cable systems were still out of action, and an uncomfortable little trip it had been too. Around them, immense machines hummed and telltale lights glowed green. These mighty engines pumped air and power into the mineworks below, mineworks idle and abandoned save for two enigmatic travellers, a handful of kids, and the strange alien entities the Doctor claimed he was trying to communicate with.

'Wasting time and money,' Florian said now.

'What?'

'You asked what we're doing here. That's what *you're* doing, Reyes, with your pointless nursemaiding. Just as pointless as all your pottering about and nosing. And all the while you're cashing your fat paycheques, funded by the hard labour of the taxpayers of the solar system.'

He had to laugh at that crude attack. 'Well, it would be hard labour if it was up to you. Come on, Florian. You're being enigmatic, to say the least. Have been ever since Sonia and Jo Laws gave you the clearance to come back here.'

'Pah. I don't need their clearance to do anything.'

'Actually you do. I'm not here to nursemaid you but to inspect what you get up to. Just remember, Florian, I haven't pressed the issue of access to your records. I'm quite sure there will be evidence in there of Blue Dolls and strange mass concentrations at the core and all the rest of it, all inconvenient to you, and all hidden away. I'll leave all that to the investigating commission. But for now – where have those young techs of yours gone? What are they doing, Florian?'

'I don't answer to you.'

'Why do you need a Demeter rocket?'

'I gave Jo Laws a written submission for it.'

'I saw that. It was so vaguely worded that Jo would never have passed it if she wasn't juggling a dozen crises at once, as you surely knew. You're going to take "spare parts" from a corroded relic like that? How old *is* that thing? Why, you don't even use the same materials any more. Using hulks like that for shelter up in the Wheel is one thing. Are you really going to stick a bit of space junk into the middle of a super-modern high-technology facility like this mine?'

'You're not technical. You wouldn't understand.'

'Oh, wouldn't I?'

She glanced at her wrist chronometer. 'Look, I've got a lot to do and not much time to do it in. If you don't mind—' She walked off, towards the work rooms at the rear of the building.

He stood to follow. Immediately a couple of Florian's guards blocked him. He called past them, 'Actually I do mind. I'm not supposed to let you out of my sight.'

'So sue me,' she called back.

'I might just do that.' He glanced at the guards, both powerfully built men in armoured suits. He stepped back. 'Well, you won't mind if I take a look around up here, right?'

'Whatever.'

He waited until she was out of sight.

Then he grinned at the guards. 'Well, you heard the lady. I'm going to take a look around outside the building. That's not restricted, is it?'

The guards exchanged glances. The marginally bigger one shrugged.

'Thanks. Now if one of you wouldn't mind running down a skinsuit check with me . . .'

42

Since Zoe and Sonia had gone back to the Wheel, Phee and the Doctor had been alone in the chamber of the Arkive – alone save for the Blue Doll called First, and Phee wasn't sure if *he* counted as company. They had been here for twenty-four hours already. They had set up a little camp, with fold-out chairs and sleeping bags and a food store brought down from the surface.

Now they were preparing for work. The Doctor had Zoe's instrument pack at his feet, the control panel in his hand. A big display flag stood before them, inert for now, showing pale blue emptiness.

The Blue Doll stood silently with them, facing the hulk of the Arkive, behind its screen of rippling light.

Even up close the Arkive wasn't much to look at, at first glance anyhow. It was a shapeless mass of some kind of hull metal – an alloy of bernalium, the Doctor said. But then he had pointed out features to Phee, and her fascination had grown. The scarring of meteorite strikes. Erosion caused by the interstellar medium, the dust that lay between the stars. Stumps that might once have supported some kind of shield, or sail. Mounts for long-vanished antennae. Even vents like rocket exhausts, scarred and scorched and clogged with debris. All this was evidence of great age, the Doctor said, billions of years perhaps; this artefact might be as old as the Earth itself.

She longed to touch that hull. To rest her human palm on the bernalium alloy. To feel age – to feel space. But nobody knew how toxic that venerable surface might be.

Certainly the hull was intact, however old it was. And inside was – something. Whatever it was consisted of huge masses. Standing close to it, she actually could feel the shifting gravity field of those masses as they rolled and churned. The Doctor speculated that the hull might contain miniature black holes, held suspended in an immensely powerful magnetic field; the holes would serve as an inexhaustible source of energy, as well as causing gravitational fluctuations – and, perhaps, were the source of the neutrino transmissions he had detected. He had said, 'Maybe these black holes, in their ever-changing configuration, even store the "mind" of this being. Its very thoughts. I've seen stranger technologies.'

Phee had stared at him, wondering, when he said things like that, talking about things he couldn't possibly know.

Whatever was inside the hull was functioning, conscious. But was it alive? Even the Doctor hesitated to use that word.

'And now we're going to try to speak to it,' Phee said.

The Doctor looked up from his preparations. 'Hmm?'

'Sorry, Doctor. Thinking out loud.'

'Well, that's the plan. But we are rather improvising,' he said with some pleasure, and Phee got the impression he was having a lot of fun. 'The Arkive is very old, and it's been stuck in this moon for a very long time. Embedded. The very substance of its hull has seeped out into the ice – that's where the bernalium came from. It's old and complicated. And the way we will have to communicate with it is old and complicated too . . . Now, the Arkive clearly has some straightforward communications systems, of which its neutrino beam is surely just one option. I suspect it's been a very long time since it's had a reply. Technologies to detect such beams are still in their infancy in this solar system.'

'Then why does it keep trying?'

'Probably because it can't help itself. And because neutrinos are important to it, given the circumstances of its birth. Neutrinos are produced in floods when a supernova detonates – a massive star explodes – and I rather suspect that's a clue to the Arkive's origins. Such choices aren't made for entirely logical reasons, Phee. These, after all, seem to be cries for help.

'And then there's the gravitational perturbation of the ring particles. I rather suspect that's an unconscious process. The entity in there, in the dark, forever alone, tosses and turns—'

'Like having bad dreams?'

'Yes! And those dreams, those dark thoughts, are stored in the tidal patterns of the rings. It must be able to *sense* those patterns, in a way; it must be aware of the subtleties of the planet's wider gravitational system, the tidal harmonies of Saturn's sixty moons . . . There must be feedback loops in place. But I'm hoping that those perceptions will be greatly enhanced when we start giving it a visual representation of the patterns, a picture of this great buffer of its own dark thoughts. It may be like an expansion of consciousness.'

'You mean, we might wake it up.'

'Exactly, Phee! Well, let's hope so. Now then . . .' He tapped his control console. 'It's all going to be a bit complicated. As soon as Zoe's translated neutrino data starts to come through, and that will be any minute now, I will start to hear it in my suit speakers, and read Zoe's interpretation and commentary on the screen here. Meanwhile MMAC will feed back the ring images directly to the flag here, with translations. I'm going to try to put all this together, and then I'll speak back to the Arkive.'

'Speak? How?'

'How? Why, with my own rather resonant voice as usual. On the assumption that First here can hear what I say, and can pass that straight back to the Arkive. For it's clear that they are in contact. The simplest way is always the best . . . Ah. Here we go. It's begun.'

The flag lit up with a swathe of ring paths, covered with a scrawl of symbols, notes and equations.

The Blue Doll started, as if given an electric jolt.

And Phee felt the black holes inside the Arkive twist and roll, felt it deep in her stomach.

The Doctor leaned down and faced the Doll. 'Arkive. Hello. I'm the Doctor. I can hear your words, in neutrino pulses. I can see your dreams, in swarms of ice grains . . . I'm here to speak to you. Answer any way you like, I'll be able to hear . . .'

There was a kind of flash, like the spark when the Doll had touched Phee's amulet.

And information, words and diagrams, began to pour across the screen, too fast for Phee to read.

The Doctor, staring into the screen, jolted upright, as if shocked. 'Oh!'

'Are you all right, Doctor?'

'Yes – yes, I'm all right. But the flood of information—'

'Doctor?'

'Its mind is bigger than mine, Phee. Bigger, and older. So much older! And it is in such pain . . .'

INTERLUDE

ARKIVE

I

She had sensed their coming. *Others.* Responding at last to one of her lures.

And she had detected the lure's own signal, timed to sound three times in every one of the gas giant's years. She exulted. Somehow the long wait for this response made her triumph all the sweeter.

She remembered how she had created the lures, oh so long ago . . .

Fifty million years ago:

Resilience. Remembrance. Restoration.

All that she was, all that survived of her – and she was all that survived of Home – was embedded in an ice moon. A moon orbiting a planet, a ball of roiling gas, that itself orbited a feeble sun.

This solar system itself had no value for her, no interest. Nor did the life forms that swarmed and died on the surfaces of its planets. A sculpture of debris and rubbish, the system owed its very existence to the destruction of Home.

She had survived in this system of garbage for billions of years.

Survived though she was damaged. The detonation of the star that had destroyed Home had been too severe. It had caught her, it had overwhelmed the elaborate survival mechanisms given her by her designers.

She had not demonstrated Resilience. She could not be certain of the veracity of her Remembrance. And she could not be sure she could fulfil her ultimate goal of Restoration. She could not fulfil her mission.

And so she had formulated a plan. A strategy. If she could not fix herself, if she could not fulfil her mission, then she would return to the arms of those who made her. Who had perished billions of years before. Who had entrusted her with all that they were, all that they could have been. Who would grant her forgiveness.

She would bathe in the light of a long-dead sun. And she would try again.

She would reach through time, even though it would take the sacrifice of this pointless little moon to do it.

She even prepared a fallback.

Deep in the heart of the moon, a kind of clock ticked. Attached to a kind of bomb. Which was meant to open a kind of door, in space and time. It was all terribly crude. Wasteful. But it might work.

She readied herself for the moment, aware that she herself might not survive what was to come. Or if she did survive she might be damaged, her mission further compromised.

But she had a backup plan. That was part of the designers' wise conditioning: always prepare a fallback.

There was intelligence in this system now, a reptilian race that swarmed upon the surface of the third world from the central star. They meant nothing to her. Nothing but an opportunity for exploitation. So she had prepared lures. If she awoke still trapped in this system, then at least, if even just one lure worked, *the past would have been changed.*

And those reptilian beasts would come swarming out here to help her. Laying aside all that they were, all that they aspired to be, to help her effect an escape. Even in her moment of failure they would come, an independent intelligent species, and become her acolytes. The spear-point of a changed history –

Searing light.

The detonation was visible from Earth. And, through a telescope, the scattering of the moon's fragments, quickly gathering in a ragged ring around the parent gas giant.

Across planet Earth, faces were lifted to the light, crowds looking up with intelligence, with curiosity, but with a cold-blooded stillness that would have seemed eerie to any human observer. Pale unblinking eyes watched, and wondered.

But for these people there was a greater emergency. A rogue planet was swimming towards the Earth. Already the reptilian race was withdrawing into the great hibernation caverns that they hoped would protect it from the calamity. The explosion was a light in the sky, soon forgotten.

And so no Silurian eye ever saw the Arkive's lures, most of which were destroyed, but one of which survived to sail through branching ruptures in space and time to travel deeper and deeper into the past . . .

II

One hundred million years ago:
From a distance the animal might have looked like a horse, to human eyes. But humans would not evolve for a hundred million years.

Even the age of the Silurians, a reptilian intelligence, lay some fifty million years in the future, on the other side of the blinding termination that was the asteroid impact that would smash a biosphere.

All that for an unimagined future. For now there were more pressing matters. Hunger. Thirst. Fear for one's eggs. Fear for oneself.

On all fours the beast followed a water course towards a muddy swamp, raising her head to graze on stubby cycads and dwarf trees. Near the water she stood up on her powerful hind legs to reach a succulent branch, balancing with her massive tail. Her front paws had five digits, with hoof-like claws on the fingers and a spiked thumb. She chewed complacently. She was in fact one of the first animals on Earth to have evolved the ability to chew, and that small advantage was the reason there were so many of her kind on the planet.

There was a rumble, like a distant engine.

The chewer stood stock still. Massive as she was, there were predators in this world bigger than she was, killers that could run impossibly fast, with disembowelling claws the size of scimitars. It paid to be wary.

And then she saw the light in the sky, dazzling and bright, like a second sun high above this humid, warm, water-logged proto-England. For an instant it appeared as if a navel had puckered the sky, like a tunnel trying to form. But the navel closed with a brighter detonation of light, and the browser looked away, dazzled.

She did not see the object that followed the wavefront of light, coming from the explosion in space.

Did not see the streak of brilliance it cut across the sky, entering Earth's atmosphere.

Did not feel anything when, almost gently, the object, small, dark, massive, ended its two-billion-kilometre journey by slicing through the chewing browser's brainpan.

Her body fell forward, already lifeless, and her front paw settled over the Arkive's lure.

III

The tunnel through time to Home did not open.

And the reptile creatures did not come for Arkive.

Alone, for long millennia no more than half-conscious, she brooded on her multiple failures.

While on Earth, kingdoms of life rose and fell.

And at last the Others came to her moon.

She sensed their presence. Their noisy drilling. Their crawling into the moon.

She created a thing that could see. She used the factory, the womb, a facility intended to resurrect her makers, to make this crude thing, an eye on a tripod.

The seeing thing met one of the Others, in a deep tunnel. A child. It was not afraid of the tripod.

She created again. This time, beings like the child. She sent them out in their turn, to observe, to learn, to explore.

Had the Others been drawn here by the lure? Perhaps. But rather than seeking her out, finding out how they could serve her, they seemed to be drilling for *her* hull metal, her bernalium, which over aeons had seeped into the cold ice around her.

She bellowed protests, blasts of pure neutrinos.

None heard her. None replied.

In frustration, her substance twisted and turned in the recesses of her hull, and her agonies, transmitted by gravitational perturbations, were recorded in the roiling rings that surrounded this gas giant. Her biography, written in whirling bits of ice.

At least these Others had come with technology. Materials that could be adapted to her purpose: to build a way to the past, a more subtle design this time. She instructed her creatures to take what they needed. To bring it to the moon from the Others' own constructs.

And to build a device, a doorway deep into the past. A doorway to allow her to go home, at last.

Once again she would pour what was left of the mass-energy of a moon into this endeavour, and more. Whatever was needed. She did not care what she destroyed in this system. The whole system was garbage, a secondary product of the detonation which had destroyed Home. Let it burn, as long as it bought her escape.

But her creatures were slow and stupid. *(Or I am.)* They tried but failed to build the machine she wanted. *(Or I have failed.)*

Then more of the Others came probing. Digging. Stealing the bernalium of her flesh, once again. She made more creatures, purely destructive now, to defend herself.

But still they came. Burning, blasting her soldiers. She drove them out of the moon. Her moon. For a brief time she was alone once more, with her creatures, her half-built time machine and her brooding.

And then one of the Others came to her. Looked into the face of her creature, so Arkive could see. Spoke, so Arkive could hear.

Hello. I'm the Doctor.

43

'No more!' The Doctor dropped the control console and staggered back, clutching his head. He stared at the Blue Doll. 'And to think she once had the capacity to recreate a civilisation. And all she was capable of, in the end, was *you*. Oh, you poor creatures . . .' His big hands covered his face.

The Blue Doll watched impassively.

Phee ran to him, took his arms, and settled him in one of the fold-out chairs. 'Doctor? Come, sit down . . . Do you want some water, or—'

'So alone. So alone!' And he lowered his hands from his face. He had been weeping, she saw, those deep blue eyes brimming with tears. 'The emptiness – to be alone for nearly half the age of the universe . . .'

Phee could think of nothing to do but hold him.

And when he was done, he told her the story.

'It needed to apologise, I suppose,' the Doctor whispered. 'And, above all, it wanted a chance to try again. To try to launch itself into the past.

'Its first attempt to build a time machine caused nothing but the destruction of a moon – and the creation of the rings of Saturn. It must have been a crude effort, a wormhole, perhaps. But it did at least succeed

263

in sending an allohistorical lure deep back into time, which, after going wildly off course, brought you and your family here. And now it's attempting to build *another* machine, to take it home at last. A more subtle design, but one likely to be just as destructive . . . What extraordinary determination, by this blind, crippled thing, sustained across aeons! Hammering away at the same simple objective – to find a way home, back to the lost past.'

'We must help it,' Phee said.

The Doctor was recovering his self-control. 'Yes. And the Blue Dolls, come to that. What a plight for them – to know you are a made thing, and made by something itself mad! For everything about the Arkive is worn down, faulty, misfiring. Its artificial womb should have been capable of so much more than these shabby travesties. Well, I have achieved one thing – no more conflict. No more armies of Blue Soldiers rising up to strike down the human invaders. I feel assured of that – as long as we keep good faith.'

Phee was trying to work all this out. 'So the supernova that ended the Arkive's civilisation gave birth to this solar system. To Earth.' She looked at her hands. 'To me.'

'Yes. The very atoms of your body were baked in the fires of supernovas.'

'But at what cost? Did *they* have to die so I could live?'

He folded her hands in his. 'That's a question not the greatest philosophers of all the ages could answer – not even the philosophers of my own people, who lived beyond the ages altogether. All life relies on the death of others, one way or another. One must merely make the best of the moment, I suppose.'

'And remember those who went before.'

'Oh, yes, Phee. Always that—'

An alarm sounded in their suit speakers.

The Doctor tapped a button. 'Yes? What is it?'

It was Jo Laws. 'Doctor – is Phee there? Are you both all right?'

'Yes, she's safe with me.'

'Good. Now listen to this. It's a recording, we picked it up a moment ago . . .'

The voice was a breathless whisper, from a mouth held close to a small skinsuit microphone. 'This is Luis Reyes. PEC ident 287/856-78. I'm on the surface of Mnemosyne. Near a mine facility, ah, Building Number 4-A, in Quadrant Four. And I'm in the rocket hulk Florian Hart brought down to the surface. The old Demeter missile. Florian's up to something. I'm amazed her goons let me climb around in this thing in the first place. Maybe they thought I wouldn't understand what I saw.

'Listen, whoever's out there. *The missile was armed.* It clearly carried a warhead. I say "carried" – I'm in the nose cone now and I can see fresh cuts in the wiring, scarring on mounts that have been sawn through, a panel cut out of the hull to take away the warhead. I know these old hulks were supposed to be made safe before being brought to the Wheel. I don't know how it got here with a warhead in the first place. I can only tell you what I'm seeing. There *was* a warhead in here, and now it's been taken out by Florian and her goons . . .'

As Phee listened to this in horror, she saw that the Blue Doll, First, was reacting. Leaning in to listen.

Luis continued, 'I think it's clear what's going on. Florian sees whatever is in the heart of this moon as an obstacle to her ambitions. All she wants is to be rid of it, regardless of the cost, human and cultural. And I think she's going to use this old warhead. I'm rusty on century-old ICBMs. The Demeters were armed with Z-bombs, weren't they? Planet-busters, they were called. I don't know how much harm might be done if she manages to set the thing off. She has to be stopped. And I – oh. Hi, guys. No, don't shoot! I'll come quietly. Empty hands, see? Oh, by the way, I'm sorry I called you goons. I meant the other goons . . .'

There was silence. He had been cut off.

'A planetbuster,' Phee said in horror. 'Do you think he's right?'

'I fear so, Phee. And we must—'

The floor shook, shuddered, threw them up in the air. They landed face down, but still the shuddering went on, and now the ice walls of this cavern creaked and cracked.

Phee stared around wildly. 'Doctor! Look at the Arkive!'

The whole of that battered hull was shaking, quivering, as if tremendous detonations were going off within it. The sense of huge energies – and, Phee thought, of huge anger – was palpable.

The lone Blue Doll stood before the Arkive, motionless, like a child standing before an oncoming tank. A great section of roof cracked off and came loose and fell with a slow-motion crash.

The Doctor said, 'It's heard what we said. It's reacting. Well, why wouldn't it? Moments after I promised it we would do it no harm, it's been threatened with annihilation!'

Phee tried to stand, grabbing for the Doctor's hand. 'We must get out of here!' She dragged him by main force to the side-shaft out of the chamber, while huge blocks of ice hailed down from the roof and walls.

And another shudder shook the whole moon.

44

Suddenly the moon ice erupted, all around the equator.

Though she was sealed up inside a windowless hulk, Zoe saw what was coming through a multitude of sensors. Saw by deep radar and gravitational sensors the churning of the singularities of the Arkive, the huge masses at the core of Mnemosyne. Saw by seismometer networks planted throughout the moon a series of massive, convulsing quakes. Saw by remote cameras mounted on MMAC and other free-flying platforms the cracks form in the surface, and huge chunks of ice breaking away and flying out from the equator of the spinning moon.

Saw that spray of lethal blocks head straight for the fragile habitats of the Wheel of Ice, which orbited in precisely that equatorial plain.

And saw a lethal shard, spinning and glittering, come sailing up towards her shuttle from the broken surface of Mnemosyne. A mass of a million tonnes, perhaps, heading straight for her, and the fragile old hulk that cradled her.

She felt no fear. Perhaps the shock was too great for that. The Doctor and Jamie were both down on the shivering moon, and might already be dead. Was this her own death heading for her, this fist of rock-ice that would swat her more casually than she would brush aside a fly?

She watched the first of the great blocks reach the Wheel and smash through the wall of a fragile ice bubble. She saw it all quite clearly, across an arc of the Wheel in which she was embedded. Air and water froze in a glittering spray, and people were sent spinning into space. She was too far away to see if they wore skinsuits. It all seemed very abstract.

Belatedly, alarms sounded in the hull.

And Casey started crying, scared by the alarm. Sitting on the floor, surrounded by her toys, the little girl's face was twisted, red. 'Ma! Ma!'

Zoe rushed to her, picked her up, clutched her close, rocked her and stroked her hair. 'There, there. Don't cry. You're safe with me. Everything will be all right.'

To lie was illogical! And yet the little girl calmed, just a bit. So there was a deeper truth than just fact, Zoe thought. A deeper communication, a deeper human truth that they were sharing. The two of them were lost in a lethal universe that might kill them at any second. But at least they had each other.

Zoe slapped a button to shut down the proximity alarm. There was an instant of calm. Chaos outside, but inside this hull with its clean-carpet smell and humming of electronic fans and air pumps, all was orderly for a moment. Casey's crying softened to a whimper.

And the ice rock fragment hit them with a sideswipe, like a mighty fist driving into the hull. Zoe and Casey were thrown against a wall, bounced away.

Zoe knew immediately it was a glancing blow, since she was not dead. The old Mars shuttle was still intact around her. But the spin gravity was gone, and she and Casey went floating up into the air. The impact must have severed the hull's connections to the rest of the Wheel, and it had gone whirling off into space.

Then it got worse. All the screens and sensor displays fritzed and turned a useless blue. The voices from the speakers were cut off. The lights blinked out. For a heartbeat they were in utter darkness, before dim red emergency lamps cut in. And the pumps of the air scrubber system rattled and died.

For now they still had air to breathe. Blinded, it seemed, the hull's comms systems and sensors wrecked. Helpless. But still alive. They were drifting in the air, the little girl still hugged close to Zoe's chest. The hull turned slowly around them, a slow rotation imparted by that glancing blow. Casey had stopped crying. She pointed, over Zoe's shoulder. 'Oo.'

Zoe turned to see the child's blue rag doll floating in the air, cart-wheeling slowly.

When the moonquakes began, Jamie, Sam, Dai and Sanjay were still at the outer shell of the Doctor's neutrino detector. They'd stayed in place to tend to any leaks or malfunctions.

Now Jamie felt the huge convulsions, the very walls shuddering around him, and he heard distant thunderclaps, it sounded like, in the thin air of the shafts. Suddenly this whole wretched moon, a big chunk of ice riddled with tunnels and shafts, felt very fragile to Jamie, as if it all might fall in on him at any minute. And that was even before this wretched Z-bomb they'd all heard Luis Reyes blab about went up.

But, as he saw with a quick glance, by some miracle the Doctor's detector was still intact, the thin remnant ice shell still holding, and containing the sloshing fluid within.

It was Sam, of the four of them, who recovered first. 'Seal up your skinsuits. There are going to be breaches, the air could be lost. And we should keep together. Come to me.'

'Good idea.' Jamie hurried towards Sam's position, through tunnels that shook, the walls cracking, huge sheets of ice flaking away. He sealed up his skinsuit as he moved, and called, 'Is everybody all right? Sanjay, Dai—'

'I'm here.'

'Me too.'

And the tunnel ahead of Jamie was about to close up, with a huge fall of ice coming down in slow motion from the ceiling. He didn't know a way around it – didn't even know if there *was* a way – he dived forward, wriggled under the fall, snatched his legs out of the way just as thousands of tonnes of ice closed up like a huge mouth.

Jamie, breathing hard, found himself looking at Sam and the others, in a short corridor.

'Nice move, granddad,' Sam said.

For a moment the four of them, reunited, wide-eyed, put their arms around each other's shoulders. Like a band of soldiers, Jamie thought, about to go into battle.

'What's going on?' Dai asked. 'Has anybody got a comms signal?'

None of them did.

Sanjay said, 'And the shaking – it's like the whole moon is having a huge fit.'

'We've got to get out of here,' Jamie said.

'Right,' Sam said. 'But how? Look.' He pointed to the side-shaft that had brought them here. It was blocked by huge fallen masses.

Jamie thought hard. 'So we can't go that way. But when one shaft closes up another must open. Stands to reason, doesn't it?' He wasn't sure how true that was – what did he know about shuddering moons of ice? – but he glanced around at their faces behind their visors, and they nodded. 'So we find another way. All we have to do is keep moving up. Right? Get to the surface. Then find some way off this thing and back to yon Wheel.'

Dai nodded. 'Lead the way, granddad.'

'Och, less of that,' Jamie grumbled under his breath. He glanced around, saw what looked like a passable way, and set off.

Well, it was never going to be easy. The old passages had been chosen by the miners for their wideness and straightness, or else had been cut through the ice purposefully. The chasms opened up by these bizarre quakes were random and they felt like it, with jagged sections of wall ready to rip through your flimsy skinsuit at the slightest misstep, and passages where they narrowed and blocked your way entirely, and you had to double back. There were no lights here, none of the handy light globes that had been scattered through the mine workings, and they only had their suit lamps. And, after a time, when they passed through a seal, no air either. But Jamie tried to take encouragement from that, because, he reasoned, if the passages were open to space there might be a way up to the surface.

The hardest thing of all, though, was telling which way up he was. The gravity was so low that there was no strong sense of up or down, and he fretted he had lost his way, like a drowning man swimming down into the depths rather than up into the air.

But he wasn't alone. The boys worked together, watching out for each other, muttering advice. They were calm, brave, sensible, even though he could detect the fear in their voices. Jamie felt obscurely proud of them. Not that he was going to tell them so, for fear of being called granddad again.

He had no idea how long they blundered through the broken carcass of the moon. He deliberately tried not to track the time. So he was oddly surprised when he pushed his way out of a crevasse, and suddenly there was black space above him.

The four of them stood open-mouthed under a sky full of the fragments of the shattered Wheel, ice bubbles and rocket hulls and severed cables, drifting apart.

Sam swore. 'It must have been the quakes . . . My mum's up there. No wonder the comms are down.'

Jamie could see the fear and anxiety in his face. In all their faces. All of their families were in peril. As were Zoe, he realised, and the Doctor. But he put those thoughts aside.

'We have to think about ourselves,' he said urgently. 'That's all we can do for now. Any idea where we are?'

Sam looked around and pointed. 'There.' A low building, visible over the moon's close horizon. 'That looks like the Quad Four facility where we landed in the phibian. We haven't come far, after all that. But where's the phibian itself?'

Dai wordlessly pointed upwards. The craft hovered in space, maybe a kilometre above the surface, a toy.

Given the moon seemed to be shaking itself to pieces, Jamie wondered why Harry hadn't brought the ship down in search of Sam and the others. And there was no movement at the surface facility.

Some instinct made him peel the blaster from his back. 'We don't know what we're walking into here.'

'We've got no choice,' Sam said reasonably. 'It's either go to that building or wait out here until our skinsuits pack up.'

'Fair enough. But be ready for trouble, lads.'

Sanjay wielded his own blaster and checked it. 'You do realise these are fixed to a baby setting, Sam.'

'Yeah, well, at least they look scary.'

'One thing at a time,' Jamie said gently. 'Come on.'

He led the way to the facility, loping over the surface. It was a relief to be in the open, to be able to move relatively freely, despite the strangeness of the low gravity conditions, the constriction of the skinsuit. But still the moon shuddered and jolted.

They found that most of the facility was open to vacuum, but a small section was still airtight, beyond an inner airlock. Inside, in an otherwise deserted personnel room with a kitchen, bathroom and a couple of fold-down beds, they found Harry Matthews and Karen Madl sitting on the floor, back to back, bound together with lengths of cable. Jamie ran over, opened his suit, pulled out his dirk and sawed at their bindings.

Harry's relief at seeing Sam was deep and obviously genuine. 'Thank heavens you're safe, Sam.'

'If not, Mum would have killed you.'

'Tell me about it.'

'What happened here?' Jamie snapped.

'Florian Hart,' said Karen savagely, rubbing her wrists. 'We were relaxing in here. Drinking coffee! She and her Bootstrap goons just jumped us. She stole our ship! Left us to our chances down here and took off to safety.'

'Just after Luis Reyes sent out that message about the Z-bomb,' Harry said. 'She must have suspected there would be a reaction.'

'So she's up in the ship now?' Jamie asked.

'Yes.'

'What about Luis?'

Harry shrugged. 'He was in the next building. Presumably trussed up just as we are.'

Sanjay said, 'I'll go and find him.' He hurried off, sealing up his suit.

'The ship's safe enough,' Jamie said. 'And Florian inside it, I shouldn't wonder. But the Wheel—'

Harry nodded grimly. 'We saw some of it. But Florian shut down our audio communications before she took off. Oh, Jamie, your friend the Doctor was trying to reach you.'

Jamie hurried over to a comms console. 'Which switch?'

'Just press the big green button.'

'– calling Jamie. Or anybody else who can hear me. This is the Doctor, with Phee Laws, we're both fine, but I need to speak to somebody, anybody—'

'Doctor!'

'This is the Doctor. If you can hear me—'

Harry called, 'Press the yellow button to transmit, Jamie.'

'Och, these gadgets – Doctor! Doctor, can ye hear me?'

'Jamie! Oh, what a relief to hear your voice. Are you all right?'

'Aye, fine. A bit shook up. And you?'

'Still in one piece, but I fear we're trapped here, near the chamber of the Arkive; its shuddering did rather a lot of damage to our escape routes, though I hope we're calming it now.'

'What about Zoe?'

'Well, she's up on the Wheel . . . I'm afraid I've no idea what's become of her. But I will need to speak to her in a minute if you can find a way – and MMAC, come to that.'

Jamie stared at the console, baffled. 'Aye – whatever ye want –'

'I'll take care of it,' Karen said, at his side.

'Thank you, Ms Madl,' the Doctor called. 'Now listen to me, Jamie, this is urgent. *We must defuse that Z-bomb.* If it goes up – well, it may or may not destroy the Arkive, the entity at the heart of the moon, but the wider damage it will do is incalculable. It must be stopped.'

'Leave it tae me.'

'If you get through to the bomb, we'll work out what you have to do with it. But you must expect trouble on the way, Jamie. Florian Hart is bound to have left it defended, even though she must know she is sacrificing her guards to do it – but that's Florian for you.'

Jamie wielded his blaster, and looked around at the young men with him. 'Trouble, eh? Who's wi' me?'

Sam and Dai, all sealed up their skinsuits.

Harry quickly printed off a map from one of the consoles. 'This is a map of the moon, the interior, a recent radar scan. The quakes are continuing, and shafts might still open or close. But look at this.' Harry pointed to a hard purple dot, deep in the moon. '*That* is the Z-bomb. You can tell by the radiation signature.'

Sam snatched the map out of his hands. 'Thanks, Harry.'

But Harry was now pulling on his own Bootstrap-issue skinsuit. 'Oh, I'm coming with you. You kids can't have all the fun.'

'Good,' said Jamie. 'The more the better. Time for a wee rebellion, lads.' He raised his blaster over his head. '*Creag an tuire!*'

They lifted their spacesuited arms and roared.

45

' F 'ightened!'

'I know, dear. I know you're frightened. But I'm not. See? Look, I'm smiling. And dolly's smiling too.'

'Wan' Mum.'

'I know you do. But all we can do is wait until somebody picks up the shuttle.'

'Wan' Phee. Wan' Sam!'

'I know. I know! And I want Jamie and the Doctor, you silly little girl. But I'm all you've got! Oh no, no, don't cry, I didn't mean to be sharp – oh, why are children such a mystery? I really am so unprepared for this—'

'Story.'

'What's that?'

'Tell me story.'

'Well, I don't know any stories. I didn't grow up with stories. I read stories now. *Brave New World* is a good story but I don't think it's suitable for a little girl . . . Oh, I know.'

'Story?'

'We used to read this funny old strip cartoon in the *Hourly Telepress*.

When we were supposed to be swotting up on dull stuff like export figures . . . Oh, I'm doing this all wrong, aren't I? Look, come here. I'll strap myself in this chair, and you sit in my lap. Now then – once upon a time there was a hero. He was a big strong fellow, and his name was the Karkus.'

'Karku'?'

'Karkus! That's right, like "carcass", I suppose. He was big and strong, and his skin was bright green – I think – and he wore purple tights and silver boots, and a mask and a big black cape. Like a display flag. I say he was a hero, but he wasn't very clever. Not really . . . Now there was a little girl, called, umm—'

'Phee!'

'Yes, all right – Phee! Now one day Phee was being a good girl, she was helping her mummy and playing with her toys. And Mummy was making, umm, an apple pie. When suddenly the Karkus burst in! Why, he just kicked the door down, and he walked in, and he had this great big gun. It was an antimolecular ray disintegrator! And he said, "Obey . . . or . . . I . . . fire!"

'Well, Phee wasn't afraid, but Mummy said, "What do you want?" And the Karkus, he was always a bit greedy, he said, "Apple . . . pie!" Because he always talked like that, you see.'

'App-oo . . . pie!'

'Yes, that's it! Well, Mummy was shocked. "What, all of it? But what will there be for Sam's tea if you eat all of it?" But all the Karkus would say was, "Apple . . . pie!" '

'App-oo . . . pie!'

'"Oh, well," Mummy said, "you'd better have it then." So the Karkus came lumbering across the kitchen, like this – he always walked like this – heading straight for the apple pie. But Phee was a very brave little girl, and do you know what she did? She stuck her leg out, and she tripped up the Karkus so he went splat! – on the floor. And she got hold of his gun, and said, "Now you're my prisoner!" '

'Ooh.'

'Yes! And the Karkus said, "I . . . am . . . your . . . slave. Command . . . me!" Because that was all you had to do with the Karkus, you see. Beat him once, and he was your loyal servant forever. So Phee said, "Well, for a start you can get up and tidy up that door you kicked in. What a mess!" "I . . . obey," said the Karkus. And he went to fix the door with his, umm, magic door repairer. And when he'd done that – oh!'

'Karkus!'

'I think somebody's trying to contact us. That green light . . . I think there's some smart circuitry in this old shuttle trying to self-repair, and fix up an emergency comms system. Gosh! I wonder who it is. Maybe it's the Karkus, coming to save us.'

'Karkus! Karkus! App-oo . . . pie!'

'All right, the story. Well, when the Karkus had fixed the kitchen door . . .'

46

Harry's map showed that the Z-bomb had been placed not far from one of the main vertical access shafts. Not surprising, thought Jamie, since that was the way Florian's emplacement team would have gone in to deliver it.

But when Jamie's amateur bomb-disposal team got there they found the shaft blocked by big ice boulders.

'Infall from the quakes,' Sam suggested.

'Maybe,' Jamie growled. 'Or Florian's bombers might have smashed it in after 'em.'

'So what do we do? Looking for another way in could take hours – days, even.'

'Time we might no' have,' Jamie said. 'Can we no' just get this stuff out o' the way?'

'With what?' Sam lifted his blaster. 'Mum set our weapons so weak they wouldn't cut a cake.'

Harry grinned, and raised his own blaster, liberated from the Bootstrap surface facility. 'This might have a little more poke.' He raised it, and fired point blank at the uppermost boulder in the shaft. They all ducked back as the boulder exploded in a spray of a kind of thin snow, settling rapidly. 'After you,' Harry said mildly.

So they worked their way down the shaft, with Harry smashing the worst of the blockages out of the way. The ladder set into the wall had been badly damaged during the quakes, but Jamie found it was easy to float from rung to rung; there was plenty of time to grab a handhold as you drifted down.

Soon they were at the bottom of the shaft. Harry, without looking up, studied his map and pointed. 'This way.'

'Ye mean,' Jamie said grimly, 'the way past yon Blue Soldiers?'

There was a mass of the figures, eerie, still, their bare artificial flesh coated with frost, blocking the passage. They hadn't formed up in a rank as humans might have; instead they were heaped up on each other at all angles, like pegs forced into a hole. But they had their heads raised, their eyes open, and they stared at Jamie and his team.

'Leave this to me,' said Harry grimly, and he moved forward with blaster raised. 'It will be nice to extract a little payback.'

'No.' Jamie grabbed his arm. 'Wait. Let's try talkin' first.'

'Talk? To those plastic monsters? Are you mad?'

'Let's at least try.'

Harry stared at him. Then he shrugged, and backed away.

Jamie fixed his blaster on its sling on his back, and stepped forward, arms open, gloved hands empty. 'I know the Arkive can see me, through your eyes. Or it can see through the Dolls, the Doctor says, so it stands to reason it can see through you too, right? So listen to me. I'm not gonna hurt ye. That's what the Doctor told ye, isn't it? But we have to get past. There's a bomb that's gonna blow us all to kingdom come, if we can't stop it. And,' he added on impulse, 'if there's anythin' of Dr Sinbad Omar left in ye Blue fellows, and he died so ye could live, then ask yerselves what he would do.'

Harry snorted, and raised his blaster. 'You're wasting your time.'

'Let's just see.'

There was silence. Time stretched. Jamie imagined he could hear ticking – a clock attached to the bomb that might kill them all.

Then, as one, the Blue Soldiers rustled backwards, squeezing back down the passageway. They didn't retreat entirely, but they left a way wide enough for the humans to pass through.

Jamie grinned. 'Told ye. Now let's get on with it.' And he led the way forward.

To get through the passage he had to step, gingerly, on plastic-smooth chests and legs and even faces. The Blues did not so much as flinch; they might have been carved from solid marble. Jamie tried not to show his own fear, to avoid sparking off some kind of incident.

At last they were through. Jamie emerged into a larger chamber, lit by a few scattered light globes. And immediately there was a flash of light, a soundless splintering of ice rock in the vacuum above his head, a hail of fragments. Sam shoved him in the back and they both fell to the ground. The rest of the party squirmed down around them.

'Och,' said Jamie, winded, embarrassed at having to be saved. 'Now some beggar's shooting at us!'

'Florian's guards,' Sam said.

'They're here to guard the bomb,' said Harry. 'That's it. Straight ahead. I recognise it from footage of the wars of those days . . .'

Jamie dared to lift his head. At the rear of the chamber the ice had been shaped into a kind of rectangular alcove. On a shelf sat an object like a fat suitcase, pearly white, smooth. It was a beautiful bit of technology. But a small console sat on the top of it, with green-glowing lights, and a display showing numbers – numbers counting down. Jamie had seen enough bombs to recognise certain unmistakeable characteristics.

Another blaster shot came zinging across the chamber, lower this time, making him duck back down.

Harry murmured grimly, 'I suppose you want to try talking to these chaps, do you?'

'Well, it's worth a try. And besides we don't know how many there are. But how do we call them? We're in vacuum, aren't we?'

'Wait a minute.' Harry tapped at stud controls on his own skinsuit neck, and then at Jamie's.

'– clear off,' came a crisp voice. 'This is Bootstrap business. And this is a hazardous area. You're advised to turn around and clear off out of here. We mean you no harm, but you may come to harm even so.'

Jamie, exhausted, his mind drained, tried to work out what to say to get past this latest obstacle.

But Sam touched his arm. 'Take a breather, granddad.'

'What?'

'I know this guy.'

'You *know* him?'

Sam shrugged inside his suit. 'The Wheel's a small place. The whole Saturn system's a small place, in human terms. You get to know people. He's OK, even though he's a Bootstrap goon. Let me try.' He pressed studs at his own neck. 'Hey, Booster. Booster Cavey?'

'What? Sam? Is that you?'

'Yes, it's me. Sam, who beat you at three-dee dodgeball in that tournament in Res Five that time.'

'Sam, who I taught everything he knows about playing the drums.'

'Sure you did.'

'Sam . . . I'd much rather not have to shoot you.'

'Well, ditto, Booster. Although,' he muttered to Jamie, 'with my mum's kiddie settings on the blaster I'd do no worse than tickle him. Look, Booster – that's a bomb you're guarding there.'

'Sure. A shaped cavity charge. Shortly we'll get the order to fall back, then it will go off, and cut a new shaft to the bernalium workings.'

Sam shook his head. 'No. You've been lied to, Booster. First of all, there won't be any call to fall back. And second, it won't be just cutting a shaft. You have to believe me . . .'

And he began to explain Florian's plot, as he understood it, with interjections from Harry and the others.

Meanwhile Jamie spoke softly. 'Doctor – Zoe – I hope ye can hear me – I don't know if ye can see what I see. There's the famous bomb. And I think I can guess what those numbers countin' down mean. I'm all for talkin' our way past these lads, but then I'm gonna need ye to tell me what to do. How do ye defuse a Z-bomb?' He peered harder. 'An answer in six minutes or less would be dandy. Five minutes fifty-nine seconds. Fifty-eight . . .'

'It's all ma fault. All o' it.'

'MMAC? MMAC! Is that you?'

'Zoe? Where are ye?'

'I'm in a defunct shuttle. A Mars ground-to-orbit ship I think. We've been patched together thanks to some miracle coordinated by the Doctor, and whoever's still alive and functioning on the Wheel.'

'I see ye. Is that wee Casey I hear wi' ye? I'll come get ye, just as soon as—'

'No! No, listen to me, MMAC. There's something much more important we have to do first.'

'Can I keep on savin' folk as we talk? I'm squirtin' around pickin' up bits o' the Wheel afore they drift too far away.'

'Of course. But, look, MMAC – we have to talk about Z-bombs.'

'Aye! Like the beast Florian Hart smuggled down to the moon. The beast I let lie in some old Demeter booster. Aye, lass, I know all about Z-bombs. And I know I failed.'

'Failed? What do you mean?'

'I was supposed tae make this Wheel safe. To build it out o' safe components. I was supposed tae check o'er all the old junk I scrabbled together – all the old shuttles and boosters and missiles. Empty out the fuel, an' toxic fluids. Disarm explosive bolts – anythin' like that. An' if I found a planetbuster bomb or anythin' like it I was tae throw it into the sun! That was ma job. An' I didnae do it.'

'You didn't find the Z-bomb warhead in that old Demeter rocket.'

'Nae.'

'*But that's impossible,* MMAC. Don't you see? There's no way you could have missed such a device. It would have violated all your programming – it simply isn't logical. MMAC, I'm sorry to tell you this, but I believe your memory must have been tampered with.'

'What? Ah, hush ye.'

'I know it's difficult to accept. But it's simple enough to do, believe me, especially with a primitive substrate like yours.'

'Wha'? I'm state o' the art! Or was.'

'Sorry. I didn't mean that. Look, I can do a simple trace – I can run it from here . . . Wait a minute. This might sting a bit.'

'Ooh.'

'It will pass . . . Ah. There. Can you sense that deleted region?'

'Yes . . . No. I know I've forgotten somethin' . . .'

'But you don't know what it is. Precisely! It's been quite coarsely done. Look at the inputs and outputs to that region, MMAC. Remember what you were handling at the time.'

'A Demeter rocket!'

'Yes. MMAC, you've done nothing wrong. You would never have let through a planetbuster bomb. But they didn't let you see it, and then deleted any memories of that moment of blindness. It must have been done long ago, all in preparation for a contingency like this.'

'Why, the schemin', connivin' – we've got tae put a stop tae this.'

'Exactly! Now, I know you can recognise a Z-bomb. But do you know how they work? In particular – how do you defuse one?'

'I'll look it up. And *then* I'll come and save ye. But Zoe, one question—'

'Yes?'

'Why's Casey wearing a cape?'

47

As soon as the data from MMAC was downloaded to the Doctor, Jamie got to work.

The Doctor's voice was an insect buzz in his ears. 'That's it. Take that second screw right out. Who would have thought that your dirk would make such a handy screwdriver?'

Jamie was crouched before the bomb. He took the loosened screw between forefinger and thumb, his hands clumsy in their skinsuit gloves, and set it aside. This was the last stage of the disarmament. He'd already worked through a series of codes, entered on a keypad. Now there was this last bit of physical disassembly to do. It wasn't particularly warm in this cavern, and the sleek body of the bomb gave off no discernible heat, but Jamie was sweating profusely. But he had no way of mopping a brow sealed up behind a spacesuit visor. And he had to shift to keep his own shadow from blocking his view; the light was very poor.

'Jamie—'

'Aye, who'd a thought that about ma dirk?'

'All right, Jamie, stay calm.'

'Don't tell me to stay calm, yer blitherin' Sassenach.'

'Well, Jamie, I'm neither blithering nor a Sassenach, as you know very well. Now, you need to take the cover off the timer unit. You might need to use your dirk to prise it free . . .'

'No, it's come away fine.' The cover was a complex box of metal punctured with holes. When he lifted it away that glaring countdown clock still remained, but he had exposed a tangle of cables, wires and electronic components underneath.

'The matter is pressing, Jamie,' the Doctor said, with only a trace of anxiety in his voice. 'As it stands the time left is—'

'Dinna tell me. It won't make me do the job better, will it?'

'Probably not, no.'

'So wha' next?'

'Now you have to isolate the wires going from the timer unit into the body of the bomb, to the detonator. They should be obvious, according to MMAC and Zoe. The detonator is actually a four-stage process, with conventional explosives triggering a fission explosion, which then sets off a shaped thermonuclear detonation, which in turn—'

'Aye, ye can draw me a picture later. *Which wires*, Doctor?'

'The red and the blue ones. A bundle of four.'

'I canna see the colours too well. The light in here—'

'The ones at the front of the timer.'

'Got 'em.' Jamie grabbed the wires and yanked them out of the bomb casing.

'Whatever you do, don't pull them out of the casing.'

'What! Ye might have said!'

'Well, you might wait to be told what to do! Since we're all still alive I take it you haven't done too much damage.'

'Get on with it, Doctor.'

'All right. Now you must take your dirk and cut the wires, in a certain sequence. Two reds, then the single blue, then the final red.'

'Which reds first?'

'Well, it doesn't matter, Jamie. As long as the blue is third of the four. It's just another code, and that's the key.'

Jamie took the wires in his hand. In the shifting light of the suit lamps all the wires looked more greyish than either red or blue. 'And if I get it wrong?'

'Well, you won't have time to know about it. I suggest getting a move on, Jamie.'

'All right, all right . . .'

Which first? One of the wires looked that bit darker than the rest – not so much blue as dark purple versus light purple. He picked one of the other wires, and cut that.

And lived. The bits of cut wire retracted, vanishing into the casing.

Now two light ones, one darker. Two reds left, one blue. He picked one of the similar ones. Cut it.

And lived. The wire snaked away.

But now he fumbled the remaining two wires, and when he picked them up again, he wasn't sure if he had them the same way around as before. Which was red, which was blue? Blue had been the marginally darker one – hadn't it? He shifted his position, trying to get a bit more light.

He glanced at the clock. *Twenty seconds.*

'Jamie, I do suggest—'

'Aye, I know. Eeny meeny miney moe.'

'What did you say?'

'Just kidding.' But he wasn't, not really. He chose a wire, cut it.

And lived.

There was a scream of rage in his earphones.

The Doctor laughed. 'Florian Hart! So you can see what we've done! The game's up, Florian.'

'Not yet, Doctor. Nobody defies me. Don't believe you can hide from my wrath.'

In the cavern of the Arkive the Doctor was gleefully hugging both Phee and an unresponsive First.

Then Luis Reyes called. 'Doctor. Reyes here. I'm with Sanjay. We're in the surface facility, code number—'

'Yes, yes, Luis—'

'I can see her. Florian Hart. She's come straight down out of the phibian ship on a scooter. She's moving at a fair lick, and I suspect she's armed.'

'You do surprise me.'

'She's heading for her new trial bore, off to the east of my position. Leads pretty much straight to the Arkive cavity, Doctor. Where you are. Nobody we've got is going to reach her in time. And, Doctor, her line about how you can't hide? I suspect she's using thermal imaging gear. Looking for your body heat. Standard issue, used to search for trapped miners.'

'Hmm. So it's not over yet. Thank you, Luis.'

Phee tugged his arm. 'Doctor, what are we going to do?'

He looked at her absently, his crumpled face rather blank; he was clearly thinking hard. 'Well, for a start, *you* are going to do nothing. Just stay here. And keep First with you.'

'Here?' Phee, uncomprehending, glanced around at the mute bulk of the Arkive. 'But this is where she's headed!'

'Quite. But I can't allow her to get here. I should think even a blaster would be powerful enough to do rather a lot of harm to the Arkive. No, no, I can't allow her to come here – and therefore this is the safest place for you two. Do you see?'

Phee tried to puzzle that out. 'I . . . think so.'

'Good, good. And then I must stop her before she has a chance to set off her accursed bomb. Now. Luis said she'd probably be using body-heat sensors to track me down.'

'Yes.'

He glanced down at his open skinsuit. 'Tell me, do these suits trap body heat? Or radiate it away . . . They must at least blur the signature.' He began to strip off his suit.

'Doctor, what are you doing?'

'Now, you seal up your own suit. I really must insist. Do it, please! And then go find somewhere to hide. Find a heap of rock if you can, rubble to burrow in – something that might mask your own body heat further.'

'While you do what?'

He pulled his suit's comms system out at the neck, and dumped the rest. 'Why, while I go and lure Florian Hart away, of course.'

'But without your suit, if there's a decompression—'

'I need her to see me, Phee. And I am an experienced space traveller, you know.'

'When Florian finds you, she'll kill you!'

'Not if I find her first. Now, enough questions. Go hide – go, go, shoo!' He all but pushed her away, towards the heaps of debris by the chamber's quake-cracked walls. And then, earnest and desperately vulnerable, equipped with nothing more than his black coat and crumpled trousers, he hurried off into the corridors of the ice moon.

Phee grabbed First's hand, he followed her unresisting, and dug her way into a bank of rubble. There, huddled up, with the Blue Doll eerily still beside her, she waited, listening to the Doctor's progress over her comms system.

'This is Jamie. Ye're sure Florian can't hear us?'

'Aye,' MMAC replied. 'I'm monitoring the wavelengths she's using. I'll switch ye over if she changes.'

'We can see them,' Luis Reyes called now. 'In the mine shafts. There's a deep radar system in here . . . I'll overlay a body-heat scanner. Yes, the image is crystal clear. There's the shaft, I see the exhaust of Florian's scooter, very bright. And I see the Doctor, approaching her. What's this big spherical mass in the ice – is it liquid?'

'That's the Doctor's new tree telescope.'

'Neutrino, Jamie,' Zoe put in, sounding as tense as the rest.

'It's difficult to see in our scan,' said Luis. 'And probably in Florian's too. Look – the Doctor is right beside its wall. He's doing something to those bits of equipment.'

'The heaters,' Jamie said. 'We put in heaters to keep the contents of the bubble liquid. He must be turnin' em off!'

'How do you know?' Zoe asked.

'Well, what else can ye do with them?'

'Cooee, Florian? Here I am!'

Jamie snapped, 'Is that the Doctor?'

'Yes, Jamie,' Luis called. 'He's jumping up and down! He could hardly make himself more visible.'

'Och, I wish I was there, I'd knock him on the heid and haul him off!'

'And get both of you killed in the process, probably,' Zoe said primly. 'I suspect he knows what he's doing, Jamie.'

'And here comes Florian,' said Luis. 'She's heading towards him from the other side of the neutrino detector – it's the way the Doctor's positioned himself, he's leading her there deliberately.'

'But why?'

'I'm waiting for you, Florian!'

Florian Hart's skinsuit was in fact equipped with milspec sensor technology, much more powerful than anything issued to the miners. The tunnel she followed was in vacuum, but her skinsuit was comfortable.

She could clearly see the Doctor by his infra-red signature, on the other side of a roughly spherical anomaly in the ice. He was evidently in air; he wore no skinsuit.

'Doctor! So glad I found you. Any last will and testament?'

'Hmmph. Florian Hart, why is it that megalomaniacs like you always imagine they are comedians too? With your disgusting planetbuster you really were prepared to destroy us all, weren't you? While you floated around in safety, up in the phibian ship, while you sacrificed the lives of those of us trapped on this moon – even your own guards?'

'Oh, I am sure they would willingly have given their lives to the cause. If I'd told them about the bomb, of course. Well, despite your petty obstructiveness all is not lost. As soon as I've dealt with you I will return to the bomb and reset it. Your muddle-headed allies are too far away to stop me.'

'What? No! Florian, surely you see that if you set this thing off you'll destroy the very thing you seek, which is the bernalium of the Arkive's hull.'

'Oh, on the contrary, Doctor. I'll be destroying the Arkive – blasting it to atoms – but the energies of a mere Z-bomb can't harm the bernalium itself. It will merely be . . . scattered.'

'Scattered? You'll smash up the whole moon! What's left of it—'

'All the better to extract the dispersed bernalium efficiently. I'm already preparing a process to do just that, Doctor. No more mining; it will merely be a questing of fielding bernalium-rich lumps of ice from the sky.'

'Fielding? What do you think this will be, a butterfly hunt? You've no idea what you're doing. Even if you merely broke up the moon itself – even just that – you could be sending a hail of meteorites through the Saturn system. Which, these days, is full of humans! And, Florian, this Arkive seems physically to be a sack of singularities. Of knots of twisted space-time. What about that? Why, it shattered the Wheel merely by turning over in its sleep! If you now blow it up – if even one of those singularities ended up in Saturn itself – you could destabilise the planet, a gas giant! And if you do that the consequences would be solar-system-wide. Even Earth would be at risk. And *in addition* you risk destroying an entity, an ancient consciousness, the last trace of a vanished civilisation – perhaps a cultural treasure of value beyond imagining!'

'The Arkive is just an obstacle. You were right, Doctor, by the way. I do know all about alien life. After the alien intervention that wrecked my father's T-Mat, I dug into some of the old records, clumsily concealed by governments, and agencies like UNIT.

'There have been extraterrestrial interventions in this solar system for centuries, haven't there? And what good have they ever done? Infestations. Clumsy attempts at conquest. Nothing but obstacles to human progress, one way or another. And so it would be now. All this Arkive of yours will do is to bring down on us more busy-body types like Luis Reyes. We'd be swarming with archaeologists and historians and bleeding-heart types, who will object to every spade we stick in the ground. No, Doctor, we can't have that. That's why my solution is so perfect, you see. The Z-bomb will eliminate the Arkive, which is less than worthless, while preserving the bernalium of its hull, which is hugely valuable, and essential for the next phase of human progress.'

'Oh, come off it, Florian Hart. This isn't about mankind. It's not about economic growth and all that balderdash. It never is! Oh, soon enough you humans will be troubling the stars, I'm sure of that. But there are always ways to achieve economic growth without exploiting others, if you're prepared to be patient.

'No, this is all about *you*. You and your childhood, isn't it, Florian? Is this revenge on those you believe destroyed your father? Do you imagine all this will help you sleep at night?'

Florian listened with growing anger. The Doctor's lecturing reminded her of the oafs she had endured at school. Counsellors. Pastoral care providers. Trying to *help* her, to *work through her issues*. They were all idiotic losers, and so was the Doctor.

'You dare to mock me, you worm. You've been an irritant since you came wandering out of nowhere in that box of yours. We should never have saved your pointless life in the first place.'

'Yes, well, fortunately that was never up to you, was it?'

'Now at last I can *rationalise* you, Doctor.' She raised her blaster, aiming at his position with the aid of her thermal imager. The few metres of ice between them would be no obstacle, to a beam set to kill. She prepared a raking sweep, starting to the Doctor's left, to ensure he couldn't escape.

She fired.

And as soon as the blaster's energy poured into the ice, a thin shell before her cracked and shattered, and *water*, liquid water, came pouring out in a gush, rushing enthusiastically into the vacuum. The blaster was knocked from her hands, and she was thrust backwards as if by a huge hand, shoved back down the passage behind her by the pressure of the water. The corridor quickly flooded, the water rising over her as she thrashed for the blaster. But *it was freezing*, almost immediately, growing thick and glutinous, some exotic cocktail of pollutants allowing the water's residual heat to pour away rapidly.

Trapping her like a fly in amber. She roared in anger, but she was already pinned.

She raised her head to glare down the corridor. Her thermal imaging system was functioning still, and she could see the Doctor. See his face, creased in a grim smile. *But he wore no skinsuit.* Now that the chamber between them was breached, she realised, he was suddenly in vacuum.

And as she watched, he clutched his chest, coughed, folded over.

She laughed out loud. 'You beat me, Doctor. But you gave your life to do it! Can you hear me, as you puke out your dying breath? Can you hear Florian Hart, laughing at you?'

And the ice closed hard around her.

Regardless of the Doctor's commands, Phee pushed her way out of the mound of rubble and ran, sweeping up the Doctor's discarded skinsuit.

The Blue Doll First followed her, with his usual efficient, eerily inhuman gait.

Phee found the Doctor quickly. There was no air in the chamber, none at all, and the temperature had plunged to the cold of deep space. He lay on his front, unmoving, a sprinkling of frost on his tousled dark hair.

The voices on the comms kept calling, asking for updates, pleading for the Doctor to reply.

'This is Phee Laws. I'm with him. I'm with the Doctor. There's no air here. He wasn't wearing a skinsuit. He wanted to attract Florian Hart to the neutrino detector. He did it. But he couldn't have survived.'

'Don't move him,' Zoe said urgently. 'Just stay with him. Don't move him!'

The Blue Doll stood and stared, and Phee wondered how much he understood.

INDEPENDENT
MNEMOSYNE

I

'Order! And that means you, Dai Llewellyn, and don't think I can't see you.

'Welcome to the First Constitutional Convention of the Independent State of the Mnemosyne Cincture. And I might say, what are you all doing here, isn't it your on-shift? Oh, I forgot. We don't have shifts any more, do we? Just kidding.

'You know me. I'm your mayor, for now, Jo Laws. Luis Reyes here has kindly volunteered to serve as an independent scribe of the proceedings, with Sonia Paley as scrutiniser. Anybody got any objection to that? If so speak up. Look, I'm serious. This is your meeting. If you have something relevant to say at any point, say it.

'Good. Second item. As far as I'm concerned I'm only here to open this meeting, because somebody has to. As soon as we have some kind of constitution in place I'll be stepping down as mayor, and I may or may not stand for re-election as – well, whatever executive role we choose to define. I'm serious, we have to do it right, and maybe I've been too long in the saddle anyhow. And in the meantime, I'll step down as chair of this meeting if anybody wants to propose a better candidate. Come on. Anybody?'

'I propose Jo Laws keeps the job, for fear of someone even worse getting it.'

'Seconded.'

'All who agree—'

'Aye.'

'OK. Thanks for nothing. Now we come to the people up here with me. We have representatives of various interest groups to lead the discussion. I know you all picked these characters by some manner or means, but we'll go through a verification that you're still happy with them. We have representatives of the classifications, As, Bs and Cs. And up here too is Sam, my own son, representing the youth of the Wheel. Who are no longer just fodder for the vast engine of labour that was the Wheel and its mine. And who are demanding a right to protection, to nurturing, to proper opportunities for education and choice of destiny – a right to be heard. That's what he's told me. Good for you, son, and I'm very proud of you, but I won't embarrass you any more.

'Third item. In this other row of chairs beside me are guests. You'll recognise Luis Reyes of the Planetary Ethics Commission, and Sonia Paley our Marshal, but who's actually attached to the International Space Command, a UN organisation. Oh, and you'll see one empty chair. We've left that for one much-loved guest who isn't with us today . . .

'These folk are to be regarded as guests; they can advise, but they aren't of the community, and they don't get a vote. But in particular I feel we need their input into how to prepare our case as a newly independent nation, to be presented to the representative of the ISC who's on her way here right now from Earth. Ostensibly she's coming to check on the legal status of our three refugees—'

'And to take home Florian Hart!'

'They shouldn't have thawed her out!'

'All right, all right. But as an independent nation this will be our first interface with the United Nations and the national and regional governments of Earth. And that gives us a deadline, the ISC rep is due here soon, so we have to get our act in order.

'Fourth item—'

'Sorry, sorry! So sorry I'm late! I just could not get away from the medical centre. Hello, Phee, can I sit with you back here? Phew! Have I missed much? I wish I'd brought some popcorn . . .'

II

'Doctor, you do make a lot of noise for a man who spent thirty minutes in a vacuum.'

'Which is more or less what your physicians have been saying. Strictly between you and me I have a small advantage. Respiratory bypass system. Does come in handy from time to time. But mum's the word – eh?'

'Speaking of Mum—'

'Doctor! You have a place up here on the podium.'

'Oh, Jo, must I? I do so hate to be conspicuous.'

'We rely on your wisdom.'

'Flattery will get you nowhere. Oh, very well. So have you made a start?'

'Well, we've tried to—'

'Of course you must rely on the best models to hand. As painfully worked out by humanity over millennia of bloodshed, but a rather magnificent effort, given that you had no help. The British parliamentary system – as crusty and robust and long-lived as a barnacle on a ship's hull. American principles of freedom and self-determination—'

'Life, liberty and the pursuit of happiness.'

'Order!'

'Exactly, Sam. You see, you know it all already, and it is *yours*; you don't need help from the likes of me. You're free now – that's the thing. You're free to negotiate with the likes of Bootstrap, to sell them your labour if you like, but you are no longer *owned* by them. Or indeed by anybody else. And you can raise your children as you see fit, not just for labour in the mines. You can go off and colonise Enceladus and Titan – do whatever you like. And I should do away with all that corporate labelling nonsense. Cs and Bs and As – humans aren't robots, you're not Cybermen, you don't fit into neat categories, and nor are you supposed to. And then there's the status of your oldest resident to consider.'

'Who?'

'Why, the Arkive, of course. After all she was here long before you were. It may not be an issue for a constitutional convention, but as a matter of urgency you must establish her official status. As an alien artefact she doesn't fit comfortably into legal systems drawn up when humanity believed it was alone. Is she property? If so, whose? Yours, Bootstrap's, humanity's? Can you *patent* her – or some aspect of her, like the Blue Doll manufacture technology? Or is she an independent entity in her own right? To be treated like the representative of a separate nation, perhaps, to whom appropriate diplomatic courtesies should be extended?'

'If I may speak? There are organisations on Earth connected to the search for alien life that have done some thinking on these issues. I'd be happy to advise.'

'Thank you, Luis. And I have some thoughts on the Arkive's long-term fate – as best we can arrange it. I have Zoe working on that. But remember the Blue Dolls! They too are independently sentient creatures in their own right.'

'They're killers!'

'Yes, they have killed, and destroyed. They did what they were pro-grammed to do. But now the war is over; I made peace, on your behalf, with the Arkive, their controller. And besides, even before the ceasefire they transcended that programming. I've seen it with my own eyes. They care for each other. They ask questions, of life and death and the meaning of their existence. They have even created art. They are made things, but they have evolved their own culture, and it deserves preser-vation and respect . . . as long as they last.'

'Doctor? What do you mean by that?'

'Well, Jo, I mean Mayor Laws, they seem to have a certain built-in obsolescence. The signs of ageing are already obvious, sadly. Though they remain child-sized. And they have no way of reproducing, of course. The same with the Blue Soldiers. So those of you who despise them can comfort yourselves that they won't be a problem for long.'

'Again we can help with that. Room can be found on Earth, or on the moon.'

'All right. Thank you, Luis. You've given us food for thought, Doctor; we'll deal with all these issues in the best interests of everybody – and I mean *all* the residents of Mnemosyne and the Wheel. But if you've done hijacking my meeting, let me get us back on track. We're here to discuss a constitution for our new nation. And though it galls me to admit it, Karen Madl, my ex-husband's partner, is not just a hotshot space pilot. Turns out she has university-level training in constitutional law. She's been taking input from you all and has prepared a draft constitution for you to consider.'

'Not really a draft. More principles to guide the construction of a draft.'

'Whatever. You want to come up here and tell us what you have? . . .'

'You'll always remember this day, you know.'

'Yes, thank you, Doctor.'

'I'm not surprised none of you are leaving, even you youngsters. This isn't about dry-as-dust documents and legal principles. You are building a new nation. Your *own* nation, one of the first independent states beyond the Earth. This is a day that will always be remembered, as long as there are people in the Saturn system.'

'Order! OK, Karen, the floor is yours . . .'

48

'Zoe! It's guid tae hear yer voice again. And ye're back in yer Mars shuttle?'

'Yes. Hello, MMAC! It's become a sort of home from home for me in here. I have to thank you again for coming to save us when we were flying off into space.'

'Och, don't mention it. Though I have tae warn ye—'

'What?'

'There's a mighty monster sleepin' not a metre behind ye.'

'Oh, you mean Casey. Or rather, the Karkus! She just won't get out of the costume her sister made for her. Her mother's going to have to peel it off her when it's time for a wash, I think.'

'Ye've a way with kids, Zoe Heriot.'

'Have I? I mean – I don't know anything about children—'

'Believe yer uncle MMAC. Ye've a way. They're all in the big house talkin' about the future, is it?'

'Yes. The constitutional convention. Which is why I'm babysitting, again. And it's what I've come here to talk to you about, MMAC.'

'The future.'

'Yes. Specifically your future.'

'Ah, whisht ye. What future? I've always done my job tae the best of my ability. And, well, I'm still handy in an emergency. But I'm obsolete, Zoe. Just a rottin' hulk whose day is done.'

'MMAC! Let me get a word in. It's not just your future I'm concerned with but the Arkive's.'

'Och, another relic who's run out of purpose! Mind you, they'll look after some bit of old alien kit better than anythin' made on the Clyde, I shouldnae wonder. Put her in a museum, will they?'

'Well, no, the Doctor has worked out something rather better than that for her. But it's all going to rely on you.'

'Oh!'

'It's going to take dedication.'

'Ah've plenty of that.'

'And a long time.'

'I've more than enough o' *that.*'

'MMAC, have you ever heard of a substance called taranium?'

'No . . .'

Taranium, the Doctor had told her, was one of the rarest, and most unstable, substances in the universe. It was capable of storing tremendous amounts of energy – and had been used in time travel applications. The Daleks, the Doctor said, had once used the substance to make a 'time destructor' which was capable of sending not just vehicles like the TARDIS, but whole *regions* through time.

Zoe gave MMAC an edited version of this.

'Time travel, ye say? Well I nivver.'

'Now the good news is that one of the few sources of this stuff taranium is in the solar system. The planet Uranus!'

'Uranus? Why, that's right next door.'

'Yes! But the bad news is that it takes a long time to extract. Decades. You'd have to process a billion tonnes of ore just to retrieve a milligram.'

'That really will take decades!'

'I imagine you'd have to take up orbit around Uranus. Perhaps use some of the scoopships Bootstrap use to extract deuterium from Saturn. Set up a very long-term operation . . .'

'Ye're makin' me slaver, lassie! That's right up MMAC's street. As ye ken verra well, don't ye? But I still don't understand. How will time travel help yon Arkive?'

'Well, that's just it, MMAC. *She's already tried.* She failed in her mission to preserve the culture that sent her out, escaping the supernova – through no fault of her own, but she's consumed by guilt. So she's been trying to *go back*, back in time, to confront her makers and—'

'And tell them she's sorry.'

'Yes! You understand. She tried once before – well, at least once. She didn't have taranium—' Or the Doctor's own TARDIS technology.

'So now the Doctor wants to help her go back. Is that the idea?'

'Well, not quite. Even with the taranium, to go back would be unadvisable. The Doctor says it's never a good idea to cross your own timeline. I mean, to go backwards and—'

'Meet yersel' comin' forward.'

'Yes.'

'Knows a lot about time travel, yon Doctor, doesn't he?'

'Oh, ha ha, it's all just theory. Goes back to Einstein, you know! And there's another problem. We couldn't send the Arkive back even if we tried! Because of what she is – or rather, what she's become.'

'Ah. All that information in the rings.'

'Yes. The Arkive has been stuck in that moon for billions of years. And in all that long time she's become – embedded. The elements of her hull, including bernalium, have seeped into the ice. Unconsciously, she has learned to store her thoughts in the shifting gravitational field of Saturn and its moons. How could we possibly transfer all that? And the Doctor speculates that there may be other natural storage media. The Arkive has done a *lot* of thinking, and has had a *lot* of memories to hold onto. Saturn's magnetosphere, for instance; you could write information into fluctuations of the magnetic field. And who knows what else, that we haven't thought of yet?'

'I see what ye mean. You can't send the whole of Saturn back in time! So the Arkive can't be moved. But what's the point of this taranium then?'

'Well, the Doctor has suggested something smaller scale. The Arkive can't go back. *But she could send a message.* A kind of journal – an auto-biography. It could be sent back to the moment after the Arkive herself was dispatched, so there would be no timeline-crossing, no time para-dox. And as a stream of information it would be much cheaper to send, in terms of taranium.'

'A letter home. She would have the chance to say sorry after all.'

'And to say what became of her.'

'Perhaps it will give her some peace, then.'

'That's the idea. And then, maybe, she can move on, and we can learn something of the people of her lost world . . . This is going to be a strange project, MMAC. The Arkive will surely be preserved where she is, here in her moon. There will be scientists studying her, and so forth. And all the while you'll be out at Uranus. But you'll have to come up with some cover story. The Doctor says this taranium is not stuff you'd want to fall into the hands of – well, of someone like Florian Hart.'

'Och, I understand.'

'This will take decades, even centuries, but—'

'But that willnae matter to me. Or to a creature that's already waited billions of years.'

'Yes. So will you help, MMAC?'

'Try an' stop me! And Zoe – thank him fer me.'

'Who?'

'The Doctor.'

'What for?'

'Ye ken verra well what for.'

'I should go, the Freedom March is due to start soon . . . Oh, I almost forgot. Speaking of letters home – MMAC, do you remember you told me about how your mother wrote to you from Glasgow? And then the letters stopped?'

'Aye.'

'Well, I was suspicious about that. Why should they just stop like that? I wondered if somebody had put a block on them deliberately.'

'Why would they do that?'

'I don't know. For reasons of economic efficiency, probably. You'd get more work done if you weren't taking up precious time and processing power reading letters from your mother—'

'Ye've found 'em, haven't you?'

'As soon as we had access to Unity House in Res One, which was Florian's own residence, I hacked into the computer store. And guess what I found . . .'

'*Fifteenth of June. Cristal Street, Glasgow. Dear MMAC, It's been a few weeks since your last message reached me but I thought I should write again. There's too much news to be kept in my head! To begin with there's your old pal Tommy Burns, who's just been selected for an apprenticeship at Clavius Base on the moon . . .*'

'It's her voice.'

'Your mother?'

'Yes.'

'These are yours, MMAC. Uploading now . . . done. You read them through. We can talk about them later if you like . . .'

He didn't say anything.

'*You must know how sorry I am about what we did. All the lies. But it didn't feel like lies at the time! You were just my little boy. Even though you were in a sort of virtual-reality tank, and I couldn't hold you or kiss you . . .*'

'I'll leave you to your memories, MMAC. And don't miss the March.'

49

The Freedom March was magnificent. Practically the whole population of the Wheel of Ice, permanent and temporary, gathered in Res One before the great front of Unity House, the corporate headquarters where once Florian Hart had enjoyed intimidating workers, elected officials and representatives of Earth's governments. Now it was a palace claimed for the new nation.

Then they all paraded anticlockwise through the whole of the rebuilt Wheel, through the six sectors, marching through the gleaming bubbles of Mnemosyne ice, squeezing with much jostling and laughter through the interleaving space hulks and fuel tanks.

Zoe, having taken longer over her conversation with MMAC than she'd planned, ended up joining the March in Recreation, the last sector before the return to Res One. Once this had been one of the most bleak and joyless places Zoe had ever seen, with corporate messages pumped out from display flags, and cinemas showing nothing but uplifting sagas of happy, toiling workers, and sports pitches and play halls where you had to pay for everything. A mixture of work camp and theme park. But now the company flags were gone, the fences around the football pitches torn down, and the March, surging through, was a mass of disorderly colour.

By now MMAC was providing a noisy commentary over the Wheel-wide PA system. The March as a whole was made up from all the Wheel's communities, the grey-clad As, purple-clad Bs, green-clad Cs, the squat Earth-born adults mixed in with their low-gravity-tall kids, wearing sunglasses to protect eyes adapted to the dim light of Saturn.

Zoe wasn't at all surprised to see Jamie front and centre, bagpipe blaring. Sam Laws, with Dai and Sanjay and others, flanked him, plucking at home-made harps and hammering drums. Even the Doctor was there, piping away on his recorder, though Zoe couldn't hear him over the din.

Once back in Res One, the March returned at last to Unity House, where Jo, Sonia, Luis and others stood on a balcony. Standing under a rank of flagpoles, Jamie led the musicians in one last air: 'The Wearing of the Green,' an old Jacobite marching tune.

And MMAC's commentary gave way to uncontrolled blubbing.

The Doctor put his recorder into his pocket, and quietly beckoned to Zoe and Jamie. They slipped unnoticed out of the crowd, and, with the Doctor leading the way, went around the grand house to a small storage building at the back.

MMAC was still weeping into the PA. The Doctor held his hands to his ears. 'Oh, what a racket! I *told* Walter Scott that all that sentimental stuff about the tartan and the heather would lead to no good. I told him! And now we've got to put up with this – a caterwauling Modular Autonomous Component!'

'Well, he has got a lot to weep about, Doctor,' Zoe said cheerily. 'You've just sentenced him to a century's hard labour, mining taranium from Uranus.'

Jamie was taking his pipes apart. 'Uranus! Not yon King George's planet! That's nae place for a good Scot!'

'Oh, don't be absurd, Jamie. But what a day it's been.' The Doctor sniffed the air. 'Freedom! Can't get enough of it. I do admire people like this, you know, at this sort of juncture in their history. People who build things – a home, a city, a world, a nation. Not something I've ever done, or ever could do, I suppose. Now, look what I've found for you . . .' He opened the storage building's unlocked door to reveal the TARDIS.

'The ship!' Zoe said. 'I thought she was impounded in Utilities somewhere.'

'Well, I suspected Florian would have had her moved. Perhaps as a long-term way of manipulating us, whom she saw as enemies. Or perhaps as an acquisition of what she may have recognised as high technology. At any rate it didn't take me long to find her, I've been popping back for this and that – for I have the key!' He produced it with a little jig of pleasure. '*And* she's ready to depart. The inhibitor circuits that locked us down because of the threat to the continuum have cleared now. So here she is,' he said, stroking the TARDIS's battered frame. 'Grumpy, grouchy, unreliable and with a mind entirely her own. But ours again!'

'Och, I coulda used my own pipes instead o' yon museum piece on the March,' Jamie grumbled.

Zoe felt mildly shocked. 'Oh, must we go now? Without saying goodbye?'

'Well, goodbyes lead to good questions, Zoe, and that's never advisable for us. And besides – look over there.' He pointed to the flagpoles fluttering in a fan-assisted breeze before Unity House. 'The flag at the end – just been hoisted . . . Don't you recognise it, Zoe?'

Zoe saw a rather grandiose circular crest: a globe, an outstretched hand, a spaceship pointing at the stars. 'That's the insignia of the International Space Command.'

'Yes. And it's been hoisted because the inspector that you cleverly requested to get us out of the jug, Zoe, is about to arrive. Earlier than expected. Been whizzed here aboard a brand new Delta-class interplanetary freighter, I'm told.'

'Ah,' said Jamie. 'Talk about chickens comin' home to roost.'

'Quite so, Jamie. And so you see . . .'

Jamie touched Zoe's arm. 'I know ye made a friend, lass. The wee bairn'll miss ye. But maybe ye'll see her again some day.'

'I somehow doubt it,' Zoe said, trying to keep a tinge of bitterness out of her voice. 'That's not how we live our lives, is it?'

The Doctor patted her on her shoulder. 'But at least we have each other. Now then, all aboard – I don't *think* anybody's watching us . . .'

In that, he was wrong.

The blue box disappeared. Just like that.

And a girl and a robot saw everything.

Phee Laws wore a jumpsuit she'd been given by Zoe, neither grey nor purple nor green but panelled with pastel colours. She walked up to the storage building, now empty, and inspected a square patch of vacated floor, dust-free.

'MMAC,' she murmured.

MMAC spoke in her ear. 'Aye, lass?'

'I followed them. I thought they were up to something. Did you *see* that?'

'Aye, I did.'

'I wonder who they were.'

'Aye. And where they went.'

'I expect Marshal Paley will be interested in this.'

'Oh, aye.'

'But she'll probably lock me up and interrogate me.'

'Aye. And impound my records.'

'Do you think we should just let them go, MMAC?'

'Thought ye'd ne'er ask. I've forgotten 'em already. But, Phee . . .'

'Yes?'

'Ye've got some explainin' tae do tae your little sister.'

EPILOGUE

TARDIS

In the vortex that lies beyond time and space tumbled a police box that was not a police box.

The brilliantly lit control room was empty, silent save for a hum of unseen engines. On the gleaming floor, in one corner, lay two modest musical instruments, a wooden recorder and a bagpipe's practice chanter.

And beside them was a ragged doll, blue, made of scraps.

Somewhere an alarm chimed faintly.

Distracted from their different pursuits, the ship's three crew hurried towards the control room.

'Och. What *now*?'

'Which of you has been meddling with the controls *this* time?'

'Doctor – Jamie – look at the scanner! What's *that*?'